"Kristy Kiernan bursts from the gate with this skillful rendering of a family's reckoning with its painful past. Kiernan peels away the layers in a lilting and luminous voice, exposing strata after strata of family secrets made murkier by the passage of time. Kiernan proves she's a writer to watch—find a comfortable spot, turn off the phone, and lose yourself in this gorgeous debut."

—Sara Gruen, *New York Times* bestselling author of
Water for Elephants, *Riding Lessons*, and *Flying Changes*

"Kristy Kiernan's fluent storytelling and fully drawn, credible characters make for an affecting novel. With effortless grace, her lyrical prose drops the reader into scenes rich with details and powerful emotions. *Catching Genius* is a stunning debut that will leave readers of Jodi Picoult and Anita Shreve clamoring for more from this talented author."

—Tasha Alexander, author of *And Only to Deceive*

"*Catching Genius* is the real thing: a rich, compelling, and deeply nuanced story delivered in language that's as luminous as it is authoritative. To judge by this affecting first novel, I'd say Kiernan's the real thing, too."   —Jon Clinch, author of *FINN*

"With precise and evocative prose, Kristy Kiernan weaves a story of family and history that is as nuanced and finely wrought as it is compelling. *Catching Genius* draws you in with its genuine characters, and it holds you there with its truthful exploration of the enduring bonds of love and family . . . This affecting novel shines a new light on the concept of genius—what it is and what it isn't. And speaking of genius, Kristy Kiernan looks like a debut novelist who will be around for a long time to come."

—Elizabeth Letts, author of *Family Planning* and *Quality of Care*

CATCHING GENIUS

Kristy Kiernan

BERKLEY BOOKS, NEW YORK

THE BERKLEY PUBLISHING GROUP
Published by the Penguin Group
Penguin Group (USA) Inc.
375 Hudson Street, New York, New York 10014, USA
Penguin Group (Canada), 90 Eglinton Avenue East, Suite 700, Toronto, Ontario M4P 2Y3, Canada
(a division of Pearson Penguin Canada Inc.)
Penguin Books Ltd., 80 Strand, London WC2R 0RL, England
Penguin Group Ireland, 25 St. Stephen's Green, Dublin 2, Ireland (a division of Penguin Books Ltd.)
Penguin Group (Australia), 250 Camberwell Road, Camberwell, Victoria 3124, Australia
(a division of Pearson Australia Group Pty. Ltd.)
Penguin Books India Pvt. Ltd., 11 Community Centre, Panchsheel Park, New Delhi—110 017, India
Penguin Group (NZ), 67 Apollo Drive, Mairangi Bay, Auckland 1311, New Zealand
(a division of Pearson New Zealand Ltd.)
Penguin Books (South Africa) (Pty.) Ltd., 24 Sturdee Avenue, Rosebank, Johannesburg 2196,
South Africa

Penguin Books Ltd., Registered Offices: 80 Strand, London WC2R 0RL, England

This book is an original publication of The Berkley Publishing Group.

This is a work of fiction. Names, characters, places, and incidents either are the product of the author's imagination or are used fictitiously, and any resemblance to actual persons, living or dead, business establishments, events, or locales is entirely coincidental. The publisher does not have any control over and does not assume any responsibility for author or third-party websites or their content.

PRINTING HISTORY
Berkley trade paperback edition / March 2007

Library of Congress Cataloging-in-Publication Data

Kiernan, Kristy.
   Catching genius / Kristy Kiernan
      p. cm.
   ISBN: 978-0-425-21435-0
   1. Sisters—Fiction.   2. Gifted children—Fiction.   3. House selling—Fiction.
4. Domestic fiction.   I. Title.

PS3611.I4455C38 2007
813'.6—dc22   2006050496

PRINTED IN THE UNITED STATES OF AMERICA

10   9   8   7   6   5   4   3   2   1

For my husband,
Richard W. Kiernan,
who makes everything right . . .

And in memory of the two finest women
I've ever had the honor of knowing:
Ruth P. Smith
and
Mary Ellen Kiernan

ACKNOWLEDGMENTS

The editor who originally bought this book remained largely unknown to me. Thank you, Leona Nevler, I will always remember that you gave me a shot.

Luckily for me, *Catching Genius* was bravely taken over by Jackie Cantor, whose wise and deftly expressed ideas were an education as well as an inspiration.

Thank you, Anne Hawkins, my agent, who makes me laugh, keeps me informed, is loyal, tough, and kind, and sent squeaky toys to my dog.

Reva Youngstein, flutist for the Gainsborough Trio based in New York, was incredibly generous with her knowledge and experience. Thank you.

Thanks to David Groisser, Associate Professor and Undergraduate Coordinator for the Department of Mathematics at the University of

Florida, and to Janna Underhill, who put me in touch with him. Janna also has a lot of titles after her name, but for over twenty years I've been honored to simply call her friend.

My heartfelt gratitude to: my critique partner, Sara Gruen, who read more drafts than I'm sure she wants to remember; Tasha Tyska, who kept me sane with her sharp sense of humor and unflagging loyalty; Barb Meyers, who kept me fed and watered; Tanya Miller, who made me leave my house and be a human being at least once a month; and B.S.R., for the use of the most beautiful mountain cabin during the writing of this novel.

The following talented writers offered support in various forms, and I am eternally grateful: Zarina Docken, Jon Clinch, Sachin Waikar, Rachel Cole, Sandra Kring, Camille Kimball, Gail Konop Baker, Terez Rose, and Elizabeth Letts.

Thank you to The Debutantes: Tish Cohen, Mia King, Jennifer McMahon, Anna David, and Eileen Cook. They are an inspiration.

Thank you to my grandfather, Robert E. Smith, for setting a storyteller's example and for being excited for me. Thanks to the Claiborne family for their interest and good wishes. The Kiernan family has been extraordinarily kind and supportive; a special thanks to Elizabeth Kiernan, my mother-in-law, for her countless everyday kindnesses.

Thank you to my mother, Judy Claiborne. There is no doubt that I wouldn't have become a writer without having developed a love of books, and she is solely responsible for that. I love you. I miss you. Be well.

And finally, because, yeah, I *am* the sort of writer who thanks her dog, thank you to Niko, who is convinced that I am the perfect companion, when it is quite clearly the other way around.

If children grew up according to early indications,
we should have nothing but geniuses.

—Johann Wolfgang von Goethe

PROLOGUE

Constance Belle Sykes

1969

Our real lives were lived in the dark. Late at night, every night, we met in the music room, stealthily avoiding the scarred legs of the piano, the stringless harp, the ⅛-size Mittenwald balanced upon the violin stand as if waiting for a musically inclined fairy. No childish nightlight cast shadows across the wallpaper; only the moon, streaming through the skylight to glow upon the yellowed piano keys, lit our play.

Some nights there was no moon at all—though Estella patiently explained to me that it was still there, we just couldn't see it because Earth had shoved its wide, round self between the moon and the sun, a social bully forcing its way into an ancient conversation—and we would reluctantly crack the door to allow the light of our parents' downstairs lives in.

We were precocious children, promising children, healthy children. At seven, Estella was tall enough to reach everything we'd ever need and smart enough to know what we could get away with. And I, younger by two years, was quick enough to flee, small enough to hide, and beguiling enough to lie convincingly.

And though we didn't know it at the time, we were wealthy children, the great-great-grandchildren of lumber baron Nathaniel Austin Sykes. A sound track of important conversation accompanied those nights we left the door cracked for light. Illustrious people: politicians, university presidents, eminent board members of museums and cultural centers, all came looking for that old, rapidly dwindling money. They laughed too loudly at our father's jokes, exclaimed over our mother's beauty, greedily ran their eyes over the volumes of rare books filling the library shelves, and scuffed their shoes against the tight nap of the Bokhara rugs.

We had the run of the upstairs on those nights. The nanny, pressed into service in the kitchen, left us alone, and the noise of the dinner covered the drumroll of our feet as we rushed from the music room to the top of the stairs and back as proof of our daring.

Sometimes we eavesdropped, glancing at each other with big eyes when we heard our father swear or our mother tell a bawdy joke. And we heard things our parents did not, like remarks about our father's age and thinning hair, and our mother's youth and lush figure. The men were as guilty as the women, and we even heard our own names in those catty conversations, about how spoiled we were and how we would grow up without ever learning to appreciate hard work.

I knew what spoiled was. Kimmy Kay Watson down the street was spoiled. She got not one, but *two* ponies for her sixth birthday, one for her friends to ride and one that she never had to share. I asked for a pony for my fifth birthday and got a tattered first edition of *Little Women* instead. So I knew I was not spoiled.

Our eavesdropping never lasted for long; we had our own rituals to attend to. We always danced first, a childish shag that our mother taught us, twining our hands together and awkwardly flinging ourselves away and then toward each other, tethered by fingers gone numb. When we finally broke apart, panting, I followed her lead, as I had ever since I could crawl after her. Sometimes we played Alligators in the Carpet, sometimes The Witch in the Attic, sometimes Schoolteacher and Brilliant Pupil or, when I got my way, Superhero Twins.

As we tired, we drew apart, to play our own favorite games. Sometimes I picked up my tiny, dilapidated violin with its fallen bridge and collapsed sound post and pretended I could play, but my stuffed animals commanded my attention more often. I arranged them in order of height, rearranged them in order of affection, or color of fur or eyes. I conducted wild animal chorales, and sometimes there was a vicious mauling and one animal would be punished while I gently nursed the victim back to life. Most often, I simply watched my restless sister at her game.

Estella loved numbers the way I loved my stuffed animals, and she arranged them in her own fashion the way I arranged my bears and elephants and monkeys. She always started at the door and stepped precisely along the baseboard on the outsides of her soles, her big toes tilted into the air, counting under her breath, always getting the same number when she reached the windows. And then her real fun began.

She snatched numbers out of the air—the date, or the number of the month, or the year, sometimes her age or mine, or all these things combined—until she reached some sort of critical mass in her mind, and then she searched for zero. She added and subtracted, or multiplied and divided, or otherwise manipulated the numbers, quickly, under her breath, eyes closed, until she got there. Sometimes it took her longer than others, and I would watch her face shining in the moonlight, her mouth working, until her eyelids finally stopped jumping, her shoulders relaxed, and a smile slid across her mouth.

Zero.

The windows that framed her looked out on the nature preserve named for our paternal great-grandfather, Henry Louis Sykes, black sheep son of Nathaniel Sykes, the man who had gathered his boot-straps in his callused hands and hauled himself, tree by tree, to the great heights that only oil tycoons and land barons could reach. Henry spent his life dedicated to replacing every tree his father felled from New England to Florida. They reconciled just before the elder Sykes' death at age ninety-four. Just in time for the will to be changed, be-deviling the other Sykes children by cutting them out completely and leaving the bulk of the wealth to Henry.

We were told this story night after night by Sebastian Henry Sykes, our father, in the beautiful language of a genteel South, liquid words and phrases that seemed born of some golden mother tongue. I loved to listen to him speak, loved that he used words that he naturally as-sumed I knew the meanings of, that caressed my ear with soft, multi-ple syllables and near-mythical imagery. As he spoke, he would point toward the land Henry had fought to preserve, the slash pines and live oaks and palms that signaled the end of civilization. Beyond them was the Everglades, where swamp took over and the alligators of our imag-inations grew to preposterous lengths and water moccasins, thick as mangrove roots, lay in wait for careless children.

Then our father would gesture toward the old cracked oil painting of Nathaniel, pointing out how firm his mouth was, how proud his nose and strong his jaw. But it was his eyes that he always came back to, the same light brown that both he and I had inherited. They were Sykes eyes, the eyes that said I belonged to him and that divided our family down the middle. My mother and Estella shared the change-able blue-green of the Gulf of Mexico. My father teased that he could tell their moods by their eyes: anger showed as clear green, joy as blue, sadness a cloudy mix of the two. I often searched my sister's eyes, pleased to have this barometer of her soul that she could not hide behind numbers.

The Sykes eyes took everything in and gave nothing away, and Nathaniel's looked down upon us sternly every night in the music room, the same way I imagined he'd looked at Henry, until his disapproval turned to admiration.

My father's sensuous Southern outpourings of respect would end later, when the money and land slipped out of his too-little, too-late grasp, but there were many professions of admiration for our forefathers in those days.

I knew that he was passing down our history, trying to instill respect for our brilliant ancestors, but I enjoyed the stories simply for the sound of the language and for the intimacy it generated among the three of us. My father and Estella were my world, and when she left for school and my father went on one of his book-buying trips, I faded away like the moon when the sun rose, leaving me a tiny scrap of silver at my mother's side. I was only fully formed when snuggled on my father's lap or when watching Estella searching for zero in the music room.

Long before the moon gave way I began to nod off and my sister's agitated mind finally exhausted itself. We came together in the center of the back wall where a long pink velvet sofa stood, covered in an immense, moth-eaten shawl our father bought in Spain from a down-on-her-luck marchioness. Sometimes I dragged a stuffed animal with me; sometimes she brought hard little magnetic numbers from the slant-top desk in her room. We would curl together, me sucking my thumb, Estella clutching sharp-edged sevens and fours, and fall asleep.

One night, a night when our parents did not have a party but rather met across the long dining table under the stairs, everything changed. Suddenly, we might no longer be healthy. For two weeks we had been taken to doctors' offices, had dutifully filled out tests, had waited alone in chill rooms while our parents were spoken to in plush offices with closed doors. The only solace was that we were not stuck with needles, though that fact in itself did not reassure me of anything. The people had names with a *Doctor* prefix, and that was enough for me. But once home the worry slid from me as easily as I slid down our blue pool slide.

We met in the music room that night, but as I began to close the door, the moon bright as a half-dollar in our skylight, Estella stopped me. We did not dance. Instead, I pulled at the fluted hem of her night-gown as she listened just outside the door. She flapped her hand, quieting me as she strained to hear our parents' muted words over the clink and clatter of silverware. Hurt, I turned away. The doctor visits were over and we never got a shot. What else could possibly matter?

I pulled the violin and sprung-haired bow from the stand and bounced the bow across the violin's empty middle, making a low thump in the air, then quickly put them down again when I earned Estella's glare. Crawling onto the sofa, I wrapped the shawl about my feet, gathering stuffed animals around me like a moat, and watched her. I was always intrigued when she was still, when her eyes did not flit from point to point and her fingers weren't tugging at each other. She never glanced back at me, and I eventually fell asleep.

I woke when she threw a stuffed animal at my head. We rarely fought, and I was shocked at the unprovoked attack. I began to cry immediately, but she shushed me from her position at the now-closed door. The moon had dipped below the skylight as though it had never been there, making the room dim as a movie theater. I searched for her eyes, hopeful that they could tell me what her heart was feeling, but they were in shadow.

"Be quiet," she whispered. "Connie, you have to listen; you can't tell anyone that we know."

I snuffled, gingerly retrieving the fuzzy duckling she'd chucked at my forehead. I checked it for injury and sullenly asked, "Know what?"

There was a pause while Estella folded her arms over her chest, posing in a dramatic stance I recognized and always responded to. It was I'm the Older Sister pose, The Sun, commanding her planets to fall in line. I listened.

"I'm sick. I am probably going to die," she said, solemn as a Siamese cat.

I could feel my mouth hanging open and shut it quickly, before she could say anything about catching flies. I slid off the sofa, the shawl tangling soft as sand beneath my feet. Estella held her hand up to stop me from running to her.

"Don't. It might be catching," she said.

My mouth betrayed me again and I gaped at her. Catching? I caught chicken pox from her so I knew what catching was. I leaned back against the sofa, my fingers clutching the velvet, and asked the only question my five-year-old mind could come up with. "But why?"

She frowned. "I have eyecue," she said. "It's bad. I have a lot of it, but I couldn't hear everything. It has something to do with my brain, or my head." She lifted a hand to her temple, gently brushed it, just a flutter with her fingertips, and then let it drop. "You can't come near me in case I give it to you too."

I fluttered my fingers against my own temple, checked in with my limbs for aches, remembered the bee sting from the previous week, my fever from the chicken pox. "But what if I already have it?"

She shook her head. "They said you were normal."

I moved toward her again and Estella took a step back, her hand on the doorknob. "Connie, stop. You have to go to your room."

I bit my bottom lip, gripped the fuzzy duck tightly to my chest. She didn't look sick. She didn't have any spots. "I don't want to," I whined.

"You have to," she insisted. "You have to stay away from me." She began touching her thumb to each of her fingertips in turn, running them faster and faster against each other as she did when she was particularly agitated.

And then it hit me, as I stood there staring at her, that yes, she was different. It hit me the same way complex issues always hit me after that, at once, with perfect clarity after a long period of fruitless effort. Now it glared at me: She was fevered, had always been fevered with disquiet. I started to cry again with the revelation, the sudden force of it, sobs beginning to hitch my stomach, the fuzzy duck jittering under my chin.

Estella's eyes rounded with worry, and I was hopeful when I saw that they glinted blue, but then her mouth straightened into a stubborn line. She turned the knob and opened the door while I stood there, frozen in fear of her lethal head eyecue.

Then she, my sister, my best friend and protector, my dance partner and ruler of planets, was gone; and though I didn't realize it that night, she took my father with her.

Estella Lianne Sykes

1979

I have been holding my own, but it is an uncomfortable feeling just the same. I am an impostor. I am not used to this absurd two-piece bathing suit. It is impractical and utterly useless for swimming.

And these boys, these beach-rat boys who've never given me a second look before, are suddenly drooling all over themselves, looking past Connie to seek me out, offering me beer, disgusting lukewarm pisswater beer.

The Gulf calls, offers to hide me, and I retreat to it, my comfort zone.

The water is warmer than the beer, and I stroke out, feeling the power in my arms, the flex and ripple of muscle and tendon pulling me through the water, sluicing through the waves. I feel the undertow around my ankles but it merely tickles, a weak river beneath the placid surface of the water.

I tread in place, waving my forearms and watching the beach rats in their faded cutoffs, knotty white strings hanging down their thighs, emphasizing their long muscles as they rush each other, proving their manhood to themselves, to each other, and to Connie.

Tate stands out, as he always does, as he always has. Towheaded, lean-muscled from the work on his father's shrimp boat, already a man beside the boys. I am free to be honest with myself out here. About this anyway. He is beautiful.

Connie will have him.

I wonder what a young man's body feels like and then flush, even out here in this salt-buoyed safe place of mine. I turn back toward the horizon, executing a gentle front somersault before popping up and treading again, facing away from the shore, away from the beautiful young people. Dolphins are feeding beyond the far sandbar, lifting, diving, lifting, diving, all fins and eyes and curious smiles. If I were braver I would join them, would grab a dorsal fin and allow the dolphin to take me down, my ears popping, exploding gases in my head.

Connie squeals and for a moment I think it is a dolphin. I turn back to shore to see her race into the water clutching a football, chased by the beach rats. And Tate. Darwin whispers in my ear, says he will outpace them, and he does, nearly catching her as they hit the first thigh-high waves. But somehow she eludes them, moving faster than I've ever seen her move in the water.

The beach rats quickly give up and return to the beach. And finally Tate gives up and returns to the beach. He flings himself down and shakes his wet hair out of his face. It stays where it lands on his last shake, pointing to the north, toward Little Dune Island. It would be absurd on anyone else. On him it only serves to underscore his confidence.

Something bumps my shoulder and I spin in the water, my heart leaping. It is only the football, bobbing in the waves. It is already several feet from me, the current carrying it farther than the others are willing to swim. I could retrieve it for them, but I don't. Instead I search for Connie.

She is not far from me and I start to call out, but then turn away, realizing suddenly that the salt on my cheeks is not Gulf water. I duck beneath the waves, and when I come up, I don't see her. Then I spot the top of her head. It disappears again. There is a flurry of hands on water, and the head appears again. She is calling out for me. I hear an edge in her voice and stroke toward her, feeling the undertow fight me, stronger this time.

She sees me. I am mesmerized by her frightened eyes, the Sykes eyes. They're brown. Nothing special. Just brown. I stop swimming. I tread water and watch her Sykes eyes realize that I have stopped swimming. Out of the corner of my eye I see that Tate has leapt to his feet and is racing for the water, yelling to the other beach rats, who also fling themselves into the surf. Tate is moving fast, but Connie and I, we are moving so slowly.

When she goes under the next time, I will go under too. I will swallow the Gulf and sink to the bottom with my secret. It is me who needs saving this time. And as Connie disappears under the water for the last time, it is all I can think, all I can scream inside my head where there is now entirely too much space free of numbers.

Save *me*!

PART ONE

CHAPTER ONE

Estella didn't have a disease. Not one you could treat anyway. Estella was a genius. She had an IQ of over 140, though I was never told the exact number. It has not given her a happy life, being a genius. In fact, of both our lives, mine is certainly the one most people would prefer to have.

Except perhaps right now. While Estella, now forty-three, was living her strange, secluded life in Atlanta, I was still in Florida, though far south of Big Dune Island, and on my way to our mother's condo just across town. It was the last thing I felt like doing. What I really felt like doing was working myself into a good lather over Gib's report card, which had arrived in the mail that morning. My oldest son was failing math. Obviously the number gene completely skipped my little branch of the family.

I checked the time as I turned into the condominium's impressive entrance, determined to be back home before Gib returned from school.

"Afternoon, Mrs. Wilder," Otto said, leaning down to peer in my car window. His little security guard hat was tipped back on his head, offering a view of a mile-long forehead speckled with age spots.

"Hi, Otto, how's it going today," I said with a smile—a greeting, not an inquiry. Last year, when nobody pulled in behind me for almost twenty minutes, Otto had given me a vivid account of his emergency appendectomy before he finally raised the gate.

But today he just waved me through, and I parked in the visitors' lot of my mother's building, carefully reapplying my lipstick before heaving a sigh of self-pity and getting out of the car.

The Gulf of Mexico was quiet. Little waves, barely large enough to break, piddled their way onto the sand, scattering the pipers searching for coquinas. The sun glinted off the windows of the building, and I wondered if my mother was watching. She had a perfect view of the parking lot and the Gulf from her fifteenth-floor condo, but spent more time gazing down to see who was coming and going than she did looking out at the water.

I came two days a week, but this had been a special summons, another *putting my affairs in order* meeting. My stomach always clenched in apprehension when she told me she'd been talking to Bob McNarey, her lawyer, financial advisor, and steady escort. And it irritated my husband, Luke, to no end that she chose to stick with Bob rather than placing her financial decisions in his capable hands, though she was never above scooping a juicy stock tip from him.

She opened the door dressed in a pink suit, her glasses perched on the end of her nose and a pen clutched in her hand. She pecked me once on the cheek before making her way to the office, with me trailing behind her.

"I've just gotten off the phone with Bob, and we've decided it's time to sell the beach house," she said. I stopped walking, my muscles forgetting how to move as I tried to process this bomb, dropped as casually as she might mention a new purse, or a change in manicurists. Her back was to me, as if my reaction did not matter. And why should it? The beach house on Big Dune Island was hers, though the move had been Daddy's idea.

His intent had been noble enough. Estella's tutors agreed, when she swallowed their knowledge whole and looked for more, that she should transfer to the college in Grantsville to study with Dr. Roy C. Pretus, the eminent mathematician. Big Dune, just an hour away, satisfied our father's need for privacy, for the wild Florida he'd grown up with. It was a different sort of wild, but wild nonetheless, with salt-stunted scrub and massive dunes as far as his Sykes eyes could see.

Luke and I had honeymooned and vacationed there, but we hadn't been back for more than four years. I had to do the math twice to make myself believe it had been that long. How had I let that happen? How had four years passed by without that beach, without that stretch of Gulf, without the escape from the moneyed heat of Verona?

My mother shuffled papers on her desk while I stood at the door, despair flowering inside me. I thought it would always be there. When I needed a fantasy, when I built a secret future in my mind where everything was exactly as I wanted it, I pictured myself there.

"But why?" I asked. I knew the answer. It was always the same answer. The money—the *real* money—was gone, the victim of several drawn-out lawsuits brought by distant Sykes relatives and the State of Florida. I'd had a small piece, my trust fund, which I'd used to buy and furnish our home and set up college funds for the boys. Mother was still wealthy by anyone's standards, but it was not the kind of wealth that could ignore a home nobody used and could be sold for a hefty profit.

"Because I'm tired of paying the property taxes, the insurance, the caretaker. It just sits there, nobody uses it." She turned her chair to face me, her beautifully preserved cheekbones in high color. "Do you have any idea how much the electric bill is? Your sister won't get those damn books out of there, so the humidistat has to run all the time, and Tate's fee is double what Len's was and I don't have any idea what he does for it. For all I know he's living there."

Her irritation at Tate, son of the home's original caretaker and the first friend I'd made on the island, was false. She loved him like one of her own and kept in touch with him often enough to make me slightly, and silently, jealous. Tate had been scarce during my family's visits to the island, for which I'd always been grateful. I didn't want to relive teenage crushes with my husband and sons there, but I kept in touch through Mother and felt closer to him than I felt to Estella, so he was the nearest thing I had to a sibling now.

"Why don't you rent it out?" I asked, beginning to feel panicky.

Mother waved her hand in dismissal. "I'm not going to get into that. Renters will ruin the place. It's time to sell. That area has jumped in value over the past few years."

"Sell it to us," I said. "It will be an investment for us. Luke would love it."

"Sweetheart, Bob's looked into it and he thinks we can get over two. I'm not sure you're in a position to take that on."

"Two million?" I asked incredulously.

She shot me a wry smile. "Well, I wouldn't be doing it for two hundred, and frankly, that's not much for beachfront property these days."

Defeated, I turned toward the windows. The dazzlingly bright sun was diffused through the thick tinted glass, and I could gaze out at the water without having to shield my eyes. The sound of the waves was diffused too, muffled by the hurricane-strength concrete and steel of the building.

When I was younger, Mother would periodically leave Big Dune to travel to New York. She said there was no decent shopping in Florida, but she always had the same pained look for days before she left, and I knew it was because of the pounding of the waves, the relentless *whoosh* and *crash* that got into her head. Here she could have the cachet of beachfront property without the invasive voice of nature.

"What's the problem, Constance?" The resignation in her voice was heavy, more pronounced than it needed to be.

"I just . . . I guess I'd always thought about being there with the boys. It's a surprise, that's all."

"You haven't been there with the boys for years."

"So your mind is made up? I have no say?"

She looked surprised. "It's *my* house, Connie. I wouldn't expect to have a say if you chose to sell your home. Now, if you want the boys to see it one last time, you can bring them along when we go to close it up."

"When *we* go?"

"Well, we certainly can't allow anyone to go through the house for us, and I can't do it all by myself. I assumed you would want the rugs and your violins. And of course Estella will come for the books."

I snorted and she looked at me sharply. "If you get Estella to come I'll be there with bells on," I said. Unfair maybe, bitchy definitely, but undeniably supported by past behavior. Estella didn't drive, had never gotten her license, in fact. Her boyfriend, live-in life partner, whatever she called him, didn't own a car either.

Estella had received the same funds I had when she turned thirty. She could certainly afford to buy a car. It was an affectation, or perhaps simply an easy way to avoid driving to visit her family. Even when a ride was offered she said she couldn't drive over bridges. She said she couldn't fly. She said she had an inner ear disorder and it was too painful.

And she said all those things to my mother, because we hadn't spoken for almost eight years. No one event, no big fight had caused our break. Rather, the years had simply eroded our already tenuous relationship. And after Daddy died there was nobody to fight over anymore, so even that died away until there was nothing to keep us together at all.

I didn't believe for a second that Estella would go. In fact, I didn't know if I was going to go. But I did want those violins, and the rugs, and if Estella didn't take her books then I would damn well take those too, despite what my father's will said. They should have been mine to begin with.

At least my father left me the rugs, proving he did still occasionally think about me: a kilim and two Bokharas taken—along with the piano—against his lawyer's advice from the family home before its contents had been categorized for auction. I should have rolled them up and brought them home when he died, but they seemed to belong to the beach house.

My violins, the tiny Mittenwald and a full-sized Vuillaume, were safely tucked away in the library at the top of the house, shabbily preserved alongside the books and the piano in their controlled environment. The violins had been beautiful at one time, long before my father bought them. Neither my mother nor I had ever been able to convince him to have them restored.

He hadn't wanted me to play them, he'd wanted me to appreciate them. He liked the names and histories, he liked the expense, and he couldn't help himself at auctions.

And so the bows and fiddles remained in terrible condition to ensure that I wouldn't actually play them. My high school graduation present had been a beautiful Stainer chosen by my mother, the same violin I play today. I hadn't bothered taking the other decrepit violins with me when I'd left for college.

"I've already spoken to Estella," Mother said. "She'll be ready to go next month. We'll drive to Atlanta, pick her up, and then go to the island."

"She won't come," I said. "She'll drop out at the last minute, you know she will. And then I'll be stuck doing everything again."

"I really can't take the martyr routine today, Constance. She promised she would come. She wants the books. I told her that I would give them to the college if she didn't take them herself."

I felt a little smirk twitch my lips, as much in glee at the thought of my mother threatening Estella as in irritation that she didn't even think to offer the books to me. "What did she say?"

"I won't gossip about your sister with you. The important thing is that she'll be coming with us. And I'd like you to be civil. I would like to have good memories of our last visit to the island. Now, when will you be able to get away?"

"I don't know." Luke would be busy with work, Carson was leaving for music camp in a few weeks, and that left Gib. "We're having a problem with Gib," I admitted. It was always Gib. I felt my stomach tense again when I realized that I didn't want him to come to Big Dune. The thought of an eight-hour car ride to Atlanta, then four more back to the island with his sullen silence was enough to make me clench my teeth. But I couldn't let him stay home alone either.

"What did Gib do this time?" my mother asked, but she was distracted, already turned back to her desk. She didn't notice when I didn't answer.

"And I've got my students," I said instead, "and the trio."

She rolled her head across her shoulders as though her neck pained her. "Connie, I think the bambinos can do without you for a few weeks."

"They're not Italian, Mom. And that was a donation-worthy comment if ever I heard one." I volunteered once a week at the Cowachobee Community Center, ostensibly teaching music to the children of mostly Haitian and Mexican immigrants, but I was little more than a glorified baby-sitter. I hit up everyone I knew for donations, especially my mother. Especially when she made comments about bambinos.

She sighed and swung back around to her desk, opening her checkbook to atone. "Five hundred," she said firmly as she signed her name. "Don't ask again until we get back from Big Dune."

I smiled and plucked the check from her fingers. "Thank you. I'll see what I can do. All we have on the schedule is the library series, and Alexander was talking about going on vacation too, so maybe we can coordinate it."

"You know he never called Cecilia," my mother said with a frown.

"Cecilia is thirty-five years older than he is, she's going deaf, and she's a woman."

"Yes, but she's rich as can be."

"It's not 1850, Mother, he doesn't need a patron. Besides, he's not struggling, he's fine."

Alex, the cello player in the trio I played with twice a month, was, in fact, struggling quite a bit. He and my mother got along famously, but she never stopped trying to pair him up with her widowed friends, despite the fact that she knew he was gay. Alex had been my best friend since my freshman year of college when we met in the string ensemble, and I was fiercely protective of him. Mother always put me on edge when she insisted on discussing him as though he were a project.

She arched her eyebrows and leaned back in her chair, studying me, but said nothing except, "So when can you go?"

"Let me talk to Luke," I said, the surest way to buy some time, and left after promising to call her with an answer.

As I drove home, I tried to focus on Gib, tried to come up with some punishment we hadn't tried before, something he might actually care about besides football. He'd taken the PSAT almost three weeks ago and we were expecting those results soon. I'd been so busy worrying about those scores that his report card hadn't crossed my mind until it came in the mail.

But as hard as I tried to concentrate on my son, my mind stubbornly returned to Estella. Despite my irritation, I wondered what it would be like to spend time with her again. I wondered if she would really come to the island knowing that I would be there, if she would brave the four-mile-long bridge. I wondered if I could stand to have her there, could bear the subtle and not-so-subtle slights and jabs that she managed to aim with disquieting perfection. Mostly I wondered if, when we were finally in each other's presence, we could manage to remember that once we had both been valued by our father, had been friends, and had danced the shag as though our lives depended on it.

Estella

I have agreed to go back to Big Dune. It has been twenty-six years. Paul has urged me to go, and after what he's done for me, I can refuse him nothing. It is for him that I am going.

I've taken to responding quickly to his needs. I am almost psychically attuned to him, if I believed in that sort of thing. I've also taken to thanking him often, with the sort of verbal gymnastics I associate with my father, for the smallest thing—a glass of water, an adjustment of my pillows, making the bed. In other words, I've taken to being abjectly grateful.

And I've taken to lying to myself about this trip.

My hair is short, and I wonder if Connie will think I'm ugly. Jealousy over Connie's honeyed curls, so unlike my own washed-out blond frizz, no longer exists. Hair no longer matters to me at all. Many things no longer matter to me.

Like the books. Connie was the one who helped our father in the library, who listened to him when he talked, who climbed on his knee and read with him. I'd never been able to match her devotion, even after he'd focused solely on me. While he talked about our brilliant ancestors, I added and subtracted dates, I rearranged the numbers, I found the relationships between them. I gazed at him with what must have looked like adoration, but was in fact merely me turning my thoughts inward, my face a blank canvas upon which any onlooker could have painted their own longings.

I never cared about the books.

Connie did, and they should have gone to her. By the time he died it was too late to take the enormous, excruciating step of handing them to her. And yet I couldn't take them with me either. So I left them, and now they're my excuse to go back to Big Dune Island. For this chance, I should be grateful. Abjectly grateful.

I look in the mirror and run my hand over my hair.

CHAPTER TWO

I passed Carson on his skateboard at the top of our street and stopped to say hello. He popped the board up into his hand and I hid a smile, knowing that he had done it strictly to impress me. And it did. He was a graceful child, not brawny like Gib, to the dismay of the Pop Warner football coaches.

Carson could never compete with Gib when it came to sports, just as I could never compete with Estella when it came to academics. But it didn't stop coaches from pushing Carson, hoping to tap a previously unknown talent, just as it hadn't stopped teachers from pushing me. The disappointment when that talent didn't materialize was thick enough to be palpable.

"Hey, Mom. I know something you don't," he greeted me.

"Benny Goodman's birthday?"

He grinned, a grin that grew more like Luke's every day. "Yeah, that too. Nope, big surprise. B-i-i-i-i-g surprise," he hinted.

"An elephant?"

He rolled his eyes, too grown-up for fantasy elephant talk, I supposed.

"Your brother home yet?" I asked.

"No, but Dad is."

"Really?"

"Race you home," he said, flinging his skateboard to the ground like a gauntlet.

"No cutting in front of me," I warned and then goosed the engine a little. He took off and I allowed him to go, only taking my foot off the brake when he was well ahead of me. I let the car pull itself along without hitting the gas and watched his slim figure bend and sway on the board as he bumped on and off the curb. He turned sharply into our driveway and I braked lightly, always fearful of hitting him during this little game of ours.

I was watching him so intently that I didn't see it at first, though it certainly couldn't be missed. I slammed on the brakes before I hit it and stared out the windshield at the massive Cadillac badge on the back of a black SUV. Only two explanations came to mind.

Either Luke had gone over the edge and bought our oldest son a brand-new Cadillac—Gib had mangled his sixteenth birthday present, a brand-new Jeep, and his no-driving punishment was nearly at an end—or he was finally done screwing the twenty-four-year-old Starbucks barista. Luke spoiled Gib, there was no question, but even he had his limits, and so I was left with the alternative.

Hello, Deanna, I thought as I turned off the engine. This was by far the most impressive atonement gift I'd received. It had started off with small jewelry, gone through a home appliance phase, and then moved on to larger, more expensive jewelry.

Jocelyn was a locket, Colleen a sapphire-and-diamond bracelet, and

Angela an emerald pendant. I rarely wore any of them. They burned my skin when he slid them on me. I did use the appliances, however, relishing Tina the vacuum cleaner sucking up dirt and Barbara the blue Kitchen-Aid mixer gooey with dough. And now I had Deanna the Escalade. An espresso machine might have been more appropriate.

Carson rapped on the passenger window and I jumped, scowling at him. His face fell and he shrugged before dropping his skateboard back onto the drive and pushing off toward the garage door, which was rumbling up. That would be Luke. He never gave presents without a floor show.

Just as I unbuckled my seat belt his expensive loafers came into view, followed by sharply creased slacks, and then a golf shirt. He was leaning against his own car, one foot cocked over the other, and before the door revealed his face I already knew the expression that would be on it. That self-satisfied grin, the grin that still made my knees weak, still made my rage at being this incredibly stupid cliché of a woman evaporate.

I hated the Cadillac. I hated the barista. And I hated myself. But somehow I could not find it in me to hate Luke when I was faced with his smile and his charm and his undeniable adoration of me. Because make no mistake, I was *the wife*, and I was publicly adored. Or at least adorned. And my friends, despite the fact that I was positive they knew of Luke's infidelities much the same way I knew of their husbands' affairs, considered me very lucky. Alexander was the only one who knew that it was slowly killing me.

This was part of it; this was part of this lifestyle and this town, and right then I was less angry than I was relieved that I could stop pretending it didn't matter and that he would be in our bed tonight, present and thinking of me. I arranged a smile on my face and got out of the car, cautiously approaching the Cadillac as though I didn't know it was for me or *why* it was for me.

Luke met me beside the passenger door and kissed me on the cheek as I gazed in the window at the elegant, pewter-colored interior.

"What's this?" I asked, raising my eyebrows at him.

Are you finished with her? Is this the last time?

"What do you think? I figured it was time you had something a little more befitting your station in life," he answered.

Yes, it's over, but just look at what I got you to make up for it. I swear it's the last time.

"I thought about one of those new Beetles," he continued, "but it just didn't have the dignity I know you crave."

I rolled my eyes and gave him a cheeky grin, scripted, expected reactions. "I think you made the right choice. It's incredible," I said, walking around the front, admiring the massive grille, the sheer size of the thing. He was right; all my friends had SUVs of one expensive sort or another. There were no gas shortages in our neighborhood, and escalating prices would not keep us from the pumps.

I liked to think that I wasn't that shallow. But Luke's childhood had been so different than mine. He had never had expensive cars or houses, had never been envied. These things were important to him.

He walked around the back of the Escalade and opened the driver's side door for me, dangling keys in his hand. I raised myself on my toes to kiss him as my hand closed over the keys, sealing our deal yet again.

"Ready to go for a ride?" he asked.

"Gib failed algebra," I blurted, offering up my child. I wasn't quite ready for the ride.

"Whoa," Luke said, pulling the keys back into the palm of his hand. "Really? What about football?"

I shrugged. "I guess if the school year's over nobody cares that he failed. Maybe they won't let him play next year if he doesn't make it up. I don't know. We'll have to find out." I pulled the report card out of my purse and handed it over to him. He studied it and gave it back to me without a word.

"What are we going to do?" I asked.

"We'll get him a tutor," he said with a firm nod, already decided, taking things in hand. "Don't worry so much, Connie. The rest of his grades are fine; maybe the teacher doesn't like him. Listen, I'll handle it. I know what Gib needs. And I know what you need too. Come on, don't you want to take that baby out for a spin? It's got a big backseat." He wiggled his eyebrows up and down at me and bounced the keys off the end of his finger again.

"His PSAT scores are supposed to be coming in any day," I said, ignoring his flirtation. "What if his scores are bad on that too?"

Luke sighed and stuffed his hands in his pockets. I felt like a child suddenly.

"First of all, I'm not worried about his *scores*. That's your father talking. It's not like Gib needs to rely on scores for a scholarship. I said we'd get him a tutor, didn't I? Let's hold on to the report card until we get the results and then we'll see if this is a problem with math, or a problem with a teacher, okay? Now come on, let me worry about this. It's time to break this baby in." With his hands still in his pockets he moved his body up against mine, leaning down to kiss my neck.

Subtlety had never been Luke's strong suit, and he became more obvious, or I became more cynical, every year. The first car we bought together, a Ford Thunderbird Super Coupe, was the first car either of us had had that was large enough to comfortably fool around in. And we took advantage of it. Perhaps he took advantage of it with other women too, I don't know. I didn't believe he began screwing around until after Carson was born, our last try for another child after two miscarriages, but I could have been wrong.

The next car was quickly christened in the same manner, and each car we bought after that brought the same lecherous act from Luke. It used to thrill me, and sometimes it still did. I wanted Luke back in my bed, to claim him, to punish him, to remind him of who I was again. To remind myself of who I was again.

But doing it in Deanna the Escalade was too much like doing it *with* Deanna the barista, and I was certain that when I crawled in the backseat and wriggled out of my pants to straddle my husband, I would not smell new car leather, but slow-roasted coffee and milky latte. A ménage à trois with biscotti and a V-8 engine.

He should not have bought this vehicle. It was Alex's voice in my ear, but it was somehow becoming mine. Something was coming apart inside me. The thought of spending three weeks trapped with my mother and Estella in the beach house, of my ever-distant child sabotaging his future, of my husband's shiny, gas-guzzling apology—they all snapped painfully inside me like rubber bands against my tender inner wrist, reminders that my life wasn't what it was supposed to be.

I stared at the keys winking in Luke's hand, wondering what would come out of my mouth when I finally opened it. I was disappointed to hear myself say, "Let me freshen up," as I stuffed the report card back in my purse and turned toward the house.

I cried afterward. Luke held me in the backseat, his chin resting atop my head. I'd cried after sex before, but it had always been because of the release, the chemicals flooding my body. Luke chuckled at my tears, convinced they were badges of his prowess, as they had been in the past.

He took the long way home. We passed Starbucks and I gazed out the window as we drove past. Did he hope that she would see us, would know that the new Escalade was mine, his, ours? I turned my eyes forward again, those rubber bands still snapping—*not your life, not your life.*

A month before that night in the music room, when Estella protected me from catching her genius, Mother went to New York to shop, and our nanny, Graciela, she of the mammoth thighs and Tabasco-tinged breath, was left in charge. She put us to bed early, which meant I had to lie there longer than usual before I could make swift down the hall to the music room.

I had little games that I played to keep myself busy, to stay calm. I might recite the stories our father told us about his grandfather and great-grandfather under my breath, faster and faster, like a prayer. Or I might try to remember the order of titles in the library, moving shelf to shelf until I couldn't remember what came next.

I never wondered what Estella did during that odd half-light suspended time until I was years older. Did she lie quietly, rearranging numbers in her head until they formed whatever configuration she was looking for? It was hard to imagine her still for any length of time. I found it more likely that she paced her room like a caged panther, counting her steps over and over, figuring how many to her bathroom door, to her window, to her desk.

My mother later told me that Estella's inability to concentrate on one thing at a time was what led to them having her tested to begin with. Having me tested was just a bonus. One that paid no dividends except to let everyone know that I was not destined for greatness.

When I finally broke for the music room, Estella was already at the banister. She held her hand up in a warning and I tiptoed the rest of the way, carefully keeping the hem of my nightgown from brushing the railing. I dropped to my knees beside her, noting with some concern that her eyes were a murky sea-grass green.

I could hear my father at the dining room table, his voice low and soothing. And there was Graciela's voice, arcing into a high giggle. I strained for a third voice and, finding none, was immediately bored. But then Estella grasped my wrist tightly in her hand and pulled me toward her, pointing with her other hand.

I pressed my face to the railing, my cheeks puffing around the edges of the bars, only able to see out of my left eye. At the right angle we could almost get a whole view of the dining room by the reflection in a large mirror hanging in the living room. But it was painful and left us with red creases on our faces, and there was rarely a situation intriguing enough to warrant it.

Graciela was seated with her back to the mirror, and her hair was loose, spilling over the chair back in a long black wave. My father was in profile at the head of the table where he always sat, and aside from the two of them the room was empty. I was just about to whisper a complaint to Estella when Graciela pushed back her chair, tucked her hair behind her ears, and crawled beneath the table.

I thought she must have dropped a piece of food, or maybe her napkin. I was forever losing my napkin—my lap seemed maddeningly slanted—and had ducked under that table many times to retrieve it.

Estella's fingers ratcheted painfully around my wrist with each moment that Graciela did not come out. My father leaned back in his chair, apparently unconcerned about Graciela and her errant napkin, but then his hands disappeared under the edge of the table, and I realized that our nanny was doing something in my father's lap.

I stared only a second longer before Estella jerked backward, taking me with her, and we thudded onto the Oriental runner. There was a sudden noise from the dining room, and we stared at each other in terror. Our father took the stairs two at a time, but by the time he reached the top I was in my room.

I trembled beneath my covers, clutching a stuffed dog, less concerned now with Graciela and her interest in my father's lap than I was with my role of sleeping innocent. He stood over my bed, breathing heavily, but he said nothing, and I finally felt his hand light upon my head. I both longed for the comfort of that touch and was repulsed by it.

He left, quietly closing my door behind him, and I heard him walk down the hall to Estella's room. Were numbers racing through her mind even then? Zero comforting her the way my stuffed animals comforted me?

The next night I crept to the music room, staying well away from the railing. Estella was not there yet, and I clambered onto the sofa and wrapped the shawl around my shoulders, already having forgotten the revulsion I'd felt when my father touched my head with the same hand he'd touched Graciela's head with. At first, all I took with me from that night was that nannies were definitely not in my future and that I needed to figure out how to pick my fallen napkins up without ducking under the table.

Estella finally stole in the door, allowing her eyes to get used to the dark before she shut it. She climbed onto the sofa with me, tugging for a bit of the shawl, and we huddled together.

"Connie?" Estella said. "You can't tell Mother what we saw last night."

This put a new slant on things. "Why not?"

"Because what we saw didn't really happen," she said. "We were dreaming, okay?"

"Oh," I said. "But—"

"It's our secret dream, okay?"

I thought about it for a moment. I had many secrets with Estella. I knew all about secrets, but I knew nothing about nannies in laps. I went with what I knew. "Okay."

I don't know to this day if our father found Estella before she reached her bed and what he said if he did. I learned how to keep a napkin on my lap. I had Gib young, married and pregnant before I graduated from college. I never got a nanny. I never told my mother. And Estella and I never spoke of it again.

But it remained fresh in my mind, like an acid etching. I kept trying to forget, but the sight of Graciela tucking her hair behind her ears and my father moving his hands down to his lap never went away, and this was what I thought of when I cried in the Cadillac.

I did not tell Luke about the beach house. I did not ask Gib about his report card. And nearly a week later I still had not called my mother with an answer. When the phone rang I considered not answering, certain it was Mother, ready to start nagging, but when I glanced at the caller ID, I smiled and picked up, always happy to talk to Alexander.

"So can we practice at seven instead of six?" he asked without preamble.

"Sure. I'm not the one you need to ask. Have you called Hannah yet?"

Hannah was our flutist, a tiny, harried woman with less free time than anyone I knew. Alexander had moved to Verona after a disastrous break-up with a high-strung conductor, and he'd initially harbored grand ideas of taking South Florida by storm. Unfortunately he wound up with me and Hannah. The mother of five kids, Hannah had to fight for her time with the trio by necessity. I had to fight for my time to play too, but my fight was against my own tendency to disappear into my family, whether they needed me or not.

Alexander, childless but for his students, wound up being our default manager. The baroque period was rich in pieces for our trio, but it took skill and time to arrange concerts, so Alexander shouldered the responsibility for organizing everything.

"Of course. She can do it. How's the Escalade?" he asked quietly. He was the only one who knew about the gifts and what they meant. This one had nearly sent him over the edge, and I'd found myself consoling him rather than the other way around.

"It's . . . large," I said, forcing a smile into my voice, but he was silent. "Everything okay, Alex?" I prodded.

"I'm not sure. Is everything okay with you?"

"Ah, did my mother talk to you? I was going to talk to you about it at practice. You did say you were ready for a vacation."

"What? No, I haven't talked to June, I just—listen, can we talk after practice?"

I was mystified. "What's going on?"

"I really want to talk to you in person," he pleaded.

"All right," I said. "We'll talk about vacation then too. I have to go close the house on Big Dune after Carson leaves for camp. I'll be gone for a few weeks."

"We'll look at the schedule," he said. "David can probably sub for you."

"Great. Maybe you could use the time to schedule some auditions?" I was constantly pushing him to find a position with the Verona Symphony, or at least get on the sub list.

"Don't start," he warned. "I'm very fragile right now."

I grinned as we said good-bye; he was always *fragile right now*. I wondered what the big mystery was. Maybe he had a new love interest. Or maybe he was looking to change the trio, find a pianist and make it a quartet. It was Hannah's main fear for some reason, though Alexander reassured her constantly.

In the beginning, I encouraged him to replace me as soon as he could. I wasn't the most dedicated violin player. My father's gift of the child's violin might not have been prompted by a desire to see me actually play, but after Estella's genius commanded all of his attention I naturally turned to something I thought might please him, might swing his beautiful language and Sykes eyes back my way.

And so I practiced. And practiced some more. And got a callus on my chin from the chin rest, one to match on my neck, a hickey on my collarbone from the shoulder rest, and an unconscious uplift of my left shoulder even when no violin was in sight. All to achieve little but a broken heart when my practice turned me into a merely competent player by the time I was twelve, not a prodigy, not a genius, nothing to rival Estella.

My gift was beauty. A fact constantly pointed out to me by my teachers, who, after discovering I was merely average in intellect, seemed to feel slighted that they didn't get their chance with Estella. Aside from the Sykes eyes, I was my mother's child through and through, and the light brown eyes combined with the blond hair and my mother's delicate features seemed to strike a chord in men, especially men like Luke. Luke didn't like the calluses, or my short nails, and so I gradually stopped practicing regularly after college. I occasionally played something soft and dreamy when Gib wouldn't go down for a nap—until it became obvious that it just agitated him.

When Carson was born I put the Stainer away and forgot it, until a friend from college came for a visit. We drank too much wine one night, and somehow she convinced me to pull the violin out. The case, stuffed behind discarded Easter baskets and outdated coats in the hall closet, was clogged with dust, and I felt a pang of guilt, as if I'd neglected an old friend for so long that I might never be forgiven, and rightly so.

After I'd tightened and rosined the bow I drew it across the strings, and from the discordant wail that drifted forth it seemed that perhaps I was indeed not to be forgiven. I worked on it for almost forty minutes, but it slipped out of tune almost immediately. My long nails made me clumsy on both the strings and the bow, and I grew frustrated as I hunted for the nail clippers I'd always kept in my case but that seemed to have disappeared.

My wedding rings kept my fingers from moving the way they should; my hoop earrings clanged against the violin; my necklace ground into my collarbone; I couldn't find a comfortable position for my left foot; I was distracted by the smell drifting from the long-shut case; my hair fell across my forehead and into my eyes. In short, it was a disaster.

My friend, bewildered by my growing irritation, poured me another glass of wine. But even after divesting myself of all jewelry, pulling my hair back, and cramping my hands awkwardly to play around my nails, I couldn't bring myself to listen to my own out-of-tune playing. I finally put the violin away in the corner and spent the rest of the night in an oddly satisfying snit.

After my friend left the next week, I clipped my nails off and worked on tuning nonstop. Once the A-string finally stayed where it was supposed to, I pulled my stack of music out, alternately sucking my sore, naked fingertips and flipping the sheets. Like lines from favorite childhood books, snippets of music ran through my mind as I shuffled through them, and I found myself excited in a way I hadn't been since I was a child at the thought of coaxing music out of the air.

When Alexander moved to town, I'd needed some prodding, but there was no denying the joy the trio brought me. Everything about my life was shared. The very food on my plate was open to the jab of a fork from Luke or one of the boys, and I could hardly remember the last time I'd had five minutes alone. Not only was the playing my own, but somehow the music seemed my own too, coursing up like blood through my heart as the bow rose, running down through my veins as the bow fell.

I worried that if I played with other musicians it would force me to share what I firmly believed to be mine, but as soon as those first notes from the three instruments met and threaded together, I knew that it was all more concretely mine than I ever would have thought. I was *giving* them the music, because it was mine to give.

Alexander's phone call was mysterious, but he had a flair for drama; I quashed the dread that he might want to break the trio up and accepted that his news would come when it came. I put it out of my mind and was later grateful for the last few days of peace that act brought me.

Estella

Connie will not set a date, and I am tempted to call the whole thing off. I don't want her here. I don't want my mother here. I don't want them to ask me why Paul and I aren't married, why we leave our doors unlocked, why we rent the upstairs, why we don't have a car, why I don't shop more, why I'm so thin, quiet.

We don't *need* to rent the rooms. We want to. We love the college students. Paul is social, and he somehow found the social animal in me and patiently coaxed it out, and now I cannot imagine life without these young people. And they have been astounding this year. They refused to allow me to notify the schools that I could no longer take students. Instead, they set up a two-sided desk next to my bed and took turns tutoring, looking to me for confirmation, teaching at the same time they were learning themselves.

The doors remain unlocked because many of the younger students

I—we—tutor need somewhere they can go that will always be available. They are the scholarship kids at private schools, and few come from happy homes. Some are talented in math and come to me for more advanced skills, some need help in math in order to keep their scholarships.

The schools send them to me because they know I'm no longer at the college and have the time. And because I do it for free now.

I don't want to explain any of this.

I tell Paul I've been tired. He looks at me sternly and tells me I'm going before he takes me to bed and holds me gently, as though I might crack at the seams. I tell him I have too much to do to bother with old memories, or old books. He shows me the bookcases he's making for me, makes me run my hands over them. They're beautiful, and I don't have the heart to tell him that I wish he would abandon them to work on his own projects.

The things he makes are permanent. He turns imperfections into bowls, split wood into sculpture, lightning strikes into art. He believes the imperfect can become perfect if he can only find the correct form, and then fit it to function. I cannot explain that there is no perfect form or function to this family.

There is nothing beautiful to be made from our lightning strikes.

CHAPTER THREE

The Haydn went better than we expected, and Alexander was pleased beyond measure. He played a quick jazz riff and twirled his cello, laughing, and Hannah and I grinned at each other as we put our instruments away. Alexander's approval was always worth the practice time.

I pulled my wedding rings out of my front pocket and slid them back on my finger as I watched Alexander wipe down his cello. I'd never gotten the knack of playing with the rings on. It was too distracting for me, too invasive, and I rather liked the ritual of it, the trade of one life for another. Without the rings I played unencumbered by earthly possessions and responsibilities, but they were always there when I finished, to remind me that my life was anchored by things more permanent than the notes that died away in the air despite my attempts at sustaining them.

Once I'd laid my case by the door, I broached my trip, showing them the dates in Alexander's date book. It was unfairly short notice, and I almost hoped they would protest so I could have a reason to cancel.

"I'll see if I can take my two weeks here," Alexander said, tapping his pen against the calendar. "And David can easily sub for this performance," he continued, circling the date we'd planned for the library.

He poked his pen at the performance scheduled for the week after my return, the night we were to play the Haydn Trios for the conservancy. "But you've got to be back for this, Connie. I'm comfortable with the Beethoven, God knows we've done it enough, and the Telemann is in good shape. Can you guys practice the Haydn during those two weeks? And, Hannah, you're still lagging on the Tartini."

It would mean taking my violin to the beach house, but it was too important to him for me to turn him down, so I agreed. Hannah, who hadn't taken a vacation since her fourth child, didn't even bother looking at the dates as she closed the case on her flute.

"Whatever you want. I'll try not to screw up too badly, darling," she said with a smile, blowing an air kiss at him.

"Can we fit a practice in . . . here?" he asked, circling the Saturday after I came back. I agreed to that too, though I knew Luke wouldn't be happy about me having practice on his first day off after I'd returned.

Hannah shrugged. "Long as you don't mind me bringing Jan and Natalie," she said. "The other kids will sell them on eBay if I leave them alone long enough."

"No problem," Alexander said, and we stood there awkwardly. Hannah and I usually walked out together, talking about kids, husbands, houses, anything but music. A trio was a careful mix. There was always eventually someone left out of something. It might be social plans, or the decision to try a new piece, or just gossip. It was like having two best friends; each covert conversation and private joke had the power to instill paranoia, altering the delicate balance.

Alexander cleared his throat. "Connie, I'm still having problems with my server bumping me off. Could you have another look at my computer?" he asked, his eyes pleading with me to go along.

"Sure," I said. "I'll see you when I get back, Hannah. Enjoy the break if the kids will let you."

Hannah's eyes flitted between us uncertainly, but she finally smiled and turned away. "Okay. Have a good time at the beach, Connie."

Alexander wrinkled his nose at me when the door shut. "Sorry," he said. He suddenly looked very serious, even nervous. I followed him to the kitchen, where he poured us each a glass of wine before perching on the stool next to mine.

"I don't know how to do this," he said and took a slug of wine.

My heart took a double beat and I licked the wine, too dry for my taste, from my lips. "Just say it," I said softly.

"I've lost lesser friends than you, Connie."

I stared at him, taking my fingers off the stem of the wineglass and twining them in my lap. "Say it, Alexander."

"I saw Luke. I saw him with someone. It was obviously not just a friend."

Time slowed and slowed and slowed. Another one? So soon. I wasn't ready for it so soon. Had it truly become this easy for him? Apparently, yes. I continued to stare at Alex, my eyes growing dry and then watering, finally forcing me to blink, to move, to breathe again, though I did so in slow motion. Those rubber bands snapped, snapped, snapped, and yet I still couldn't speak. If I didn't speak then perhaps I would not have to listen.

But my tongue betrayed me and I blurted, "When? What did you see? Oh, shit—what did she look like?"

Alexander had tears in his eyes, and I could have cried for him if I hadn't been so intent on not crying for myself. "I'm so sorry, Connie. I really debated whether to tell you at all—"

I held my hand out. "It's fine," I said forcefully, almost aggressively, and then quickly dropped my hand when I saw him lean back away from me, wide-eyed, as though afraid I might strike him. "Just tell me . . . please."

He took a deep breath. "Okay. I had a lunch date—" He paused. I knew this was big news and that I should be happy, but I couldn't think about it right then. I took another swallow of wine and waited.

"Anyway, we went to Bruccia's, you know, with the fountain?"

I nodded. I knew the place. It was sensual, with jeweled silk pillows in the private booths and a massive stone water fountain in the middle of the room providing cover, privacy. "When?" I asked.

"Friday," he said, watching me carefully. "I was sitting by the far wall, in a booth, and I saw them walking up the sidewalk and through the door."

"What did she look like?" I asked again.

"Long black hair, thin, tall . . . and young. Sort of, oh, I don't know, hippie looking."

Deanna. The barista. It shouldn't have hurt as much as it did. *Thin* hurt, though I was still damn trim myself; *young* hurt worse, but the real twist of the knife was that it was Deanna, that it was—what? A relapse? To my knowledge, Luke had never seen any of the other women again after breaking it off. Deanna was now a compound fracture.

I considered the Cadillac. Was it the end-of-the-affair apology I'd thought it was and he simply couldn't stay away? Or had it merely been an expensive decoy, taking our unspoken agreement to a new level to see how I might cope? A thought suddenly occurred to me and I slowly lowered the wineglass to the counter. *Was he in love with her?*

"Connie?" Alexander said.

"Did he see you?"

He shook his head and poured more wine. The neck of the bottle chattered lightly on the rim, making me wince. "No. No way."

"How did you know they were together? I mean, that they weren't just friends?"

He looked down into his glass, swirling the wine, pretending to inhale its fumes while he decided what to tell me. "It was obvious, Con. He had his hand on her waist when they came in, he put his arm around her shoulders when they talked to the host, they sat on the same side of the booth." He stopped and looked up at me. "There was more."

I nodded. I believed him. How could I not? My mother's old advice, given years ago, to maintain a stiff upper lip as long as Luke was discreet, ran through my mind. I wondered who else had seen him. I was as scared as I was angry, and I wasn't sure which emotion I wanted to win.

"Connie, tell me I've done the right thing," Alexander said. His eyes were sad, and in a moment his lip was going to start trembling out of control. I leaned forward and put my hands on his shoulders.

"Of course you did. Yes, you did. Thank you," I said, feeling not the least bit ridiculous for thanking him. He moved quickly to enfold me in his arms and I let him comfort me, but by the time I left, red-eyed and slack-faced, I still didn't have any idea of what I was going to do. I drove around for almost an hour before I headed to Mother's.

But it was Bob McNarey who opened the door when I knocked. "Connie," he said, "how nice to see you. I was just asking June about you and the boys."

He was the last person I felt like seeing. I leaned in to accept his pursed lips on my cheek and then walked past him. Mother took one look at me and tilted her head toward her office. "Bob, we'll be a moment. Perhaps you could find a glass for Connie?"

Bob hustled toward the kitchen and my mother followed me into the office, shutting the door behind her.

"What is it?"

"Luke," I said quietly.

"A woman?"

I nodded, and then I was crying again. She stayed where she was, backed up against the office door. "There are tissues in the top drawer," she said, and I fumbled for a minute until I found them. "Is it serious?" she asked.

I shrugged. "Looks like it," I said, and blew my nose. Mother watched me clean myself up and then crossed the room to sit in the chair beside the desk. She laid one hand on the desk and tapped a manicured nail on the blotter in front of me.

"And what are you doing about it?" she asked.

I looked up at her and told the truth: "I don't have any idea. I just can't do this anymore, Mother. I can't. It's just one after another. It's never going to end. I think I want—"

"What?"

"I want out." It was almost a whisper.

She was quiet for several moments. "I suggest you make sure that's what you want before you talk to Luke," she finally said.

"Could you be on my side for once?" I snapped at her. "Just once?"

Her face softened. "I am always on your side, Constance. Always. Sometimes women don't know what divorce will do to them. You're not a young woman anymore."

I snorted. "When I was a young woman you talked me out of it too. When exactly is the right time?"

She was silent again, and then said, "When you've lost yourself."

"Well." I thought about that for a moment, but just a moment. "Then it's time."

My mother nodded once, decisively. "Do you know how to go about this?"

I stared at her. How to go about it? How else? "I guess I'll have to talk to Luke," I said.

The look of horror on her face might have been comical if it weren't for the subject matter. "Do no such thing," she said. "You need to know where you stand first."

"What are you talking about? I think I know by now where I stand."

She shook her head. "Not with him, Connie. Financially, where do you stand?"

I sat back in the desk chair and stared at her, stunned. The fact was, I had no idea. I had become everything my friends and I swore we never would. I had allowed Luke to control everything financially. It was his business, it was what he did, and did well. I knew how much was in the household account, and that was about it. I paid the bills out of it every month, I bought clothes for the family, food. But there was never more than a few thousand in the account at one time.

I allowed Luke to handle all the investments. In fact, I had even, years ago, waved my hand at him when he'd been explaining our status. I had done it to myself. I had created and then embraced the role I now found myself in. I felt sick.

"What do I do?" I whispered.

She pushed a legal pad and pen in front of me. "Are you sure you want to do this?"

I picked up the pen. I wasn't sure what she wanted. An affidavit declaring my intentions? "Yes," I said, "yes, I'm sure. I can't do it anymore."

"List everything. Luke and the kids' full names and Social Security numbers. All account numbers you can remember. Every creditor. Everything you can get your hands on. Do not, under any circumstance, tell Luke what you're doing. Get started. I need to talk to Bob."

I stared up at her. "How—how do you know to do all this?" I asked.

She stopped as she was reaching out for the doorknob and stood with her back to me for a moment, then slowly lowered her arm and turned around. "Just because I never did it doesn't mean I wasn't ever prepared to do it, Connie. Even if you don't wind up going through with it, at least you'll be prepared." She nodded at the pad in front of me and then left the room, closing the door on my shocked face.

When Mother returned to the room she had Bob in tow. He sat down in the chair she'd vacated while she stood by his shoulder.

"I'm sorry to hear about your troubles, Connie," Bob said. He held his hand out for the pathetically short list I'd made, and I ripped it off the pad and handed it to him. He looked it over and gave me a pained smile. "Is this it?"

I nodded. "I don't know account numbers off the top of my head. It's not like I've been planning this."

"Planning is exactly what you need to do," he said, leaning forward in the chair. "Have you considered counseling?"

I looked at my mother and could tell that she was remembering the visit I'd made to her seven years earlier. I'd left Luke, showing up at her house with a packed car, a baby on one hip, a sullen eight-year-old trailing behind me, and a startling case of chlamydia.

Luke had already called her and she was ready for me. She allowed me to stay for two weeks to clear my head. Then she gave me her theory: The wealthier the man, the more affairs he had, and if I were to be married to such a man then I could appreciate all the fine things that came with it, or I could raise two children alone.

Her advice had seemed hopelessly outdated, and though I listened patiently to her over the dinner table, in her guest room at night, with my fist stuffed against my mouth and tears running from my eyes, I rejected every bit of it. But the chlamydia cleared up quickly with medication, and Luke and I saw a marriage counselor.

Luke made promises, the counselor proclaimed us healed, and I moved back into our home. In the end, we could have saved the money. My mother knew more about marriage and men than I'd given her credit for.

"We've tried counseling before," I answered.

"Same reason?"

I nodded.

"Try to find all the paperwork related to those sessions—receipts, canceled checks. Is he a serial cheater?"

I gnawed on my lip and nodded again.

"Any proof?"

"Not unless chlamydia—"

Bob grinned. "He gave you an STD? That's great."

I flinched. "It's gone now," I stammered, suddenly horrified at what this man knew about me now.

"Doctor receipts for that too," he said. "Now listen, don't you breathe a word of this to anyone. You're vulnerable right now. If he gets to your assets before we know what's going on it's going to get ugly. You have to think self-defense right now. How many years have you been married?"

"Seventeen."

"Excellent. Still just the two boys?"

"Yes. Gib just turned sixteen, and Carson is eight now."

"Good, good. Keep them completely out of it, not a word."

"Of course not," I said, offended that he'd even mentioned it. But he either didn't notice my offense or didn't care.

"This week get everything you can, but be careful. Rent a PO box and get me the address in case we need paperwork to come through the mail. Get a safe-deposit box at a separate bank and put all your jewelry, all your legal documents in it. Don't call attention to yourself. He can't know you're removing your jewelry from the house, it's a sure tip-off."

My mother sat in the chair next to him and reached out to take the legal pad and pen from my numb fingers. "Give me a list of what she should look for, Bob," she said quietly. I remained speechless, taken aback at the amount of work suddenly thrust before me, the sleaziness of it all.

"Tax returns, credit card statements, insurance policies, business records, any itemized phone records you can find. Marital assets, family cash flow, credit lines. Look, if it's got dollar signs or tits attached, I want to see it."

"Jesus, Bob," Mother said, shooting him a pained look.

Bob took one look at my face and stammered an apology. "Hey, sorry, sorry. Look, just keep your normal schedule and mention nothing to Luke. Get together everything you can, and call me Monday."

"Keep my normal schedule? How—well, I can't go to Big Dune now," I protested.

My mother started to speak but Bob raised his hand. "You should definitely go. Tracking all this stuff down is going to take time, and the farther away from your husband you are during it the better. You'll have less opportunity to slip up and say something. Some say it's a risk, leaving the home, but from what your mother tells me you bought that home with your trust fund?"

"Yes," I said, surprised by the fact that my heart didn't leap when I thought about losing the house the way it had when I found out Mother was selling the beach house.

"Then the law is on our side. When are you going?"

Mother raised her eyebrows at me.

"I guess I can go after Carson leaves for camp," I said. "As long as I can get Luke to agree."

"Agree to what?" Mother asked. "Agree to have three weeks to himself? I don't think you'll have a problem, Connie."

I realized she was right. "Okay," I said. "We'll leave next Saturday."

Bob made notes on the paper, and then met my eyes. "Have you ever been unfaithful?" he asked. "Anything I need to know about? Surprises can really screw things up."

"Absolutely not," I said, infuriated by the question.

"Hey, the questions will get more personal than this, so get used to it. Divorce is ugly. I should know, I've done it twice, and frankly, I advise against it. But if you're determined, then I'll get the ball rolling. I'm not a divorce attorney of course, but I have plenty of them working for me. I'll be close by during the whole process, looking out for you."

I nodded wordlessly, suddenly aware of the enormous step I'd just taken by giving this man, a man I'd always vaguely distrusted, my family's personal information. He stood, pecked my mother on the cheek, and then he was gone.

I sat back in the chair and accepted the glass of wine my mother proffered.

"You can stop this at any time," she said. "And you can trust Bob. He knows where all the bodies are buried in this town."

"My God, Mother," I said, my hand at my throat. "It's like he's your—your—"

"My what?" she asked coolly, raising her eyebrows.

"Your henchman or something," I finished.

"I owe more to that man than you know, Connie. He'll take good care of you. Now, what will you do tonight?"

I shook my head. "I don't know. I guess I'll go home. The kids are probably starving."

"Okay, then. Go home. Act normally, not a word to him, do you hear? You've got almost two weeks to get the rest of the information for Bob. You can come over Monday and we'll go through this together. And you can always change your mind." She looked at me, her eyes more focused on me than I'd seen them in years. "You're going to be fine, Connie."

I agreed with a nod, but on the drive home I knew that she was wrong. I couldn't do this. And I wasn't going to be fine.

Estella

A date. Connie has finally set a date. It's close to my appointment and I find myself hesitating, thinking of lying to Mother on the phone.

"I don't know," I say, looking at my calendar as though she were in the room, watching me. "I've got some appointments—"

"Connie said she's looking forward to seeing you," she interrupts, and my heart pounds in my chest, responding to the comment, as though it can take over the conversation for me.

"She said that?" I ask. I don't believe her. My mother lies easily and convincingly.

"She did," she says.

My heart still pounds, and its beats turn into words: "Well, as long as I'm back home by the thirtieth."

"Then it's settled," Mother says, and as I hang up the phone Paul comes in. His hair is filled with sawdust, and old, dried varnish streaks his shirt. He smells amazing, and I inhale deeply as his arms encircle me from behind. I pull a red pen from my desk drawer and circle the day they will come for me, draw a line through the next three weeks, and circle the day they will return me to my home, three days before my appointment.

"It's going to be fine," Paul whispers in my ear, and I nod.

I don't know which *it* he's talking about, but I know the odds of both better than he does. And I don't know which I'm more afraid of. Those red-circled and -lined dates, or the one penciled in, silvery and glinting in the light. The numbers on the calendar fight for space in my head.

I breathe Paul in again.

CHAPTER FOUR

I avoided Luke, and even the kids, as much as I could that week. But I often caught myself staring at one of them as they spoke, watching their lips move, forgetting to answer. I continued to get Carson ready for camp and agreed to a parent-teacher conference with his music teacher for the following Wednesday, though I'd never have remembered it if I hadn't attached a note to the refrigerator.

The things I forgot that week could have easily filled a psychiatrist's hour: lunch with a friend, overdue library books, dry cleaning, Luke's favorite beer, Gib's favorite cheese crackers, Carson's favorite everything. I was scattered and short with everyone, but as soon as I was alone in the house the silence snapped me out of my haze, and I hurried to gather information.

I stealthily riffled through the papers on Luke's desk while he was gone, feeling like an intruder in my own home. I went through my jewelry, through our insurance papers, through Luke's drawers. The distance I managed to put between myself and my family in such a short period was frightening. I felt like an island, with my family eddying and flowing around me, unaware that I had become immovable. They did not change, and did not notice that I had.

Gib remained aloof and out of the house and Luke was "working hard" at the office. I purposely did not follow up on his whereabouts, and he was not home when Gib's PSAT scores came that Saturday.

I'd spent the morning fitting my fingers to Haydn, trying to lose myself in it. The sunroom where I practiced, filled with my orchids and flooded with light, was next to the kitchen, but I hadn't heard anyone come in and felt a certain satisfaction that the music had engrossed me enough to cut the rest of the world off.

Carson was playing in the pool and Gib was nowhere to be found, but when I broke from practice the mail was already on the kitchen counter, the long, nearly transparent envelope peeking out from between bills. I hadn't heard Gib leave, but I also didn't hear any bass from his stereo, which usually meant that he wasn't home. Perhaps he'd seen the envelope and was making himself scarce. I tore it open.

His reading scores, good. Writing, good, both in the slightly-better-than-average-but-not-so-much-as-to-attract-attention land that Gib had perfected. But math. How could a child with the genes this child had score so abysmally on math?

Luke's theory had been wrong. This wasn't a teacher who didn't like Gib, it was something else altogether. Could he have done it on purpose? That would be typical Gib, the same way the circumstances surrounding the test had been typical Gib.

These results were from a makeup PSAT. Gib had intercepted the notice that had come in the mail about the first test, and the date had come and gone without our knowledge. It wasn't until I went online to browse the school website that I found out he'd missed it. Luke wasn't concerned, pointing out to me that the test was voluntary to begin with.

Instead, he'd shaken his head with a mock-weary smile and told Gib to be ready to take the makeup test, winking at me behind our son's back. I was as irritated with him as I was with Gib. I knew that just because they call it the *preliminary* SAT, as though the test were merely practice, it didn't mean that the numbers wouldn't be in their permanent files. Though I didn't know that for sure and was practically superstitious about asking for more details from the school, those numbers were important to me.

Numbers had governed Estella's life for so long, gained her entry and kept her apart at the same time. That was why I had not wanted Gib's or Carson's IQ tested. I wanted them to grow up to be normal, accepted, happy.

Like me.

But with the PSAT, numbers had again assumed significance in my life, and I wanted to stress their importance to Gib. He had managed to maintain a solid B average throughout middle school, neither failing nor excelling, never giving reason for us to be more involved. And then high school had crept behind our backs and changed our child into a sneaky, untrustworthy cynic. Luke refused to believe that anything had changed. As long as Gib was still playing football, Luke was happy. Gib was at the end of his sophomore year, halfway through his high school career, and Luke was still insisting that he simply hadn't settled in yet.

He reminded me that he understood Gib better than I, that Carson was my domain, my responsibility, while Gib was his buddy.

Gib was Luke's, right from the moment he plucked him, red-faced and screaming, off my chest in the delivery room. Luke could always calm him. Luke was the one he ran to when he got hurt. He walked early, talked early, and potty-trained early. Though I never voiced the idea to anyone, I was certain that his motivation in achieving those milestones was sheer determination to get as far away from me as quickly as he could.

His shoulders broadened after he turned fourteen, and in the two years since, he'd steadily packed on muscle as easily as he packed on attitude, thrilling his coaches, making his father proud. And while I resorted to avoiding my oldest child and his aggressive maleness, Luke sought him out. He was making Gib into the man's man he'd had to wait for so long to turn into himself.

Carson had been different right from the beginning. He cried when Luke tried to pull him from my arms, and I admit that I clung the tighter to him for it. He needed me all the time. At eight he was starting to pull away slightly, but once his friends had gone home and dark fell, he was my boy again, anxious to earn my laugh. His trip to music camp that summer would be the first time he'd spent away from me, and worry was already gnawing at my stomach.

Gib and Carson were as different as Estella and I were. And it was that difference that made me push them together as often as I could. I wanted them to be friends. I wanted Gib to be kind. I wanted to watch Carson light up when his older brother walked in the room, rather than slink out, hoping to not be noticed.

Luke protested that if I forced them to be friends now, against their will, they would not be friends later in life, when it mattered more. He said this as though he knew what having a sibling who was alien to you was like. But Luke was an only child, and his theories meant little to me. Estella and I were never forced to be friends, and now, later in life, we still are not friends.

It was in this spirit of togetherness that I had wrangled Carson into the car when I drove Gib to the makeup PSAT. Gib, his barely used driver's license burning a hole in his wallet, alongside the condom he had no idea I knew about, fought to drive himself, but I was sticking to one of the few punishments I had control over. Gib punished me with silence and a straight-lined mouth as I drove, while Carson and I made careful conversation about music camp, mindful of the tension Gib radiated like a fever.

"Geek," Gib muttered when Carson mentioned Benny Goodman for the eighth time in as many minutes.

"Knock it off," I said.

"Mom, how many eight-year-olds even know who Benny Goodman is?" Gib asked. "I only know because he won't shut up about him. Seriously, Mom, you're turning him into a total geek."

Carson fell silent, too hurt to continue, and I threw Gib an exasperated look. He raised his eyebrows at me, his arms crossed over his chest, daring me to do what? Something other than what I always did, I suppose. Which was nothing.

We rode the rest of the way to the school without a word, and Gib slammed his door shut as soon as he got out, forcing me to lean over the console to open it so that Carson could push the seat forward and slide out. He'd climbed into the front seat, settling himself into the area his older brother had just left, taking up so much less room that I suddenly felt the danger of all that extra space around my younger son. He pulled his seat belt on without waiting for me to ask, and I smiled to myself. He felt it too, the vacuum his big brother left.

We'd watched Gib retreat, waving to his friends, and I remembered how I felt when I watched Estella leave for college. I imagined that Carson must have been feeling much the same way, and I felt the sweet heartache of a bond that only two younger, left-behind siblings can feel. And then he'd turned to me with a relieved smile and asked, "So, can we go to the mall now?"

What did I know? I wasn't the genius in the family. I headed toward the mall.

"Can we go to The Gap first?" Carson asked, sliding a CD in the player. I glanced over at him with a distracted smile, still thinking of Estella leaving for college, nothing in her hands but a large leather satchel. My father was her proud chauffeur, my mother was in her rose garden, which she'd been trying to interest me in for years, and I'd stood on the front steps alone, swatting late summer mosquitoes and watching them drive away.

She was twelve years old.

"Sure," I'd answered. I couldn't imagine Carson being mature enough to handle himself at camp, much less college, though it had been my decision, made without even consulting Luke.

Carson was mine and Gib was Luke's, and now I stood with the calamitous results of that decision in my hand, nearly convinced that Gib had sabotaged the test on purpose and wondering how I was going to leave him alone to go to Big Dune Island. I still hadn't broached the subject to Luke.

I heard a splash in the pool and looked out the window. Gib hadn't left, he'd simply decided to bother his little brother. I could see him holding Carson's head under the surface, water splashing up violently around them. I dropped the test results on the counter and slammed the sliding glass door open.

"Gib! Out of the pool and in the house. Now."

I stalked back to the kitchen and pulled his report card out of my purse, placing it on the counter next to the test results. Gib came through the door with a grin on his face, toweling his hair off, his muscles still taking me by surprise.

"Mom, that kid's never going to learn how to defend—"

"Sit down." I pointed to the stool across the counter from me. His eyes widened, but he sat, his gaze finally falling on the two pieces of evidence before him.

He started to speak but stopped when I slapped my hand down on his report card and pushed it toward him. "This came on Wednesday. Did you know you were failing algebra?"

He licked his lips and shook his head, but said, "Yeah, I guess."

I pushed the PSAT results toward him. "And this came today. You want to explain it?"

He looked at the report card first, then inspected the test results. He read them and shrugged. "I guess I'm not good at math."

"Really? When did this happen? Because you managed to pass every math course before this. You never indicated you were having a problem."

His face settled into sullenness.

"Explain this to me, Gib."

He rolled his eyes and sighed, but I continued to stare at him and he finally spoke. "Well, I didn't fail on purpose," he said.

"Then what's the problem?"

"I don't get it," he said simply, cutting his eyes toward the pool. I felt a sinking in my stomach when I realized that he was looking to make sure Carson didn't hear him. He was telling the truth. "I mean, I can do all the other stuff, but I don't get all the unknown numbers. You know, the x's and y's to the third power of pi, or whatever."

"But Gib, why did you let it get this far? Why didn't you tell someone? We could have gotten you a tutor."

He shrugged again, that maddening teenaged shrug. "I don't know."

"Well, now you're going to have to go to summer school to make up for it. And I don't know if you'll be able to play football next year either, Gib."

He gnawed his lip. "You going to tell Dad?"

"Of course. He already knows that you failed the class, we were just waiting for the test results."

"Why?" he asked.

"He thought the teacher didn't like you. He thought your test scores would be good."

"You didn't think that though, right?"

I said nothing, suddenly feeling naked, suddenly aware that Gib knew more than I realized about our roles when it came to parenting him. "No," I said quietly, gathering the papers up and folding them together. "I didn't think that."

Gib glanced out the window at Carson playing in the pool, his face sober and older than his years. I saw where his first wrinkles would show up, around his eyes, across his forehead, what he would look like when he was my age and had his own children to worry about, to make mistakes with and feel guilty over. I felt like crying suddenly, tears welling in my eyes and my throat closing, when I saw how much he looked like my father.

"What did you think?" he asked.

I couldn't tell him that I thought he was doing it just to anger me, just to force my hand somehow. "I don't know," I finally said, realizing a second too late that it was the same nothing phrase I hated when it came out of his mouth. I shook my head and pushed my fingers against the back of my neck, working at the crackling knots from my violin practice. "We'll talk later, after your father gets home."

His mouth twisted and he jerked his head, acknowledging the fact that I'd chickened out. "Yeah, well, Jamie's picking me up in an hour. I'll be home later."

"No. Call Jamie and tell him you're not going anywhere. You have five minutes, then bring your cell phone and your keyboard down to me. Until we figure out what we're going to do, you can consider yourself grounded. No phone, no computer, no television."

He stopped for a moment and then walked on, refusing to look back at me. My lunch forgotten, I watched Carson swimming circles in the pool, his hand held straight up in front of his head like a shark fin. Both the kids were terrific swimmers, but I couldn't help watching them anxiously whenever they were in the water.

Swimming was a skill that not only had I never mastered, but that left me with vague feelings of dread I didn't want to fully explore. I could stay afloat, could paddle about with determination, but it frightened me more than anything else ever had, especially in the warm waters of the Gulf of Mexico. It was more than the fear of sharks, more than the unknowable depth; it was the living water itself. It twined around my legs, its currents slipping their fingers about my calves, tugging at my ankles. It felt fat between my toes and fingers, as though its molecules weren't willing to slide apart for me as easily as they did for everyone else.

Estella was the swimmer. When we moved to Big Dune Island, my parents worked out an arrangement with Dr. Pretus that Estella would stay with him and his wife four days a week, something that would never be allowed in this day and age I'm sure, and would come home for long weekends. With an atypical bow to her age, she was forbidden to bring work home with her, and she spent most of those days locked in her room or exhausting herself swimming in the Gulf.

Estella was transformed by the water, a mermaid worthy of her own fairy tale when she came up for air, her lips parted and her eyes half-lidded with exertion. Her slicked-back hair revealed beautifully arched eyebrows, her eyelashes spiked together as if she were wearing mascara, and water droplets clung perfectly to her lips. I would never have told her how beautiful, how sensual, she looked in the water. All I had in my family was my prettiness, and I wasn't about to give that up to Estella too.

When she retreated to her room, I imagined that she pulled out pencil and paper and devised her own mathematics course, because she would often go in wild-eyed and emerge serene, as though she'd gotten her fix.

The doctors initially put her on a medication to calm her constant agitation, but our father felt that it dulled her genius, made her less agile-minded, and discontinued it himself. I don't know what my sister thought of her medicated days, but I do know that I saw her smile more, and saw less of the rapid blinking and teeth clenching that made other people stare.

Had our parents ever wanted to punish her for anything they could have easily found the method. Take away math and swimming at the same time and she'd be desperate in days. I wished Gib were so easy to figure out. Taking away the phone, the computer, the television—it had all been done before.

I glanced at the clock again. Fifteen minutes had passed. With a sigh I headed upstairs and could hear him talking as I neared his room.

"Gib, let's go. Off the phone."

He glanced up as I reached the door and held the receiver out to me. "Gram called while I was talking to Jamie. She wants to talk to you. Why didn't you tell me we were going to Big Dune?"

I took the phone without answering him and pointed to his keyboard before I greeted my mother. She was already talking as I raised the phone to my ear.

". . . had the courtesy to at least call me back."

"Hi, Mom," I said, pretending I hadn't heard her. "Sorry. Are we still on for Monday?"

She was silent for a moment, mollified.

"Yes. I take it you don't want Gib to come? He hadn't heard a thing about it. And what's this about him being grounded?"

"He failed algebra without telling us he was having a problem, and he stole notification about the PSAT test from the mail."

"I thought he just took those tests."

"That was a makeup test, which we were lucky enough to find out about."

"Well, it's not as if he robbed a bank, Connie—"

"Thanks, Mother. So, I'll see you Monday?"

"I spoke with Estella yesterday."

I was surprised into silence. Two conversations in one month. It was surely a record. "And?" I finally asked.

"She's looking forward to seeing you," she said.

"She said that?" I didn't believe her. She was just trying to soften us up before we saw each other. She'd probably told Estella the exact same thing.

"Yes, she did. And this is a perfect time for the two of you—"

"I get it, Mother," I interrupted. "I'll talk to Luke."

When I hung up I gathered Gib's keyboard and cell phone and stashed them in my closet just as I heard the garage door rumble up. I met Luke in the kitchen and held the test results out to him as he walked in the door. He put his briefcase on the counter as he read them and then looked at the report card again.

"So he takes summer school," he finally said, shrugging.

"But don't you see that this is a bigger problem than just taking summer school?"

He sighed. "No, I don't. What's the problem?"

"He's hiding things, Luke. Even from you."

He looked startled. "All kids hide things from their parents when they become teenagers," he said, but he sounded less certain. "I'll talk to him."

"He's in his room. I took his phone and keyboard and told him no television."

"Damn, Connie," Luke protested. "You should have waited until I got home so we could decide what to do about this together."

"I'm his mother. I did what I felt I had to do, and you weren't here, were you?"

Where were you, Luke?

I remembered Bob's advice, remembered the paperwork I'd been gathering, the trips I'd made to a new bank, the jewelry I'd hidden there. We both had our secrets, and my questions went unasked.

He shook his head at me and walked out of the kitchen. Carson came in, wrapped in a big towel, and I made him a snack while Luke talked to Gib. When Luke came back downstairs his face was sober.

"Hey, buddy," he said absently to Carson. "Want to give me and your mom a few minutes alone?"

Without a word, Carson picked up his plate of fruit and gathered his towel around him again, heading for the sunroom to eat among the orchids.

"I don't think it's quite as bad as you've made it out," Luke started, putting his hand up to stop me when I began to interrupt. "We'll sign him up for summer school and get a tutor if he still doesn't get it. He's got this last week of school and then I told him I wanted him to get a job."

I raised my eyebrows. "Really?"

"Well, if you're going to Big Dune with your mother—"

"I was going to talk to you about that," I said quickly.

He shrugged. "It's fine, Gib told me. He doesn't want to go, and I'm not going to have time to baby-sit him. Summer school gets out early—he can work after school and we'll get home around the same time. We'll be bachelors. It'll be fun."

"All right," I said. "I'll plan to go to Big Dune right after Carson leaves for camp, but Luke, you're responsible for making sure he's going to school. I don't want to get back here to find out that it didn't happen and you never knew about it."

He leaned down to peck me on the lips and then gave a mock salute. "No problem, Sarge. What's for dinner?"

On Monday I fairly flew out of the house after Luke left, arriving at my mother's breathless, a sinking pit of quicksand for a stomach and a large box containing my entire marriage clutched in my hands.

Estella

I wait until I hear Paul close his finishing room door and then drop to my knees beside our bed. The box is back there somewhere. My fingers wiggle, stretch, and finally brush against cardboard.

I have to see her.

I have to see me.

The box is heavier than I remember, or, more likely, I am weaker than the last time I pulled these memories out. The last time I had been drunk, and I cry easily when drunk. I am sober now, and I am, thankfully, not prone to sentimentality when I am sober.

And yet my heart is racing.

For Whom the Bell Tolls, a gift from my father, reproaches me when I lift the flaps. It has not weathered the years well. I use it merely for its weight, to keep the envelopes from sliding around and damaging the pictures within.

I wrinkle my nose as the musty smell hits me, and then I put the book aside and open the first manila envelope. These are pictures of Connie's family that Mother has forwarded, pictures of her beautiful home, her beautiful husband, her beautiful children.

It used to infuriate me, the thought of Mother writing cheerful descriptions on the back of each photo, sealing them in an envelope, writing out my address, mailing them off. The very effort she made of getting them to me angered me beyond reason. But I kept them, and didn't tell her to stop sending them.

I stuff them away; they don't interest me right now. I don't bother with the next two envelopes, filled with newspaper clippings, commendations, and awards, the stuff of childhood genius. It is the last envelope I am interested in.

The pictures tumble out across my thighs and spill facedown to the floorboards. The old, ivory-bordered photos warm against my skin while I replace the other envelopes in the box and smooth the empty one on top of them with its flap open, ready to hide us at a moment's notice.

The first photo I turn over is an anomaly: Connie and I are together and we are both smiling. I don't remember it being taken. I don't remember smiling with Connie after the genius. I shuffle through the rest quickly.

Connie, Connie, Connie. Smiling, shining like our mother.

Me. Not smiling. And nothing like anyone I knew.

I stuff them back into the envelope. Jam the book down on top. Shove the box beneath the bed.

It is only when I stand that I realize I am still holding the first picture. It is clutched in my hand like a lottery ticket, full of promise, but doomed to disappointment. I place it on my nightstand and pretend that my hands aren't shaking.

I leave it there, crumpled at one side, the side I am in, and my warped smile mocks me out the door.

CHAPTER FIVE

Mother flipped through the box of documents I brought and nodded before pouring me a cup of coffee. "You're still determined to go through with this?" she asked, watching me carefully.

I nodded slowly. "I think so."

"That's not good enough. 'I think so' doesn't deserve a consequence as serious as a divorce."

"Mom," I said, and she winced. She hated *Mom* as much as I hated *Constance*, but I needed the closeness of it, the informality. "Tell me why you were prepared to leave Daddy. Please. I need to know."

"Well, no, you don't *need* to know anything. This is your life you're talking about changing, not mine."

It had always been this way. I knew little to nothing about her childhood, about her parents, who'd both died before we were born. All she had told us about them was that they were God-fearing Christians, good, sturdy people who'd raised her with a firm hand and a steady nature, if without material wealth.

When I asked for stories of her childhood, she gave me one of two versions. If she was feeling happy she told me fairy tales about swimming in moonlit creeks, talking frogs, and shooting stars zooming so close to Earth that they kissed her sleeping cheek on their way by, leaving the delicate smattering of freckles I'd inherited from her.

If she was feeling irritable or unhappy she told tales of a tiny, cramped house full of ghosts, beating off a pack of snarling dogs under a stormy sky, and teachers who'd sent her home for the humiliating offense of not having shoes. I had no real image of her as a child, no pictures, no mementos; and for the first time I felt that absence keenly.

"Mother, I don't know what to do. You're right, divorce shouldn't be an *I don't know*. I am thinking about changing my family forever. Daddy's dead; it can't hurt him now for me to know." I closed my eyes against her implacable face. "Help me for once, Mother; just help me."

"Open your eyes, Constance. You can't go through life with your eyes closed. And it's not your father I'm worried about hurting. Dredging up the past rarely makes people happy."

I opened my eyes, feeling chastised. "How bad was it?"

She took her coffee to the glass doors leading to the patio and slid them open, and I followed her with my cup. She settled herself into a patio chair and gazed out at the Gulf, the morning sun unforgiving on her un-made-up face. I sat in the chair to her left and looked at the water too, giving her time.

"You know your father wasn't faithful, don't you?"

I thought of Graciela. "I figured," I said. "Do they all do it?"

"All men? No, no, I don't believe they do. I read an article once that linked money and power to affairs, though. Makes sense. Money and power attract women, and men who make a lot of money are more likely to travel for business, more likely to have alibis. And I think women married to men with money, especially if they don't have money of their own or if they have children, are more willing to look the other way. I did for a long time, and I don't regret it now. But sometimes it's time to put a stop to it."

"And you did?" I asked with a half-smile. It was hard to imagine my mother forcing my father to do, or *not* do, anything.

"Yes," she said, "I did. You find that hard to believe?"

Embarrassed, I bit my lip and looked away from her. "Well, I just mean you and Daddy always seemed so happy, like everything was fine. And it wasn't like he was a serial cheater or anything."

The hand holding the coffee cup halted about halfway to her lips and she slowly lowered it back down to her lap. "You think you had it tough, don't you?" she asked softly.

I flinched inside. I must have flinched on the outside too, because a bit of coffee spilled on my knee, and I set the cup on the small table in front of us. I'd heard that tone before, but rarely heard it turned on me. Suddenly, I felt expansively sorry for myself because yes, I did think I'd had it tough. My own mother didn't have any idea what my life had really been like, how I'd struggled.

She hadn't had a superior older sister to live up to, or a father whose attention was so easily stolen by the promise of greatness, or the dread of going to school to face the disappointment of teachers, or the struggle to carve her own identity out of thin air.

"You know, you're a great one to talk," I said, standing up and walking to the rail before turning around to face her with my arms crossed beneath my breasts, holding myself in, keeping myself together. "You've always had everything you wanted. You didn't have to compete with a genius, or any sister for that matter. And Daddy might not have always been faithful, but he obviously didn't flaunt it in front of your friends, and he spoiled you—"

"Spoiled?" she interrupted. "You have no idea what you're talking about, Constance. You don't know what a tough life is."

"I don't remember things being so tough for you. I remember you having nannies, and maids, and a rose garden, and plenty of damn shoes."

She shook her head and firmed her lips into a straight, severe line, her too-angry-to-talk look. I turned back toward the Gulf, the railing pressing heat into my belly, my eyes watering at the glare of the sun on the water.

"I was born with nothing," Mother said quietly, bitterly, and I froze. These were not words I'd heard before, and I didn't want to startle the story out of her by turning around. "I was born on Salt Island, off the coast of Georgia. No hospital, no doctor. The men on Salt were good ole boys, and I was lucky enough to be born to one who didn't think it was his right to start touching me when I turned eight. Most of my friends weren't so lucky.

"We had to take a boat to the mainland for school. And I *was* sent home for not having shoes. I skipped most days, especially after the twins were born."

That made me turn around, my eyes wide, my heart beating wildly in my chest. "What? Twins? You had twins?" I whispered.

She looked startled and then gave a sharp bark of a laugh. "No, Connie, no, I didn't have twins. I was seven when my mother had twins, my sisters. She named them April and May, if you can believe it. Now, let me talk. If you interrupt me again I won't be able to get through this, and I won't repeat myself."

My mother had sisters. Two sisters. I stumbled back to my chair and lowered myself into it, and then turned to her, to ask the thousand questions that were forming in my mind, but she started to speak again, and I struggled to remain quiet.

"My daddy had been a fisherman, but he was a gambler at heart. He lost the boat after the twins were born, and then he took off, but he came back—and he had money. I didn't know where it was from, and I didn't ask. Mama asked, though. She'd gotten Jesus after he'd left.

And when she found out he'd won it playing cards, she left. With the minister. I took care of the twins. But then she came back too.

"It went like that for a long time. Daddy would leave and come back, then Mama would leave for a while. After I turned twelve, she didn't come back. The twins were only five. I took good care of them, but there was never enough money. I fished for food, gigged frogs for their legs. Daddy stayed awhile, but he couldn't make any money, and so he stocked us up and left. He promised to be back in six weeks.

"In four weeks a hurricane hit the island. We didn't have radar, or television, or weathermen. We just had fishermen, and they knew a storm was coming, but not that. They didn't know about that."

She stopped with a shudder and I wondered if I should say something, but I left it too long. When she started again her voice was different, with a tremor in it that I'd never heard before.

"Anyway, it hit, and I took the twins and hid in our parents' bedroom, under their bed. The girls were under me; I just tucked them up, shoving a little leg or a little arm under whatever bit of me I could, trying to shield them. The house disintegrated around us; the roof collapsed, hit the bed. It had these wood slats that kept the mattress up and they cracked me on the head, knocked me right out.

"The girls probably thought I'd died, and when the storm passed I was still out cold. The water started coming, the storm surge. I know what that means now, but then I didn't know that would happen—that it would just suck all that water away and then throw it right back at us. When I woke up I was choking on water, and the girls were gone. I imagine they were going for help. We found them the next day, caught in the root cavity of a tree taken down by the storm. They'd drowned. Their clothes had been torn right off by the water, and they were naked except for their shoes."

Tears were rolling down my face, but I barely noticed them. Mother stared out at the water, dry-eyed, and I reached out and put my hand on her arm. She shook it off and turned her head away.

"You started this, might as well hear the rest," she said harshly. I put my hand over my mouth. I wasn't sure I wanted to hear any more.

"Daddy came back when he heard the news. And I left with him that time. There was no house left for me to stay in anyway. Seventy-six people lived on Salt. More than half of them died in that hurricane, died or just disappeared. Most of the rest of them left when we did. Nobody said good-bye to each other, we just all hit the mainland and melted away. We rented a room in Atlanta, and Daddy worked out something with the landlady, so she watched me after school and made sure I had dinner, and then he left to find work."

She stopped for a moment and took a deep breath, her eyes fixed on the horizon but appearing to look far beyond it. I stayed quiet, afraid to jinx the outpouring of information, and felt triumphant when she gave her head a little shake and began to speak again.

"He took me on one of his business trips once, for my birthday. We stayed in a fancy hotel in Louisiana, and he gave me money to have my hair done and to buy new clothes, and he had a new suit. We looked good. People stared at us, and one man in particular stared at me. He was a rich man, a man on vacation with a woman who wasn't his wife, and he was so handsome.

"I had my seventeenth birthday at the hotel, and the man asked me to dance after dinner. I'd never danced with a man before, but he knew how. My feet just followed him."

Her voice had grown dreamy and the angry lines of her mouth had softened. I risked a question. "Was it Daddy?"

She turned to me with a half-smile. "Oh, yes, that was Sebastian. Anyway, he tried to make friends with my father. Kept trying. He sent the woman he was with away, and my father stayed in the room with me at night to make sure I didn't sneak out. It was . . . like a dream, just like a dream. Daddy told him that he was in town looking at investment property, but was sticking around for a big poker game he was in on. Sebastian got in on the game too."

"Daddy played poker?" I asked incredulously. I couldn't imagine it.

"Lots of men did back then," she said. "You want to hear this or not?"

"Sorry."

"My father was winning, but your dad was giving him a game, and it came down to the two of them. I was watching from a corner, and on the last hand, Sebastian pushed all of his chips in and said, 'I want to marry June.' I nearly fainted. Daddy looked at me and laid his cards down. He'd won, and he took Sebastian's money. And then he said, 'If you marry her tomorrow, I'll stand up with you and give you back the pot.'

"And we were married in the morning. Daddy told me to never tell your father where we came from, and I never did. Daddy left the next day, and I was a wife."

I leaned back in my chair. Shock left me speechless for a moment, but the thrill of discovering this whole other life, this life of Southern poverty and motherless traveling, this life of deceit, made the questions come quickly and thoughtlessly to my lips.

"How could he do that? It's like you were a horse to be traded or something! A poker chip to be won."

"My father?" she asked, shooting me a look of surprise.

"Yes, your father!"

"Were you listening to anything I just told you, Connie? He wasn't trying to get rid of me, he was giving me the gift of a life. What do you think would have happened to me? I was seventeen, with a fifth-grade education and a father who was always on the road. He gave me to him out of love, Connie. Parents do all kinds of things that might seem heartless, to their children. But they are done out of love."

"But you were only seventeen, Mother. You could've—"

"What? Gone to college?"

"I—no, I guess not. But what about Daddy's family? God, they must have had a fit."

She laughed, nodding. "Oh, they did, they did. He wrote long letters to his father, and got little telegrams in return. He was already in trouble, traveling around, spending their money. I think his mother finally pointed out that if he was married he might finally settle down. I don't know what all went on, but a few months later he got a telegram telling him to come home, and to bring his wife. And they were good to me, in their own way."

"Did you ever see your father again?"

"Oh, yes," she said. "He was still traveling, but I sent him money out of my allowance whenever I could, and we met in Atlanta and then later New York."

"I wish I'd known him," I said.

"He died when you were just two."

"Oh. I'm sorry, Mom. Did you ever tell Daddy? About April and May?"

"I wanted to tell him, but my father wouldn't let me. He knew the kind of family Sebastian was from. It was bad enough that he'd sprung a seventeen-year-old unknown on them. They would never have accepted me if they'd known about my life on Salt, about my family. He didn't want to ruin the life he'd given me. It was the right decision, Connie. Your father would never have understood, and I got by. I learned to read better, learned a lot of things just by watching you girls grow up. Did you know I used to sneak in your room and borrow your schoolbooks?"

I shook my head in amazement. "No, I never knew," I said. And I really hadn't. I'd never suspected anything about my own mother's past. But then children grow up believing what their parents tell them. It simply receded into background that I didn't care about as I got older.

And I was as guilty as my mother. I'd never told my own children about my childhood. I never told them about the library full of books, or the music room full of memories, the loss of my sister, or my father. But at least Mother's father had given her a better life. She still knew he loved her.

"I wish I'd known sooner," I said to her, and this time it wasn't an accusation, but sympathy for the history she'd carried by herself for so long. When I placed my hand upon her arm again she didn't twitch it off.

"Go get my hatbox," she said, still gazing out at the Gulf. "The one with the blue stripes. It's under my bed."

I didn't question her. The hatbox was large and round; I dragged it from under the bed by its short ribbon handle. It was light, and I contemplated a quick peek, but Mother called me and I hurried out to her, placing the box on her lap. Her hands fluttered over it like butterflies before settling on the edges of the lid and lifting it off. I stood beside her, looking alternately at her drawn face and the box while she peeled back layers of brittle ivory paper.

Her hands obscured the contents, and they shook as they hovered in the tissue, then stilled as she laid them atop whatever lay within the box. When she finally withdrew her hands, my breath escaped the astonished O of my lips, as though my lungs had been punctured along with my heart. Pinched between my mother's thumbs and fingers were two tiny stained and creased pairs of shoes.

She thrust them toward me, and as soon as I held my hands out she placed the shoes in them, scraped her chair back, and left me there on the porch, the brilliant sun illuminating the ghosts of my aunts in heartbreaking detail. I didn't follow my mother. I couldn't do anything but stare at those little once-white Mary Janes, their warped and gritty soles resting as lightly on my palms as memories. The little metal buckles bled rust across the sides, and I bent toward them and inhaled. They smelled like time and water. I felt the tears on my cheeks, but I couldn't put the shoes down to wipe them away.

When Mother returned she didn't say anything, and I held my hands up like an offering to her pale, drawn face, where I saw the evidence of her own tears. She took the shoes and nestled them in the box, carefully replacing the tissue around them and snugging the lid down firmly.

"Well," she said, shaking her head as if to ward the memories off, but clutching the hatbox on her lap to keep them safe at the same time. "None of that was supposed to be the point of this conversation. The topic was divorce."

Incredibly, during her story I'd forgotten about Luke.

"Yes, Sebastian cheated on me. And yes, I was often angry and jealous enough to consider divorce, but I knew he loved me in his way. And I had you girls and a nice life, a life I certainly never believed I'd have. I probably would have gone on like that until he died, but then we had to move."

I suddenly understood. "The island," I said. "You didn't want to live on the island."

"No, I did not. I couldn't imagine living on a tiny, stinking island again. All I could see were April and May, stuck naked in those roots, still holding on to each other. And I almost told your father then, I almost told him everything."

"Why didn't you?"

"Because of you."

"Me?" It thrilled me to think that I might have had some influence on my family, after believing Estella had held all the power. But my thrill was short-lived.

"You and Estella. I had nothing to give you. All I had was my wits, and your father's estate, which his father had been foolish with, and which was being pulled right out from under us. We would have had nothing left if it weren't for me threatening to divorce your father, Connie. I went to Bob McNarey."

"Bob! You knew him back then?"

"That's when I met him. I was lucky. He was just out of law school and knew all kinds of things I didn't. I made your father put as much as he could in my name, I made him set up the trusts for you girls, and I made him sign the deed to the house and land on Big Dune over to me. And I let him believe it was all because of his affairs, but it was really so that I could stand living on an island again, for you and Estella, for your futures, Connie.

"And I didn't live on that damn island for fifteen years for you to get taken in a divorce because your husband can't keep it in his pants."

She glanced at me, angry now, and I saw the iron gray of a storm-buffeted Gulf in her eyes. "Do you know what people are saying about Luke, Connie? Do you know that he's lost a lot of clients a lot of money?"

"What? What are you talking about?" I sat up straight in my chair, all warm sympathetic feelings for my mother forgotten, ingrained defense of my husband surging to the fore.

"I'm just telling you what I've heard."

"From who?" I demanded. Luke was a lousy husband, but his work was his life and he took pride in it. *I* still took pride in it—it was the last bit of pride I had in him. "Bob McNarey? He just doesn't want you to take your money out of his control. I can't believe you'd even listen to that kind of—of nasty gossip."

"First of all, *I* am in control of my money, not Bob, and I'll remain in control of it until the day I leave this world. Bob is not the only one to mention this to me; for your information, most of the people who have mentioned it have done so out of concern for you, not to gossip. He's losing clients left and right, Constance."

"I don't believe that for a second."

I stood and pushed the sliding glass door back with a protesting rumble. I grabbed the box of paperwork on my way to the door, ignoring my mother's footsteps behind me.

"Connie, stop. Just stop and let's discuss this."

I turned around with the box still clutched in my hands, my heart beating erratically. "It's just mean-spirited gossip. I can't believe you've been talking about us like this."

"Calm down. Put the box down. I wasn't sure before, and I didn't want to hurt you with rumors. But since your last visit I've spoken with several people who've recently fired him. You have to protect yourself and the boys, Connie. You could wind up with nothing."

I hesitated. I couldn't help myself. After all, I was the one who'd said I was ready to leave Luke, I was the one who told Bob McNarey that my husband was unfaithful, I was the one who'd aired my dirty laundry. Who was I to turn tail and run when some of it was shoved back at me? Mother took the box from my arms and set it on the hall table before she took my hand and led me back to the living room. She'd left the sliders open, and the Gulf filled the condo with its incessant whisper of waves.

"Would you rather I hadn't told you?"

"Yes," I said softly, but of course it wasn't true. Everything—my marriage, the person I thought my husband was, Gib, even what I thought I knew about my mother—was all crumbling around me, and I had no way to keep it together.

When I left my mother's condo almost an hour later, I left the box, with her promise that she would drop it at Bob's that very afternoon.

It took fewer than twenty-four hours for the first of the bad news to come in.

Estella

Fewer than twenty-four hours have passed since I left the photo on my nightstand, and Paul has already framed it in beautiful maple— which perfectly matches Connie's hair, I can't help but notice—and placed it on the shelf in the dining room. I haven't said anything about it, but it looks inevitable there. There is no denying what is happening.

My mother and Connie will arrive in four days. Lisa, the quantitative sciences major, has generously agreed to move in with Chelsea, a statistics whiz who rents the room across the hall. On Friday I will blitz Lisa's room so that Mother and Connie will have someplace comfortable to spend the night. They'll have to share a bed, but unless one of them wants to sleep on the downstairs sofa, there's no other choice.

The college students have been helping to clean the house, taking the broom from me as I sweep the tile, shooing me to the living room when they see me drop to my knees to clean the oven, which I've never done. Ever.

They leave me the smaller tasks, or talk me out of the impossible ones. Two days ago I decided that I should plant the flower garden I've been putting off for eight years and began drawing up a list of supplies.

When Paul suggested that it might be a bit late for it and stuffed the list in his pocket, I drew up another list with ingredients for beef Wellington and baked Alaska, which I've always wanted to learn how to make but never actually have. This list was also confiscated and spaghetti gently suggested.

And now it is four days away.

I have packed three times.

Fours and threes.

The easy answer is seven, of course.

Facts about seven:

Seven is the smallest integer that is not the difference of two primes.

Seven is the only prime that can be the digital root of a perfect square.

There are seven deadly sins: pride, envy, gluttony, lust, anger, avarice, and sloth.

I force myself to stop before I fall off the edge. I quiet my mind, limit myself to just the three facts.

And now, with all the nervous energy that I am not allowed to expend writhing inside of me, I sit at the front window looking for a distraction. The college students are out for the night and the young ones I tutor have eaten their dinners and retreated to whatever broken homes they come from. The house is quiet but for the steady, gritty sound of Paul sanding the curve of a new bowl, the door to his workroom propped open in case I need him.

The sound is the same *swish, slow, swish* of the Gulf of Mexico, and I close my eyes and imagine that I am already there.

The sanding stops, and soon I hear his steps in the kitchen and the vacuum of the swinging door as he pokes his head in to find me. I don't turn around, and I hear the swinging door settle back in place.

Music, Van Morrison, streams through the living room. I cannot help but smile. Paul takes my hand from my lap and I allow him to pull me up and into him, easily lifting me and placing my bare feet on his boots. He sways in place, and then we move together, and we hit every inch of the floor, because I do not need to look down, because Paul has me, and he will not let my feet touch the ground.

Four days.

I have nothing left to do but dance.

CHAPTER SIX

I needed more time. Four days was not nearly long enough to get everything done. I had no time for the mundane chores of everyday life in our household, and yet I couldn't escape them.

I was watering the orchids when the phone rang. Luke gave me my first orchid almost seven years ago, when he saw me reading *The Orchid Thief*. Good book. So was *Seabiscuit*, but I had no desire to train racehorses after reading it. Nonetheless, it was a sweet gesture, and perhaps I overdid the gratitude, because for every small occasion since that first purple phalaenopsis, Luke has given me another orchid.

I learned how to care for them, and even discovered, thanks to the local Orchid Society, that an orchid was named for my great-grandfather, Henry Louis Sykes. The 'Sykes Spike,' a cattleya with large, deep yellow flowers, a dark red lip, and a snowy white throat, was found in 1887 by Francis X. Gestain, a botanist who disappeared in Asia a few years later.

Henry's largesse allowed Francis to spend his time orchid hunting rather than cataloguing endless hybrids, though he might have been safer had Henry not been so generous.

Luke immediately acquired one, and when visitors exclaimed over the sunroom of orchids he would proudly point to the 'Sykes Spike' and recite the story. He was pleased to have ancestors he could tell a story about, even if they weren't his own.

The orchids took up an astonishing amount of my time and I grew to resent them, like an older sibling forced to care for a brood of youngsters. But what I grew to dread the most was Luke's presentation, running his fingers along the lips, caressing the throat, gazing at me slyly. Much like a new car, a new orchid was foreplay to Luke.

He also went through a Georgia O'Keeffe phase when we were first together and bought me several prints. After a while I couldn't even look at an O'Keeffe without thinking sex, seeing swollen vulvas, delicately colored clitorises. Frankly, it pissed me off. I used to enjoy looking at Georgia O'Keeffe's work. And now he'd ruined orchids for me too.

So there I was, surrounded by all the petaled sex, when the phone rang. The caller ID showed Bob McNarey's name, and I snatched the phone up furtively, though nobody was home. He dove right in after my tentative hello.

"I don't have good news, Connie."

I stumbled backward into a kitchen stool and waited.

"Did you know that Carson's college fund has been wiped out?"

No, I had not known that. My jaw was rigid, frozen in place, not allowing me to scream out *What are you saying?* the way I was screaming it inside my head. I managed a whisper.

"No."

"And Gib's has been dipped into recently, though the majority is intact. The house seems to be untouched, no liens have been attached, and it's clearly and legally in your name. That's all I've been able to get so far. Do you want me to continue?"

I fingered my wedding band—*twist, twist, twist*—a nervous habit I thought I'd conquered long ago. "Yes," I said.

"Right. Okay then, I'll be in touch at Big Dune. Keep things normal around there, just go on your trip like nothing is happening, okay?"

"Okay."

He hung up. The whole conversation, only four words on my part—*hello, no, yes, okay*—was enough to leave me gasping for breath. I hung up the phone slowly and very carefully, as though it were crystal. My hands felt too large for the skin they were in, the muscles of my arms tight and ready to burst.

I returned to the sunroom, to the orchids. I gazed at them, all so different and yet alike: spiky, olive green, light green, bulbous bases, slender stalks, gracefully drooping over the rim, shooting straight into the air. I felt the flower of the one closest to me, the 'Sykes Spike,' in full bloom and velvety soft, even where the edges ruffled slightly. I pinched the lip between my thumb and finger and plucked it away from the rest of the flower before letting it drop to the floor.

The scarlet lip lay on the slate, quivering, like a drop of freshly spilled blood. It was more beautiful there on the floor than it had been on the plant; defenseless, shocked, shocking. I reached out, cupped the rest of the flower in my palm, and crushed it, ripping it off the spike, and then moved on to the other blooms.

I stopped for a moment, staring at the denuded spike, still rigidly, defiantly thrusting itself toward me. And then I tore it apart. I stormed through the room in a fury, smashing the pots on the slate floor, separating spikes from stalks, leaves from pseudopods, petals from throats, bellowing in rage. The massacre took less than five minutes and left me panting and trembling on my knees, my palms stained green, nursing a gash in my thumb that welled blood. Bits of petal clung to my hands, rolled against my cheeks as I wiped tears from my face.

All around me plants lay unrecognizable, a battlefield of awful dismembered limbs. My fury settled into something approaching satisfaction when I realized that at least I no longer saw sex when I looked at the orchids. And then I was horrified to realize that I preferred thinking of a battlefield to thinking of sex.

I had trusted Luke. Perhaps not with another woman, but certainly with our children. He could betray me with his body, but I would not let him betray Gib and Carson with their future. Bile rose in my throat when I remembered his glib reaction to Gib's test scores and grade. Was that why he had taken Carson's first? So he would have time to replace it?

But things must have been worse than I could comprehend, because he was beginning to dip into Gib's too, savings we would need in just two years. That did not leave much time to replace the missing funds. Was he even planning on replacing the money? And if not, how did he think he would get away with it? By encouraging Gib to fail in school?

I couldn't answer the questions. Only Luke could, and I couldn't ask him. I slowly got my feet under me and stood, still panting, wiping my dirty palms on my shorts. I surveyed the littered sunroom and glanced at the clock too late to change anything. Carson would be home in minutes.

I grabbed a few trash bags and had one of them filled by the time he wandered in, stooping under the weight of his ridiculously large backpack.

"Stop!" I called, before he could step into the sunroom. "Got shoes on?"

"Whoa," he breathed, slumping his shoulders to allow the backpack to slide down his arms and onto the floor. "Yeah. What happened?" he asked as he picked his way across the sunroom, crouching beside me to scoop up debris and dump it in the second open bag.

I sat back on my heels, gazing at my son. He simply pitched in, as though coming home to an orchid explosion was a regular thing. Gib would have looked in, shook his head, and then disappeared to his room without a word. I felt a sudden rush of love for Carson and leaned over to kiss him on the cheek. He immediately raised his shoulder to wipe it off and continued to gather up broken pots and scattered flowers.

"Well, I hit a bad note on my violin and the pots shattered, all at once," I said.

He didn't even bother looking at me, just said, "Mom," and rolled his eyes.

"I don't know, honey," I said. "I was watering them, and it was bugging me that I had to do so much work on them, and I got careless and knocked one over. It broke, and I just sort of tipped over the rest. It was a little fun, you know? Like orchid hockey."

He sat back, his hands cradling a smashed pseudopod, and scanned the damage as though assessing the validity of my story. "Well," he finally said, resuming work, "what're you gonna tell Dad?"

I didn't have an answer. What, indeed, would I tell Luke? All the things I *wanted* to say to him were unspeakable.

I sighed. "I don't know."

"You could tell him it was a snake," he said, matter-of-factly.

"A snake?"

"Yeah, like a big snake got in and you were trying to chase it out and knocked over all the plants. He'd believe that. Remember when you broke the table when the wasp got in?"

I did remember that. A wasp had landed on my arm just as I had been placing a heavy orchid on the glass-topped coffee table, and I dropped the pot to flail at the wasp. The pot had shattered the tabletop, bringing Luke, Gib, and Carson running. I was lucky I still had all ten toes. I felt a stab of guilt over my young son so calmly providing me with an alibi, and, even worse, instantly understanding that an alibi was called for.

We'd been confidants before, but I'd never felt guilty about it, perhaps because I'd always been the one protecting him. Now our roles had been reversed, and I was ashamed of myself. I felt as though I should retrieve my old journal, the one I hadn't written in for well over ten years, and mark the day that I damaged my youngest son, the day he would remember and repeat in his thirties to a therapist as the day his mother made him lie to his father, the start of all his troubles.

"If we get this all cleaned up quickly enough, I think I'll just tell him that I donated them to the Orchid Society," I said, glancing around. Not one orchid in the sunroom had been spared. Not one sex organ had survived. A snake sighting just wasn't going to cut it. "Would you feel okay about that?"

"About what?"

"Actually, you wouldn't have to say anything at all. We'll just pretend that you weren't here, and the Orchid Society ladies came and picked them up."

"Yeah, sure," he said with a shrug.

I gave him a bemused smile and barely managed to stop myself from kissing him again. After the sunroom had been scrubbed clean of all orchid corpses, I took him to the ice cream shop before we went to the Cowachobee Center for my music classes.

Maybe one day I would tell him the story of the orchids that gave their lives so he could go to college. Maybe I could even get it in there before he went to therapy. I hoped I would come off better in twenty years than I had that afternoon.

Carson had a crush on one of the little girls at the center. A shy, beautiful little violin player named Luz. Her mother and aunt attended citizenship classes while she practiced scales with me on one of the violins I'd donated to the center.

Other than Luz, none of the children were very interested in music. They'd all spent the day in school and were restless, so time spent trying to teach them how to read music was most often time wasted, and instead I allowed them to blow off steam by wailing away on recorders and beating tambourines.

Carson had been coming to the center with me since I'd started volunteering, around his second birthday, and he was as comfortable there as he was at home, perhaps more so as there was no older brother waiting in the wings to humiliate him, or worse, to ignore him. In the past few months that I had been working with Luz, Carson had begun to sit and watch us rather than poke around the center looking for something to interest him.

He watched as I went over the notes to a beginning piece with Luz, and then sat down at the piano when I stopped playing to loosen Luz's wrist and adjust her fingers. When we began to play our awkward duet again, I was surprised to hear notes plinking from the piano behind us, but I tuned it out and trained my ear to hear only Luz and her fledgling efforts.

But on our way home that night I remembered Carson's fresh boredom with Luz and was pleased that he turned to music rather than searching out a new crush. I wasn't ready for either of my sons to have a love life, and it made me ache especially for Carson. Gib had started getting calls from girls as early as the fourth grade, all those young cheerleaders already impressed with the cocky athlete. But I knew that Carson would have a harder time with romance.

"I have a conference with your music teacher tomorrow after school," I reminded him. "Do you want to wait for me or take the bus home?"

He grinned at me. "I'll be there," he said, and I raised my eyebrows at him.

"I don't think Mr. Hailey is going to let you sit in on the conference,"

I cautioned him, but he didn't seem perturbed in the least, merely turned the radio up and bobbed his head along with the music.

Luke bought the Orchid Society story, but was furious anyway and questioned me about my motive until I wanted to scream and show him the cut on my thumb and the garbage bags in the bin at the curb. He was especially upset over the 'Sykes Spike,' his pride. It was only when I told him that they would all have died without constant care—which was absurd, they were fairly hardy plants despite their reputation—that he finally let up.

He needed to punish me, though, and he played computer games with Gib for the rest of the night, leaving me to pack for my trip and climb into bed without him. He woke me on purpose over an hour later, reaching for me, but I instinctively pulled away, breathing regularly, curling into my pillow, and he finally turned away.

I opened my eyes in the gloom, staring at my nightstand. An orchid stood there in a pierced ceramic pot. It was a young plant, and its green-tipped, searching roots seemed vulnerable to me, as though they sensed that an orchid murderer slept close by. It was right to fear me. Had I remembered it was up there I would have destroyed it too. I wanted to reassure it that it no longer had anything to fear from me. It had merely been one of many before. Now it was special, a fact I was suddenly envious of.

Its solitary existence seemed an omen. I'd never believed in omens before, but then I was doing many things I'd never believed I'd do before that Escalade showed up in my driveway. Confiding in my mother, agreeing to spend time with Estella, lying to my husband, and denying him my body as well.

I had been doing what I was told, keeping everything as normal as possible, keeping everything hidden from Luke, but it had not been easy. It went completely against my nature, as well as against the habit of simple daily disclosure I'd developed over seventeen years of marriage.

You think your relationship is one thing for so long, think you're in control despite affairs or disagreements, and one day you wake up and with the gift of an expensive car or another sexy flower you realize it is something else entirely, and you haven't been in control of anything for a very long time.

Estella

Paul says we've wasted too much time. He stands beside me, his touch reassuring, and we look at the calendar—not to check on the dates for Big Dune, they are too close for me to forget. Instead, he wants me to settle on a date next year. The calendar is clear after my appointment. I've refused to schedule anything and until now Paul has indulged me. I am grateful to him for that.

Perhaps I should be grateful again.

My finger shakes slightly as I run it down the Saturday column, through all those months, all that time. It stops on the second Saturday of April, and I calculate the dates in my mind, finding zero, and then back up to an even hundred, divided down to my age, a prime. Fighting to stop it is as useless as fighting a facial tic. It happens unconsciously, within seconds, without Paul being aware of it.

Psychosomatic, he would say, as the doctors have said, keep saying.

He nods, looking at the date. "Yes, I think that would be fine," he says. "And it gives us almost a year to plan."

Almost a year.

I am trying to get through these three days, and then I must try to get through the three weeks on Big Dune, and then the three more days to Dr. Fellows. Three days, three weeks, three days.

Three facts about three:

Three is the first prime Delannoy number.

Three is the smallest Fermat prime.

Three to the third equals three squared three times.

It happens in a split second. Dr. Fellows will say I am imagining things. Playing Go with Lisa I see the black and white disks form the old shapes before my eyes, I see the grid rise off the board and rotate in front of me, showing me where to place my piece.

And now I am calculating dates, zipping through simple number facts. It is child's play, a bright fourth grader could do the same. I don't believe in psychosomatic. I believe in what my past has taught me.

Paul wants another year, and I cannot help but feel that he is asking for too much. But I circle the second Saturday in April anyway, and he is pleased.

CHAPTER SEVEN

Streams of chattering fourth graders flowed around me as I walked down the hall toward the music room, their faces bright with anticipation of summer vacation. Mr. Hailey was waiting for me, smiling like an excited boy, and I imagined he was as pleased about school ending as the students were. He led me down the hall, away from the music room, and opened the door to the auditorium.

When I saw the stage, I marveled at what a wonderful teacher Mr. Hailey was. Luke had wanted to send the boys to private school, but I'd somehow won that one, and Mr. Hailey was just the sort of teacher who reminded me that I'd made the right choice. He was also one of the first teachers who accepted Carson for who he was and not a clone of his popular older brother.

Carson sat on the stage, with a string-bass player on his right and a pianist on his left. I glanced around for the other parents, but Mr. Hailey and I were the only members of the audience. Carson waved at me and nervously shuffled his music as we took our seats.

"Mrs. Wilder, I'm very excited about this," Mr. Hailey said, turning toward me in the tiny upholstered seat.

"I've never seen him play with bass and piano," I said. "I didn't even know he was working on anything like this. Is this how his Benny Goodman fixation came about?"

"I've played some Goodman records, but I think this piece is more reminiscent of the Blue Wing Trio."

"I'm not familiar with them," I said. "Jazz?"

He nodded enthusiastically. "Yes, yes, but what I'm most excited about is that you, well, you know music, so you'll understand. I've seen your trio."

"Really?" I said, truly surprised.

"You're all very good," he added and I nodded my thanks. "But, please, listen, not just to Carson, but listen to the composition. That's what I really wanted you here for."

Warning bells sounded in my head. "The composition? You know I really don't play professionally—"

He looked startled. "Well, certainly you do, Mrs. Wilder. But maybe we should just sit back and listen. Ready?"

I nodded, but a feeling of dread was coming over me. Obviously Mr. Hailey had composed the piece we were about to hear, and he hoped that by placing Carson in the jazz trio I might give him an entry into the local music scene in return. Had it not been my son up there I would have made my excuses and rapidly left.

Not only did I have no influence on the local music scene, I wouldn't even know where to begin with a jazz composer, or a composer of any stripe. Mr. Hailey would be sorely disappointed to discover that the only real contact I had was a down-on-his-luck cellist.

Mr. Hailey nodded at the players and raised his hand. The clarinet, Carson, led. It was a bit wavery, a bit weak, but strengthened quickly, and then the bass and the piano joined in and a bouncy, New Orleans–flavored jazz number filled the auditorium.

I forgot all about Mr. Hailey and his dreams of launching a composing career off the backs of schoolchildren, and watched my son in amazement. He wasn't great; in fact, the bass player and the pianist, both older than him, could likely play rings around him. But he was obviously having a ball, and it lent his playing a new, more powerful and confident sound.

The piano backed off and the bass surged, leaving Carson to find his way, the music wallowing a bit, and when the piano took off again with the bass in tow and left Carson once more out of the loop, I began to pick apart the composition. It was a fun piece, and Hailey was obviously talented, but it lacked polish, as if he had the raw stuff but perhaps hadn't studied as much as he should have.

The piano dropped out, and then the bass, and the final notes, like the first, were Carson's to play with. As the cry of the clarinet faded away I stood and began to applaud, as did Mr. Hailey.

"Yes, oh, fantastic, just fantastic," Mr. Hailey cried, his enthusiasm carrying him away. "Thank you, Tabitha, Kyle, you're dismissed," he called across the auditorium. "I'll see you in class. Great job today. Carson, why don't you pack up and we'll meet you in the music room. I'd like to speak to your mother for a few minutes."

Carson nodded and raised a hand to me before gathering his music and trotting off the stage. Mr. Hailey turned to me again, his eyes bright with hope.

"And what did you think about *that*?"

"It was very nice," I said, trying to be kind but noncommittal. "Carson's playing has really come a long way, and the bass player and pianist are terrific."

His face fell a little bit. "Well, yes, he's a good student; he practices, that's half the battle right there. But what did you think of the music itself? The composition?"

I swallowed. I had never been good at letting people down. "I thought it was very nice, but, ah, I'm afraid I really don't have the sort of connections you might need. Perhaps you should get in touch with a jazz group in the area? I'm sure they'd love to discuss your work."

Mr. Hailey stared at me, obviously puzzled, but then he opened his eyes wide. "Mrs. Wilder, do you think *I* wrote that piece?"

"I, well—" I stopped, uncertain of where he was going.

"Carson wrote that," he said, with a soft smile.

"Carson? Carson—*wrote* that?"

"Yes, yes, he did. I'm sorry, I thought you understood."

I began to laugh, first out of relief, and then out of sheer astonishment. "But how? I didn't know anything about this."

"It happened several months ago, after I brought a Blue Wing Trio album in for music theory class. We'd been listening to jazz, some Miles Davis, Charlie Parker, Bill Evans." He smiled ruefully at me. "I hate to say it, but it's stuff that puts most of the kids right to sleep. But it was obvious that Carson was fascinated, and the Blue Wing album just seemed to click with him. He started asking me questions about why we didn't play that sort of music in class, why didn't everyone play that way, how did they know how to play the music like that, just full of questions. It was the most I'd ever heard him say at one time. After a few days I started to realize that the core of his questions, what he was really intrigued by, was composition, the building of the music itself, the form, especially with these three instruments.

"He seemed to understand strings well enough—he said he's been watching you since he was a baby—and then showing him the scales on the piano was the next logical step, and then I started working with him on his study hour with composition basics. You know, some people believe that musical composition can't be taught, but he took everything I showed him and ran, just ran with it. It's really quite amazing."

"So, what are you saying?" I asked, my initial astonishment slowly being replaced by a chill of fear.

Mr. Hailey leaned toward me with an earnest look. "I'm not saying he's a prodigy exactly. He's not Beethoven, he doesn't automatically know what to do as if born with the knowledge already. Gifted? No question. Genius? Perhaps. I think time and instruction will tell."

And there it was. *Genius.* My neck and face felt as if they were on fire. Mr. Hailey looked at me in concern, and I realized that I was twisting my rings again, as though trying to unscrew my finger. I tried to remember that to most people it was a good word, a word that most parents prayed they might hear one day.

Mr. Hailey was still staring at me. "I'm sorry," I said, falling back on good manners, my only cover. "You've just caught me by surprise."

"But are you—aren't you pleased?" he asked, inclining his head toward the stage, indicating that of course I must be, I had to be. But I wasn't. I was terrified—I wasn't ready for the roller coaster to begin with Carson, especially not this particular ride.

"I am, I'm very impressed," I finally said. "Thank you for allowing me to watch, and I hope you have a nice summer."

I hope you join the Peace Corps and go to some distant Third World black hole, I thought fiercely. And if he didn't, then I would look into private schools.

Mr. Hailey laughed, as though I still didn't comprehend the wonderful news. "Mrs. Wilder, I don't think you understand—"

"I understand everything," I said. "I understand that you think you have some right to make decisions for my child. But you don't."

He cut his laugh off and slowly stopped smiling. "I haven't made any decisions for your son. Carson made his own talents clear. He really has something here. Don't you want him to follow this gift?"

"Mr. Hailey, what exactly is in this for you?"

"I'm not sure what you're implying."

"What's in it for you? Why are you so interested?"

"I'm a teacher, that's my job."

I nodded. "In a small-town elementary school. But you're a musician too, aren't you? It might be a good way for someone to notice you, maybe get you a better job."

He flushed, and when he spoke his voice was hard and tight. "Yes, I'm a piano player. Not a genius, not even particularly gifted or talented. And now I'm a music teacher, and that is exactly what I was put here on this earth to do. And I don't want to be anything else."

"Really? Then why this performance? Why didn't you notify me before this? Why the secrecy?"

"Mrs. Wilder, it was Carson who wanted it to be a surprise, and quite frankly, I resent the implication that I have something to gain from this. Do I hope that one day a Schumann or a Nyiregyhazi will walk through my door? Sure, but neither of them turned out to be very happy people, did they? That's what I'm concerned with: finding out what makes my students happy."

"As his mother, I am better qualified to decide what will make my child happy."

"I don't think any mother can decide what makes her child happy," Mr. Hailey said quietly. "Carson doesn't have a lot of friends, which I have to assume you've noticed. This is the first time I've ever seen him truly excited, truly passionate about anything. I can see his mind working, taking the music apart, figuring out how it was done. It's startling and wonderful. Does it excite me to think I might be a part of that? Of course, but I have no designs on your son."

"I've seen people like you before, and I won't allow you to ruin Carson's life."

"Ruin his life?" Mr. Hailey repeated in bewilderment. "And what will you do when Carson grows up and wants to know why *you* didn't allow him to pursue what he so obviously loves?"

"That's not something you need to worry about, Mr. Hailey, as you won't be around to find out. My family history gives me an edge when it comes to children and genius. I have more experience than you in this matter."

He raised his eyebrows. "You have more musical geniuses in the family?"

"No, my sister is a math genius. She went to college at twelve. Do you know what that does to a child?"

"Ah," he said, "well, that makes perfect sense."

"How is that?"

"Music is math, math is music. And for what it's worth, suggesting Carson be accelerated because of this never crossed my mind. Composing isn't exactly a common course, except at a basic level, and not at all existent in the primary public school system. This is something that should be taken care of by private tutoring, mentoring. He's too advanced already for standard classes. He'd just be bored. There are workshops, camps he can attend."

"Good-bye, Mr. Hailey. And if I find out that you've continued any relationship with my son, I will file a formal complaint."

"You don't need to threaten me, Mrs. Wilder," Mr. Hailey said, stiffening.

I stood, grasping my purse like a shield. "I don't see that you've given me any choice."

I left him sitting in the auditorium, fairly vibrating with confusion and indignation. I hustled Carson out of the school as though the building were on fire and tried not to speed as I drove out of the parking lot.

Carson was jittery on the way home, flipping through a stack of music that Mr. Hailey had given him. I saw the names flash by out of the corner of my eye: John Lewis, Billy Strayhorn, Ornette Coleman. They rang distant bells, but nothing concrete came to mind.

When I felt as though I could speak with a steady voice, I said, "That was great, honey," interrupting his inspection of a piece of music. He was humming and continued for a few bars before he stopped to acknowledge what I'd said.

"Did you really like it?" he asked, his cheeks and forehead flush with color, as though he'd been in the sun too long.

"Sure, it was good," I said, my stomach clenching when his face fell at my faint praise. "Wasn't it kind of boring, though, writing it?" *Oh, God, forgive me. It's for your own good,* I silently pleaded with my son.

"No, it was so cool, Mom. I was watching you and Luz, you know, at the center, and I was thinking about how you showed her the notes, and then she did it real slow, and it just sort of came to me. I mean, I could figure out the clarinet part, but I didn't get how the bass would do it, except with the same notes, but then that wouldn't be very good would it, and then you were playing, and Luz was playing, and I just figured it out, how the sound was different, you know, and so the notes had to be different, they had to go around each other. And then Mr. Hailey showed me on the piano, how the notes would sound different too, and I just had this melody at first, but then with the other notes I figured out the harmony, and it was so cool. I like . . . I almost *saw* it."

"Wow," I managed to say. I was speechless and nauseous at the same time as I eased the car to a stop at a yellow light and looked over at him. He looked just like Estella when she'd tried to explain the Goldbach Conjecture to me, or the Banach-Tarski paradox, or any of the number of theories she'd tried to explain and would then give up on when I just stared at her.

The thing was, I did understand some of what she was saying, at first anyway, when I was still listening. I wasn't staring because I didn't get it, I was staring because she was transformed. Her words came fast, her eyes widened and shone, and she became short of breath in the mad rush to get the words out, as though they were piling up at the back of her tongue faster than she could roll them forward and out her lips. And now Carson looked, and sounded, exactly the same way.

"That's interesting," I said, measuring my words, desperate to be delicate. "It'll be nice to take a break from it for the summer, though, huh?"

"But Mr. Hailey said I could work on my own whenever I wanted," he said, looking up at me in surprise. "I was gonna write at camp. And he says I should have piano lessons too, Mom. Can I?"

I hit the brakes before I could stop myself, making us both lurch forward before I eased back up to speed. Camp. Pure music. Twenty-four hours a day with music professionals, all eager to find the next prodigy. Carson was slipping through my grasp as though my hands were oiled.

"Hey," I said, ignoring his request, making my voice bright and happy. "Why don't you come to Big Dune with me instead. Wouldn't you like that?"

He looked at me in confusion. "But what about camp?" His voice was rising in pitch, a warning sign I ignored.

"Wouldn't you rather play on the beach?"

He shook his head emphatically. "We get to try different instruments, and Tim, he's from my class, he's going too, and we said we would ride together on the bus, and I want to try this one thing I was working on, and—"

"But we're selling the house up there. This will be your last chance to see it. Gib won't be there, and we can go swimming and eat shrimp and—"

"No! No, Mom, no!" Carson was nearly panicked. His voice trembled and his face turned bright red, tears already beginning. "I want to go to camp, please, I *have* to go to camp!"

"Okay, okay," I soothed him. "It was just a suggestion. We'll talk more about it tomorrow." He didn't look soothed, though, and I felt near panic myself. If I didn't let him go to camp he was going to have a full-blown, three-day fit, a fit impossible to hide from Luke. And I couldn't tell him about this, not now, not when I couldn't trust him with anything, not when he had already proven that he was willing to compromise Carson's future.

What if he was like my father? What if he thought Carson could give him the credibility he constantly strove for? And worst of all, what if he took him over? What if he took my youngest boy?

Carson was staring at me, his tears spilling down his face, breathing heavily through his mouth. It had taken Mr. Hailey a school year to figure this out, how bad could it be in four weeks of camp?

"Okay, sweetie, but remember, you're there to play clarinet, not write music. They don't even have classes in that."

The change was dramatic. His face cleared and he rubbed the tears away, taking great gulps of air. "Okay, Mom, I'll get really better," he said, ducking his head to his sheet music again, his breathing returning to normal.

"Much better," I murmured, but he was already engrossed. The notes, the doubles and quarters and eighths, swam on the page as I stared at them, re-forming themselves into fractions and decimals and logarithms, a language I understood not at all, separating me from my son. A horn honked behind me. The light had turned green.

I drove home with a stranger in the car.

At least things at home were beginning to shape up. Gib had managed to get a job with his friend Sean, the son of a general contractor. The boys would be learning to hang drywall, and at first I'd thought it was a terrible idea. For one thing, I didn't like Sean. He flirted outrageously with me, and when he wasn't overtly staring at me, he was smirking behind my back.

But I hoped Gib might get something out of the hard physical labor, might feel some sense of pride in seeing something tangible resulting from his work, something concrete, unlike those numbers he swore he didn't get.

We enrolled him in the second session of summer school, so I would be back to make sure he attended after all. And Sean would pick him up each morning for work, so my Saab was safe again, though to be certain I wrote down the mileage on the odometer so I could check when I got back. There was nothing left to do for my oldest son.

Carson was already packed for camp and I was as ready to leave for Big Dune as I was going to be. That only left Luke—two more days of pretending.

We went out to dinner on Thursday night, but Luke was obviously distracted and blamed it on a meeting with a new client the next afternoon. I hated the lies. And now that I was lying myself, I hated them even more.

McNarey had cautioned me to be careful, but I couldn't help myself. On Friday I drove by Starbucks, looking for her car, telling myself that even if it wasn't there, it didn't mean anything. Luke could easily have a new client, though it had to be one who hadn't heard the rumors that had spread through my mother's group, and Deanna could easily have the day off for something legitimate.

It was not my first stakeout of the Starbucks parking lot. I knew she drove an old, light blue Celica with no rear bumper and a rubber Mickey Mouse head on the antenna. I steered the Escalade up and down the rows and didn't see the Celica. But there was a new, bright yellow Beetle parked at the end of a row, the dealer's paper tag still on it. With a Mickey Mouse head on the antenna. I parked in the next space, careful to hold on to the Escalade door to keep it from bumping the rounded front quarter panel, and peered into the Beetle. A top-heavy spike of orchid blooms tilted in the little vase beside the steering wheel.

Perhaps I was no genius, but neither was I an idiot.

That night Luke and I had sex. Going away sex. *Gonna be gone for three weeks*, he'd joked. *I'll be a maniac by the time you get home.*

But I was the one who wanted to make love, and I concentrated on myself. How Luke's back felt under my hands, how the ends of his hair brushed against my lips, how my skin felt where he touched it. He'd had too much to drink, something that had been happening more often over the past year, and it took him a long time, but I was patient, even loving, oddly embracing the realization that I would be sore the next day.

When I woke in the morning I lay on my side and watched him sleep. He was still a beautiful man. A sadness washed over me, as inevitable as the tides.

He was awake by the time Carson and I drove away, waving to us from the open garage door. He'd turned around to go back inside before I'd taken the Escalade out of reverse at the end of the drive.

We picked up greasy breakfast sandwiches, eating them in the parking lot of the elementary school while we waited for the camp buses to open their doors. Kids greeted each other and clutched instruments, while their parents held duffel bags and looked either terrified or relieved. I felt both in alternating waves.

I chewed on the rubbery croissant, trying to decide if I was brave enough to simply take off, kidnap my child, and spirit him away to the beach where I could hide him. I wasn't quick enough. Camp employees taped signs to the bus sides, A–M on the first bus, N–Z on the second, then positioned themselves at the open doors, clipboards in hand, and began checking kids in.

"There's Tim," Carson cried, pointing to a boy clutching a French horn case and waiting near the last bus. He reached out to open the door, and I put out a hand to stop him but connected with only an empty seat. I helped him with his things, and somehow managed to keep from falling to my knees and hugging him to me when he turned away.

When he disappeared into the bus, closely following Tim, a chill, clammy rush of air brushed the back of my neck, and I searched the windows for his face, seriously considering pushing my way onto the bus and dragging him out with me. He finally appeared toward the back and joined the rest of the kids in sticking their arms out the high windows and waving steadily.

The buses rumbled to life, and then they were gone. The deserted parents filed back to their cars in the silent, humid morning. I sat in the Cadillac and waited until everyone else had left the parking lot before I headed for my mother's.

On the way up in the elevator I wished I had someone with me to make a bet on whether Estella had called that morning to tell us to go on without her or not. Mother's door was cracked, waiting for me. I pushed it open and inhaled the scent of coffee.

"I'm here," I called, noting the fact that her bags weren't waiting in the hallway as they usually were when she was leaving on a trip. "Are you ready?"

"In the office," she replied, and I found her at her desk, dressed in a teal suit, hair coiffed and high heels waiting beside her chair. Not Mother's traveling outfit.

"Are you ready?" I asked when she finally looked up at me.

"I've had a bit of a change of plans," she said briskly, closing her checkbook and sliding it into the file drawer.

"Okay," I said, cautious, watching her as I would a wild animal. "Want to share them with me?"

"I'm afraid I've gotten myself too involved in the hospital charity, and with the fund-raiser only a month away I just won't be able to—"

"Oh, no," I said. "No, absolutely not. If you're not going, I'm not going. You can't do this, Mother."

"Don't be ridiculous. This is a perfect opportunity for you to get away from the Luke situation, to take some time for yourself—"

"How is packing up that entire house time for myself?"

"Well, Estella will be helping you."

"You can't seriously think Estella will even go now?"

"Why not? Besides, it means so much to me that you and Estella are finally getting a chance to be together. She's so looking forward to seeing you. I absolutely insist that you go."

"I can't believe you've done this," I said, slowly shaking my head.

"I didn't plan it, Connie."

"Of course you did. You knew exactly what you were doing. Come on, get your stuff together. I'm not doing this alone," I insisted, and turned toward her bedroom to haul her suitcases out myself. I flung two of them onto her bed, then opened a dresser drawer and pulled handfuls of underwear and bras out, throwing them in the first case before I moved to the other side of the bed, where a tall chest of drawers held nightgowns and stockings.

I nearly tripped over the hatbox. The top was still on, but tissue hung raggedly out the sides, as though she'd hastily replaced the lid. I knelt and gently pulled the top off, carefully replacing the tissue paper around the little shoes, tucking them in as gently as I'd tucked my own children into their cribs. As I slid the box under the bed, my mother appeared at the door, but came no farther.

We regarded each other silently, me still on my knees beside the bed.

"This is completely unfair," I said under my breath. Her eyes flickered over the underwear strewn across the bed, and she nodded slightly.

"Call me when you get to the island," she said, then returned to her office and shut the door.

I sat in my car in the parking lot, listening to the Gulf whisper against the sand while I tried to decide what to do. My choices were limited: Go back home and try to live with Luke as though nothing was happening, go pick up Estella, or take a vacation by myself at the beach house and leave the packing up for Mother to take care of herself after I returned home.

One way or another, sitting in the parking lot wasn't an option. I took one last look up at Mother's condo windows and then slowly drove out of the lot, with no idea of where I was going.

Estella

Connie is speaking urgently, but we, my father and I, are leaving and her words are lost as my father drives away. I am seated backward, so I am able to watch her recede out the rear window, a leather satchel that is larger than I am pressing into my thighs, and I read her lips grotesquely over-forming the words: *Watch for alligators!*

My eyes fly open, and I swing my legs around under the covers so I'm sitting on the edge of the bed in one fluid movement. I look at the clock, certain that I've slept through the alarm. But it is still over an hour from going off, and I recline again, slowly easing my legs back onto the bed.

Paul snores softly, undisturbed. I listen to him and stare at the ceiling, regretting my decision to go now that the day is finally upon me.

I don't have much left to do. I'd done all the cleaning with the help of the students that week, and even the shopping for dinner tonight is done. I'd been in a panic to make sure everything was completed in time and now I regret it deeply. I wish for bathrooms to scrub, for floors to mop, grout to bleach, anything that will keep me from slowly going insane waiting for my mother and Connie to arrive.

Paul grumbles and turns over, taking the covers with him and exposing me to the chill of the air-conditioned room. I'm not going back to sleep, so there is no sense lying there, disturbing Paul with my unsettled aura.

I carefully get out of bed and turn the alarm clock off, padding to the bathroom to take a shower. The steam loosens me up; I take my time getting ready, as though I am going on a date. I even shave my legs.

I am wiping the counter and mirror with my towel when I hear the phone ring. I run to get it, hoping it won't wake Paul, but Chelsea already has it. She holds it out to me, smiling at my wet hair.

"Your mom," she whispers, and I make a face and shake my head, pretending I won't take it. I imagine she's calling to tell me they've already left and are currently *x* hours away. My mother loves cell phones, and I'll doubtless get approximately eight of these calls today. Chelsea just grins and hands me the phone.

"Hello," I say, trying to sound cheerful. "Where are you?" *Ha*, I think, *beat you to it.*

"I'm home, sweetheart, I won't be able to make it," Mother says. Confusion floods me, and is then quickly replaced by clear, sparkling relief.

They're not coming.

I am off the hook. A smile spreads across my face and my knees actually go a bit soft. I immediately begin to look forward to the house full of people who will be here tonight, the students, the people I love and who love me, whom I've invited tonight to distance myself from my own family, to insulate me, and whom I will now simply get to enjoy.

"But I don't want you to worry," Mother says. "Connie left about an hour ago and should be there by five."

So Connie is coming. Alone.

The hours pass the way hours do when waiting for pain medications to kick in: slowly, with a tension that infects everyone within range. By four o'clock, I am nearly quivering. I had hoped that Connie might call to tell me she wasn't coming, and in fact, the phone did ring this afternoon, but when I answered it, whoever it was simply waited for a moment and then hung up.

Almost everyone is here: Chelsea and Lisa; Chelsea's boyfriend, Steve, and his friend Hal; and three high school students I tutor, Chris, Phil, and Julia. They are all having a good time together.

I step out onto the front porch, away from the laughter, away from the warm, spicy aroma of spaghetti sauce, away from Paul, who seeks me out with his eyes every few minutes to make sure I'm okay.

The magnolia tree on the corner wafts its scent all the way down to me. I inhale with my eyes closed and think I might like to have a few of the blossoms. The house on that lot is for sale and has sat empty for over a year. All the neighbors snip the flowers as freely as though it were their own tree, and we all harbor a little hope that the house will never sell.

My surrogate family's laughter follows me down the block.

CHAPTER EIGHT

A private security car followed me on my third trip around Mother's block, and I finally admitted to myself that I wasn't going to march back up to the condo. I waved to the guard and turned away from the expensive condominiums and toward the interstate. I still wasn't sure what I was doing.

I looked down at the directions to Georgia, thinking of the time it would shave off my drive if I went straight to Big Dune. I could be installed in the house with a plate of shrimp by about the same time I would have arrived at Estella's. I had six hours of steady driving ahead of me before I had to decide, before I had to make the turn left toward the island or veer toward Atlanta.

I spent the first two hours figuring out and refining all the things I could have said to Mother. I even said them out loud, turning the music down so I could hear my voice, righteously angry, admirably tough as it reverberated through the cavernous leather interior.

But as I calmed down, I began to wonder what her motivation had been. Had it been simple laziness? Did she just need me and Estella to close up the house and knew we wouldn't go if she weren't there to buffer us? Had she, feeling mortal and motherly, been trying to force us to deal with each other? Or could she simply not bring herself to go to the island again?

I couldn't get the image of her little sisters snagged in the tree roots, two naked little girls, identical in their lives, identical in their deaths, out of my mind. I wondered if they knew how much their older sister had loved them. I knew how much Estella had loved me once. I had felt that fierce protectiveness, and at the age that April and May had died I would not have been surprised to have had Estella protecting me from a hurricane with her own body. I would have expected it.

But in the years after that night in the music room, I'd been a free agent. Estella was no longer my protector, my father was wrapped up in her rather than me, and my mother, I now knew, was ensnared in her own drama of learning how to be a wife and mother moving in educated circles.

After all those years of trying to win his attention by playing the violin, I had finally realized that I would not get my father back. He was lost to me. And so I turned my energy to Estella instead. Our relationship had finally achieved some common ground, based simply on the fact that we were growing into adolescence. I had lain awake nights scheming how to expand upon it, waging a quiet war to win my sister back.

I had been a pretty baby and was turning into a pretty girl. And my shopping trips with my mother ensured that I was always in style. My sister, however, got the Sykes crooked teeth and missed out on the shopping trips, an unfortunate combination. Add her appearance to the fact that she spent all her time with adults, and she was destined to fail in the popularity contests that all childhoods are.

I, on the other hand, was practically the center of the neighborhood. Except for Kimmy Kay and her damn horses. But fortune was with me that year leading up to Estella's college entrance. Kimmy Kay's guest horse came down with some horse illness that necessitated a quarantine, and the neighborhood kids congregated at our house. Estella hovered in the background and eavesdropped on conversations, like Fossey trying to fit in with gorillas, and it was a wonder to watch her exercise the social instincts that had been hiding for so long.

She was only a size larger than me, and I took great advantage of my mother's generosity on our shopping trips by slipping clothes for Estella in with mine. I would casually toss them on her bed, muttering something about them being too big for me. She never thanked me, but whenever kids filled the house she would invariably show up on the fringes wearing something I had chosen.

I managed to get her braces by making fun of her teeth over dinner, forcing my mother to take notice without calling attention to the fact that I was trying to help. And truth be told, I was secretly pleased to make my father acknowledge that perhaps his prodigy might be flawed in ways that I wasn't. It still pleased me a little, just a little, to remember it, his eyes flitting from her teeth to mine and back.

My interest in reading never waned, but without my father's guidance, I moved from the classic and obscure tomes that filled our library to mainstream novels far beyond my years. Perhaps it was simply to spite Daddy, but I began to leave these books in Estella's room. Stephen King, Danielle Steele, even Harold Robbins made their way onto her nightstand. They were never in sight when I looked in her room, but she never gave them back either.

But before she even had a chance to shiver with me over the creepy twins in *The Shining*, she left for college, to learn about complex variables and combinatorics. All my work had been for nothing. I may as well have spent my time deadheading roses and spraying aphids with my mother; my experiment at socializing Estella failed before I'd made a dent.

I was minutes away from having to make my decision to continue on to Georgia or turn toward the island when I picked up the phone and dialed my sister's number with a shaking hand and my heart in my throat. With one hand I held the phone to my ear and with the other hand I steered, ready to flip my directional and take the exit that would carry me along Florida's panhandle and out to Big Dune. But just as Estella answered, rather than taking the exit I kept to my lane, steering straight toward Atlanta. She said hello twice, and I hung up without a word.

I turned the radio up, allowing the music to take my mind off my mother, off Estella and Luke and my sons. But the flat length of Florida's I-75 seemed designed for brooding, and by the time I arrived in Estella's neighborhood hours later, I was exhausted and close to tears.

I slowed considerably when I turned onto her street. The house on the corner, a dilapidated old Southern monstrosity, boasted an extraordinary magnolia tree in the front yard. Its blooms were the size of dinner plates, and its leaves fluttered green and copper in the light wind.

I caught a quick glimpse of a dervish in a gauzy blue skirt twirling beneath the tree, magnolia-laden arms extended in a joyful, frenzied dance. Whoever it was must have seen me staring at her as I came around the corner, because the gauze quickly disappeared around the back of the house, bare feet flying, before I could get a glimpse of her face. I laughed out loud, thinking the woman was someone I'd like to know, or perhaps someone I'd like to be.

I glanced in my rearview mirror as I drove down the street, but she never reappeared, and I nearly missed Estella's house. I pulled into the driveway, stopping behind a beat-up old Cutlass, surprised that they'd finally gotten a car. I stared at the house for a moment before I picked up the cell phone again and dialed home. It was an exercise in procrastination. There was no answer. I hadn't expected one.

I grabbed my overnight bag and approached the porch, wishing I were visiting the magnolia dancer up the street instead. I felt naked as I stood there in the fading light, trying to compose myself before I rang the bell. I could hear music playing, and voices, lots of voices. I reached out to touch the doorbell, but the door flew open before I could, and I took an involuntary step backward.

Paul stood there, towering above me with his long wiry limbs tensed and worry creasing his face. "Connie," he said, looking over my shoulder as though he expected someone else.

I silently cursed Mother before I stuttered a reply. "Paul, hi. It's just me. Mother couldn't make it."

His eyes met mine again, and he stood back to allow me in, reaching to take the overnight bag I was clutching tightly to my side. "I know," he said. "I hoped it was Estella."

"Estella?"

He had been heading for the stairs with my bag, and he stopped and stood there for a minute before he turned around. "She's gone."

Before I could respond, a group of young people came around the corner in a smiling wave of chatter, engulfing me in their midst. Paul walked up the stairs and out of my sight as they reached toward me.

"—so cool, we've heard so much about you."

"—and this is my boyfriend, Steve."

"—long did it take you?"

"—check the spaghetti sauce."

I shook hands with everyone, confused about exactly who they were and why they were here. They continued to talk to me and among themselves as they moved me toward the living room. One of the girls pressed a glass of red wine into my hand. I found myself in the corner of a long sofa, staring at Estella's old Escher prints on the wall. Paul finally reappeared to make formal introductions, and I almost forgot that Estella wasn't there, as a portion of her life completely unknown to me revealed itself.

She'd never mentioned that she tutored kids. Or perhaps she had and I simply hadn't processed it. But I never knew that she had college students living in her home. I thought back to Estella on the fringes as an adolescent, trying to find her way in by the crumbs I'd dropped. And now I was the one flummoxed by the activity, stunned into a shy, bewildered outsider. Then I remembered that my sister wasn't even there. I carefully set my glass of wine on the side table and stood.

"So, Paul, where is Estella?" I asked.

The group of students quieted and began to excuse themselves, moving out of the living room and into the front hall. I heard a swinging door and then silence. Paul shrugged, a sharp, quick movement of his shoulders.

"I don't know," he said. "She was on the front porch watching for you, and when I brought her a glass of wine, she was gone. I was about to go look for her when you arrived. She couldn't have gone far, she didn't even have shoes on."

I felt loathsome tears at my eyes. Maybe I hadn't been crazy about seeing her, but to think that she'd run away from home rather than face me hurt more than I thought possible. I suddenly felt like a child again, pushed away from the one person I wanted most to be near. The fact that she didn't have shoes on struck me.

"What was she wearing?" I asked Paul, who was tying the laces of his boots, preparing to go search for Estella.

He didn't look up at me. "Long skirt, short-sleeved shirt, that's about it."

"Long blue skirt, sort of full, gauzy?"

That got his attention. He looked up at me in surprise. "Yeah, did you see her? Where?"

"Close," I said, placing my hand on his arm. "Paul, would you mind if I went to get her? Maybe she'd be more comfortable if I saw her alone first."

He cleared his throat and finished lacing his boots. "No offense, Connie, but why do you think all these people are here? If you'll just tell me where you saw her—"

"But she left," I interrupted. "So maybe she didn't feel as comfortable as she thought she would."

I walked past him and out the door without waiting for his permission and heard him follow me. To my surprise, he stayed on the front porch while I walked down the steps and turned toward the big magnolia tree on the corner.

Had we waited a few more moments we wouldn't have had to go through the little power struggle. A few houses from the corner I saw the blue skirt and white top slowly coming toward me, their owner's arms filled with creamy magnolias glowing in the half-light. She stopped when she saw me, her features still indistinguishable, but she recognized me, and I was crying even before she dropped the flowers and ran toward me, like a child, her arms crooked at her sides. I started a half-jog too, and then her arms were around me, and mine were around her, and we were both crying, whispering each other's names in the magnolia-scented air.

She felt tiny in my arms, so much smaller than I remembered her. It was like hugging a child. I loosened my hold, just a bit, afraid I was hurting her. We slowly let go of each other and stepped back without saying a word. Her hair was short, shorter than I'd ever seen it. But it suited her, framing her thin face, making her into a pixie of a forty-three-year-old.

She reached out to run a hand over my own long hair. "Still so pretty," she said with a smile, and I laughed out loud.

"Well, it is getting dark," I said, "and obviously your eyesight's failing."

As our laughter faded I felt a distance, a shyness come between us again, and Estella backed up a few paces as if she felt it too. She turned suddenly with a cry.

"I was bringing these for you," she said, running back toward the magnolias scattered across the sidewalk. We gathered them together, avoiding each other's eyes.

Her face was flushed when she stood upright, and she smiled warily at me before she glanced down the block. Paul was on the sidewalk outside their home, turned toward us, watching intently. She raised her arm, waving a magnolia at him, and he turned and disappeared into the shadows.

"He was worried about you," I said as we began to walk back to the house.

"Yeah," she said. "Sorry about that. I got—a little nervous."

"I know," I said softly.

When we walked into the house it was as though Estella had been gone for days. The students rushed her, but she batted them away with her thin arms and laughter. I watched in wonder. I'd never seen my sister so easy in the presence of others, and I'd never seen a group of people so obviously enamored of her either.

I stood to the side, with the scratchy magnolia branches in my arms, and felt as out of place as she must have around my friends. But then she turned to me, inclining her head toward the swinging door beyond a long dining table, and said, "Come on, let's get these flowers in something."

I followed her into the kitchen where Paul was stirring a huge pot of spaghetti sauce. A few of the students followed us in while the rest scattered around the living and dining room, as comfortable in Estella's home as if it were their own. I felt a pang of jealousy for the easy feel of it. Estella dropped her flowers in the sink and then went to Paul, who bent down and whispered something in her ear. I studiously avoided looking at them as I dropped my flowers in the sink too, and moved out of the way when one of the college students nudged me with her hands full of containers for the blooms.

I looked around for something to do, but within seconds Estella had broken away from Paul, who glanced at me over her head and smiled. It was the first real smile I'd received from him, and I felt a warm blush of approval, as though I had been looking for it all along.

"Let me show you your room," Estella said. I followed her out the swinging door and through the dining room, where two of the high school students were setting the table. Now that I wasn't surrounded by students or worried about Estella, I finally noticed my sister's home. The dining table was made out of one long, narrow slab of golden, highly figured wood, and a single wide shelf ringed the entire room, holding books and polished wood bowls, sculptures, and picture frames.

The floor throughout the downstairs was tile. Not surprising in South Florida, but a surprise to me here in Georgia, especially considering the age and style of the house. It was lovely, though, rustic terracotta with little animal pawprints every few tiles. Estella led me up the stairs, pointing out doors to me as we walked down the hall.

"This is Paul's finishing room. You'll get used to the smell. He put in a ventilation system and plastic around the door, so it's not nearly as bad as before."

I did catch a whiff of something pervasive—varnish? sawdust?— but not altogether unpleasant.

"And Lisa is bunking in with Chelsea for the night, so here's your room," Estella said, turning into a room toward the end of the hall. My bag was on the bed, and Estella walked around nervously, straightening a lamp, pulling at the comforter.

"It's beautiful," I said, trying to put her at ease, and she flashed a smile at me.

"Well, be sure to tell Lisa, it's all her stuff. We let them do whatever they want with the rooms. Would you like to freshen up before dinner? Nothing fancy, I'm afraid, just spaghetti and salad."

"That would be nice," I said, nervous now that we were in it, now that the rush of being greeted, inspected, acknowledged was over. I moved out of her way as she left the room and followed her to the bathroom.

"You'll have to share with the girls," she said apologetically as she handed me a stack of towels, but I waved her off. *The girls.* I still couldn't process this Estella.

"I'll be fine," I said, and then we fell silent. She moved first, suddenly, as though shocked back to life.

"Okay, then. Take your time, dinner's easy to put together. We'll be waiting for you downstairs."

"Great," I said, a smile stiff on my lips. "I'll be down as soon as I can."

She was already walking down the hall. "No rush," she called back to me as her head bobbed out of sight down the stairs.

Estella

Oh, God.

I am clutching the banister, stuck between the upstairs and downstairs, between childhood and real life. I know I'm out of Connie's sight, and I haven't been noticed by the students or Paul yet. I wonder how long I can stand here in limbo, clutching this railing. I sink to the steps and just sit there. I would say that I was catching my breath, but my breath is caught just fine.

It's my mind that's racing.

I need to catch my brain, I think, and a manic giggle piles up in my throat.

She is as beautiful as she always was, those light brown eyes and dark lashes so striking with that thick sheaf of blond hair. But there is something different. Maybe it's just age, or maybe it was that unguarded moment when we first saw each other. Maybe that stamped her with temporary uncertainty.

She flinched when she saw my hair, and I felt her draw away when she hugged me. I take a deep breath and let it out.

Three weeks of this.

Paul comes around the corner before my mind can begin to reconfigure this into a formula, and his foot hits the first step before he sees me. I grin at his look of surprise, the way he has to stop his long body from continuing the climb before he folds his legs beneath him and sits on the step below me.

"How you doing?" he asks.

"Oh, I'm fine," I say, and I realize that I am. In fact, I realize that I haven't felt this rush, this crazy mix of emotions, in over a year, and I feel strong with it. I lean down and kiss Paul on his beautiful lips, surprising him. I am surprised too. The numbers have fled my brain and for a moment he is all I need.

"Let's do this thing," I say, inclining my head down the stairs, and he grins at me, feeling my strength. He stands and pulls me forward and I join my downstairs life, accepting a glass of wine and looking forward to dinner.

With my sister.

CHAPTER NINE

Halfway down the staircase, I faltered and considered turning around and burrowing into my borrowed bed. But I heard laughter filtering from the kitchen, and then music, and knew that for this house, the night was just getting started. I took a deep breath and found myself walking through the swinging door into the kitchen.

"Hey," Paul said, "there she is."

They all turned to look at me. Estella sat at the kitchen table, drawing something on graph paper for one of the students, and she motioned me over, startling me again with her ease among so many vibrant young people.

"Let her through," she said, and the students parted and Chelsea pulled a chair out for me. I murmured a thank-you as I sat, and nodded another thank-you as Paul poured me a new glass of wine.

"Lisa?" I asked, looking around, and the blond young woman with the startling blue eyes lifted a hand in a little wave. "Thank you so much for giving up your room. It's lovely."

"No problem," she said with a grin. "Chelsea and I will have a sleepover, just like high school. It'll be fun."

"Can I come too?" Steve piped up, and Lisa slapped him lightly on the arm. I sat back and relaxed a little, looking over at Estella. Her head was bent close to Chris's, the two of them inspecting something on the graph paper.

Chelsea leaned over them, pointing with a pencil and saying something about a devil's curve and polar equations while Phil watched quietly, his lower lip caught in his teeth. I felt another pang, and realized with a start that it was jealousy. We'd had nights like this at our house, before Gib perfected his distance, before Luke started screwing baristas, before we seemed to want to be anywhere but in the same room together.

"Soup's on," Paul announced, and everyone grabbed something to bring to the dining room. A breadbasket was placed in my hands, and I followed Estella, who was carrying a huge wooden bowl of salad, out to the table. Julia, one of the high school students, smiled shyly at me and patted the seat next to her. "You can sit over here, Connie."

"Thank you," I said, and took the chair. The usual flutter of passing bowls and plates commenced amid good-natured banter, and I realized with surprise that I was hungry. I took a good helping of everything and was about to raise my fork to my lips when Paul stood, his glass of wine raised.

"A toast, please, quiet down," he said, and everyone found a glass of wine or soda. "A thank-you to our family for being here tonight to welcome Connie to our home. We've provided sustenance so you won't eat her, a Go board in the living room so you won't force her to dance for your entertainment, and wine, except for you poor underage folk, so that she may see us all through the fuzzy haze of liquor and won't speak too badly of us when she returns home."

Everyone stood and leaned in to clink glasses and I said, "Thank you," touched by such hospitality from Paul, who'd looked anything but hospitable when I'd arrived on the porch. As the serious eating got under way the conversation turned naturally toward classes and teachers. I stayed silent, listening to the foreign math terms and the gossip about professors, and much of the humor flew completely over my head.

I saw the looks that passed between Paul and Estella and found myself reassessing Paul. I'd always thought of him in a rather vague *Estella's friend* way, but it was obvious that they were still deeply in love after more than ten years together. In fact, everyone seemed solicitous of Estella. She was less, I realized, like a popular friend and more like a protected mother figure. For the first time, I wondered if she was sorry that she hadn't had children.

The wood pieces around the room caught my eye. I'd never seen any of Paul's work up close before, though Mother had shown me pictures of his bowls and sculptures. The pictures hadn't done them justice. The bowls were exquisite, shaped out of the burls of trees, and highly polished so that the grain was revealed in stark contrast.

The sculptures were all free-form, and many had blackened centers, with pieces of the wood flowing up like flames around them, as though he'd burned right down to their hearts and then carved them from there. My gaze froze on a picture frame. Most were empty, but this one was filled. I recognized the photo, and I glanced at Estella, looking for something I couldn't define.

"Your work is beautiful," I said, flushing when I realized that I had interrupted a conversation, but Paul smiled openly at me.

"Thank you," he said with a nod. "I don't usually keep so many pieces here, but a gallery is having a show next week and I'm stocking up for it."

"Oh," I said. "I'm sorry we won't be here for it."

He shrugged. "No big deal. There's always a show going on somewhere. Estella's been to enough of them to last a lifetime I'm sure."

"You finish the pieces here?" I asked, recalling the room upstairs.

He nodded. "If I had more room here I'd move my entire workshop. I do the major work a few blocks away, and I used to finish everything there, but after Estella—"

"I got tired of him coming home late," Estella interrupted, with a bright smile at Paul.

Paul agreed. "So I fixed the guest room upstairs into my finishing room. I try to stock up on pieces, do the turning on several at once, and then bring them all home. That way I can be here for long stretches of time. Stinks up the house a little, but at least I'm here."

"It must be nice to have him home so much," I said to Estella. It was such an odd pairing. I had always pictured Estella with an older mathematics professor, or maybe a scientist, or, most often, alone. "It's interesting that you two got together," I blurted out and instantly regretted it. Paul looked at me quizzically.

"How's that?" he asked.

"Estella's so . . . math-oriented, that's all. And your work is creative. It's just an interesting mix."

"Math and creativity?" Paul asked, and my mouth dried up when I realized I had the whole table's attention.

"Yes, you know, opposites attract and all that, I guess," I finished lamely, feeling more out of place than ever. But to my surprise, everyone began speaking at once.

Paul waved his hand to quiet the students and took a sip of wine. "Actually, math enables creativity, it supports it. I work with a natural medium, and Nature is the most exacting mathematician there is. My work has only benefited from Estella's knowledge."

"How do you mean?" I asked.

"This is an old, old discussion," Estella said to me with a smile. "Not just around this table, but in the math world, the art world, the music world."

I nodded, thinking of Carson and my own music training. "Music is math, math is music," I said, repeating Mr. Hailey's words as if they were my own. I felt my cheeks burning.

"Exactly," Lisa said. "Look at Berg's 'Lyric Suite.' Everything's based on twenty-three and its multiples. He did that on purpose, planned it out."

"Beethoven and Shubert too," Julia said.

"Yeah, but they didn't do it on purpose, and it wasn't twenty-three," Phil argued, looking to Chelsea to see if she approved.

"How do you know they didn't do it on purpose?" Julia contested.

"And what about poetry?" Estella said, steering the conversation, obviously used to the little skirmishes.

"Omar Khayyám," Hal mumbled around a mouthful of spaghetti.

"*The Rubaiyat*," I said in surprise, and Hal nodded, swallowing and taking a big gulp of wine as he waved a piece of garlic bread at Chelsea to indicate that she should enlighten me.

"He introduced a solar calendar superior to the Gregorian calendar in the eleventh century," she said.

Hal finally took a break from all the chewing. "Twelfth," he said.

"Eleventh," Steve said, coming to his girlfriend's defense, though he looked uncertain. "He also published a treatise on algebra. There have always been people like that, who've mixed mathematics and art of one kind or another. Look at da Vinci."

"Well, it was only a matter of time before someone brought him up," Paul said with a smile.

"Language is math too," Phil said, apparently full of one-liner facts. "Hebrew is math."

"And you've been watching *Pi* again, haven't you?" Julia shot at Phil. "That's numerology, not math."

"What do you know?" Phil asked. "You've never even seen it."

"The Great Pyramid, the Parthenon, they used Nature's numbers, divine proportion and all that, even before da Vinci came along. I think he just put stuff down in writing before a lot of people," Chris said.

"That's one theory," Estella said. "But if we're talking about that Leonardo we can't forget—"

"Fibonacci," Lisa interrupted. "Three hundred years before da Vinci, Chris."

"Yes, but da Vinci was the first to introduce the principles in great art," Steve said.

"That's debatable," Hal said mildly.

"Raphael, Rembrandt, Chagall, Dalí," Chelsea said. "All geniuses, whether they even knew they were doing it or not, they were all fascinated by dynamic symmetry in nature."

My head was spinning. I had no idea what they were talking about. Estella, grinning at the discussion, saw the bewilderment on my face.

"Dynamic symmetry encompasses what's known as the golden rectangle, the golden triangle, and so forth. The divine logarithmic spiral, which da Vinci was intrigued with, is found in Nature all the time."

"I'm sorry." I shook my head. "This is all a bit over my head."

"No, it's not, it's just the terms you're unfamiliar with. Think of a ram's horn, a spiral galaxy, the bands of a hurricane. There are specific proportions that repeat themselves over and over in Nature, which you would think would mostly concern mathematicians and scientists. But artists and poets and musicians throughout history have either consciously or unconsciously used those same proportions in their work. Math is connected to creativity in all kinds of ways we don't completely understand. You should know that, Connie, you're a wonderful musician."

"Bees are mathematicians," Phil said. "Hexagonal tiling. Plants too. Phyllotaxis." But everyone was looking at me.

"What do you play?" Lisa asked.

"Violin," I said. "But Estella thinks too much of my talent."

"Not true," Estella said quietly, and when she looked directly at me across the table it was as if the rest of the people in the room disappeared. The moment passed quickly. "She's very talented."

"Will you play for us?" Hal asked, still shoveling food into his mouth.

"Oh, no. Besides, I don't have my violin," I lied.

"Yes, she does," Chris said, and Phil shot him the sort of *shut up, stupid* look I'd seen passed between my own sons, but Chris either didn't see or chose to ignore it. "It's in the backseat. Case is, anyway." He finally looked up to see everyone staring at him, and he ducked his head in embarrassment. "Uh, I really like the Escalade. We were just checking it out. I didn't touch it or anything."

"It's okay," I said. "I'll let you look at it after dinner."

Chris shot Phil a smug look. "Cool."

"You brought your violin?" Estella asked. "Would you play?"

"No, I couldn't," I said. "I'm exhausted, and besides, I don't have anything prepared." Which was another lie. I was forty years old. I had plenty of pieces I could have played with my eyes closed.

"I play piano," Chelsea said. "Got a keyboard upstairs. Come on, they make me play all the time. It would be nice to have some accompaniment."

I shook my head again, beginning to feel a little desperate, and Estella stood and grabbed her plate. "Let's clear and get ready for dessert," she said, taking the attention off me.

Everyone took their own plates and began to make their way to the kitchen, with me following, my own hands full too. "What's for dessert?" I asked, and they all started laughing, turning toward me with grins.

"What?" I asked, just as the high school students, as if waiting for the question, all yelled "Pie!" at the same time.

It took me a minute, and then I shook my head. "Who knew math was so funny," I said, rolling my eyes at the continuing giggles as we milled around the kitchen, getting in one another's way as much as we were helping.

After pie, after coffee, after more useless protestations, I took Chris and Phil out to inspect the Escalade, and Chris carried my violin in to the living room. I tucked my wedding rings in the case and dragged out my preparations, tightening and rosining the bow, tuning, fussing with the shoulder rest. I was ready to play just as Chelsea got her keyboard set up. I was almost hyperventilating. I'd never had a problem with performance anxiety before, but here in my sister's house, thrown off by the entire happy household vibe, I struggled to find where I fit, and came up empty.

"What's your poison?" Chelsea asked.

"We've been working on 'La Rejouissance'," I said hopefully, looking at the sheet music at the top of my stack, but Chelsea shook her head, flipping through her music.

"Nope, love Handel though. How about Vivaldi?"

" 'Spring'?" I asked.

"But of course," she said with a grin.

This is knew I had. I riffled through my music but Chelsea was already holding the pull-out violin section from her own music, and I smiled a thanks at her. She nodded, allowed me to set up, make a few more adjustments, and after a couple of abbreviated starts, we were off, alternately looking at our music and watching each other.

Spring did indeed return with the first notes swooping down like the birds from the trees, and the birds sang for me, joyfully and with only a few errors that nobody else seemed to notice. As always, "Spring" seemed to make everyone happy, and Lisa rose and pulled Julia up with her and they performed an impromptu, technically doubtful but joyful ballet across the tile.

The birds were closely followed by the fountains and they flowed easily, bouncing along in their constant movement, challenging me. Chelsea and I played well together, and when we finished we took exaggerated bows and curtsies.

Prodded by Estella, they talked me into a short Tartini solo, and then Chelsea put my own carelessly phrased playing to shame with an accomplished Beethoven sonata. We finished together with a choppy, laughing "Flight of the Bumblebee," or what I could manage to chime in with anyway, and I was sure that Chelsea toned down her obvious talent to match my own rusty performance.

"Encore, encore!" Paul shouted and the rest of them took up the cry, but I demurred, claiming exhaustion. Chelsea looked pointedly at her watch.

"We've got to get these kids home anyway," she said, nodding at the already protesting high school students. "I'll drive them, it's too late for the bus. I'll need to get out," Chelsea said to me as I was putting my violin away, and I remembered the Cutlass in the driveway. Of course it was Chelsea's, not Paul or Estella's. But it didn't irritate me as much as it once might have.

Once the students left, Estella and I cleaned up the dessert and coffee dishes, and I started a hundred different conversations in my mind, but each time I opened my mouth, Estella turned away to open a cupboard or hang up a towel.

"Well, I guess I'll get to bed. Long day," I said, but her back was to me as she rinsed cups.

"Good night," she said. "You played beautifully."

I was already out the swinging door when she said it, and I'm sure my thank-you was lost.

I lay awake, unable to drift off. Estella and I had spent all but the beginning and the end of the night surrounded by other people. I could distill our conversation down to a few sentences. We hadn't even discussed Mother's absence. Tomorrow we wouldn't have the distraction of Paul and the students. Two people in a car on a long ride are very alone if they aren't talking to each other.

I heard Lisa and Chelsea giggling in their room, occasionally breaking out into full-fledged laughter, and felt those pangs of jealousy again. Estella was so lucky, I thought, and then immediately listed the reasons why I was luckier, but they seemed hollow. A sweet aroma tickled my nose, and I thought that the girls lit some incense, but I laughed softly when I recognized the smell of pot within a few moments.

I lay there for a few more minutes, arguing with myself, and then made my decision. For the first time since college I was alone. Not just alone, but lonely. The evening, surrounded by young people without the weight of divorce hanging over them, without the hostility I felt in my own home, made me desperate to feel part of something again. There was nobody to worry about but myself. No kids, no husband, just me.

I crept down the hall and knocked lightly at their door, whispering, "It's just Connie." Lisa cracked the door and peered out at me. When I grinned at her she giggled and opened the door enough to allow me to slip in, welcomed back into that old familiar place of girly friendship that I had lost long ago.

As I settled onto the bed, I wondered if I should go get Estella. But then Chelsea put the radio on softly, and Lisa set black and white game pieces on a board in the middle of the bed, and I thought about how lucky Estella was, and stayed right where I was. She was probably asleep anyway.

Estella

I hear Connie's door squeak open, and my heart leaps in my chest. Paul snores lightly, naked, curled on his side away from me, the hill of his shoulder jutting toward the ceiling. Perhaps she is simply going to the bathroom. I listen hard, trying to tune my ears to the weight of her.

The squeak comes, but it is to the left of her door, not the right, the way the bathroom lies. No, she is turned toward the stairs. She steps farther down the hall, and I levitate by degrees, careful to not wake Paul, until I'm sitting up.

The late hour makes me giddy with something I struggle to define, a certainty that *something* is possible. I realize that I am hopeful, a pure emotion, unencumbered by resentment or anxiety as it might be in the light of day. I envision us meeting at the foot of the stairs and smiling conspiratorially before we make our way, silently, to the kitchen—there is no music room here—where we might finally ... what? Talk? Dance?

There is no squeak of the first stair. But I am already out of bed, poised with one foot raised, stepping into my pajama bottoms. There is a soft rapping, and then silence. I ease my foot into the soft cotton pants and snug them up to my waist as I listen, actually moving my face forward, my neck elongating, as though this will help my ears to isolate the noise.

Chelsea's door. A click, pause, click, silence. Footsteps across the floor and the squeal of bedsprings. I remain still for a long moment wondering *what the hell*, and then I finally pad my way out of the bedroom, moving tile to tile, and then up the stairs, avoiding the squeaks I know by heart.

The air outside Chelsea's door is heavy with the musky sweetness of pot, and I smile to myself. It doesn't bother me. They're big girls, responsible. They might even be giggling about boys, though they're more likely playing Go.

I slide my feet past their room and peer at Connie's door. It's open. I poke my head around the corner and focus on the bed. It's empty.

"Con," I whisper. "Connie?"

No answer.

I look down the hall to the open doorway of the bathroom. It's dark; there's no one there. I suddenly realize that Connie is in the bedroom with Lisa and Chelsea. *In there.* At the sleepover. Probably oohing and ahhing over the Go board, pretending, charmingly, that she's too dumb to learn it, like she tried to protest playing the violin tonight and then dazzled.

And smoking pot.

At first, I am simply shocked. I lean against the wall and stare at the closed door. My perfect little sister. Forty years old, perfect mother of the perfect two boys, perfect wife of perfect financial planner Luke, was inhaling, or pretending to, perfectly, in the next room.

And then I am pissed.

Because she's done it again. Somehow, she's done it again, and I am an outsider in my own home. I would have been happy to crawl on the bed, to snort and hack my way through a few tokes while studying the black and white stones of Go. I would have been happy to giggle about boys.

I walk back down the stairs. Passive-aggressively. Purposely hitting every squeak I know—there are six of them.

Three facts about six:

Six is the first perfect number.

All numbers between twin primes are evenly divisible by six.

Six is the product of the first four nonzero Fibonacci numbers.

I reach the tile, step carefully to the center of each one. Every third one, I skip one to the right—forty-three in all.

Three facts about forty-three:

There are forty-three three-digit emirps.

Forty-three is the smallest prime that is not the sum of two palindromes.

There are forty-three verses in *Beowulf*.

I finally gain our bedroom, where I remind myself to be wary of hope in the middle of the night.

CHAPTER TEN

My juvenile little middle-of-the-night party left me dry-mouthed, headachy, and nervous, and it was difficult to meet Estella's eyes in the morning. When we finally left, both of us were buzzing with raw nerves and too much coffee. We spent the first hour talking about directions, although there had only ever been one way to drive to Big Dune. I pointed out the OnStar system as if it were an old friend who would get us out of any jam, be it directional, mechanical, or medical. She didn't seem nearly as impressed as Chris and Phil.

Once we'd exhausted the subject of interstates, exits, and the marvels of modern technology, Estella began to yawn. When I encouraged her to lean her seat back and close her eyes she didn't protest, and we rolled along in silence. She woke when I stopped for gas and dug money out of her purse, but I waved it away, slamming the door while her arm was still stretched over the console. She was waiting by the car when I returned.

"Would you like to switch?" she asked, and I laughed, but her face was completely serious.

"I thought you couldn't drive," I said.

She shrugged. "I don't get much practice, but I can drive. I got my license a couple of years ago. Paul taught me. Although I've never driven anything this big," she said doubtfully, looking at the Escalade.

"No," I said, shaking my head. "That's all right."

She set her mouth in a thin line, said, "Fine," and climbed back in the passenger side.

As the miles crawled by, the silence became oppressive.

"So, I guess we'll need to get boxes for the books when we get there," I said after nearly an hour had passed.

"Hmm."

"And our first stop should be the store. There won't be any food there."

"Uh-huh."

"Plus we'll need toilet paper and stuff like that."

"Connie, you don't need to talk."

"Are we not going to talk for three weeks?"

She was silent for a long moment, and then said, "What do you want to talk about?"

"You haven't even asked about the kids," I pointed out.

"How are the kids, Connie?"

At least it would take up some time. "Gib is—well—Gib is not great. You'll love this: He's failing algebra."

That got her attention.

"You're not serious," she said.

"Oh, yes. He never told us he was having a problem. Got a twenty-seven on the math section of the PSAT. He'll be going to summer school after I get back."

"But what exactly is the problem?"

"He says he doesn't get the x's and y's," I said.

She nodded. "Have you gotten him a tutor yet?"

"No. By the time we found out, it was too late to help his grade. Luke—I'll get him one when he starts summer school, though."

"Hmm," she said. I glanced at her quickly. She was looking out the window again.

"What?" I asked. "What did I do this time?"

"I just don't know why you didn't call me, I mean, this is what I *do*, Connie. I teach math."

I was flabbergasted. It had never crossed my mind to call Estella. "What would you have done?" I asked.

"I could have given you some names, suggested books, I could have worked with him online, I could have done a lot of things. You know, sometimes it's just a matter of the teacher not understanding what the student is missing, or how he learns. Who knows? I might have made a difference with just a phone call to find out what the missing piece was for him."

I tapped my fingers against the steering wheel. "Well. I didn't realize that," I said. "You've never been particularly interested in his education before."

"He's never had a problem before, has he?" she asked, her voice cold.

"No, he hasn't," I said, matching her tone. I pressed my head against the backrest. She'd returned to staring out the window.

"How's Carson?" she asked softly after a moment.

"He's great," I finally said. And then I couldn't help myself. "In fact, it looks like he got a few genius genes from you."

"What's that supposed to mean?"

"Nothing, Estella, nothing," I said with a sigh. "He's evidently a very talented composer."

"*Really?*" She shifted in her seat, placing her shoulder blade against the door and facing toward me.

"*Really*," I answered.

"How did this come about?"

"His music teacher called me—" I stopped when she suddenly bent over and rummaged in her purse, pulling out a pad and pen. "What?"

"His teacher," she said. "What's his name?"

"Why? You gonna have him whacked?" I asked with a laugh.

"No, but I might have him checked out. You know, there are people out there, teachers, professors, who are just looking for kids like this—"

"You think I don't know that?" I asked vehemently.

She looked startled.

"I was there too, you know. You weren't an only child. You didn't exist in a vacuum."

"No, no, of course not," she said. "I was only trying to help, Connie. Really. I—I don't always say things the right way. I was only trying to help."

This was exhausting. It was as if we were both sunburned, flinching and shrieking at every touch, real or imagined.

"Dan Hailey," I said. She looked at me for a moment and then wrote it down. "Heron Pointe Elementary," I continued before she could ask.

"So tell me," she said. I nearly sighed in relief. This, at last, was something we could agree on. Estella was an adult now, and though we'd never spoken of it—the jealousy, the anger, the ruined childhood—she'd obviously come to the same conclusion I had: It had been a mistake, forced upon us by a father more interested in living up to his ancestors than in creating a happy family. Here, finally, was someone who would support my decision to keep Carson's childhood intact.

"He started clarinet about two years ago," I said, "and he was all right. You know, he practiced, but I never heard anything that led me to believe he was particularly talented. But he stuck with it, and then Hailey went over some composing basics this year, and I guess Carson caught on quickly. He'd already learned how to read music from me and he'd had a beginning music theory class. But it sounds as though it really came together when Hailey brought in some jazz records—"

"Jazz?" she asked, looking surprised.

"Yeah, jazz. Funny huh? He sort of got into Benny Goodman last year, went through a swing phase, but it was this one particular group, the Blue Wing Trio, that got him all excited."

She was nodding slowly. "It's interesting, actually. I don't think about jazz in a composing vein the way I do, say, chamber music. Benny Goodman? Big orchestra, lots of instruments, right?"

I nodded. "Not all of his stuff, but it's what he's most known for, yeah."

"And this other group, it's a trio?"

"Right. Cello, piano, and clarinet."

"Huh," she said.

"What?" I asked.

"Once he heard just the three instruments, he figured things out?"

I looked at her in surprise. "Yeah, his teacher said something along those lines. Like, Carson had the clarinet part, and says he thinks he understood the cello quickly from watching me play the violin. Then Hailey showed him some things on the piano, and he said Carson just seemed to get it. Carson himself said something about suddenly getting how the instruments played around each other."

Estella sat up straight. "See, a lot of these kids just need that *thing*, that one thing that makes it make sense for them. It's like a key that opens the door. Suddenly all this understanding pours out, and *bam!* They don't just understand the one more thing, they get it, totally get it, the whole thing. It sounds like Carson just needed some of the extraneous instruments shut down."

"You think that's what happened?" I asked, feeling something blossom in my chest when I thought of a door of understanding being thrown open in my child. It was rather amazing, and completely different from the panic that blossomed when it was labeled as genius.

"It sounds like it," she said. "And this is what I was talking about with Gib too."

"How's that?" I asked, failing to see any correlation.

"Well, the same way that just one piece of information can be the key to entire understanding, it can also be just a piece that holds *back* all understanding. Now Gib, he's never had a problem before, so that leads me to believe that he's just missing something. If I could discover what it is, then we could clear it up and the other basic knowledge won't be held back anymore."

"The fate of the world might hang on understanding just one thing," I said in jest. But she looked at me solemnly and nodded.

"You'd be surprised. So now the real question is, what are you going to do about it?"

I laughed. "What do you think? I already told Hailey that if he ever even mentioned composing to Carson again I would file a formal complaint. Now I'm just hoping that nobody at camp notices. I talked to Carson about keeping it low-key—"

"You did what?" she asked, her voice full of disbelief and something else I couldn't define but that sounded close to disgust.

"I—I told him to keep it low-key," I faltered. "What?"

"You find out your son is a genius—"

"Nobody ever said he was a genius," I said. "And what the hell am I not getting? I thought you'd be the last person to encourage this."

"Me? Why wouldn't I?"

"Are you kidding? You'd want my son to grow up like—"

"Like me?"

"No," I protested. "That's not it at all."

"Oh, bullshit. Just because I'm not married and don't have kids and didn't join the Junior League doesn't mean—"

"I didn't join the Junior League."

"Did you even think about what it would do to Carson to tell him to hide his genius? Do you want him to be ashamed of what he can do? Make him feel like a freak? Most people would think this was wonderful, Connie."

"Stop saying that. Nobody said he was a genius," I nearly shouted.

"You're making this about you, Connie. And what do you know about classifying genius, anyway? What is he, then? Talented? Gifted? An ordinary genius? A magician?"

"What the hell are you talking about? An ordinary genius? A magician? You're not making any sense, and I'll remind you that Carson is *my* son, not yours."

"Look, Connie, you need to figure out what's going on with *your* son, and you're going to have to let some people into your life to do that. Maybe he's just talented, maybe he just has a knack. But if he has genius and a passion for it, then you won't be able to control it. And if you try to keep him from it, he'll just wind up hating you."

My breath was coming hard. This was not at all what I had expected from her. "And how am I supposed to do that, Estella? This isn't a Harry Potter world. There's no magician school to send him to."

"No, it's not like that. Look, there are ordinary geniuses, people who sort of follow a logical path to doing something, something that other ordinary geniuses—really smart people—could do if they'd been so inclined, had the right tools, education, and so on. But then there are the magicians, people who just *know*. Their process isn't clear; we don't know how they manage to learn what they learn, produce what they produce. How their minds work is just . . . incomprehensible to the rest of us, no matter how smart we are."

"Is that you? A magician?"

"You can't be serious," she said, and I saw at a glance that she was utterly taken aback by the question.

"You did sort of seem to just know things," I said.

"That's completely untrue. I had a knack, that's all. I played number games."

"Estella, please; people with just a *knack* don't go to college at twelve."

"Sometimes they do."

"Well, don't worry," I snapped. "I have no intention of disrupting my entire family just to further one child's *knack*."

I could feel her staring at me, but I kept my eyes on the road and we passed the halfway mark without another word between us. After another silent hour passed, the previous night and the argument started to catch up with me, and I began to yawn. When Estella finally spoke her tone was soft, but it was still startling.

"We only have a couple of hours left," Estella said. "Why don't you let me drive the rest of the way?"

"Are you sure?"

"Well, I'm a genius, right? I guess I can figure out the gas and brake pedals if you can."

"Fine," I said, heading for the approaching exit. *Let her run us off the road*, I thought. *At least it would put an end to this.*

I topped off the tank at a gas station and when I climbed into the passenger side, I made sure she knew where the directions were, then leaned back and pretended to sleep.

But my pretense got the better of me, and I actually fell into a deep, surprisingly restful nap. Estella woke me gently, turning the music up a bit and placing her hand lightly on my knee. I opened my eyes and stretched, luxuriating in the space the Cadillac afforded. I popped the seat up and took a drink of water as I tried to figure out where we were.

"We'll be making the turn to the bridge soon," she said.

"You want to switch?"

"No, I'm fine."

"Can you drive over the bridge?" I asked in surprise.

"Sure," she answered. "Why wouldn't I?"

"Your inner ear thing," I said, pointing to my own ear.

"That's altitude that affects it," she said. "And besides, it doesn't bother me anymore."

"Hmm," I said, pressing my lips into a thin line. I knew it.

We made the turn, and I could see the bridge stretching out in front of us, almost four miles of gentle slope. A curve to the right brought it to the island, but it was hazy and I couldn't see the land on the opposite side.

"Remember the bridge?" Estella asked, and I knew she was asking about the old bridge. Of course I remembered it. The original bridge to Big Dune had really been two bridges. Both had two lanes; one led to the island, while the other led off. They had been constructed close together, low over the water, and ran parallel to each other on barnacle-covered concrete pilings.

The year before we moved to Big Dune a barge hit the off-island bridge, collapsing the center of it for almost two miles, sending concrete and cars filled with islanders into the water below. Eleven people died, and a year later the boat's captain took his own life.

During the construction of the new bridge, island traffic was forced to use the one remaining bridge—one lane on, one lane off—and that, combined with the new, horrific view of the damaged bridge, made traffic often slow to a crawl. It took three years for the new bridge to open, and the sight of the old bridge gave children more nightmares than the stories of pirate ghosts on Little Dune Island.

Each end of the damaged bridge had survived, but their seemingly stable lanes led to nowhere. They were left as they'd been on the day of the accident, with huge slabs of concrete hanging from the rusty rebar embedded in the center of the bridge. Pilings that hadn't collapsed entirely had been left standing, jutting out of the water at varying heights, holding up nothing but the salt-laden air.

After the initial shock had worn away, the barricaded bridge became a favorite haunt for fishermen and pelicans. During the summer, teens with more time on their hands than sense daredeviled on the bridge, crawling over the end and shimmying down the rebar like circus performers, hand over hand, bare feet scrabbling for purchase, until they were standing on the chunks of concrete that swayed over the water. Some stopped there, paralyzed by fear, while others were brave enough—or stupid enough—to dive off the concrete into the dark water below.

I remembered getting my first "real" kiss there, from Tate, the taste of beer and cigarettes foreign in my mouth, but the shape of his mouth perfect and familiar. I looked over at Estella, wondering if she remembered the one night she'd been there, but Estella was concentrating on the gradual climb up the new bridge and didn't look my way.

Once the new bridge was complete, they'd collapsed the center of the other span, removed the pilings, and turned both old bridges into fishing piers, complete with steel guardrails and a little bait shop. I could see people fishing out at the ends, and I rolled down my window to breathe in the air.

It was tangier than the air of the Gulf farther south, redolent with the metallic scent of oysters and shrimp, and my mouth practically watered at the thought of popping a cold boiled shrimp, fresh off the boats and dripping with more horseradish than ketchup, into my mouth. A tingling joy rose up in me when we crested the top of the bridge and were greeted with a wave of dragonflies flowing around the car, taking me completely by surprise.

We could see the island now, and the Gulf beyond it, calm and green, with the unmistakable silhouettes of trawlers coming in. The grin on my face was uncontrollable, the muscles stretched taut, and again I looked over at my sister, certain that nobody could possibly keep the smile from her face when confronted by the beauty of Big Dune. But I was wrong.

Estella looked just as she had as a teenager, coming home to the island on the weekends. She looked like someone had taken her math away.

Estella

I can still see the old bridge as we drive over the new one. And in my mind, I can still see the rough edges of the concrete glowing in the moonlight as I'd hung my head over the edge of the shattered bridge. I can still see Connie and Tate walking toward the deeper shadows, bent toward each other. I never knew for sure if they'd actually become lovers; no one detail had revealed itself to me as the final clue. And she'd certainly never told me.

But my imagination had been merciless.

Connie draws her breath in as we crest the bridge, and I am thankful to have the excuse of keeping my eyes on the road when I feel her looking at me. She rolls her window down, and as soon as that gamy air hits my nose, my head begins to throb and my mind begins methodically picking its way through Zorn's Lemma, equivalent to the Axiom of Choice and the well-ordering theorem. It soothes me for a moment.

I grip the steering wheel tightly and feel the bottom of my stomach drop when the island comes into view, the Gulf backing it like an escape route, spreading green to the horizon, vast, so many places to swim out and disappear. A swarm of dragonflies engulfs the car like hundreds of hostile, iridescent dive-bombers and I almost panic, certain I will be blinded and will drive over the guardrail and plunge into the water below, but they clear almost immediately.

The panic remains.

I want to go back. To Atlanta, to Paul, even to the college students I'd been so disappointed in last night. I would marry Paul tomorrow if he could somehow transport me from this ridiculous behemoth of a vehicle back to my flawed but suddenly desperately beloved life.

Connie is wearing the demented grin of a homecoming queen, and I cannot quite believe that she could possibly be looking forward to being here again.

With me.

PART TWO

CHAPTER ELEVEN

Tate met us at the end of the driveway, his near-white hair and tan the only recognizable reminders of the teenager he'd once been. Estella braked hard, and I leapt out of the passenger door and ran to him with a joyful scream. He caught me under the arms and swung me around. My flip-flops flew off, and when he set me down, none too gently, my feet sank into the sand and oyster shells that made up the path to the house.

We both laughed out loud, barely audible over the waves, and I pushed my hair off my face to inspect him. He was no longer a child, that was for sure. The years had hardened him in places, softened him in others, as I supposed they did to all of us.

"Well," he said, drawing it out with his thick accent, "Connie Sykes, you get better every year, don't you?"

"Flirt." I laughed, hitting him on the chest. Estella glided up behind us in the Escalade, and we moved out of the way as she maneuvered between the pilings and eased the car under the house.

Tate raised his eyebrows over his sunglasses as the Cadillac passed. "Guess Estella's done all right then."

I was embarrassed to admit that it was mine, but he merely appraised me again and nodded.

"So how'd you know we were here?" I asked as we waited for Estella to pop the hatch.

"Your mom called," he said. "I missed her, but she left a message."

I laughed. "Dodged a bullet," I quipped, expecting him to laugh with me, but he looked at me askance and shrugged.

"I like talking to June all right," he said.

"Well, yeah," I said, embarrassed. I turned away from him and rapped my knuckles on the back window. What was taking her so long?

"What do I hit to open the back?" she asked, opening the door and leaning out. I walked up to the front and she got out. Rather than walking to the back to greet Tate, she leaned in with me and watched while I punched the button to release the back hatch, and then followed behind me.

"Hello, Tate," she said, stretching her arm out from a distance, as though afraid to get too close. He took her hand and pumped it once.

"How you doin', Estella?" Tate asked. It was an easy question, as easy as Tate himself was, but a forced current underneath it caught my attention and my hands stalled on the bag I was reaching for.

"Good, and you?"

"I do all right."

Tate reached out for a duffel bag at the same time Estella reached for a suitcase, and they both looked relieved to have something to do. I groaned as we struggled up the stairs to the front door. The house, built on stilts like most of the houses on Big Dune, was a nightmare of stairs. Six separate flights in all: from the ground to the first floor, where all the bedrooms were, then to the second floor with the living areas and kitchen, and then the third-floor library, another flight from the library to the widow's walk—never used because the humidity might damage the books—and then two separate flights outside on the beachfront side of the house, leading down to the boardwalk that skimmed over the dunes to the beach.

Estella was breathing heavily when we reached the first floor. She turned away from me and headed down the hall toward her old bedroom. I watched her retreating back for a moment and then turned toward my bedroom with Tate following me.

He dropped the bag on the bed and opened the curtains of my sliders. The room flooded with the golden light of the late afternoon sun, and I smiled as I took in the familiar view. When I came here with Luke we'd stayed in the master bedroom, but it was this room, the room of my teenage years, that could make me happy just walking into it.

Gib had refused to stay in the girlish, lemon-yellow and white room, preferring the severe white walls and plain furniture of Estella's old bedroom. Carson, by younger brother default, stayed in my room without complaint.

The house was set behind the dunes and I couldn't see the Gulf from this floor, but the strange, stark beauty of the dunes was as arresting a view in its own way. The porch, wide slats of unpainted wood, stopped at a waist-high railing; beyond that, great mounds of sand and oyster shells anchored a wild profusion of vegetation that would have horrified the average Verona homeowner.

There were no manicured lawns here, no splashy rows of impatiens and hibiscus, no orderly ficus hedges for privacy or stately royal palms. Instead, pale yellow beach roses spread their runners through clumps of scrub and sharp-edged cabbage palms. Sprinkled throughout, sea oats tried to gain a hold, gracefully arching their grasses over everything, slender stalks topped with plumes shooting toward the sun.

Pearlescent oyster shells gleamed in their backdrop of white sand;

underneath it all, the invasive, impossible-to-eradicate sticker plants scattered their vicious, dun-colored pods. Crab holes, some large enough to house a cat, freckled the dunes, hinting at unseen lives beneath the sand.

This untamed landscape was part of what had drawn our father to the island to begin with, perhaps thinking it would be a private haven from the hordes of homebuyers who had steadily moved in on his childhood property. He was only half right.

Big Dune Island was wild, but it was still beachfront, and by the time our father built our home there, seventeen other wealthy families had already staked their claim to its changeable shore. Thirty-two houses on the island, most built of coquina tabby and plopped directly on the sandy soil of the interior, were owned by natives and had been passed down by generations of fishermen.

The two groups avoided each other for as long as they could. As the island began to change with the advent of commercial fisheries, the hurricanes that reformed the shoreline, and the textile mill that polluted the bay, the natives saw what was happening long before the new families did. They saw the dead oysters, the sick fish, the ever-narrowing beach.

The wealthy families, prepped from years of community service, banded together with the natives and did what they did best: made powerful people listen. Len, Tate's father and caretaker of our property, had been unofficially elected to a leadership position representing the natives, and he found his counterpart in our father, a man with time on his hands and a desperate need to catch up to long-dead ancestors.

Big Dune Island—and uninhabited Little Dune Island to the north, where an old lighthouse was slowly making its way out to sea—were brought back in the spirit that Henry Sykes would have been proud of. Parachukla Bay, the body of water between Big Dune and the mainland, became officially protected by the government. The world-famous oysters thrived again; the dunes were rebuilt and their sea oats protected from housewives who would cut them to grace their family rooms; the sea turtle eggs were protected from poaching, curious tourists, and porch lights.

The lighthouse on Little Dune and its accompanying tender dwelling were shored up and stabilized, and the island became a popular day-trip destination. Canoes and kayaks regularly crossed the small inlet that separated the two islands, and though no homes could be built on Little Dune, braver souls occasionally set up tents and stayed overnight.

I cared nothing about Big Dune Island when we moved there. All I cared about was the fact that, once again, my sister's genius was changing my life in ways I had no control over. We could have gone anywhere after leaving the family home, but the college and Dr. Pretus, its esteemed mathematician, were in Grantsville, and since my father couldn't stand the bustle of living in a college town, to the island we went. I didn't blame the move on the lawsuits—those would have happened no matter what. I blamed it on Estella.

She ended our sisterhood, she took my father, she blazed a path impossible to follow or live up to, and then she took all I'd managed to build in our hometown and swept it away, just when I'd finally gotten a foothold in my own life, out of her shadow.

Though I'd had to start over, I eventually came to love the island. It just took me a long time to realize it. And now, as I gazed out at the dunes, I felt that open, raw feeling in the pit of my stomach again, the one that had started when Mother said she was going to sell.

"Miss it?" Tate asked, making me jump.

"I do," I admitted. "I'm surprised, but I do."

"Gets to everyone," he said. "People don't even know what's missing until they come back."

I turned away from him and cleared my throat. "That's Estella's," I said, pointing to the duffel bag. Tate picked up the bag and headed toward Estella's room, while I went downstairs to unload the rest of our things. They were on my heels before I made it to the Escalade, and we all made two more trips before we dragged ourselves up to the second-floor living room.

Tate had turned the air-conditioning on before we'd arrived and the downstairs was cool, but the second floor hadn't lost the stifling heat of the day yet. I turned all the ceiling fans on, flopping down onto the sofa and allowing their breeze to chill me.

Estella walked over to the wall of sliding glass doors that ran across the beach side of the house and began to pull the curtains back. Tate started on the other side, and the wall soon became an expanse of glass. I squinted in the sun and rose to my feet, joining them as Tate opened a slider and walked out onto the screened porch.

If the view downstairs had made me nostalgic, this one nearly made me cry aloud with its beauty. I couldn't keep the grin from my face as I looked out over the deserted beach and the Gulf of Mexico stretching before me. The expanse of army green seen from the bridge became a hundred different colors this close: deep blues, light grays, jade, emerald, teal.

I no longer cared that I was there to work. I no longer cared that I wasn't sure Estella and I could speak civilly for more than ten minutes. And, for just a moment, I didn't care that Bob McNarey was probably at that very second finding out some horrible new truth about my marriage. All I cared about was that I was there.

Estella, with her arms crossed in front of her and keeping a distance from Tate, stared down at the water as Tate bustled around, checking the tracks of the hurricane shutters, jiggling the loose handle of the screen door.

"It's beautiful, isn't it?" I asked. "I'd forgotten. I don't know how, but I had."

Estella didn't look at me when she surprised me with her answer. "It is," she said. "It really is. I think maybe I'll go for a swim tomorrow."

"Well, right now I think we'd better get to the store and get some provisions," I said. "I'm already hungry for some shrimp."

"I brought dinner," Tate said. "Shrimp's in the fridge, oysters too. I picked up some beer, hope you don't mind," he said, shooting a glance at us. Both Estella and I shook our heads. "And I picked up some supplies to get you started," he continued, "so if you want to wait until tomorrow, you can."

Estella and I looked at each other and smiled. It could wait. At that miraculous moment we were in agreement.

We ate on the screened porch, greedily slurping fresh oysters from their rough shells and moaning in delight over the three pounds of Gulf shrimp Tate dumped, steaming, across the newspaper-covered table.

I leaned back in my chair and propped my feet up on the table supports, one hand on my satisfied belly and an icy beer in the other. Estella had leaned back too, her eyes closed, and I watched a smile play about her lips.

"So how's your father, Tate?" I asked.

Tate frowned. "As well as can be expected, I suppose," he said. "He doesn't recognize me anymore. He thinks I'm still in Kuwait. Tells me all about myself when I go see him. I'm evidently quite a hero."

Tate's mother had died of leukemia when he was only four. Len raised Tate by himself, taking him out on his trawler every day and teaching him the secrets of the island and the Gulf. A jaded veteran of Korea, Len was furious when Tate joined the Marines at the ripe age of twenty-five. Old enough to know better, Len told anyone who would listen.

At twenty-nine, one year away from getting out and taking advantage of the GI bill to finally go to college, war broke out in the Gulf, far from our own peaceful Gulf of Mexico. Tate went to Kuwait, and two weeks before his return Len had a heart attack while winching up a net full of shrimp. The heart attack was quickly followed by the heart-breaking diagnosis of Alzheimer's. Tate took over the shrimp boat and the caretaking business for absent homeowners while taking care of his rapidly deteriorating father, before finally admitting defeat and placing him in an assisted-living facility on the mainland.

I had good memories of Len, a gruff bear of a man, a Hemingway figure even to the island natives. Stories of him filled the nights around beach bonfires, and Tate had always been his most ardent fan. I couldn't imagine the pain it must have caused him to place him in the facility, and worse, to not be recognized by him.

"Do you still have *Jessica*?" I asked, remembering scanning the Gulf before dawn, picking out the ghostly outlines of trawlers heading out, their mast lights glowing dimly over the water, trying to imagine which was theirs. Tate shook his head.

"Nah. I was never the shrimper Dad was," he said. "I sold it a few years back, fixed the house up. I make enough to stay afloat. Don't need much."

"Leonard Tobias could bring in more shrimp than any five shrimpers combined," Estella intoned, her eyes still shut, and we all burst out laughing. It was the way most of the stories about Len began.

"He could," Tate said, "he really could. What about you, Estella? How's the genius gig going?"

She slowly opened her eyes and stared at him. "About as well as the shrimping gig for you, Tate. I'm a tutor, not a genius."

Tate seemed unfazed, but I jumped to my feet and got busy, folding the wet newspaper over the piles of empty shrimp and oyster shells, holding the entire soggy mess as far away from my clothes as I could. Tate opened the slider for me and Estella closed her eyes again, leaning her head back against the seat and allowing us to clean up.

As Tate and I dried our hands on the same towel after the kitchen had been put to rights, Estella walked by, placed her empty beer bottle on the counter, and muttered a terse good night before heading down the stairs without a look at either of us. Tate looked at me and raised his eyebrows. I shrugged.

I followed Tate downstairs and stood on the front porch as he backed his pickup out the driveway and drove away. As I locked the door, Estella's light went out, and I stood in the dark corridor, listening to the hum of the air-conditioning and the swish of the Gulf, wishing I had come alone after all.

Estella

I leave them alone, the way they prefer it, and head to my room. I thought I had stopped embarrassing myself over Tate long ago. I love Paul desperately, and I cannot figure out why the perpetual beach rat can still affect me like this. The thought that I am simply still competing with Connie enters my mind, but I will it away.

I listen to her lock up and quickly turn out my light so that she will not be tempted to knock on my door. I am too mortified to face her.

My head hurts.

I blame it on the beer, and then wonder if I should have eaten raw oysters. I lie on the bed and gently probe my stomach with my fingertips, searching for pangs, forewarnings of a contaminated oyster, but feel nothing amiss. I ache to hear Paul's voice but don't reach for the phone.

Instead, I remember pulling Tate toward the sofa upstairs by the front of his T-shirt. His protests and my insistence. Connie had been off with Luke, our parents were in New Mexico, and I'd arrived on Big Dune with a plan.

He left me there on the sofa, untouched and humiliated. He'd been kind, apologetic, and that made it even worse. I can feel the shame of it even now, twenty years later, creeping up my neck and making my face warm. My stomach cramps, and I gasp and turn on my side, curling around the pain as the tears roll down to the pillow.

I didn't get a bad oyster.

I got a bad memory, and more are on their way.

CHAPTER TWELVE

I slept later than I intended the next day, my dreams a mixture of memories and strange, watery visions of Estella and Tate. When I finally arrived upstairs Estella was already gone. I made myself some coffee and took it out to the porch. A couple was walking their dog on the beach, and I watched the mutt bound up to a woman who was stretching in front of the boardwalk next door. She patted it and it frolicked around her for a moment before racing back to its masters.

She continued her stretch, and as I watched her I recognized the movements of tai chi. She looked as if she were swatting at no-see-ums in exquisitely slow motion. It was mesmerizing. I watched until Estella caught my eye.

She was in the water, swimming, but her strokes weren't fluid or elegant as they had been years ago. I didn't know how long she had been at it, but it seemed to me that she was struggling.

She chose that moment to stop her stroke and head for the beach, hauling herself up the gentle slope as if truly exhausted. I watched her flop herself down on the sand and could see the heaving of her shoulders as she caught her breath. She turned her head and watched the tai chi woman bend and turn. In a moment she rose, and, slapping sand off her rear, slowly approached the woman, who stopped for a moment and then shook Estella's hand. I wondered again at this Estella, an Estella who walked right up to strangers and shook their hands.

Estella pointed up toward our house and the woman turned, her hand over her eyes, and looked up. I shrank back into the chair, although I knew she couldn't see me behind the screen at that distance. Then they both turned and looked at the house next door. The woman nodded, and I was surprised to see Estella take up a stance next to her and carefully follow the woman's movements as she began again.

Estella was like a naturally graceful dancer trying out a new routine. Her movements were fluid but imprecise as she tried to follow along. Occasionally the woman stood in front of her and adjusted Estella's arms, or showed her with her own movements what she was doing wrong. My coffee grew cold as I watched.

Estella finally stopped and gave a little bow to the woman, who bowed in return, and then Estella started toward the house. I could feel the vibration of her steps as she came up the boardwalk, and called out to her when I heard the door open.

"I'm up here. Coffee's ready."

"Great," she called up the stairs. "I'll grab a quick shower and be right up."

I got my phone calls out of the way: to Luke, leaving a message with his secretary; to Gib at home, leaving a message there too; and to Carson at camp, where I was told he was at field practice. The feeling of being cut loose from the needs of my family might have been freeing last night, but here in the light of day, with the weeks stretching before me, I felt a slight sense of panic. I kept myself busy making a shopping list until Estella appeared and poured herself a cup of coffee.

"Hmm," she breathed, smelling the coffee before she took a sip. "I went swimming," she said.

"I saw. You met the next-door neighbor?"

"Yes, Vanessa. Did you see her? I took a couple of tai chi classes at the hospital and really enjoyed it."

"The hospital?" I asked.

"They had a wellness seminar I went to," she said quickly, taking another sip of coffee. "Anyway, she says she's down there every morning. You should try it."

"Maybe," I said, uncertain if it was an invitation to go with her or just a general observation. "I was making a list," I said, holding it up for her inspection. "I was thinking we should get ourselves set up before we start packing so we don't have to go out after a long day."

"That's a Very Sensible Plan, Connie," Estella said. I flushed, and she gently pulled the list from my fingers, reading over it. "Should we call Mother?"

We hadn't talked about Mother yet. I shrugged. "You can if you want," I said.

"So, why didn't she come?" she asked.

"She said she had too many things to do," I said. I didn't tell her about Mother's sisters, the hatbox. I was uncertain whether she wanted Estella to know, though she could have told her years ago and kept me in the dark, parceling out important history when it suited her. Why I felt any loyalty to Mother at that point was beyond me, but I hadn't been in the habit of confiding in Estella in a very long time, and so I said nothing.

"You think she wanted to get out of the packing?" Estella asked.

"Maybe," I said. "Call her if you want, but I don't feel like talking to her right now." Estella looked at the phone and then at me without comment. We finished our coffee in silence.

Our shopping trip to the mainland was uneventful, and by the time we returned and hauled our groceries and the stack of collapsed packing boxes up the stairs, we were too tired to bicker about anything. Estella made sandwiches for lunch and we ate sitting on the sofas in the living room.

"Have you been up there yet?" Estella asked around a mouthful of chips.

She meant the library, of course. The jewel box that sat on top of the house. Container of all that was prized in our family. The rugs, the piano and violins, the books, the oil paintings.

I shook my head. "You?" I asked, thinking she might have poked around, anxious to have a look at her books.

"Nope. I guess that's where we should start. Everything up there stays in the family, right?"

"I have a list," I said and retrieved it from my purse. Whatever Daddy hadn't been explicit about in his will, Mother had been explicit about in her instructions. "She wants the paintings," I said, as Estella read over the list. "We'll have them packed and shipped. All the books go to you, rugs to me. She said we could choose whatever furniture we wanted, what we don't want offer to Tate, what he doesn't want we'll donate to the Parachukla Youth Haven. They have a truck and they'll pick up for free."

"Think we'll be able to fit all those books?" Estella asked.

I hadn't given it any thought. They were hers; she could do whatever she wanted with them. "Whatever we can't fit you can have shipped," I said. "The small rugs will fit, but I think I'm going to have to have the big Bokhara shipped, and the paintings for Mother, so we'll be making trips into town to do all that anyway."

She continued to read the instructions and didn't say anything. I cleaned the lunch dishes, taking longer than I needed. Estella watched me load the dishwasher, making me nervous when I saw her brows knit together as I separated the silverware and rearranged the glasses Tate had placed in the top rack the night before.

I finally dried my hands, and we climbed the stairs to the library together. I had to lean on the door to get it open. It finally began to move, slowly, with the familiar low *shhhh* of the foam moisture barrier that wrapped the edges of the door as it slid across the wood floor. The library seemed to expel musty paper air and then pulled in fresh air around us, like an ancient tomb unsealed.

The entire third floor had been built to keep the pervasive and damaging humidity away from the books. A humidistat was in constant use, a separate air-exchange system ran in cycles, and all the windows had been sealed. The widow's walk could be used, but never had been. Its door, set into the ceiling atop yet another short flight of stairs, had been sealed with foam, locked, and never opened.

We stepped over the high threshold in quiet reverence, like pilgrims entering a shrine. Light-blocking drapes pulled over the windows cast the library in shadow, even in the midday brilliance, and I switched on the desk light. The rugs, with their thick pads underneath, felt lush as grass under my feet, and I breathed in the leather scent of the club chairs that flanked the desk and the odd, vaguely metallic scent of the piano.

A shaft of sunlight cut through the room as Estella pulled the drapes, widening across the back wall where the gallery of Sykes ancestors hung. Their faces appeared startled as the white light hit them, revealing closed-mouth grimaces, strong chins, high foreheads. There were eleven paintings in all, only two portraying women.

My gaze flitted from painting to painting, and I repeated the names I knew by heart, saw my father in their faces, saw, to my surprise and fascination, my own sons. Especially Gib. I was suddenly filled with a longing for my boys.

"Creepy, huh?" Estella said from behind me.

"No," I said. "I used to think so; now, I don't know. It's sort of sad, I guess."

We toured the library together, running our fingers over the spines of the books.

Estella leaned against the shelves with a slim volume in her hands, carefully turning the pages with a fingertip. "I want this one," she said.

"You get them all," I reminded her.

"Yeah, but I really want this one." She sank to the rug and began reading aloud, looking at me every few minutes. It was an old game. I searched my mind to place the characters and smiled when I found it.

"The Awakening," I guessed, and she nodded. I sat next to her on the rug and she handed me the book. The raised-band spine was slightly browned and there was light wear on the cover, but it was otherwise in excellent condition. I looked up the tall expanse of shelves and wondered how many books the library contained.

"Is it worth a lot?" I asked Estella as I handed the book back to her. She shrugged.

"I don't know," she said. "I guess we should pull Daddy's records out and get some idea of what we've got here."

I didn't bother pointing out that she'd used the collective rather than the singular again. *We* didn't have the books, *she* did.

"Well," I said as I got to my feet, "I'll go get the boxes." I clattered down the stairs without waiting for her, and when I returned, breathless, with a stack of boxes under my arm, Estella was holding my tiny Mittenwald, peering inside the f-hole. It was even smaller than I remembered it. And more decrepit.

I let the boxes fall and Estella jumped, looking up at me guiltily. "The violins are mine," I said brusquely.

"I know," she said. "I was just looking. What are we going to do about the piano?"

I sighed and shook my head as I looked at it. It would fit in my house. I could see the perfect spot for it, just as I knew exactly where the rugs would go. But it had been swung in by crane and the back of the house built in after it, and it wasn't coming out again except in splinters.

"Goes with the house, I guess," I said. She plinked a few keys while I built boxes, then finally joined me. We worked slowly and silently under the watchful gaze of our ancestors. By late afternoon we had a stack of empty boxes lining the back wall, waiting to be filled, and had spoken to each other only when necessary.

The doorbell rang as Estella taped the final box, and she seemed as relieved as I to have something outside our own Sykes world to distract us. It was Tate, his sunglasses hiding his eyes, with a red cooler. He held it up and grinned as I opened the door.

"You guys up for scallops?" he asked. I wanted to tell him we were up for anything that might prove to be a buffer between us, but instead I took the cooler and led him upstairs to the kitchen.

"You can't keep feeding us," I said as he unpacked the cooler. He gave me a bemused look as he dumped the scallops, glistening white and light pink, into a colander.

"Why not?" he asked. "I'll stop coming by if I'm bothering you."

"Oh, God no," I protested. "It's great to see you again. I just don't want you to think you need to check on us. I'm sure you have other things to do."

He shrugged and began sorting the scallops, his long, tanned fingers like a school of fish searching for the most succulent morsel to dine on. "I don't have anything better to do, Connie," he said quietly. "It's nice to see people in the house. See people I know."

"Everyone's a renter now, aren't they?"

"Not everyone, but most. You should see the way these people leave the houses. Makes me shudder to think what their own homes look like." He stopped sorting scallops, his hands stilling in the colander, and stared at me with an intensity I hadn't seen from a man in years.

"They don't give a shit about this island," he said, and I almost flinched at his vehemence. "All the work our families did to preserve it—they don't know, and they don't care." He shook his head and looked up as Estella came down the stairs.

"What'd you bring us tonight?" she asked. I was relieved that she was making an obvious effort to be nice.

"Hey, Estella. Scallops. You up for them?"

She nodded. "Sure. And Tate? Sorry I was snippy last night. I was pretty tired."

He shrugged it off. "No problem. I was pokin' at you anyway. I deserved it."

"That's true," she said seriously and laughed when he threw a tiny scallop at her.

"These will keep for a while," Tate said as he placed the scallops in the refrigerator. "Y'all want to walk down to the cut?"

The narrow band of water that separated Big Dune Island from Little Dune Island had been aptly, if unofficially, called "the cut" for almost fifty years, when a hurricane had swept through the Gulf, leaving a devastated coast and slicing through the north tip of Big Dune Island like a knife through the end of a finger, forming Little Dune. The lighthouse was now an official Historic Landmark along with the old tender dwelling, a tiny, two-room stilt house.

No other man-made structures stood on Little Dune, which had been allowed to revert to its natural state. Native scrub, cabbage palms, live oak, slash pines, and a small tidal marsh provided refuge for hundreds of varieties of wildlife. Whitetail deer and wild hogs roamed freely, and ospreys, peregrine falcons, wood storks, and bald eagles all made the island across the cut their home.

Growing up on Big Dune, Tate and I had spent more than a few sunsets at the cut, watching our group of friends split into couples, merge into groups, and then split into different couples. I didn't flatter myself that Tate might want to relive those sunsets, and I wouldn't have known what to do if he had. Broken down sobbing over my marriage, most likely. But there was no hint of romance in his invitation, and the three of us set off down the beach with a bottle of wine and a few plastic cups. The sand was softer beneath my feet than I remembered, and the coastline was empty up and down island.

"I can't believe nobody's out," I said as we walked.

"It's like this every day," Tate said. "All the renters go inside, bathe the kiddies, overcook their shrimp, and turn on the television. Some come out on their screened porch for the sunset, but the beach itself is pretty deserted. It's the best time of day."

"Just because the tourists are off the beach?" Estella asked. "Don't they sort of keep you in a job?"

"It's not that the tourists are off the beach; it's more than that."

He stopped for a moment, and I sneaked a look at him in the fading sun.

"It's like it's my own secret, you know?" he finally said. "This is magic time, and they don't even know it. There's a different feel to the air, the dolphins come out to feed, the birds can eat without being bothered. Everything sounds different, even the waves sound different, like it's new again."

"How do you explain that?" Estella asked dryly, pointing toward the row of houses behind the dunes. Two new ones were under construction side by side, shotgun houses, thin and deep in order to fit as many as possible on a small expanse of beachfront. A construction crane stood between the houses, ready to haul trusses up to the roof, looking as out of place as an airliner.

Tate, walking between us, veered toward Estella and nudged her shoulder with his own, making her stumble for footing. "Well, don't look *that* way," he said. "Look *this* way."

We kept our gaze to the beach and the water, and we reached the cut just as the sun began its descent at the edge of the water. I leaned back against a small dune and felt my eyes grow heavy with the warmth of the sun on my cheeks. Tate and Estella continued to try to bait each other, but mildly. I listened to them without hearing their individual words, and eventually they grew quiet as the waves smoothed their prickly edges.

"Green flash time," Tate said when the sun was just a sliver on top of the water.

"Never seen it. Have you?" I asked. I'd stared, unblinking, into more sunsets than I cared to remember waiting for it. Most people I knew claimed to have seen it, including both my parents.

"Oh, sure," Tate said with a sly smile. "Twice."

"I haven't," Estella said, and gave me a conspiratorial smile.

"Blue eyes are weak," Tate said serenely. Estella punched him on the shoulder as I laughed.

"Connie hasn't seen it, and she's got *the Sykes eyes*," Estella said dramatically.

We all flopped back against the dune and laughed like kids, giddy with wine and the pretentiousness of our father. It was only when the no-see-ums started biting that we hauled ourselves up and headed back to the house for our scallop dinner.

Just as we finished eating, to my delight, Carson called from camp. He sounded excited and babbled about the friends he'd made in his cabin. I told him about the dolphins and the birds, and felt that longing for him again. I watched Tate and Estella on the patio as I talked to him, and wondered that neither of them had ever had children.

Especially now, especially being apart from them, they seemed like the only decent thing I'd done in my life. I was feeling so sentimental by the time we hung up that I called home again, hoping to talk to Gib, even if I had to talk to Luke to do it. But there was no answer.

Tate and Estella came in from the porch with their hands full of dishes, and Estella refused to allow us to help as she cleaned the kitchen, an unvoiced apology for the night before. Tate and I took coffee to the living room, and I sat on the sofa while he meandered through the room, shuffling through the old albums on the shelves under the stereo.

"Hey," he said, sliding an album out, "want to listen to some music?"

"Sure. What'd you find?"

He grinned and flashed the album cover at me after slipping the record out. Ray Charles smiled in profile, his head tilted up as though on the verge of praising the sky. Tate fiddled with the arm of the record player, and then carefully closed the lid as "Early in the Morning" started, coming from the tall speakers like an old whiskey-and-cigarette-voiced friend.

I settled back into the sofa. Tate sat beside me, propping his bare feet on the low coffee table. The sounds of Estella washing dishes mingled nicely with the music, and I had a sudden flash of what my life might have been like if Tate and I had married. Sitting in the beach house, listening to Ray Charles, the Gulf, and our child cleaning the kitchen. I laughed out loud and Tate looked at me quizzically.

"Oh, nothing," I said to his unasked question, sobering up and taking a sip of my coffee.

"So, what's going on, Connie?" Tate asked.

"What do you mean?"

He shrugged. "You're . . . quiet. You seem awfully guarded. I've never thought of you that way."

"Getting philosophical with me?" I teased, but he merely looked at me and I felt a blush on my cheeks. I twisted my rings. "My husband is having an affair," I said abruptly. "I'm thinking of leaving him."

He continued to look at me, his shoulders drooped, a picture of sympathy I wasn't sure I could stand. "Aw, shit, Connie. Are you sure?"

"Sure about leaving him, or sure he's cheating?"

He shook his head and shrugged. "I don't know. Both?"

"I'm definitely sure he's cheating. It's not the first time, not even the second time."

"Well, then I suppose you should leave him."

"It's not that easy," I said, looking toward the kitchen, careful to keep my voice low.

"Why not?"

"We have a long history. We have two kids, two great kids who don't deserve the upheaval it's going to cause."

"What about what you deserve?"

"It's different when you have children, Tate," I said. "Things aren't so cut and dried."

"Hmm," he said, leaning back in the sofa, cupping his coffee against his chest. "Well, I'm real sorry, Connie. Anything I can do?"

I shook my head. "Mother's got her lawyer looking into some things. It looks like Luke has been spending money, or losing money, I don't know. Maybe he's just hiding it. He bought me that Escalade downstairs, but I think it was just a diversionary tactic."

"How's that?" he asked.

I told him about the gifts, the jewelry, the appliances. He grinned when I listed them by name, but his smile faltered when I told him about Deanna's new yellow Beetle.

"She know?" he asked, inclining his head toward the kitchen, where it had grown quiet. I shook my head in warning just as Estella walked in, bearing a plate of sugar cookies. She slowed and then stood still.

"Am I interrupting something?" she asked.

"Not at all," I said quickly. "We were just talking about the albums. Mother didn't mention them. Do you want them?"

"I don't think so," she said, placing the cookies on the table and then sitting cross-legged on the floor and flipping through one of the stacks. "People pay a lot of money for these now, though. Hey, what about Carson?"

I shot her a look full of warning, and she looked pointedly away.

"Carson likes music?" Tate asked, sitting on the floor beside Estella to peruse the albums.

I nodded, trying to keep my voice steady. "Sure, music, swimming, he's into all sorts of things."

"What about Gib?" he asked. "What's he interested in?"

"Other than football, Gib is mostly interested in Gib," I answered, and Tate raised his eyebrows at me.

"How old is he now?"

"Sixteen."

"Tough age," Tate said.

"I don't remember it being so tough," I replied.

Estella and Tate looked at each other and burst out laughing.

"What?"

"Oh, yeah, you were a regular little teen angel," Estella said, still laughing.

"What are you talking about? I was a good kid!"

Estella snorted, and Tate scanned the ceiling innocently.

"You, my dear sister, were a pain in the ass," Estella said.

"She was a cute pain in the ass, though," Tate said, as though that might mollify me. I threw a piece of my cookie at him, which he caught and popped in his mouth.

"You don't have anything to complain about," I said to Estella. "Watching you mope around was no picnic either, I can tell you that."

"I think I had a little more to worry about than you did, Connie," Estella said.

"Please. What were your big worries? If Daddy loved a sand dune more than you? Whether you were going to graduate from college at sixteen or seventeen?" I jabbed back.

"As usual, you have no idea what you're talking about," Estella said, getting to her feet, leaving the stack of records on the floor.

"Hey, hey, come on," Tate said, placing a hand on Estella's calf. She shook him off and stalked out of the living room and down the stairs.

"See? Just like when she was sixteen," I said. The sugar cookie tasted like chalk, and I put the other half back on the plate, feeling slightly sick to my stomach.

Tate shook his head at me. "No, it's like you're both sixteen again," he said.

"Sorry," I muttered.

"Don't tell me," he said. "Let her cool off for a while. But I think the evening's over." He straightened the albums and slid them back on the shelf and then stood and stretched. His shirt rose over the waistband of his jeans, and I could see that his stomach was as flat as it had been as a teenager. I averted my eyes.

"I won't be around much this week, but y'all want to go to Little Dune Saturday? We can bring lunch and spend the day."

"I don't know," I said. "We have so much work to do here."

"Oh, come on. You've got four days before Saturday—you have to take a break sometime. A day's not going to set you back. I'll help the next day to make up for it. Ask Estella. I'll be going whether you do or not."

"All right," I agreed. "Thanks, Tate."

I stayed upstairs when he left, and just after I heard the front door close I heard the porch door open and shut, and then felt the vibration of someone on the boardwalk. I peered out the sliders. Estella was walking down to the beach. I sighed and slowly walked downstairs and followed her.

The moon was hidden behind a bank of clouds, and I considered turning on the boardwalk lights. I'd taken a few headers off the side as a child, sending crabs skittering and driving those maddening stickers into various tender parts of my body. But I left the lights off and felt my way until my eyes became used to the dark. I caught up with Estella at the water's edge.

"What are you doing?" I asked.

"Taking a walk," she answered.

"Mind some company?"

"Whatever you want to do, Connie."

We walked along silently, allowing the warm water to lap our feet, stepping over tiny phosphorescent jellyfish.

"We've got a lot of work to do," I said.

"Yeah," she said.

We were silent for another moment.

"We have to figure out a way to get through this," I finally said.

"I know," she replied quietly. "Sorry."

"Me too."

She tugged my arm and I followed her up to the dry sand, collapsing beside her in front of a dune.

"It's me," she said, holding up a hand as I started to protest. "No, let me finish. I think it's Tate. Did you know I had a terrible crush on him when we were younger?"

"Lord, who didn't have a crush on him, Estella? But I don't remember you mooning over him, no. I mean, it's not really the sort of thing we talked about, anyway."

"No, we didn't, did we? I think I kept it hidden pretty well. I tried to seduce him once."

I gaped at her and then burst into disbelieving laughter. "When? What happened?"

"When Mother and Daddy went to New Mexico. I stayed in the house, and when Tate came over to check on the place I tried to—well, you know."

"What did he do?" I asked. I couldn't see it, couldn't fit the mental image of the two of them into any sort of romantic situation.

"Nothing," she said, bitterness flavoring the single word. "Besides, he didn't really like me at all, even as a friend."

"Tate likes everyone, Estella. You were just . . . different. Maybe he didn't know how to be friends with you."

"No. It would have been laughable," Estella said, and I heard real pain in her voice. "He was interested in you, not me, not the math geek."

"I don't know what to say," I said, feeling inadequate, remembering what she was like as a teenager. The last year Estella had spent any time at the beach house was the year before she graduated. That summer was the last time we spent any time together at all. Daddy had surprised Mother with a European tour for their anniversary, and after much debate they decided that Estella, seventeen and more mature than most thirty-year-olds, could be trusted to watch me for the month they would be gone.

I'm sure Estella had been mortified, but I was thrilled. I assumed she would spend all of her time swimming or in her room, and I would be free to roam the island. But to my surprise, Estella had not been interested in her math books. She seemed to want to stick close to me for the first time since she went to college. And now, with her confession about having had a crush on Tate, I saw why.

"So that's why you wanted to hang around that summer?" I asked, oddly hurt by it.

"Part of it, maybe," she said. "I did want to be friends with you, Connie. It seemed like maybe we were starting to, and then . . ." She trailed off.

I knew the *then* she was referring to. Then I had gotten in trouble, big trouble, in the water. We'd never talked about it. In fact, I didn't even like to think about it now, more than twenty years later.

It had been a heady two weeks without our parents. For the first time, Estella wasn't restricted to the fringes of society. She spent time on the beach in my borrowed bikini and her pale skin turned golden in the sun. She had developed a woman's body, with hips and breasts, actual round melon breasts that bounced and jiggled just like those of the women on television. They were astonishing. The boys, especially Robbie Deckers, hadn't been able to take their eyes off her. She'd seemed to blossom overnight, lush as a hibiscus bloom.

We were all growing up that summer. I'd gotten my first real kiss from Tate, and we had been sneaking plenty of time away from the group to practice. I was looking forward to more of the same when he arrived with most our friends in tow that morning, and we pulled a cooler full of beer down to the beach.

I had more to drink than I should have. Estella tried to slow me down, but I ignored her and she went swimming in a sulk while the boys started a game of football, prompting the girls to steal the ball. It was thrown to me, and I took off into the water, boys in hot pursuit.

I had enough of a head start to feel confident and was floating easily, buoyed by beer and infatuation. Kissing made me lighter, made me effervescent and dreamy, and I harbored fantasies of Tate and me twirling about in the water as his mouth moved on mine. The other boys gave up, and to my disappointment, Tate did too. Once he was back on the beach I no longer felt so effervescent. In fact, I was tiring quickly. I felt the current brush the bottoms of my feet, a tickle, a warning.

I let go of the football, stroking for the beach. But suddenly the current wasn't just at my feet but was pulsing up my ankles and then my calves. The waves, gentle and rolling just moments before, had turned choppy and disorganized, and the football bobbed in front of my face, startling me.

The first time I went under, I swallowed a bit of water and panicked, plunging my arms down in a sweeping motion, raising my head above water for a moment, long enough to draw a lungful of air. But I slipped back down so fast that water immediately followed the air down my throat. I swallowed and felt it rise back up in my throat. The football hit my left cheek and I gasped, inhaling more water.

I called for Estella, I saw her coming, I knew she would save me. I saw her eyes, the exact same green as the Gulf water that was swallowing me, and I knew that I would be okay. Her eyes comforted me so assuredly that I relaxed and gently went under the waves in slow motion.

And then everything sped up, a choppy, spluttering fast-forward in which everything was a confused mass of churning water and limbs. Somehow Tate got to me first, and then Estella was there, and together they hauled me onto the beach, where I collapsed to my elbows and knees, my back bowed like an old mare's. My hair hung like seaweed in my face, and I choked water out and gasped air in before finally vomiting a humiliating gush of seawater and beer onto the sand.

The party was over. Tate and Estella half-dragged, half-carried me into the house, where Estella, sobbing, helped me shower and then installed me in our parents' bed. She closed the house to everyone except Tate and refused to allow me out of bed for two days.

Tate came to see me every day, but it was the end of our childish romance. We became closer friends, and I've never forgotten the fact that he and my sister saved my life. I bought him a new football for Christmas that year to replace the one that disappeared.

When our parents returned, we told them nothing of our month except that we'd had a nice time, and neither of them ever found out. I knew Estella felt responsible, but I was the one who had gone beyond my capabilities, and I knew it. I'd been behaving like a fool and had been punished for it by nearly drowning, and then by Estella's determined renewal of the chasm between us. She spent the rest of that summer with Dr. Pretus and his wife, and the next year she graduated from college and left for Atlanta without spending another day at Big Dune.

I shuddered, remembering how hot and salty the water had been in my throat, how thick and grasping the current. I felt Estella stir beside me. She reached out her hand and I took it. We both leaned back against the dune and gazed at the stars, and I felt that sense of friendship with her again for the first time in a long time.

"So Robbie Deckers wasn't your first love, then," I said, anxious to relegate the memory of the water back where it belonged.

"Hardly," she answered.

I rolled over on my stomach and propped my head on my hands.

"Who was your first love, Estella? I've never known a thing about your love life."

"Paul was my first love," she said, keeping her gaze on the Milky Way.

"Oh, come on," I said. "Give me something. Was Robbie your first kiss? Or was it a college boy? I always wondered if you met a lot of frat boys."

"I met a lot of college boys," she admitted. "But they weren't interested in a fourteen-year-old weirdo like me."

"Stop, Estella," I said.

"Anyway, no, Robbie wasn't my first kiss."

"I knew it! Come on, tell," I demanded.

She was silent for a long time, and I finally prodded her side, making her yelp and wiggle away from my finger. She looked at me and worried her lip with her teeth. "All right, yeah, it was a college guy."

"I knew it! Come on, details, I want details."

"No, you don't," she said quietly.

"Jeez, Estella." I sighed. "What's the big deal?"

"It was Pretus," she finally said.

Pretus? I'd only met him a few times: a middle-aged man balding early, prone to wearing bow ties, and startlingly dismissive of anyone who wasn't in his daily math-driven world.

"Not that kind of kiss, your first *real* kiss," I said. She looked at me, and when I saw her face, still and serious, I realized in horror what she was telling me.

"No," I said.

"Yes."

"My God, Estella. What happened? When?"

"He came into my room at night," she said. "He just talked to me at first. He kissed me for the first time right after my fifteenth birthday."

"Jesus," I breathed. "Did you say anything?"

"To who?"

"Daddy? Mother? Anyone?"

"Daddy was caught up in the island. All he wanted to hear was how well I was doing. Pretus told me we had to keep it a secret."

"But—Estella," I started, afraid to voice the question. "Did he ever try . . . anything else?"

"Not until I was sixteen," she said.

"Oh no, Estella, no. That bastard, that sick bastard." My voice shook with the enormity of it. Estella, so vulnerable and shy, thrown into college too young, given over to the protective care of the brilliant professor and his wife. "What about his wife?" I asked.

"I didn't think she knew at the time," she said thoughtfully. "But I do now. I think she knew."

"How?" I whispered. "How could it happen? How long did it go on?"

"It stopped that last summer," she said.

"But you stayed with them after that, before you graduated."

She nodded. "I had to graduate. I couldn't leave, not that close to getting out of here. I threatened to tell, he threatened—"

"What?" I asked, incredulous that Pretus could possibly threaten anything.

She was silent a moment, and then propped herself up. "Connie?" she finally said, looking at me hard, searching out my eyes in the starlight. "Could we drop it? It was a long time ago."

"But—"

"We can talk about it again, just not tonight, all right?"

I couldn't help it, I opened my mouth to protest. But the words died on my lips. The clouds slid away from the moon, and in its light I saw the pain in her eyes, the muddled gray of a churning Gulf.

"Please," she said.

I was disappointed, but nodded, thinking of all the things I wasn't telling her, thinking of Luke and his twenty-four-year-old barista, of the life Estella thought was so perfect that was actually out of control and on the verge of collapse. Perhaps this was enough disclosure for the night. At least we'd both seemed to agree that Carson was off-limits.

I felt closer to her than I had since we were children, and to my astonishment, it was because of her. I had always thought it would be up to me, that I would have to lay myself bare and beg her friendship. It was a start, made by her, and I was grateful for that much.

"Thank you," she said quietly and lay back against the dune. I flopped over with a sigh and joined her in gazing into the night sky, desperately searching for something to take her mind off Pretus.

"So. Tate, huh? How was he?" I asked, and she laughed.

"You don't know?"

"No," I said, surprised she had to ask. "No, that summer, that was it."

"Well, I wouldn't know either. He stopped it. It was pretty humiliating, actually. I went back to Atlanta the next day. This is the first time I've seen him since."

I suddenly understood the tension between them.

"Yeah, well," she continued. "I guess it all came back, being here." She glanced at me quickly. "Don't worry. I'll get over it."

"I hope so, because we're going to Little Dune with him on Saturday," I said, rolling toward her again.

She groaned. "Give me back my city," she said. "You two can have all this nature stuff. What're we going to do on Little Dune? Wrestle gators? Admire Tate while he rows us manfully across the cut?"

"Maybe he'll take his shirt off," I suggested with a leer, and she laughed before she pushed me over with her legs, covering me in sand and memories. "Come on," I said, jumping up, pulling her with me despite her protesting groan. We stood with our opposite hands clasped and I pushed her away and then pulled her toward me, and just like that we fell back into it. We danced in the soft sand, stumbling and giggling and reacquainting our adult bodies with the easy rhythm of the surf and each other.

We worked our way back to the house tethered to each other with our fingers, never breaking contact as we twirled under and around, and followed the moonlight home.

Estella

I feel cleansed with telling her, as though my lungs had been filled with sand and now had finally been blown out. My head is not pounding now, the way it had been since we crossed the bridge. But when I look past the relief, I know we have not talked about what we should.

Connie makes jokes and dances, but it lies between us like the cut between Big Dune and Little Dune. It is a cut itself. It pains me, slit open again like it is. I want to take stitches to it. Scars can be prevented when sewn up with care, but I've not been taught that particular skill. My stitches will be ragged, clumsily done. How many will it take?

We have been here for all of three days, and I have to keep pulling them out and starting again. Connie doesn't even know how I've bungled it. She is the patient, out on the table, sedated with her perfect life in Verona.

My head begins to throb again. It is back. I hear the faraway thunks of the front door dead bolts again, hear Connie climb the stairs, thirteen of them.

I close my eyes. *Thirteen.*

Three facts about thirteen:

The first prime gap of thirteen occurs between one hundred thirteen and one hundred twenty-seven.

A Chinese abacus has thirteen columns.

Thirteen is the smallest permutable prime.

The three facts won't be enough tonight. I could keep going:

Thirteen is the smallest prime that can't be part of a Sophie German pair.

The olive branch on the back of a dollar bill has thirteen leaves.

Ptolemy's treatise, *Almagest*, is thirteen volumes.

Thirteen is the concatenation of the first two triangular numbers.

I think about Connie and me dancing in front of the dunes and fall asleep.

CHAPTER THIRTEEN

Estella obviously had a better night's sleep than I did. I heard her climb the stairs in the morning while I was still trying to stop my mind from racing around her confessions of the night before. My hands felt branded from her touch, as though she'd communicated as much through her sand-covered palms as she had with her words.

She was on the phone when I finally pulled myself out of bed and arrived upstairs. She grinned when she saw me, and I knew the previous night had been real. She pointed to the phone and mouthed *Mother*.

"So you're getting caught up on all your work then?" she said, her voice all honey and concern.

I shook my head at her with a smile.

"I'm sorry too," she said. "She's right here, hang on." She covered the mouthpiece. "She's still under a bit of pressure, poor thing."

I took the phone. "Hello, Mother."

"Hello, dear. Is everything going okay up there?"

"Everything's fine," I said. "We haven't gotten much done yet, but we're going to head upstairs as soon as I get off the phone."

"Has Bob called?"

"No. Why? Do you know something?"

"No, he won't discuss it with me," she said, sounding miffed.

I felt a bit of grudging respect for Bob, though I didn't doubt that he would let plenty slip in the coming weeks.

"And how are you two getting along?" she asked, lowering her voice as though Estella might hear.

I could have said, *We're as different as we always were.* I could have said, *I have no idea, it changes every hour, but last night gives me hope.* Instead, I said, "Fine, just fine."

"I'm so pleased to hear that, Connie. Have you spoken to the boys?"

"Carson called from camp last night. He seems to be very happy. I tried to catch Gib, but nobody was home."

"Well, that's how teenagers are, I suppose, always out with their friends."

"I suppose. We'll call you later in the week, Mother. Love you," I said. She reminded me once again that she wanted the oil paintings and finally allowed me to hang up. Estella slid a mug across the counter and poured me a cup of coffee.

"I'm going for a swim," she said. "Do you want to come?"

I looked out the sliders and saw the next-door neighbor warming up on the beach. "Sure," I said. "No swimming for me, but maybe I'll talk to your friend. And then we have to get to work."

"Her name's Vanessa," she said. "And she's from New Zealand."

Vanessa had a charming accent, and she was considerably older than I had thought. She stretched and swayed while I sat nearby with my coffee and watched my sister struggling in the Gulf. By the time Estella flopped down next to me, sending little droplets of water showering to the sand, I had made plans for the two of us to watch the sunset from Vanessa's widow's walk that night. Estella was breathing heavily, and I looked at her chest heaving up and down in concern.

"Are you all right?" I asked her as Vanessa carefully rotated an invisible ball and set it on the sand in front of her.

Estella flapped her hand at me. "Fine," she panted. "I'm fine, just out of shape."

When she finally caught her breath we headed back to the house, showered, and with twin grimaces climbed the stairs to the library. Estella started with Daddy's desk while I pulled paintings off the wall and stacked them downstairs. My calves were screaming by the time I got all eleven of them. Estella hauled down a few bags of trash from the desk, and then we spent the rest of the afternoon checking off books on Daddy's records. There were almost seven hundred volumes, filling six bookcases.

Most of Daddy's collection, easily triple what was currently in the room, had been put into storage before the estate had been auctioned off. He and Estella had spent weeks going through them, choosing which ones to take to the new house on Big Dune.

I'd watched from the doorway, consumed with jealousy, remembering that before he foisted me off on my mother he had told me that one day we would open a bookstore together. I held on to that fantasy for years after I'd given up on Daddy being my partner in it. I loved the feel of the books, loved the smell of them. Now, as I went through the list with Estella, I thought of it again, wondering how much it might take to set up, if it could be profitable enough, if people even bought rare books anymore.

It was the first time since my twenties that I considered what I might have done differently with my life. I fell into the fantasy the way I once imagined that Daddy and Estella would grow tired of each other and math and would return to being my ardent admirers and playmates.

"How did you and Daddy choose these?" I asked.

"It wasn't very scientific," she said with a smile. "He made me choose three subjects. Every book that fit in them, I got to pull out. He chose three subjects too."

"What were yours?" I asked.

She gave a nervous little laugh. "I hardly remember," she said.

"Come on," I pushed.

"Um, well, I remember I thought anything having to do with islands was appropriate. And math, of course."

"And what was the third?"

"Music."

"Really?" I asked, surprised. She shrugged and turned away from me.

"I thought you might like them sometime," she said. My heart nearly stilled. I wasn't sure I believed her. But how I wanted to. She turned with three books in her hands. "Look," she said, holding them out to me.

I looked at the titles: *Antonietta*, *Works*, and *The First Violin*. I'd never read any of them.

"Daddy said they all had something to do with violins, one way or another," Estella said as I handed them back to her.

"What did Daddy pick?" I asked.

"The sea, in general—that's why *The Awakening* is here—astronomy, and the South. But he had pretty broad parameters. It didn't have to be about the South, exactly, he just had to remember something specific in the book about the subject. If he could remember it, we saved it."

"And he remembered things in all of these?" I asked, impressed by my father. Over the years, I had developed a sense of how others had seen him, and his father before him, and it wasn't very flattering. When we were children and listened in on the parties, our father had seemed like the most influential of men, but once the estate was gone he had been diminished—not just in the eyes of society, but in my eyes as well.

He disappointed me, year after year, and I hardened my heart against more hurt by developing a weary, dismissive attitude toward him. It had been faked at first, but over time it had come to be a part of me. I was ashamed that I felt genuine surprise when faced with having to remember the things that had impressed me to begin with.

"He says he did, but he stopped opening them to find the passage he was looking for soon enough," Estella said, betraying her own doubts about him. "I swear Mother knew more about his books than he did," she continued, pulling an empty box from the back wall and heading for the first bookcase.

"Mother?" I asked.

"She knew where every one was. She had her own little Dewey Decimal System right in her head. He'd remember a title, but have no idea where it was. He was incredibly unorganized for a book collector. He'd call her in, and she'd point to the right shelf and just toss off *to the left*, or *in the middle*. And there it was, every time. I thought, even back then, that I got my number thing from her. Of course, I never said that. Daddy would have keeled over. To tell the truth, I really am sort of sorry she's not here. I would have liked to ask her about it, how she knew all that."

"It's probably better that she's not," I said. "We wouldn't get as much done."

She stopped packing for a moment to look at me. "Did you two have a fight or something? Is that why she didn't come? Why won't you just tell me?"

I bit my bottom lip. "No, not exactly. I think she just didn't want to come back here."

She shook her head. "There's something you're not telling me. Is it me? She acted like she wanted to see me. Did I do something?"

"No. No, it's not you."

"Then what's the problem, Connie?"

I owed her. I owed her for last night. "Did Mother ever tell you about her parents?"

She shook her head. "Just that they died when she was young. A hurricane, right? They drowned? God, it's awful that I don't even remember," she said, looking up at me in astonishment.

I checked my watch. "I'm starved," I said. "You want to get cleaned up and go to the mainland for lunch?"

"Connie," she said in exasperation. "What do you know?"

"I'm going to tell you, but it's too big a story to tell like this. Let's go to the Oyster Bed and eat oysters and drink beer till we pop."

She stared at me speculatively for a moment and then looked around the library with a sigh. "We're never going to finish this."

"Yeah, we will," I said. "Besides, we can send Mother the paintings while we're over there."

We loaded the paintings in the Escalade, carefully layering bubble wrap between them. By the time we arrived at the Oyster Bed we both felt as though we'd accomplished the first step of making the house ready for sale. Rather than feeling uplifted by it, though, I felt a profound sadness. It had truly begun.

I wished I had brought the boys. I wished I had turned around at the gates and marched back up to Mother's and carried her to the car, hatbox and all. It was hard for me to believe that this was it. The end of the beach house, the last place I had memories of Daddy. The end of my marriage, the end of my family as I knew it.

Estella seemed subdued too, and she didn't press me to tell her the story until after we'd ordered. The beer was cold, and the first one went down quickly, loosening my tongue. Estella was a perfect audience, and I stretched the story out, perhaps elaborating little details, but staying true to what Mother told me, ending with the feel of the little shoes in my palms.

"I can't believe it," she said when I finally finished. She had stopped eating her shrimp roll halfway through the story, and now she looked at it as though unsure of how it had appeared in front of her. "When did she tell you this?"

"The week before I left," I said.

"But what—I mean, why, after all this time?"

I thought about telling her. About Luke, about all of it. "Going back to the island," I finally said. "I guess I should have realized that she was trying to tell me that she couldn't go."

"I just can't believe it," she repeated. "And Daddy never knew?"

"Mother says he didn't. He just plucked her up, swallowed their story, and never gave it a second thought."

She crunched into her shrimp roll and chewed, swallowing before she spoke. "He really loved her though, didn't he?"

I nodded. "I think he did."

"Poor Mother, to find her sisters like that. I can't believe we never even guessed there was anything interesting in her past. Daddy was supposed to be the fascinating one." She shook her head in amazement. "Did she tell you not to tell me?"

"No, not exactly," I said. "She didn't say one way or the other."

"So, if her father didn't die in the hurricane, then how did he die?" she asked.

I frowned. "I don't know, actually. We mostly talked about her sisters."

"You didn't even ask?"

"I—well, no, I didn't think to."

"I'll have to talk to her about it," she said, slowly bringing a french fry to her mouth.

"You could come back with me," I said. "We could ask her together."

She immediately shook her head. "No, I couldn't," she said quickly, so quickly that it was obvious that the very idea horrified her. "I have an appointment. I can't."

"Okay, okay," I said, astounded at how quickly the tides changed direction between us. "Relax, nobody's going to force you to do anything. What's the appointment for, though?"

Estella shook her head, looking at the table. "It's nothing."

"How can it be nothing, if you have to go?" I persisted.

"It's nothing you need to worry about, okay?" she said, staring me down.

"Fine."

"Fine."

I called for the check.

We found the packing store, and Estella helped me haul the paintings in, stacking them against the high counter as the woman worked out the bill. It was astonishingly pricey, and when Estella pulled her wallet out I allowed her to pay for half without protest. As we left our ancestors there in a stack, I couldn't help feeling as though we were abandoning them.

We wandered around Parachukla for a while, working off our beer and seafood, and I found myself enjoying the town. Verona was beautiful, but without the cultural history of Parachukla. That, combined with the influence of the nearby university in Grantsville, had developed Parachukla into a haven for artists, and the main street was lined with small galleries, shops, and cafes. There was plenty of money here, but it was quiet money, not desperate and ostentatious as it was in Verona.

The people in the galleries were friendly, and many even had their doors propped open to encourage browsers. If I had been here with my friends from Verona, we would have exclaimed over how quaint it was. Now, without my armor of jewelry and with my hair loose and curly from the humidity, I found it peaceful and beautiful.

We were both tired from the mid-afternoon beer, and we drove back to the island in silence, looking forward to our visit with Vanessa. I was even going ten miles an hour over the speed limit, eager to get back to the island, to breathe in the air and feel the sun. I slowed down. It would still be there. For three more weeks.

*   *   *

Vanessa greeted us wearing a bright blue-and-white batik muumuu and silver sandals. Her tan glowed against the blue, and she looked liked a Hawaiian postcard as she gracefully opened her arms to beckon us into the house. Like ours, it was arranged with the living area on the second floor, and we followed her up the stairs, glancing around us in wonder.

The walls were covered in bright watercolors—swimming, liquid shapes that it took me a moment to realize were flowers. Swaying hibiscus and gardenias wavered and flowed over the canvases, stretching their petals as fluidly as Vanessa stretched on the beach.

"Did you do these?" I asked when we reached the living room and saw more of them.

Vanessa nodded and smiled as she poured sangria into tall, icy glasses. "Yes, do you like them?" she asked, handing me a glass.

"They're amazing. I have orchids," I said before I could stop myself. "Well, actually I don't anymore, but I used to."

"I have a black thumb," Vanessa said cheerfully. "Can't grow them, so I paint them."

"Do you work here?" Estella asked, sipping her sangria and wandering around the living room to inspect the unframed paintings.

"Upstairs," Vanessa said. "The light is wonderful. Do either of you paint?"

"I can't even draw a straight line," I said with a laugh.

"Ah," replied Vanessa, indicating her paintings, "nor can I, my dear. That never stopped me. After all, where is a straight line in Nature?"

"She's a violinist," Estella said. I blushed. It was never how I defined myself.

"I play a little," I said. "Mostly I take care of my children."

"Hmm, never a straight line in them either, is there?" Vanessa said. "My own took long, crooked paths to find their lives."

"How many children do you have?" I asked.

"Two daughters in New York City," she said, "and a son in Alaska. I worry about him, but my girls, they have each other."

Estella and I avoided each other's eyes.

"The sangria is delicious," I said, changing the subject.

"Cinnamon," she said with a conspiratorial wink. "Shall we go upstairs?"

We followed her to her third-floor studio, so different from the dark library at the top of our home. Here, there wasn't a single blind or drape on the windows, and all of them were thrown wide open. The rich gold of the waning sun flooded the space, illuminating her easels and canvases like torches. Brushes in glass pots stood at attention, as though patiently waiting their turn to be ignited and held aloft.

The clean, fresh smell of paint and sunlight woke my senses, and I breathed deeply, feeling a little dizzy. Estella was taking it all in too, turning her face to the rays coming through the windows. Her hair, short and choppy, lit up in pieces like a mirror mosaic, bouncing light about her head.

"It's wonderful in here," I said.

"Yes," Vanessa said. "I come here every day whether I'm working or not. It's good for the soul to get closer to the sky, don't you think?"

Estella turned and smiled at her. "Yes, I do," she said to my surprise.

Vanessa's comment, indeed, her very personality—vaguely spiritual, slightly eccentric—seemed exactly the sort of thing that I'd always imagined Estella had little patience for.

"Well then, let's get a bit closer," Vanessa said, leading us to the widow's walk. The stairs to the walk consisted of two short flights, the top one doubling back on the first to save room. Halfway up the second flight, Vanessa turned the handle of the door, which was set into the ceiling like a trapdoor, and pushed it up on sliding brackets until it locked in place.

She set her sangria over the high lip of the doorway and then somehow, even in her muumuu, managed to climb out onto the roof gracefully. Estella and I handed our glasses to her, and then hauled ourselves over the deep lip, neither of us able to mimic Vanessa's skill. The roof was flat and painted a cool white, as were the railing and long benches built into the sides.

Vanessa left the door open and beckoned us to the front rail, where the roof fell away at a steep angle. It was dizzying to be up so high, and I turned around in a slow circle, the astonishing view making me catch my breath. Estella was doing the same thing, and she caught my eye and said, "We are opening the widow's walk."

"Yes we are," I agreed emphatically. "I can't believe we could have had a view like this and Daddy kept it locked up."

The island was visible from its south end to its north, from the bridge in the east to the expanse of Gulf in the west. Little Dune was clear, the lighthouse like a thumbtack, skewering the island to the earth, though the tender dwelling remained hidden under the greenery. If I stayed long enough I could count every home on Big Dune and every boat in the bay.

A flock of pelicans, so improbable looking, soared over our heads, close enough to reach out and poke their fat gray-brown bellies, their massive wings. I tilted my head back and saw the bright yellow eyes of the last bird, the leathery folds under its long bill, and I laughed out loud.

When Estella and I had had our fill of the view, the three of us settled onto the west-facing bench and watched the sun set. Vanessa was right, I did feel closer to the sky. The orange and pink rays of the sun fell upon the edge of the roof, lighting the white railings like fire, and I played my fingers through it, held my glass of watery sangria up to it, making purplish rainbows against my skin.

A sliver of a new moon appeared like a ghost in the sky before the sun dipped beneath the horizon. Venus was already shining. We stayed as long as we could, pointing out new stars as they became visible, only climbing back over the lip of the doorway when the bugs drove us in. My head felt stuffy as we descended the stairs, as though the air became thicker with each step down, and I was sorry to say good-bye to Vanessa.

I couldn't wait to open our widow's walk and imbue our house with that magical light. If getting closer to the sky was good for the soul, being held up in those rays of the sun was good for my entire being. I was suffused with the light, and Estella's dreamy look told me she was too.

As we walked into the front entry of our house she said, "I think I'm going to call Paul," and walked down the hall to her bedroom while I went upstairs to make us dinner.

I waited for her for almost an hour, and finally ate my pork chops and zucchini alone, making a plate for her and putting it in the oven to keep it warm, jealous that she had someone to talk about the widow's walk and sunset to, a confidant.

I couldn't look to Estella to be that for me. I wondered if this was how Mother felt, hiding her life from everyone, even her own family. My aloneness took on a sheen of nobility for a moment, and then was just as quickly gone.

Estella

"So your mother had this whole life you girls knew nothing about?" Paul asks.

"Can you believe she never said a word?"

"You haven't exactly been up-front with her either," he says, his voice empty of rebuke, simply stating a fact.

I say nothing.

"How are you feeling?" he asks.

"Fine," I lie. I don't tell him about the headaches, or the number games that have filled my mind again. It is coming back, I can feel it, but Paul does not trust intuition. Paul trusts doctors, and scientists, and modern medicine.

"I miss you, Estella," he says, and I can hear in his voice how much he does miss me, and my heart swells with ache for him. I wonder if this is how Connie feels about Luke, if this is how Daddy felt about Mother.

"I miss you too," I whisper.

We hang up, but I stay in my room, willing my headache away. I think that perhaps I'll go for a swim, but it is fully dark out, and the water is a different thing at night. The swimming has been good for me. I can feel my body becoming stronger even while my mind weakens. Edison didn't believe in exercise. He believed that the body was merely something to cart his brain around in.

But while my brain has betrayed me, my body hasn't.

And I am no Edison.

I am looking forward to opening the widow's walk. Connie seemed so content up there. I would very much like to see that again. She is constantly on edge. She had always been so relaxed that I had been envious of her easy ways. I hate that I make her so nervous and defensive.

If I go back to Atlanta without resolving this, I never will. Thinking of it is not helping my head, but I know what will. I stare at the ceiling and count the vents in the ceiling fan motorcase. There are seventeen. Just as there always have been.

Three facts about seventeen:

The Parthenon is seventeen columns long.

This makes me pause. Paul says he will take me there on our honeymoon.

Three facts about seventeen:

The square root of seventeen is irrational.

Seventeen is the smallest Trotter prime.

Seventeen is the age I was when I got pregnant.

CHAPTER FOURTEEN

I was sweating. Despite the air-conditioning, the little double-backed staircase leading to the widow's walk trapped heat, and I was crouched as close as I could get to the door, wielding a flathead screwdriver and a dinner knife in an attempt to slice away the foam sealant piped around the door's edge. It was slow going, and old, crusty bits of yellow foam were caught in my hair and clinging to my shirt.

Estella took a turn while I packed books, and we had succeeded in working almost all of the sealant off. Now Estella was packing while I grunted and sweated on the staircase. I finally managed to dig the last of it out.

"I think this is it," I called to Estella. She appeared at the half-point landing, and I handed her the knife and screwdriver. The key to the padlock slid in and turned easily, a triumph after the nightmare of the sealant, but we weren't home free yet. The door handle wouldn't turn, and I finally banged on it, bruising the heel of my hand.

"Let me try," Estella said, and I gratefully switched places with her. She banged on it too, but she persevered, and it finally turned. She pushed. Nothing happened. She scrabbled for purchase on the stairs, and finally bent over at the waist, pushing her back against the door, and pushed up, her legs doing all the work. She looked like Atlas, lifting a flat, silver world on her shoulders, thigh muscles quivering.

The door popped without warning, and Estella shot up like a bottle rocket, banging the back of her head into the door, sending her stumbling down the steps. I caught her just before she plunged head-first into the wall facing the top flight, and we panted there for a moment, our hearts beating wildly. Estella began to laugh, and I couldn't help but join her.

"God," she said, pulling away from me and rubbing the back of her head with her hand. "We're going to be lucky to get out of this place alive."

I squinted up the staircase into the rectangle of sunlight. "Shall we get closer to the sky?" I asked breathlessly, flinging my arms out.

"Don't you dare make fun of her," Estella said, still laughing. "She's a lovely woman."

"Yes, she is," I agreed. "I'm sure I'm going straight to hell. Come on." I led the way up the stairs and crawled over the lip, cautiously getting to my feet. Estella clambered after me and we stood close to the door, nervous about the condition of the roof.

The widow's walk was the twin to Vanessa's, with a white railing and built-in benches, but they couldn't have looked more different. Years of neglect had left the white coating peeling in patches, and bird-poop stains freckled the roof, railing, and benches.

I slid my foot forward, slowly putting weight on it, testing, but the roof felt solid. Estella took one half, I took the other, and we walked across every foot of it, finally satisfied that it was perfectly safe, if disgusting. We spent the rest of the afternoon scrubbing it down, hauling buckets up and sloshing water about until the walk gleamed.

It was hot, dirty, exhausting work. Storm clouds gathered in the late afternoon, obscuring the sunset. We finally shut the door behind us just as the rain hit, grumbling about the waste of water we'd carried up.

The thunderstorms continued for the rest of the week, trapping us inside. We made grimly cheerful comments about how it was a good thing because it forced us to work, and work we did, silently and carefully, skirting around anything more serious than what was for dinner. By Friday almost thirty boxes of books were stacked against the wall on the first floor.

I had carefully wrapped my violins and packed them, clearly labeling the box and placing it in my room. We rolled the rugs up, carrying the small ones down together, but we nearly killed ourselves with the large Bokhara. Pulling it out the door didn't work; we had no leverage. Pushing it didn't work either; it was too ungainly.

We finally left it, hoping that Tate might have an answer, or a willing pair of strong arms and a stubborn back. Friday night we leaned against the windowsills, watching the rain lash the beach, lightning splintering the night in gorgeous displays over the water, followed by house-shivering thunder.

Our father had loved thunderstorms. He often woke us up to watch the lightning show while Mother snugged herself under the comforter in their bedroom. All three of us had laughed at her fear. Now I felt shame for the things we said, the superiority act of our father's that we'd readily bought into and emulated.

If I'd had the choice between her and our father, I would have chosen him every time. He led us to believe that Mother was base—not stupid exactly, but certainly not brilliant the way his family was. His sense of self had been tied up in oil paintings on a wall, not the imperfect flesh-and-blood people our mother had been born of.

"Remember Daddy and his storms?" Estella asked quietly. Her face lit up with a flash of lightning.

"Yeah," I admitted. "I was thinking about Mother too. I never gave her enough credit—"

"And we gave him entirely too much," Estella finished for me. I nodded.

"I'm sorry she didn't come," I said.

"She'd never have allowed us to open the widow's walk."

"Like that did us a lot of good," I said. We hadn't been able to watch a single sunset since we'd pried it open and scrubbed it down. I turned slowly around, surveying the room. "If I lived here I'd make this my bedroom," I said.

"It is beautiful," Estella agreed, looking around. "It seems so different now, so much bigger."

"I'd paint the bookcases white and leave the windows bare," I continued.

"Paint the bookcases," Estella repeated, sounding horrified. "Don't let Paul hear you say that. He's morally opposed to painting wood."

"Did you ever bring him here?"

She shook her head. "No. He suggested coming a few times, but it was just never convenient."

"I wish the boys had been able to come," I said. "They'd have loved the widow's walk. What a shame we did all that work for nothing."

Estella shrugged. "It's supposed to be clear tomorrow."

"Tate's coming in the morning," I reminded her.

"Do I have to go?"

I laughed. "You sound like my boys."

She sighed. "We'll see."

"Well, I'm going, with or without you," I said.

And when Tate showed up the next morning, a morning bright with sun and no rain clouds in sight, she stayed in bed while we set off for Little Dune Island. We bounced along in his pickup truck with the windows down and a big cooler and fishing rods jostling in the bed behind us.

Once at the end of the road, Tate carefully bumped the truck off the edge and onto sandy soil, following a path so narrow that branches dragged against the sides and over the roof. He finally stopped when the greenery closed in, turning the sort-of-a-road into barely-a-footpath, and he held the fishing rods in one hand while we carried the cooler between us. I had two bags slung over my other shoulder, but we managed to get through the scrub without dropping anything. We pushed through some cabbage palms and then we were at the cut, the very end of Big Dune Island. We dropped our loads on the beach, and I sat on the cooler to catch my breath.

It was just after sunrise, but the day was heating up already. It had the same feel as those long-ago summers, as though the day might never end. I heard Tate rustling in the brush behind me and turned to see him sliding a canoe out along the sand. The nose of another, smaller canoe poked out beside it. I helped him drag the canoe to the water's edge.

"Steer or paddle?" Tate asked.

"Steer," I said.

He pulled off his shoes and threw them into the canoe, then walked out in the water, pulling the canoe behind him until just the back edge remained on the sand. He climbed in the back and moved to the front while I steadied it, and then I pushed it forward, climbing in the rear at the last minute. We hauled ourselves forward and were soon off the sandy bottom, floating easily toward Little Dune.

The little intricacies of steering the canoe came back effortlessly for me, and Tate paddled us across the calm water at a good clip. In less than ten minutes we were on the shore of Little Dune. The island was just waking up; birds were calling through the trees, making a racket I hadn't heard for years.

We unloaded onto the beach and Tate pulled the canoe up to the scrub line. I sat on the cooler again and surveyed the island and the Gulf from this new, wilder vantage point, pleased to have the day stretching ahead of us.

Estella was probably right to stay home that morning. She was only good for the beach in short spurts, and going to Little Dune was an all-day affair. She'd have been miserable by noon. I rose and stretched while Tate inspected the fishing rods, and then I opened the cooler to see what he'd brought, plunging my hand deep into the ice to find the hidden treats. Soda, water, a beer apiece, turkey sandwiches, a container of grapes and strawberries, and two frozen chocolate bars. My stomach rumbled, and I quickly closed the cooler.

"You want to fish or check out the lighthouse first?" Tate asked.

"Lighthouse," I answered immediately. Tate carefully stored the prepared rods in the canoe, and I helped him stash the cooler under a cabbage palm before we set off down the beach. Tate pointed out birds as they flew overhead and quizzed me on calls. I was rusty, but the names eventually came back to me with a little prodding. We were laughing over the sandpipers scurrying before us when Tate put his arm up in front of my chest, stopping me in my tracks.

"Look," he said, pointing to the sand in front of us. Long slashes in the sand, alternating on each side of a shallow furrow, marked the tracks of a sea turtle. He grinned at me and we followed them, keeping carefully to the side, until he pointed out the nest. He pulled a small notebook from his pocket and, looking around for landmarks, drew a little map.

"I'll come back later and put some wire down," he said.

"Should you notify somebody?" I asked. He shrugged and started to brush the turtle tracks away, camouflaging the nesting site, and I knelt beside him and helped.

"People call me about the nests now," he said. "On Big Dune I report them. They come put little signs in front of them, put tape around some poles. But it just makes people more curious. Nobody comes over here anymore, and if they do, they're usually here because they respect the area. I hide the nests as best I can, put chicken wire over them to keep the raccoons and hogs away, and hope for the best. I've only lost a few over the years here on Little Dune, but they've lost a lot more on the big island. So I'm going to just keep it up until someone catches me."

"What would they do?"

"I'm not sure. I don't worry much about it."

He stood and surveyed our work, used his foot to shuffle another spot. Then, seemingly satisfied, he turned toward me. "Not going to turn me in, are you?" he asked lightly.

I laughed. "Of course not." We headed toward the lighthouse again, keeping our eyes open for more tracks.

"You never know," he said. "There's not a lot of gray area for most folks these days. I miss your dad for that. He really knew how to look between both sides to see what was important."

I snorted, thinking of how easily he'd polarized our house. "Well, maybe when it came to the islands," I said. "Not so much with the rest of the world."

Tate stopped walking. "You keep making comments like that, but your dad was a great man, Connie."

"My dad was a great man for everyone except his family," I said, my face heating up. Tate shook his head.

"What are you talking about? You and Estella seem to have turned out just fine. Do you have any idea how much he did for this place?"

"Estella and I turned out fine *despite* him, Tate. And from what I remember, your father was the one who knew what to do with the islands. My father just saw something he could stamp his precious Sykes name on."

"Jesus, Connie, listen to yourself," Tate said. "Since when do you hate your father?"

"I don't hate him," I corrected him. "I just see him more clearly now. He's no legend, no mythical figure. He was a man who didn't do much with his life. He got interested in one thing and did it halfway, or screwed it up and moved on to something else."

"Bullshit, Connie. Like what?" Tate asked. He squared his shoulders at me and leaned forward. I imagined the intimidation worked on plenty of people, but I'd never been afraid of Tate. He'd hit a nerve and I wasn't willing to back down now.

"Like all his collections, all the auctions he went and bought crap at because educating himself about what was really valuable took too much time. The violins he bought and would never get restored. Moth-eaten rugs simply for their names." My voice steadily rose, making the birds flap away from us. "What about me? As soon as he found out about Estella, he dropped me like a bad habit. He—"

"So this is all about you," Tate interrupted, raising his voice to match mine and jabbing his index finger at me.

"Okay, how's this? He cheated on Mother. No matter how much he loved her, he still fucked somebody else!" I yelled at him. "That's not about me, now, is it?"

"Oh, Connie," Tate said quietly, his shoulders slumping. "Yeah, I think it is."

No birds called, no waves swished, the beach was silent for a long moment.

"Fuck you, Tate," I said as evenly as I could, stalking back the way we'd come. I was leaving; he could swim back. He caught up to me and grabbed my arm, but I shook it off and kept going. He grabbed for me again, and I whirled on him. "Leave me alone!"

"No. Talk to me, Connie."

"We're not best friends anymore, Tate. I'm not fifteen."

"Well, yeah, I mean, the gray hair makes that obvious."

I started walking again, and again he caught up to me and reached for my elbow.

"Hey, come on, I'm sorry. I was trying to make you laugh. You're gorgeous, you're fabulous. You look fifteen."

I slowed down, feeling ridiculous trying to march through the shifting sand. "I certainly don't look fifteen," I finally said.

"I'm sorry, Connie," Tate said, serious this time. "Your husband is an idiot. And I didn't know Sebastian cheated on your mother. He seemed to adore her. He was an idiot too. For that, anyway."

I sighed and ran my hands through my hair, raking my nails against my scalp. "I'm tired of everyone thinking how wonderful Daddy was. I know he did good things. Maybe he was trying to make up for what he'd done to us. I don't know."

"Hey, my father wasn't always the man in the stories either. He could be mean when he was drunk. You know why I joined the Marines?"

"So you could go to college?"

"I joined to punish him."

I gaped at him. "For what, Tate?"

"For raising me on this island, for not keeping my mother from dying, for being the man in the stories. He was a lot to live up to."

"Tate, I had no idea. I thought you loved growing up on the island."

He took a long drink of water and handed me the bottle. I drank, the cool water slipping down my throat and soothing the harshness of shouting and sand. He shrugged. "I did, I just didn't know it. I hated shrimping. He wanted me to take it over. And he'd hated the military. So I did what I thought would piss him off the most."

"Did you hate it too?" I asked. Tate had rarely talked about his time in the Marines, and never about his time in Kuwait.

"Oddly enough, no, I didn't, not at first. I loved it. It was the first time any of my knowledge was actually appreciated. Hell, it was the first time I even knew I was knowledgeable about anything. We were in deserts all the time. Sand I knew—or, I knew it better than grunts from Minnesota did, anyway. It was different there. Here you can dive in the Gulf if sand gets anywhere you don't want it to."

"Please, don't elaborate," I said with a laugh.

"Whatever you're imagining, make it worse. Heat I knew. But it was different there too. Better in some ways. And I'd always been good with my hands. Stuff like that is sort of taken for granted here. All the men are tough, they can all fix engines, they can all fish, and drink, and shoot. They were all legends here, you know?"

I did. There was something about the South, especially the islands before the conveniences of man made them livable, that made men of a certain age and a certain temperament into hard gods, into Hemingways and Sykeses. And of course my father had been trying to live up to his forefathers, just as Tate had.

"So why did you come back?" I asked.

"It's who I am," he said simply. "I don't have to beat my father anymore. This is where I belong."

"How come you've never married, Tate?" I asked. "How come you don't have any kids?"

"I'm not fit to be a husband, Connie. And I'm certainly not fit to be a father. It's good that I know that."

"How can you say that?" I asked, dismayed. "Think of all the things you could pass on—"

"Hell, Connie, I don't even sleep in my house half the time. I live outside. I'd rather fish than make money. That's no example, and God knows no woman would put up with it. And I don't want to change. I have a girl I see on the mainland once in a while, sometimes a tourist over here catches my eye and I get to flirt for a few weeks. It's plenty."

"Really?" I couldn't imagine it, but his face gave nothing away, just like the island men who went before him. "I guess I'm happy for you, then."

He grinned. "Don't do that," he said.

"What?"

He started to laugh. "That *well, you just don't know what's good for you but I'll eventually convince you otherwise* thing. I've been worked on by the best, Connie. I'm good. It took me a long time to get that way, but I really am. I wish you were too."

"There's plenty that's good in my life," I said. "I just have to cut the other stuff out."

"So, are you really going to leave him?"

I considered. "I think my friends in Verona, except Alexander, would suggest counseling," I said slowly. "They'd say I owe that to my kids."

"What do you say?"

"This lawyer friend of Mother's, Bob, he's gathered all kinds of information about Luke. I have a bad feeling it's going to get worse. I think I've been waiting for Luke to make a decision so I won't have to."

"No decision is still a decision."

"Yeah, thanks, Dr. Tate, you're a tremendous help."

He smiled at me. "I might not be husband material, but I'm still a damn good friend. Let me know what I can do when you're ready."

"Thanks," I said. "So, are you going to take me to the lighthouse, or what?"

We trekked the rest of the way in silence. I was lost in thoughts of Luke and our children, and of my father, and I think Tate was just so used to being alone that he didn't need conversation anymore.

We reached the lighthouse and stood beneath the sloping canvas awning that had been bolted to the building and drank our water. A small fire pit, lined with stones, bore the blackened remains of a recent fire, and a small pile of kindling was stacked against the lighthouse. A green anole poked his head out from under a piece of charred wood and stared at us, ready to skitter away should we prove dangerous, and the scrub around us rustled and snapped with the sounds of unseen animals.

The lighthouse was well locked, but Tate had the keys to every dead bolt and padlock. We toured it as though we'd never been there before. The coquina tabby inside had been painted often, and I could see several different colors where it had flaked away in the humidity and heat. Tate led me up the crumbling steps to stand in the open arc of the window and gaze out at the water.

"You know that old story about pirates is true," Tate said.

"The loot hidden on the island and all?" I asked, smiling. We'd all tried to scare each other with stories of Captain Taylor Packard, said to have had a short but profitable career as a pirate. Legend had it that Captain Packard deposited all his wealth on the interior of Big Dune, but near the tip, so now the fortune was supposed to be on Little Dune. Nothing had ever been found to support the claim—not a doubloon, or emerald, or pirate skull—but the legend persisted. Captain Packard's crew, supposedly murdered on his orders, was said to haunt the scrub of Little Dune, and Captain Packard had himself died an equally grue-some death from syphilis in France before he could claim his treasure.

"I've done some research," Tate said.

"Wow," I said, needling him, "research, huh? Will you share the treasure with me so I can buy a vacation house up here?"

He shook his head. "Nope, if I find the treasure, I'll buy everyone out, collapse the bridge, and tear down all the houses. Except mine maybe."

"Thanks a lot," I said, swatting him on the shoulder.

"All right, and yours."

Our futures settled, we locked the lighthouse back up. Tate gath-ered wood to add to the pile for his next camping trip.

"How often do you come over here?" I asked.

He shrugged. "Once or twice a week. Depends on how much work I've got on Big Dune. If it rains hard enough I sleep in the lighthouse," he said as we hiked past the tender dwelling. "I tried sleeping in the house, but the floor is rotted almost all the way through. Found that out the hard way. There's not enough money in the budget to repair it, so I've been trying to buy supplies a little at a time and fix things myself."

"But why bother if nobody's allowed to live there?"

He sighed. "I don't know, Connie. It's just important to me."

I felt chastised somehow, and we hiked back to the beach in silence. I was ravenous when we finally got back to the cooler, and I ate most of my share, washing it all down with the ice-cold beer. The afternoon was passing us by quickly, and I lazily casted in the surf while Tate fished with more serious intent. By four I was ready for a nap, and I spread my towel out on the sand, tilted my hat over my eyes, and fell asleep to the waves and the birds.

Tate woke me just after five and handed me a bottle of water and my chocolate bar while he packed the cooler with the fish he'd caught. We sat on the beach watching the tide go out and then finally shoved the canoe back in the water and returned to Big Dune.

The current was strong as we paddled across, requiring more effort from me than a simple turn of the blade. The trip over had taken about ten minutes; the trip back took almost forty, but the effort felt good on my shoulders, though I knew they'd be sore tomorrow.

Tate slid the canoe into the scrub next to the smaller one, and we loaded the truck, bone weary and happy. The weather had stayed clear, and I couldn't wait to take a shower and watch the sunset from our roof for the first time.

"We opened the widow's walk," I told Tate proudly as we jounced back along the path toward the road. "Want to stay and watch the sunset?"

"Sure," he said. "If I can use your shower, I'll even make y'all dinner. I caught plenty today."

"It's a deal," I said.

I knew something was wrong as soon as we turned into the driveway. Estella was standing on the stairs, holding the phone in her hand,

and when she saw the pickup she rushed down, meeting me as I was swinging the door open before the truck had come to a stop.

"What is it?" I cried. "Is it Carson?"

She shook her head and handed me the phone. "I don't know. Everyone's been calling," she said. "Luke called twice, he wouldn't tell me why, and then Gib—"

"Gib called here?" I interrupted, already dialing home. Gib wouldn't willingly talk to me unless something was drastically wrong.

"No, wait," Estella said, grabbing the phone from me. "Mom called, she said to call her first. Gib is over there. And someone named Alexander called too."

"What? What's going on?" I took the phone back and dialed my mother's number as I raced up the stairs for my keys, ready to dive in the car and tear home.

Mother snatched the phone up on the first ring. "Connie?"

"What's happening, Mother?" I said as I hit the second flight.

"Everyone is fine, Connie. Calm down, nobody is hurt, nobody is dead."

"Then what the hell is going on?" I shouted, my hand finally clutching the keys. I turned to run back down the stairs.

"Honey, there's been a little problem between Luke and Gib."

I froze halfway down. Both Estella and Tate were looking at me from the bottom of the stairs, their faces tilted up with twin expressions of dread. I waved my hand at them and mouthed *It's okay*, though I hadn't gotten that thought through my own mind yet. "What problem?" I asked cautiously.

"Apparently Gib was supposed to spend the night at a friend's home but decided not to. I believe they had a fight. When he arrived home . . . your husband had a guest at the house."

I sat down on the top step, still gripping the keys. "A guest," I repeated, already knowing who. "Deanna."

"Yes, honey."

"Oh God," I said, dropping the keys and shielding my eyes with my hand as though a searchlight had suddenly been turned on me. "Oh God," I repeated. Estella slowly climbed the stairs and sat in front of me, her hands clutching my knees.

"He's there?" I asked. "How is he?"

"He's sleeping. I gave him a Valium—"

"You did *what*?"

"Relax, Connie. The child is at least eighty pounds heavier than I am, he'll be just fine. He was in quite a state when he got here, though. From what he says, he attacked Luke."

I felt the color drain from my face. "He attacked him? How? Is he all right?"

"I told you, he's fine. And Luke has already called here, so he seems to be fine too. I called the gatehouse and told Otto not to allow him in."

I took a deep, ragged breath, shaking my head. How could it have possibly come to this? "Hang on," I said to my mother and told Estella and Tate that everything was fine so they would stop gawking at me.

"We'll go upstairs," Estella said. They stepped past me, and I raised the phone to my ear again.

"Tell me everything," I said.

"Gib called me from his cell phone—"

"He's not supposed to be using his cell phone," I said.

"You can ground him later, Connie. Anyway, he called and asked if he could come over. I said of course he could, and he was here within a few minutes. He was just like a little boy, Connie. I could cry just thinking of how he looked when he walked in that door."

Tears came to my eyes. Gib had never come running to me in need as a little boy, so I had no frame of reference, but my imagination worked quickly.

"All he would tell me was that he and Sean had a fight, and when he came home Luke was—well, he said he was in the hot tub with a woman, and they were nude."

"Oh, no," I moaned, leaning my head against the railing.

"I'm so sorry, dear."

"What then?"

"Luke got out, and that was when Gib attacked him."

"What does *attack* mean, Mother? Did he hit him, did they fight?"

"I don't know. Gib looks fine; I didn't see a mark on him. His clothes were damp, and he was obviously upset, but other than that he looked fine."

"What did Luke say when he called?"

"He asked if Gib was here, I said he was, and he said he was coming to get him. I told him I didn't think that was a good idea and he hung up. I called down to the gate, and Otto knows not to let him in. If there's a problem he'll call the police."

"Oh, God, Mother. Don't call the cops," I said, horrified.

"What would you like me to do? Let him come up here and fight it out?"

"No, no, of course not. You were right. Okay, I'll pack my bag and be there tomorrow. I'll leave early; I can be there by afternoon."

"No. Gib and I are coming in the morning."

"What?"

"Why not? I don't want you coming back to town like this, and Gib could certainly use the break. Bob thinks it's a good idea too."

"You told Bob?"

"Yes, of course I did."

I was silent for a moment, trying to absorb it all. And why not? I had been missing both my boys. I was the one who'd been wishing I could show them Little Dune. Hell, I'd even regretted Mother not being here.

"Do you remember how to get here?" I finally asked. I could almost feel her smile.

"There's my smart girl," she said quietly.

Estella

Tate and I pace upstairs. I can hear Connie, but I'm trying not to listen. Tate is avoiding my eyes, and I wonder about their day. My mind inevitably touches on the possibility that he made a pass at her. I know she didn't make a pass at him; she's too proud of her marriage to ruin it over an old flame.

Obviously, Gib has gotten into some kind of fight over a girl. I bring his face to mind, mentally going through the photos Mother sends me. But what I see instead are the Christmas cards we receive every year with a family photo on the cover, the four of them dressed in matching shirts, or with little Santa hats on their heads. I remember Gib is tall, taller than his father, but he has Connie's coloring. Carson, the younger boy, has Luke's darker good looks, though arranged in a more delicate way.

With that sorted out, my mind jitters, looking desperately as it does in times of stress for something else to occupy it. I realize that I am stepping carefully in the center of each tile, avoiding the grout lines. But knowing that I am doing it and stopping it are two different things. Instead, I pull a chair out from the kitchen table and force myself to sit, my knee jiggling.

I wish I had a pencil and paper. All my muscles have been placed on high alert by my unquiet mind. Tate is staring out the sliders. I can smell the faint odor of Gulf and fresh fish on him.

My head pounds.

Connie comes up the stairs. Her face is ashen. I stand so quickly that my head swims.

"Is Gib okay?" I ask.

She nods and then sighs, rubbing her forehead, and looks at Tate.

"Should I go?" he asks.

"No," she says. "Tate already knows, so I might as well tell you, Estella. Luke is having an affair."

I am so shocked that I sit back down in the chair wrong and almost fall off the edge of it. I catch myself and stare at her.

"I'm leaving him," she says and gives Tate a pained smile.

She leads us to the living room, and for the first time since we've been here I don't give a thought to my head, and there are no useless numbers competing with each other for space in my mind. Instead, I am fully focused on my little sister explaining that her perfect life is not perfect.

To my surprise, when she finishes the story she leans, not toward Tate, but toward me, and I put my arms around her and rock with her there on the sofa while she cries. For this, a gratitude flows through me.

We are family.

CHAPTER FIFTEEN

The phone rang just as I finished humiliating myself in front of Tate and Estella. Estella pulled slightly away from me and looked carefully, embarrassingly, into my face.

"Oh, go ahead," I said, wiping my face.

She answered it, and I could tell by the calm chill in her voice that it was Luke. I started to hyperventilate a little. Tate reached out and held me around the shoulders.

"You don't have to talk to him right now," he said, but I shook my head. Estella reluctantly handed me the phone.

"I'm here," I said.

"Why haven't you called me?" he started, on the offensive. "I've been worried sick."

"Cut the crap, Luke. I've already talked to Mother."

"Listen, Connie, I don't know what she said—"

"Was it Deanna?" I asked.

Luke was silent.

"I know about her, Luke. I know about all of them. I know about the Beetle, I know about your lunches."

"Oh, God, Connie," Luke whispered. "I didn't want it to be like this."

"I guess you should have thought about that a long time ago," I said. "Is she still there?"

He hesitated, and then said, "No."

"Liar."

"She's upset. I didn't want her driving."

"Well, I'd hate for her to be upset, Luke. Mother and Gib will be here by tomorrow afternoon. I want to talk to Gib before I speak to you again. So, can I count on you to be able to soothe Deanna enough to be free by five?"

"Connie, please, it doesn't have to be like this," Luke said. "If you would just be reasonable—"

"You don't get to tell me how to behave, Luke." As soon as I hung up the phone my composure ran out of me like water, and I sagged against the counter. Estella and Tate stood behind me, uncertainty freezing their features. I shook my hands out, as though getting rid of something sticky.

"What am I supposed to do?" I asked, aware there was no answer.

But I was in good hands. After a brief consultation, Tate and Estella decided to get me well and truly sloshed. They swung into action like a superhero duo. Estella ran out for liquor while Tate cleaned the fish. We finally got to watch the sunset from the widow's walk, and we waved and shouted to Vanessa.

By eight o'clock, I was showered and eating dinner, laughing at Tate and Estella, who were arguing about the Velvet Underground. They'd already argued the ethics of breeding purebred dogs, the theories of some poor sap named Tesla who apparently was afraid of pearl earrings, the politics of cloning, and whether I was drinking enough or not.

"Y'all should get married," I finally said. That shut them up for a while.

By ten o'clock, and several rum and colas later, we were back on the widow's walk. I stood, or rather, leaned heavily against the railing, laughing at Tate and Estella again, now arguing about constellations.

I made it over to one of the benches, away from the Andromeda and Perseus talk, and lay down. The slats were damp, but I didn't care. I gazed straight up into the sky, drunkenly able to perceive the stars whirling and rotating above me. I don't know how much later Tate shook me awake.

"Hey there," he said softly. "Come on, you can't sleep up here."

"Why not?" I asked. "It would be wonderful to sleep up here, wouldn't it?"

"You'd get eaten alive by mosquitoes."

He was right. Little specks of black were flying in my face, and my bare arms were already itchy. He held my hands and helped me to sit upright.

"Where's Estella?" I asked.

"She's setting up a little surprise for you," he said. "Come on."

I moaned as he pulled me to my feet. "What? I hope it's not more rum."

He laughed. "No, no more rum for you. In fact, there *is* no more rum."

Standing made me dizzy, but after a few deep breaths my head cleared. Tate was still holding my hands to keep me steady, and I pulled them away with a laugh. "I'm okay, I'm okay."

"All right, but I'm going to help you down." He pulled the door up, calling down, "Estella?"

Estella smiled up at me, holding her arms out, beckoning me down the stairs as though she were planning on catching me. With Tate holding me by one arm, I swung my leg over the lip and made contact with the stairs, finally making my way down them safely.

The library glowed softly, and I looked around in surprise. They'd dragged the two sofa bed mattresses in front of the open windows, on top of the Bokhara rug, and made them with fresh sheets. One of the end tables from the living room sat between them, with a few books and two tall glasses of water.

"We have to make room for Mother and Gib anyway," Estella said, looking almost embarrassed.

"It's wonderful," I said. I fell upon the closest mattress and crawled beneath the covers. The pillow felt heavenly.

"I'll come by tomorrow to see how she is," Tate said. He sounded like he was in another room, his voice far away and deep. Estella said something, I didn't know what, I didn't care; then I heard footsteps going down the stairs. Estella slid under the comforter on the other mattress, and I turned on my side toward her, drawing my knees to my chest and smiling at her across the short space.

She turned on her side too, and reached her hand out. I touched her finger with mine and then drew it back under the covers.

"We're having a sleepover," I said, inordinately, drunkenly happy about it.

She nodded. "Yeah, sorry I don't have any pot or anything."

For a moment, I had no idea what she was talking about, and I stared at her blankly. Then I remembered Chelsea and Lisa from her house in Atlanta, and shame flooded me.

"You knew about that?" I asked.

"It's okay," she said.

But it wasn't, and I knew it. I should have gone and gotten her that night. Or I should have skipped the girls' room and gone and gotten her anyway.

"Sorry," I said. "I just couldn't sleep. I didn't want to bother you."

"You wouldn't have bothered me—and I said it's okay."

She turned over on her back and folded her hands beneath her head. She had a beautiful profile, and I stared at her, trying to see the girl in the woman's face. It was there, especially in the worried brow, the teeth nibbling her top lip.

"It's going to be weird being here with Mother," I said. Estella turned on her side again, and I could see her eyes shining in the dark.

"How are you doing, Connie?" she asked.

"I don't know," I said.

"So, this Deanna, you think she's at your house right now?"

I considered it. I didn't see why she wouldn't be, wrapped around Luke in our bed, maybe wearing something of mine, more likely wearing nothing. "Probably," I said.

"Who's Alexander?" she asked, and I sat upright, then fell back down just as quickly as a wave of nausea washed over me.

"Damn, I forgot all about Alex. What did he say?"

"He just wanted you to call him. Is he involved in this?"

"I don't think so," I said. "He's the cello player in the trio. He probably just wants to make sure I'm practicing."

"You're not," she pointed out.

"How do you know?" I asked, annoyed. "Maybe I'm practicing while you swim."

"Your case hasn't moved from under the staircase since we got here," she said.

"Oh. Well, I'll practice soon."

"So his call was just coincidence?"

"It must be. He knows about Deanna—in fact, he's the one who told me that Luke was still seeing her. But I don't see how he could know about any of this."

"Why do you keep turning your rings?"

"What?" I asked, startled at her sudden shift and realizing in embarrassment that I was indeed twisting my rings. I quickly put my hands back under the covers.

"Your wedding rings. Tonight, whenever you set your glass down, you turned your rings, and you were just doing it again."

"I don't know what you're talking about." I could feel myself blushing and was grateful for the dark. Now it was my turn to flip over onto my back, avoiding her eyes, but she wasn't ready to let it go.

"You turn them in groups of three. I saw you. Three times, each time. Why do you do it?"

"Why do you hate it when anyone calls you a genius?"

"I'll tell you if you'll tell me."

"You go first."

"No, you go. I swear I'll tell you."

"Okay, but it's stupid. I used to do it all the time after we got married. It was just a habit. I don't know, a superstition, I guess."

"But for what? If you turn them around three times your marriage is safe?"

I hadn't thought of it in those terms. It was simply something that had become natural in times of stress. I thought I'd broken myself of it years ago, when I developed an irritation on my ring finger. "I'm not sure," I finally said. "If that's what it was, it didn't seem to work, did it?"

"What else do you do?" she asked, raising herself on her elbow to look at me.

"What do you mean?"

"I've seen how you load the dishwasher. You won't put a fork in with another fork unless there's no choice. You divide them all up."

"What are you doing? Studying me?"

"No, they're just things I notice, that's all. Paul touches his knuckles to the door handle before he opens a door."

I laughed. "Why does he do that?"

Estella lay back down and laughed too. "I don't know. He doesn't know."

"What do you do?" I asked.

She snorted. "What *don't* I do?"

"Really? Tell me," I said eagerly.

"Well, I count steps—"

"I remember that," I said.

"You do?"

"You used to count the steps to the windows in the music room."
She smiled. "That's right. I'd forgotten about that."

"What else?"

"I check for a dial tone after I hang up the phone. After I lock the
front door dead bolt, I try to open the door three times. I won't use liquid soap unless it's in a clear bottle."

We were both laughing out loud as she recited her list, and I realized that I had my own things to add. "I can't watch anything cook in
the microwave," I said.

She laughed. "Why?"

"Because I'm quite sure I can feel my eyes vibrating from escaping
microwaves," I said.

"I can't step on grout lines," she said.

I drew in my breath in sudden understanding. "That's why you
walk funny."

"I don't walk funny!"

"You do! I mean, I noticed that there was something different about
the way you walked around your house—Estella! Your house, why
would you tile your whole downstairs?"

She started giggling again. "I was trying to break myself of it. It
works sometimes, but if I have a single glass of wine, or I'm up too late
and get tired, that's it. I'm steppin' mighty careful."

"Oh, Estella, that's awful," I said, unable now to stop laughing.
"But why? What does it feel like when you step on the grout?"

"Like nothing."

"I don't get it."

"It feels like there's nothing there. You know how your feet feel
when you're looking a long way down, from the top of a tall building,
or over the edge of something? They sort of tickle? It feels like that.
That's how I fell in love with Paul," she said, her laughter fading away.

"He grouted your tile?"

"No, smart-ass," she said, reaching out to poke my shoulder. "He dances with me."

"What do you mean?"

"We started dating just before I had the downstairs done, and I could barely walk to my kitchen, and here he was, trying to get me to waltz around the living room on my new tile. I was hopping around, trying to get my feet in the middle, and he finally just lifted me up onto his feet, and that's how we dance."

"That's beautiful," I whispered. She was silent for a moment and then burst out laughing. It was impossible not to join her.

"Okay, your turn," I said. "Why do you hate it when people call you a genius?"

She sighed. "Because it's a stupid term. It was based on an IQ test, and that's just too much pressure, especially for a kid."

"But, Estella, you *are* a genius."

"What do you think I'm a genius at, Connie?"

She had me completely confused. "At math, right?"

"I had a facility for numbers, for games. What I did was arithmetic, not mathematics, Connie. There's a difference. Don't you realize that you turning your rings and me playing number games are the same? Or they come from the same place, anyway."

"Well, now I really do feel stupid, because I have no idea what you're talking about, Estella. Some little obsessive-compulsive trait certainly doesn't make me a genius."

"That's my point. Yes, I was smart—I had a high capacity to learn and the number games led everyone to believe that it meant I must be a math genius."

"Well, aren't you?"

"Yes and no."

"Oh, God, Estella, you're killing me here."

"My IQ is over 140 and that labels me a genius, that's it. Like you having big boobs labels you a D-cup."

We started laughing again.

"Okay, bad analogy," she admitted. "A genius is someone capable of new ideas, of an ability to think differently about an old problem, not just learn them. There is nothing that I've ever done that could be considered new or unique. I've never come up with an answer to an unsolvable problem, I've never invented anything."

"But Estella, you went to college when you were twelve. *Twelve*."

"Why do you think that means anything? Ever notice that NASA wasn't exactly beating my door down? Connie, didn't you ever think about the fact that Daddy gave most of his book collection to the college?"

I was bewildered. "What are you saying? He didn't *buy* your degree. Did he?"

She sighed heavily. "Not exactly. When I first went, I had something, I'll admit that. But I plateaued, I evened out—hell, Connie, I lost it, okay? It went away."

"But when?" I asked. "Why?"

"I don't know. I had headaches. I wasn't concentrating. I don't know."

"But how were you able to stay? How did you graduate?"

Estella was silent.

"Estella?"

"I guess it was partly the book collection," she finally said. "And nobody wanted to admit they'd been wrong. Not Dr. Pretus, and definitely not Daddy."

At the mention of Pretus' name I shuddered. "Estella, what really happened?"

"Pretus told me that he would keep me in school, would keep the secret as long as—"

"As long as you had sex with him?"

"Something like that. I wasn't ready for that environment. Every-one treated me like I was an adult. I wasn't old enough to realize that I could have gotten Pretus in a lot more trouble than he could get me in. I had leverage. I just didn't realize it until much later."

"So, did Daddy know or not?"

"About Pretus, or about me losing it?"

"Either."

"He never found out about Pretus. But he knew my 'talents' went away. Pretus told him. Daddy donated more books and Pretus got the credit for it."

"So Pretus was, in effect, blackmailing both you and Daddy?"

"If you want to look at it that way, yeah."

"God, Estella, how else could you look at it?"

"Don't forget that Daddy really wanted this; I did too, or I thought I did. Daddy didn't see it as blackmail; I think he just thought of it as extra tuition. And, to be fair, he never made me feel as though I had done anything wrong."

"So, when you say it went away, you mean your IQ went down?"

"No, not exactly. It was more like my mind stopped seeing the rela-tionships between things in new ways. See, it was all about connections. People see connections all the time, I just did it at a faster rate, and I could figure out how they fit the theories and equations that were being taught, so it looked impressive. And then the connections just weren't there anymore. Like something had flipped a switch in my mind."

"That sounds scary," I said.

"It was at first," she admitted. "It was a relief too. Some people see patterns all the time, and sometimes they're authentic, like in mathe-matics, and when one of those people finds math they can concentrate all that extra energy on authentic patterns and connections. The prob-lem is when those patterns aren't authentic; because if they can't stop their minds from making those constant connections, they come to believe that some cosmic revelation is coming to them, when there is no revelation. It's enough to drive someone mad."

"You thought you were going crazy?"

"I think I was confused. Between what was authentic, and what wasn't. Numbers will always make connections, patterns, because that's their nature. If a thing exists, it can be counted. Even invisible things—time, distance, space. Our entire universe can be broken down to numbers. That's a powerful concept for somebody who sees patterns."

"And you don't know why you stopped seeing them?"

"I have my theories."

"Like what?"

"Nothing I can prove. I went to see a doctor. I went to see more than one. They said it was psychosomatic. That I was under so much stress that I turned it off myself. I'm glad it stopped."

"Are you serious?" I asked.

"Totally serious. I never want it to come back," she said fiercely.

"I'm sorry. I'm so sorry I didn't know."

"I'm not, not anymore. It was a long time ago, Connie, and none of it was your fault."

The rum and the day caught up with me, and I fell asleep on the crest of her absolution.

I called Alexander as soon as I woke in the morning. Estella was already in the Gulf, doing a strong, fluid crawl, and I watched Vanessa doing tai chi as I waited for him to answer.

"Thank God," Alexander said by way of greeting.

"And what if it hadn't been me?" I asked.

"Who else calls me at nine on Sunday mornings? My priest gave up on me years ago. And the caller ID tipped me off. Tell me you're coming home early."

"No, I'm afraid not. Why? Is something wrong?"

"Everything is wrong. Everything is awful. David broke his clavicle."

I gasped. David didn't just fill in for me once in a while, he was a full-time member of the Verona Philharmonic. But while the orchestra had a sub list a mile long for violinists, our trio didn't. "How?" I cried.

"Car accident. It snapped, just like a twig, under the seat belt. Not another scratch on him, though his car's totaled."

"Oh, Alexander, I'm so sorry. Please give him my best."

"He'll be fine. But what about me? I can't possibly find another violinist."

"I'm sorry, I can't come home. Especially after last night."

"What happened?" he asked, lowering his voice conspiratorially. "Luke?"

"Gib came home and found Luke and the Starbucks girl naked in the hot tub."

Now it was Alexander's turn to gasp. "What did he do?"

"I don't know exactly. Mother called last night. Gib spent the night with her and they're driving up right now."

"Connie, what are you going to do?"

"I'm leaving Luke. We talked briefly last night, but she was there—"

"She was still there? Slut."

I had to laugh. "Yeah," I agreed. "So, we're going to talk tonight. I want to hear Gib's side of the story, but my mind's made up. I don't see how we can come back from this one."

"Are you okay?"

"Oddly enough, I am. I've known this was coming for years. At least the waiting is over."

Alexander sighed. "Wish I could see you," he said. "I'd pump you full of Syrah and chocolate, and then we'd go do something really immature and vindictive."

"Ugh," I groaned. "Trust me, the liquor-soaked night has already been taken care of. And I have no interest in revenge. I just want to get through this, that's all."

"And now you'll have June there to tell you how," Alexander said with an obvious grin in his voice.

"That's right. I'll be in coral pantsuits and playing tennis at the club before you know it." I felt a little niggle of shame at making fun of Mother. "Actually, I'm glad she's coming. She's been more help than I ever would have thought."

"Well, at least she'll be concentrating on you instead of trying to get me to go straight."

I laughed. "Don't get too comfortable. She'll never give up. Now what will you do about a violinist?"

"There's nothing to do. I'll have to cancel the performance," he said, sounding panicky. "This is a disaster. It's such short notice, they'll never hire us again."

"That's not true," I said. "But it might not be bad for you if they didn't."

"Don't start again," he pleaded.

"I'm sorry, Alexander, but you belong in an orchestra, and you're going to have to get yourself back out there."

"I have an audition," he said quietly.

"Why didn't you tell me?" I asked.

"It just happened. I'll probably only be able to get on the sub list, but I guess it's a start. And I told the personnel manager about the library series. He said he might come to the performance, nothing official, just to check it out."

"Oh no! Couldn't you contact the orchestra and see if there's someone else to fill in?"

"I've got the word out, but the phone's been quiet."

"Maybe I can drive back just for the night," I mused aloud.

"That's crazy," he said. "And you'd be no good by the time you got here anyway. I couldn't ask it of you. Go lie on the beach and think good thoughts. I'll call in a few days to let you know what happens."

We hung up, and I did as instructed. I spread a towel down on the beach and watched Vanessa stretch and Estella swim, and let the sun fall on me like a lover while tears I had no control over fell from the corners of my eyes and filled my ears.

Tate arrived in the early afternoon, bearing a cooler full of fresh shrimp, and we waited on the widow's walk, trying to spot Mother's red Lincoln coming across the bridge. Tate let me use his binoculars, but that flash of expensive red never crossed. Instead, my black Saab turned onto the road leading to our house, and I spotted Gib at the wheel.

"Why, that little brat, he took my car," I said, but I couldn't work up any real irritation over it.

Tate took the binoculars and followed their progress up the road. We started waving high over our heads as the car came within sight and heard the answering horn when they spotted us. I felt a surge of excitement at seeing Gib, despite the reason for his arrival. If anything, I was relieved that it was finally out in the open.

My mind had already been made up; I just wasn't willing to admit it to myself yet. In fact, I realized that I had been shutting myself down by degrees from the moment eight years ago when Luke began cheating on me. Each year that passed, each gift I received, blocked off one more little piece. And to my shame I had applied that block unilaterally to include my sons.

Or at least the son who had looked up to Luke as the one member of the family worthy of his attention. Raw satisfaction that Luke had been exposed—in more ways than one—filled my belly before I could stop it, quickly followed by the thought, whiny and insistent, that perhaps now I would finally get some respect from Gib.

Gib pulled in beside Tate's pickup truck, and I heard Tate draw his breath in sharply at how close Gib came to swiping the side-view mirror off the Saab. Mother eased her door open and waved up at us with a brilliant smile.

"How'd y'all get up there?" she yelled up at us, shielding her eyes from the sun. "Your daddy would have a fit."

"I warned 'em," Tate called down.

"He's a liar, Mother," Estella said. "He did it himself."

"No, I didn't," he argued back.

"Well, get on down here and help us," Mother said, and we clambered into the door and down the stairs. Gib still hadn't made an appearance, and by the time we reached the car, he was hidden by the raised trunk lid.

Mother greeted Tate first, protesting when he lifted her off her feet and jiggled her up and down a few times.

"Let me down, you fool," she cried, slapping him on the shoulders. "Make yourself useful."

"Yes, ma'am," he said, setting her gently on the driveway.

"My girls," she said, opening her arms, and we dutifully entered them, enduring a three-way hug that allowed neither of us to really get close to her.

She released her grip and inspected us as I strained to get a glimpse of Gib. Tate moved around the back of the car, and I quickly followed. Tate was holding his hand out to shake Gib's, but Gib was merely looking at it distrustfully. Anger bloomed in my chest.

"You remember Tate, Gib," I said, narrowing my eyes at him. He reluctantly took Tate's hand and mumbled a greeting. Tate grabbed a couple of bags and winked at me, leaving us alone behind the car. My anger melted in expectation of a warm hug, perhaps even a new current of understanding from Gib. I was sorely mistaken.

"Here," he said, thrusting one of my mother's garment bags into my arms, effectively placing a physical barrier between us, before turning back to the open trunk.

"How was the drive, Gib?" I asked lightly, trying not to let him see how much it hurt.

It was an adult question, and he paused, gauging my intent. "It was okay," he said, guarded. "Gramma talked the entire way."

"Yeah, she'll do that. Come on, I want you to see Estella."

He hefted his shoulders, settling the bags more firmly, and followed me. Tate and Mother had already entered the house, but Estella was waiting at the bottom of the stairs, and she stepped forward and startled him with a kiss on his cheek before he could step out of range.

"Good Lord, you're huge," she said, and I almost laughed. Estella had worked hard to rid herself of her Southern accent, but within moments of Mother being around it came back strong as ever.

"Oh, hey," Gib said. "You cut your hair."

Estella laughed. "Since you last saw me ten years ago? Yes, I have. Looks like you did too."

Gib wasn't sure what to make of the teasing and stood awkwardly, hunching his shoulders to relieve the strain of the luggage. Estella reached out to take a bag, but Gib shied away as if afraid she might try to kiss him again.

"No, I got it," he said, edging past her and taking the stairs two at a time. We watched him disappear into the house and then looked at each other and grinned.

"Awkward age," I explained. "You know, from birth to twenty."

"Boy," she said, "this is going to be interesting."

"I guess it is," I agreed, and followed her up the stairs, my equilibrium somehow restored.

Upon reaching the foyer, we ran into Gib, minus the bags. "Hey, there's stuff in my room," he said.

"You'll be in my old room," I said. "That's Estella's room."

Gib looked from me to Estella and back again in disbelief and then turned abruptly and stomped back down the hall to retrieve his bags.

"Sorry," I said, embarrassed. "Please don't feel as if you should move."

Estella smiled at me. "Don't worry," she said. "I'm used to this age. I sort of get a kick out of it. So much drama, just like his mama."

I shot her a warning glance and she laughed softly. We could hear Mother in the master bedroom, opening closets, and found her with enough clothes for a month.

"Hand me those hangers," she said as we crowded into the closet. I held them out and as she took them, she gave us both a critical eye. "Have you girls been wearing sunscreen?"

"Yes, Mother," we said simultaneously.

"Because the sun will wrinkle you quicker than it turns a grape to a prune," she warned. "Now look at me. I always wore a hat, even when—"

"Prunes are from plums," Estella interrupted.

"Don't correct your mother," Mother said sharply, and Estella and I grinned at each other. "Look at me, come on, look close." She turned her face up into the light, arching her neck and widening her eyes, holding her mouth carefully to ensure no stray wrinkles got away from her and ruined the effect.

"You're gorgeous, Mother," I said.

"Like a twenty-year-old," Estella confirmed.

"Don't make fun," Mother said. "I know I look good, and never spent a moment under the knife."

I snorted.

"That's an ugly sound, Constance. And peels don't count," she said.

"Mother, you look wonderful," I said. "Where did Tate go?"

"He said something about shrimp," she said, turning away from us to resume hanging her clothes.

"We should probably give him a hand," Estella said. "Take your time and freshen up, Mother, we'll see you upstairs."

"I'd like to talk to your sister a minute," she said, and Estella left with a sympathetic smile at me. I sat on the edge of the bed and watched Mother work, placing her things just exactly so, color coordinated, long-sleeved to short, slacks to shorts. "Gib's been looking forward to seeing you," she said.

"It doesn't look that way," I said.

She finished and took a step back to make sure everything was hung to her specifications. She switched a blue shell for a green one, and then nodded in satisfaction before coming to sit beside me on the bed. She patted my knee, leaving her hand there, her rings sparkling in the sun coming from the sliders.

"Try to understand, Connie," she said. "His pride's hurt."

"*His* pride? Luke didn't cheat on him. How do you think I feel?"

"Like a mature woman who had some warning. And of course Luke cheated on him. He cheated on your whole family. Gib is the one who saw it up close and personal—naked."

I sighed. "He doesn't seem like he wants to talk to me," I said.

Mother looked at her watch. "I'm going to take Estella and Tate down to the beach. We'll walk, we'll catch up. We'll be down there for an hour. Give it another try."

"Fine," I said, feeling like a recalcitrant teenager myself.

"Bob said he would call tomorrow to get the story."

"Fine," I repeated. When I reached the doorway, my mother called to me.

"Yes?" I said, turning, one hand high on the frame.

She looked around the room, out the sliders, and then finally back at me. "I'm glad we came."

I smiled, but it felt as tired as I did. "Me too, Mom." I trudged upstairs to help clean shrimp before I was left alone with my angry son.

I downed a glass of wine after Tate, Estella, and Mother left, and then went downstairs and knocked on my old bedroom door. There was no answer, but I could hear the bass from the little stereo, and I knocked louder. The bass cut off.

"What?" Gib called.

"May I come in?" I asked, very nearly gritting my teeth.

There was no answer, but in a moment the door opened a crack and Gib looked out the slim opening at me. "What?" he repeated.

I pushed on the door, and he initially resisted but finally let me push it open. He turned away and sat down on his bed, turning the music up again, just a hair lower than it had been.

"I think we need to talk about what happened last night," I said, sitting on the edge of the bed.

"Why?"

"Because it's important. Because it's going to affect our lives. Because you're obviously upset and you have every right to be."

"I'm fine."

"I don't believe you."

He shrugged. "Whatever."

"Why did you leave Sean's? Did you have a fight?"

He avoided my eyes. "It's no big deal."

I pressed my palms to my face and rubbed my eyes with my fingertips. My fingers still smelled slightly of shrimp. "I can't do this, Gib. I can't help if you won't talk to me."

"I don't need any help!" he shouted. I flinched, pulling my hands from my face and standing in one motion. "You're the one who needs help!"

I headed for the door, hoping I made it before my knees gave way. "You can stay in here until you're ready to speak civilly to me," I said without turning around.

He responded by turning the music up loud, and before my foot hit the first stair the bedroom door slammed, making the house quiver. I grabbed the banister to steady myself, and then turned around and walked out to the beach. Tate, Estella, and Mother were far down the beach to the left, so I turned right, unable to face them.

By the time I turned around I was calmer, but I felt as fragile as a sand dollar. I met Estella on the way back, and she joined me without a word. We climbed the stairs to the house, and before we walked in she touched my arm and said softly, "It's going to be okay."

I wasn't a genius, and she wasn't a mother, and I didn't believe her.

Estella

Seeing Gib is a shock. He towers over me, his shoulders are broad, and he moves with a strength and surety unusual in a kid his age. My sister is intimidated by him. And he knows it. Perhaps not consciously, but instinctively he knows it, and he uses it to his advantage.

It pisses me off.

Walking the beach with Mother and Tate, I remember the story Connie told me about Mother's other island life—little April and May. I want to bring it up, but Tate is ambling beside her, entrancing her with stories of sea turtle nests and bald eagles, showing off in general. All the island boys had crushes on Mother at some point, and he is behaving in that way adults do when in the presence of childhood crushes.

Oh, God. Tell me I haven't been acting that way around him.

But I'm afraid I have. I am mortified, and feel disloyal to Paul in a thousand different ways although he, of all people, would understand that our childhood places and people make us behave in ways we never would in our real, adult, well-loved lives.

Tate blathers on to my mother while we walk the beach, the three of us pretending not to know that Connie is back at the house trying to get her son to talk to her. And he won't. He will be silent and angry, because that is what teenage boys do.

We finally turn around, and just as we reach the house, I see Connie coming from the other direction. She is alone. Neither Tate nor Mother see her; they are only paying attention to each other. When we reach the door, I allow them to enter ahead of me.

"You coming in?" Tate asks.

I shake my head. "I think I'll stay out here for a while," I say and hurry down the boardwalk to meet Connie.

She looks relieved to see me, but it's obvious that she doesn't want to talk, and so I just walk beside her, wanting to tell her that it will be all right, that Gib will eventually come around and appreciate her, that one day this will be a distant memory. I want to tell her about me, and about Paul, and most of all, I want to tell her about that summer, because I am full to bursting with it, and I know that she should know.

Or maybe I just want to tell.

We shuffle up the boardwalk side by side, and just as she opens the door, I get the courage to reach out and say to her, "It's going to be okay."

But it is too late, and I don't think she believes me.

CHAPTER SIXTEEN

L uke called at five, just as I returned from the beach. I took it upstairs in the library, shutting the door, hoping the sealing might
serve as soundproofing.

"Did June and Gib arrive safely?" he asked. He sounded profes-
sional, as though I were a client. Not at all what I'd expected.

"They got here fine," I replied. "Is Deanna still there?"

"No," he said. "Are you going to tell me what Gib said?"

"No," I answered, unwilling to admit that I couldn't get him to tell
me anything. "Are you in love with her?"

He was silent, and I felt satisfied that I had taken him by surprise,
hit him hard, on the offensive. And then he took me by surprise.

"Yes, I am."

All my bravado evaporated. My breath began coming in shallow gasps, as though I'd forgotten how to inflate my lungs. Neither of us said anything. I was stunned at the admission, so quickly given. I had expected a drawn-out fight; I'd planned to have him groveling, pinned, knuckled under; I'd expected to be the victor, the conqueror, all the metaphors for violent victory.

This wasn't our deal. I was the wife. The *wife,* dammit. The only reason I'd put up with this over the years was because my position afforded me certain protections and guarantees, and one of them was *my* right to leave *him.*

I wanted the fight. I deserved the fight. I was *owed* the fight. I had things prepared, for God's sake. Apparently so did he.

"I want out," he said.

"You're in love with her?"

"You wouldn't understand."

For some reason that made me want to smash the phone receiver into bits. Not that he was in love with her, but that I *wouldn't understand.*

"Try me," I said, feeling acid rise in my throat. My hand was fisted so tightly around the old, gnarled cord of the phone that my nails dug into my palm. I squeezed tighter, feeling the blood pulse in my wrist with the pressure.

"She's simple," he said, and I felt laughter bubble in my chest despite my rage.

"Well," I said, "she'd have to be, wouldn't she?"

He was silent and then said, "I didn't mean it like that. She's down-to-earth. She doesn't need all the . . . the stuff, the big house, the cars."

"How lovely of her. And who exactly were those things important to? Not me, Luke. You're the one with the poor-childhood chip on his shoulder. And if cars don't matter to her, then how did she feel about her new yellow Beetle?"

"I didn't use any of our money for that car," he said.

"*Our* money?" I asked. "*Our,* as in you and me? Or *our* as in Gib and Carson's college funds? Did you buy the Escalade or the Beetle with Carson's? And why the Escalade? Was that a diversion? Trying to keep me quiet until you could get things set up?"

Dead silence. I'd hit it.

"Be careful with me, Luke," I said, despite knowing it was unwise. "I know more than you think."

"What exactly are you threatening me with, Connie?"

The venom in his voice matched mine, and I was suddenly fascinated, as though watching a stranger's marriage disintegrate. How could two people who had loved each other, who spoke kindly to each other just days ago, suddenly be filled with such hatred? I took a deep breath and let it leak slowly from my pursed lips.

"Luke? We're getting divorced, right?" I said quietly.

"I—well, yeah. Yes, I want a divorce."

"We have these two boys—"

"I'm warning you not to try to hold me up for some insane support agreement, Connie."

"It never crossed my mind," I said. "But we do need to think about how we're going to treat each other."

"You're the one who came out swinging with the threats."

"And you're the one who's been cheating on me for eight years and who stole our children's money, Luke. I think I've earned the right to be angry."

He was breathing heavily, as though he'd been playing basketball with Gib. I wondered whether that would happen again.

"I'll be coming home in two weeks," I continued. "I suggest you find somewhere else to stay in that time. And keep Deanna out of my big house. I don't want to offend her down-to-earth sensibilities. My lawyer will be in touch."

"Your law—"

I hung up, gently, took my hand off the receiver, and carefully unwound the cord from my palm. I sat in my father's big oxblood leather chair and swiveled back and forth in the empty library.

* * *

When I came downstairs for dinner nobody asked me how the phone call had gone. They were subdued to the point of mournful, and I didn't have the energy to pretend that I was fine. I was shaky all night, my hands betraying me whenever I was asked to pass a dish at the table. Gib stayed in his bedroom through dinner. Nobody asked me where he was, and I didn't offer any information.

Tate and Estella flipped through albums on the living room floor and played music while Mother and I tried to remember the rules to the backgammon game we'd opened between us on the sofa. When Gib's door opened downstairs we all raised our eyes and looked at one another, hands poised mid-move, sentences silenced mid-word.

As his feet fell upon the stairs we all calmly went back to what we were doing by unspoken agreement. I put Mother's white piece on the bar, Tate showed Estella an Etta James record, Mother rattled the dice in her cup.

Gib topped the stairs and walked into the kitchen without glancing our way.

"There's a plate in the oven for you," Mother said, and I shot her an irritated look. She'd offered to clean the kitchen, and I hadn't seen that she'd made a plate for Gib. I didn't want him to starve, but providing him with a ready-made plate made it entirely too easy on him.

Mother had always had a way of spoiling the aggressor, harboring the fugitive. If the rest of the world were punishing a transgression, she would feed the transgressor. It used to make me crazy. Apparently neither of us had changed a bit.

Gib pulled the plate out and banged it on the counter. I ignored it. Then he pulled a drawer open, rummaged for silverware, and slammed it closed again. I ignored that. When he opened the refrigerator door hard enough to bang it into the wall, I'd had enough.

I leapt to my feet and walked to the kitchen with tight, controlled steps and tight, controlled lips. He didn't look at me when I crowded in on him.

"You get yourself under control right now," I said under my breath. "Your family is here, and I will not have you making a spectacle of yourself and making them uncomfortable."

He looked right at me and stuck a shrimp in his mouth, then spat it out into the garbage can. "These taste like shit," he said.

"You watch your mouth, young man!" I snapped. Out of the corner of my eye I saw Tate and Estella hustle down the stairs. Gib turned to me, and I involuntarily stepped backward. His handsome face was contorted, the corners of his mouth pulled down in a grimace I'd never seen before. I shrank before I could marshal my forces.

"Now, Connie, the boy's upset—"

"Be quiet, Mother," I said. I might have been afraid to be angry with my son, but I'd had plenty of practice being angry with my mother, and she proved a lightning rod just in time. "I'm sorry that you had to see your father in such an ugly scenario, Gib. But you'll do well to remember that I am your mother—"

"What's wrong with you?" Gib shouted, spittle flying from his lips. He wiped a hand savagely against his mouth even as he made his next attack. "Maybe if you weren't such a bitch he wouldn't have had to—"

Before I could react I felt my mother move. With a speed I hadn't been aware she was capable of she flew around me and then between us, and then I heard the sharp smack of her hand slapping my son across the face. Gib cried out, clutching his cheek, and then she had him by the shoulders as he collapsed forward and sobbed. She patted him on the back for a moment, and then looked at me, standing frozen in shock, and motioned with her head for me to move closer.

I stepped forward and she stepped back, transferring him to me like she had when he was a colicky baby and she'd finally managed to get him to sleep. I held my big son, whispering soothing noises, as Mother left.

"Okay now," I said as his sobs slowed down. He finally straightened up, hiding his face by bringing the bottom of his T-shirt up, exposing his stomach, making him as vulnerable as an overturned turtle. I wet half of a dishtowel and placed it in a hand I pried away from his face. He clutched at it and finally let the T-shirt drop, scrubbing his face with the towel.

"Come on," I said, taking him by the hand and leading him toward the stairs. He followed without protest. I led him through the library and up the stairs to the widow's walk. He forgot his tears trying to figure out the best way to climb onto the roof, and I let him wander around the railing while I sat on a bench, watching the moon's lacy silver path widen on the water.

Eventually he sat beside me, leaning his elbows on his knees, breathing hard, but regularly. I rubbed light circles on his back and felt his muscles relax beneath my hand.

"I didn't mean it," he whispered, and then, as though the words had been a cork, his shoulders started to heave again.

"Shh," I whispered. "Come on, now, stop. It's okay, everything's okay, Gib."

"How could he do that?" he asked, not looking at me.

A hundred tart comments ran through my mind, but I held them. "I don't know, honey," I answered. "Do you think you can tell me what happened?"

"You're going to get mad," he said.

"I already knew your father was having an affair," I said, choosing my words carefully.

"No, you're going to be mad at me," he said.

"Honey, none of this is your fault," I said, pulling his shoulder back so he had to turn toward me. He looked at me quickly but dropped his eyes again.

"I wasn't at Sean's," he said. "Not at first, anyway."

"Where were you?" I asked, bewildered.

"I was with Velvet," he said, and I suddenly had a mental image of Gib astride a horse, jumping oxers.

"Velvet?"

"My girlfriend—my ex-girlfriend. We broke up."

I wasn't sure what surprised me more: the fact that Gib had a girlfriend I'd never heard anything about, or that her name was actually Velvet. "Okay," I said slowly. "How long have you been with . . . Velvet?"

"Five, maybe six months."

I was stunned. "Six months? Gib, why didn't you ever tell me?"

He shrugged, and I could almost feel him pull away from me again, like a tide. I struggled to find the right note. "You cared about her? Obviously, you cared about her. I'm sorry. Are you all right?"

He shot me a glance as if trying to judge whether I was really interested or not, but then he nodded. "I guess. She cheated on me. With Sean."

My heart broke for my son. To break up with his first girlfriend—the first girlfriend that I knew about anyway—because she was cheating on him with his best friend . . . *cheating* on him? The lightbulb went off.

"So, you and Velvet were—intimate?" I asked. It had been a long time since I'd checked his wallet for that condom.

"Jeez, Mom," he said, avoiding my eyes.

"Well, you said cheating, so I assume you were, were—"

"Yeah, okay? Yeah."

"Did you use protect—"

"Yes, Mom."

"Don't cut me off. This is important. Especially if she wasn't faithful. Protection isn't just about preventing pregnancy."

"Mom," he pleaded. "Please, I know. I used a condom, every time, every single time, okay?"

I was mortified and mollified all at the same time. "Okay. And, you know, if you have any questions—"

"Mom."

"Okay. So, you broke up with this girl—"

"Velvet."

"Yes, you broke up with Velvet, and then you went to Sean's?"

"Yeah. I was going to kick his ass," he said, and I quailed.

I did not want to think about my son having sex. I did not want to think about him kicking anyone's ass either. He saw me flinch and muttered, "Sorry." For the *ass* part, I assumed.

"Anyway, she must have called to warn him and he wasn't there. So I figured I'd go home."

"And you've been driving my Saab," I said, just that second recalling it.

"Dad said I could," he said.

"It's fine," I said. "So you went home."

"And I came in and heard voices on the patio. So I go through the kitchen and there's this whole meal out on the counter. Lobster and champagne and stuff, and I figure you must have come home early, so I go out there and there's this . . . this . . . *slut* in the spa with Dad."

I didn't bother correcting his language this time. He looked at me, his eyes wide, as if confronted with the scene all over again.

"They were naked. In the *spa,* and she's on his lap, and I can totally see her tits and everything, and I don't even want to think about what the hell they're *doing*. It wasn't even dark yet!" He shuddered.

"Okay, I get the picture," I said. "Then what?"

He took another second; no doubt trying to separate his view of live, grown-up boobs in his spa from the fact that they belonged to the woman his father was having an affair with. I could practically see the therapy bills.

"Then he almost drowns her."

"Really?" I asked, close to an incredibly inappropriate giggle.

Gib, hearing the humor in my voice, warmed to his story. "He's flailing all around, trying to hide her, trying to get out, trying to get a towel. It was pathetic. And she's yelling *oh my God, oh my God, Luke, Luke*," he said, making his voice high and girlish.

Suddenly it wasn't amusing anymore. Gib dropped the voice.

"Anyway, he finally gets out, and she stays in there, holding her arms all crossed over her tits—like I'd want to see them—and he's holding his towel with one hand and reaching out like he wants to hug me or something," he said, making a disgusted noise deep in his throat. "And he's all, *now, son, don't worry*, like I'm an idiot or something. And I just got so pissed off, I hit him."

The punch line, so to speak, came so abruptly that it took me by surprise and I gasped. "You *hit* him?"

"Well, not very hard," he admitted. "I pulled it back at the last second and went low, so I got him on the shoulder. And knocked him into the pool."

Now I had to laugh, but Gib's expression sobered me.

"Don't be too hard on yourself," I said. "I'd have felt like doing it myself."

"Mom, how can you laugh about this? You guys are going to get divorced. Aren't you?" He looked at me accusingly.

"I don't see that we have much choice," I said quietly. "He says he's in love with her."

"You're shitting me," he said, his eyes wide. He got up, jamming his fists into his front pockets, and began pacing in front of the railing. "You're shitting me," he repeated. When I shook my head, his shoulders slumped. "What an asshole."

I couldn't have agreed with him more, but I didn't say anything.

"So, what happens now? Do you want me to talk to someone? I'll stand up in court and tell everyone what an asshole he is," he said.

"Stop saying that," I said. "In fact, stop swearing in general. It doesn't help, and I hate hearing it come out of your mouth. It's vulgar."

He fell onto the bench with his hands still stuffed in his pockets. "It's true, though."

"Maybe," I acknowledged.

He looked over my shoulder out at the water sullenly. "I won't go live with him," he said. I felt a surge of victory and just as quickly clamped it down.

"That's not something anyone has to decide right now."

"I already decided."

I sighed. "Come on, let's get you some dinner."

He allowed me to reheat his plate, and he ate the shrimp without comment while Tate, Estella, and Mother sat on the porch and watched the stars come out. We joined them quietly and listened to their conversation without joining in.

When Tate turned to leave he clapped his hand on Gib's shoulder and said, "I'm going fishing first thing in the morning. Want to come along?"

Gib slid his shoulder out from under Tate's hand and shook his head without saying anything. Tate took it well.

"Maybe another time," he said lightly, and then left, promising to stop by the next day to make sure Mother had settled in all right.

"So your mom tells me you need some help with algebra," Estella said to Gib after Tate had gone.

He shrugged. "It's stupid," he said. "Now I have to go to summer school to make it up."

"Maybe I can help," she offered, and I gave her a grateful smile.

"I have to go to summer school anyway," he said.

"Let's talk about this tomorrow," Mother said, getting up and tousling Gib's hair. "You need a haircut. I'll give you one tomorrow, and then we'll spend the day on the beach. Now come on, I'm exhausted. Time for bed."

Nobody protested, and I walked up the stairs to the library, crawled on the bed, and stared into the darkness of the empty mattress beside me.

Estella

Vanessa and I stretch to the sky, greeting the sun, and then swoop down to the sand, inhaling up, exhaling down. She continues into downward dog before moving into her tai chi routine, and I take off for the Gulf, slipping in with a shiver, allowing the chill to motivate me to get moving.

I breaststroke in the trough down to the dome-shaped house, then turn and begin my crawl, and within minutes my mind is blank but for my breathing. I occasionally catch glimpses of Vanessa, and then I see Connie take up her spot with her coffee cup in front of the dunes, and soon she is joined by Mother.

On my next pass, I see Gib coming down the boardwalk, and by the time I have turned and am heading south again he is in the water, stroking beside me, gliding as effortlessly as a ray. I flip in front of the dome house again, sticking to my routine, and he turns with me, and we are in tandem again.

He pulls slightly away from me, and I pull harder, catching up. He pulls away again, and now I understand that he is playing with me. I have no hope of beating him, and so I play too. I flip once more, long before I usually do, and head west toward the horizon.

The depth of the trough abruptly turns to shallow sandbar and I am ready for it, but he is not and he explodes out of the water, spluttering, staggering to his feet. I am standing in water that only comes up to my knees and laughing at him as he looks around in bewilderment.

He spots me and grins. I recognize that look in his eyes, but before I can dive off the sandbar he grabs me and flings me over his shoulder.

"Stop, stop!" I yell, pounding his back to no avail.

He bumps me along, sloughing through the water as though it doesn't push back. He screams a primordial boy scream and dives with me off the far edge of the sandbar, where the water is black and the currents run fast. I am plunged deep and come up gasping for air but laughing still, turning quick circles in the water to spot him. He doesn't come up.

I turn once more and see Connie on the beach. She is at the edge of the water, holding a hand over her eyes and squinting into the water.

Oh, shit.

I turn again, willing Gib to come up, and just as I am ready to panic, something grabs my ankles and I am pulled under again, with no notice and no time for a gulp of air. I struggle, kicking, and connect with something hard, and then we both come up, gasping for oxygen. I am no longer laughing; not only is Gib not laughing, he is clutching his nose with both hands and blood is pouring out from underneath them.

I struggle toward him, more afraid of Connie than of sharks, and grab his arm. He lets go of his nose, and we stroke toward the sandbar. I stand and wave my arms over my head at Connie. Gib does the same, and she waves back, too far away to see the blood yet.

"Oh, Gib," I say. "Let me see."

He falls to his knees on the sandbar and I inspect him, but soon he is blowing little snorts of laughter at my panicked face, and I start to giggle too.

"Stop now, your mom's going to kill me," I say.

"Uh-huh," he agrees, sounding like he has a sinus infection.

"We can't stop it out here," I say, "and she's not going anywhere. You ready?"

"I guess. Crap, she's going to make me stay in all day now."

"That's what you get for trying to drown me. For extra punishment I might make you do some math."

He groaned. "Do you swim every morning?"

"Yeth, I thwim ebry moanig," I say, making fun of him.

"Me too?"

"Yeah, okay, but no more funny stuff."

"Okay," he agrees, and we head back to the beach. As soon as Connie sees the blood she is on her feet and running, splashing into the water before we can emerge from it, Gib protesting that he's fine.

She shoots me a single murderous look and then hauls him up to the house. I fall to the sand beside Mother, who is chatting up Vanessa about rising real estate costs. Mother looks pleased and seems to have completely missed the little drama.

She finally stops talking, and sees me for the first time. "Oh, did you have a nice swim?"

I flop back on the dune, laughing—though it is not funny, not funny at all—while she looks on.

CHAPTER SEVENTEEN

I could hear Estella's laughter follow us up the boardwalk and my fury turned white-hot. I hustled Gib into the downstairs bathroom and got him seated on the edge of the tub.

"What the hell happened?" I asked, squeezing his nose with a towel.

"It wasn't her fault," he said, his answer muffled through the towel.

"Just stay out of the water, okay?"

"What? We're at the beach, how can I stay out of the water?"

I was shaking with anger at Estella. I'd seen plenty of bloody noses on Gib before, but to see them so far out in the water, struggling, and then to have him stagger out with blood streaming down his face, absolutely infuriated me.

"Stay out of the water when Estella's swimming, then," I said. "No argument."

He shook his head but didn't say anything. I was sure that under his closed lids he was rolling his eyes at me, but I didn't care. I gingerly pulled the towel away, watching for signs of blood. It seemed to have stopped.

"Go lie down on your bed," I instructed. "I'll come down to check on you in half an hour. If it hasn't started bleeding again you can get up."

He obviously wanted to protest, but he remained silent and went to his room. I rinsed the towel in cold water and left it in the sink to soak before I headed upstairs to find Estella. She and Mother were frying eggs for breakfast.

"What the hell were you thinking?" I demanded. They both turned around, Mother in surprise, Estella in resignation.

"Is he all right?" she asked.

"Connie!" Mother admonished me. "It certainly wasn't anyone's fault."

I ignored Mother. "Gib has enough problems right now. I don't need you encouraging him to go out farther than he should and fooling around. One of you could have been seriously hurt."

Estella nodded, not meeting my eyes. "Absolutely," she said. "I'm really sorry, Connie."

"Don't patronize me, Estella."

She held her hands up in front of her. "I'm not. I'm sorry. It really was an accident, and I'll make sure that Gib is well away from me while I'm swimming."

She was saying exactly what I wanted to hear, but something wasn't sitting right with me. I braced my hands on the counter and took a deep breath, trying to slow my heart.

"Okay?" Estella asked. Mother watched in perplexed silence while the eggs burned.

"Connie? Are you okay?" Estella asked again.

"Yeah," I said. "I'm fine. I—" I stopped because I didn't know what I was. I just knew that I didn't want Estella anywhere near my child.

"Connie?" Mother asked.

"I'm fine," I finally said.

Mother nodded, but she was looking at me in that piercing way she had. I turned away and headed for the living room. "Do you want these records, Mother?" I asked, beginning to pull the albums out. It was time to get back to work on the house. We'd been acting like this was a vacation, a family reunion. It was no such thing. I was there by necessity, as was everyone else, and it was time we remembered that.

"No, I don't think so. Are you sure one of the boys won't want them?" she asked while Estella tossed the burned eggs and started fresh ones.

"If the boys need anything I'll get it for them," I said.

While everyone ate breakfast I gathered more boxes from downstairs and began taping them together in the living room. Gib left for the beach, and Mother and Estella went grocery shopping while I divided the second floor items into trash, charity, and possible keepers. Everyone seemed unnerved by my sudden burst of energy. If *I* could have gotten away from me, I would have too. But eventually the work soothed me, a salve on my frazzled and uncertain nerves. My heart didn't even jump when the phone rang.

"Hello," I said absently, wiping sweat off my brow.

"Connie? It's Bob. I've got Angela DeSantis on the line with me. She'll be handling the divorce. Angela?"

"Hello, Connie," she said. She sounded young. "Please call me Angie. I'm sorry we're not able to meet in person just yet. Bob has brought me up to speed, and I have all of your paperwork here in front of me. Is now a good time to discuss a few things?"

Bob must have sensed my hesitation because he didn't wait for me to answer. "Connie, I want you to know you're in good hands here. Angie is the best divorce lawyer in southwest Florida. She'll be keeping me posted on every aspect of the case, and you can always call me if you can't get ahold of her."

For the first time since I'd known Bob he was in business mode, and I had to admit that it was impressive. "All right," I finally said.

"Take good care of her, Angie," Bob said. "Connie, tell your mother I miss her." And then he hung up, leaving me to his colleague.

"So, Connie, tell me about you and Luke."

Telling her about me and Luke, and Luke and Deanna, and Gib and Carson, took longer than I expected. Estella and Mother returned and put groceries away while I talked, occasionally ranted, and once, to my humiliation, cried. Luckily, Gib remained on the beach. When I finally finished the phone call, I was exhausted.

Mother and Estella hovered near, pretending to rifle through the boxes I'd filled, but in reality they were simply waiting, like nurses, to see what I might need next. What I needed was to be left alone.

"I think I'm going to go for a walk," I said.

They both nodded, and I noted with amusement that they had the same tilt to their head, the same pointed chin bounced up and down at the same tempo. I wished I had a camera to capture it and then show them how alike they really were. They were more sisters than Estella and I. They seemed a pair, and in their twin show of understanding, they made me feel even more alone.

I walked toward the cut, scattering sandpipers and crunching through patches of coquinas. The tide had pulled back, revealing rills of sand that kept small pools of water on the beach, some shallow enough to qualify only for puddle status; some calf deep, trapping confused pinfish.

Once past the small cluster of houses on the north end of the island, the cut came into view. Two men fished in the surf. Not wishing to exchange pleasantries, I nearly turned around.

But as I drew closer, I saw that it was Gib and Tate. Both were reeling in, but only Gib's rod was bent with the weight of a fish. I quickened my steps in time to see him pull a stingray from the water as Tate secured his pole in a length of PVC pipe stuck in the sand.

"Mom, look," Gib shouted as I came upon them. The stingray, light tan with gray eyes set close together on top of its head, such as it was, fluttered its wings against the beach and lifted its tail in the air, its barb searching.

"Okay, watch it now," Tate said. He held the tail down carefully and maneuvered the stingray over, letting his tail go at the last second and then holding it down again once the ray was on its back. The underside of the ray was a soft, vulnerable white, with a tiny mouth locked in an almost comical smile. Tate used small pliers to release the hook and then, careful of the tail, he carried it to the surf and let it go. It disappeared before our eyes.

"It seemed kind of small for how much it fought," Gib said, his face already bright red from the sun.

"They're strong," Tate agreed. "They head down, where a fish will head out, so it feels like there's more pressure on the rod. How's it going, Connie?"

"Were you looking for me?" Gib asked.

I shook my head. "No, honey, you're fine. I'm glad you're having fun. No, I was just taking a break from packing. How'd you two meet up?"

Gib shrugged. "I was just out looking around. He had another pole so I thought I'd try it."

"Looks like you liked it," I said.

"I caught a lot more than that. Look," Gib said, his eyes shining as he pointed to a small cooler. Tate opened the top and I could see several pompano nestled in ice. "Tate says he'll show me how to clean them, and then we can roast them in palm fronds on the beach."

"Sure," I said, shooting Tate a grateful smile. Gib was excited in a way I hadn't seen in years. Luke had taught Gib how to play sports, but they were the sports of suburbia, not survival. The house had been filled with basketballs, footballs, hockey sticks, golf clubs, baseball bats, and soccer balls. They were initially plush, brightly colored toys, but had evolved into the dirty real thing. They took up room in all the closets, bounced out of the garage and into the street, and smelled of leather, sweat, dirt, and boy.

Fishing, shooting, hunting of any kind had never entered the play realm. Gib's skills enabled him to fit in to the society of businessmen, weekend warriors, and the hierarchy of high school, while Tate's skills were, or had been at one time, essential to live in a harsh environment.

It had never crossed my mind that Gib might be missing out on anything. But if he enjoyed learning this side of life, I certainly wasn't going to stand in his way.

"Got another pole?" I asked, to Gib's surprise.

"No, but I'm ready for a beer," Tate said. "You can use mine."

Gib reached into the bait bucket and held a live shrimp up as I pulled Tate's pole out of the pipe. "Okay, Mom, here, I'll show you."

Tate popped the top of his beer and laughed out loud. "Son, your mom could show you a thing or two about fishing. Don't insult her or you'll get a hook somewhere unpleasant."

"Really?" Gib asked, not entirely convinced.

I rolled my eyes at Tate and stuck my hand in the bait bucket, pulling out a shrimp and threading it expertly onto the hook. It was a good thing I'd gotten some practice casting the other day on Little Dune, because my arm remembered the motion easily, and I made a graceful first cast, getting the lead out to the trough with an impressive whine of the reel.

"No way," Gib said, looking at me with his mouth hanging open.

"Way," I said, enjoying the feel of being something more than the woman who made sure his clothes were clean. "Go on," I said, bringing my line in a little. "Bait up, boy, let's see who catches the first fish."

Gib was quick to take the challenge and busied himself with the hook and shrimp. His cast fell just beyond the trough, landing on the sand bar, but he pulled it back quickly enough and wound up in the right spot. We walked slowly, allowing the current to take us, playing the line, reeling in; and then a fish hit his shrimp, his pole snapped down and he brought his wrist up quickly, hooking in.

Almost immediately I got a hit too, and I snapped up. We reeled and played out, watching each other out of the corners of our eyes, but I was more experienced and got my pompano up first, swinging it close and netting it with the little hand net Tate had been waiting behind us with.

I secured the pole and held the net up, crowing in victory as Gib pulled his catch in. Another pompano, but Tate took a quick look at it and declared it too small to keep. Gib watched and moved his hands in tandem with mine as we unhooked the fish. Mine went into the cooler, Gib's went back into the Gulf.

I quickly rebaited, and we fished the rest of the afternoon, occasionally allowing Tate a turn. By the time the sun began to lose its strength, I was wiped out. The three of us trudged home, Tate and Gib carrying the full cooler between them and me carrying the poles and bait bucket. Estella and Mother called to us from the widow's walk, and we waved back, spying Vanessa with them.

I started up the boardwalk, but Tate held Gib back.

"We're not even close to being done," Tate said. "We need to dig the pit, we need good, dry driftwood . . ."

I continued up to the house, allowing Tate's instructions to fade away, chuckling to myself as I remembered the work involved in cooking on the beach. Gib had no idea what he was getting himself into, and Tate was a no-nonsense taskmaster.

I washed up and joined everyone on the widow's walk. Estella and Mother searched my face, but I had nothing to hide. I was sun-tight and tired. I invited Vanessa for a dinner of roasted pompano, which she happily agreed to.

"Carson's camp called," Mother said, and my great mood disappeared.

"I can't believe I missed him," I wailed. "Damn, did he say I could call back?"

"Carson didn't call," she said. "The camp director did. He wouldn't tell me what it was about, just that Carson was fine and he needed to speak to you. The number's on the pad by the phone."

I hurried downstairs and called the camp. I wasn't particularly worried, since Carson was okay, but I was nervous. I wasn't ready to start the fight over my son that I knew was going to begin when people in charge, people like Dr. Pretus, decided that he might be a genius. I said a little prayer that Carson hadn't done anything brilliant.

I identified myself to the man who answered the phone, and poured myself a glass of wine while I waited on hold. Finally, the director picked up.

"Mrs. Wilder, thank you for getting back to me so quickly. Carson is fine, but I'm afraid I have some bad news."

"Okay," I said, confused.

"We had a little fire last night—"

"Oh my God," I said, forgetting my wine. "Carson's all right?"

"Yes, he's fine. Unfortunately, he and two other boys were the ones who started it. I'm afraid I have no choice but to ask that you pick Carson up immediately. We can't allow him to complete his time here. Please understand, we're not pressing charges. We feel that it was accidental. The boys seem very contrite, but I'm sure you understand that we do have to take this measure."

"Carson? Carson started a fire?" I could not accept it. Not from Carson. From Gib perhaps, but Carson? "How? What other boys?"

"Two boys in his cabin. The three of them have become quite close, something of a Three Musketeers. You know how boys are. They were playing with fireworks one of the boys brought from home, and unfortunately one got lodged in the shakes of their roof. There's minimal damage, but had they not immediately notified someone we could have had a terrible tragedy."

I sat down heavily on the barstool behind me, shaking my head, speechless for a moment.

"Mrs. Wilder?"

"Yes, yes, I'm here. The other boys, are they being sent home too?"

"Of course. Rick has already been picked up and Pat's parents will be arriving tomorrow. We're not placing sole blame on Carson, we're trying to be as fair as possible. And Mrs. Wilder? For what it's worth, I am sorry to see Carson go. He's a very talented young man. Aside from this incident, he's been a joy, and I think he's benefited from being here."

"Thank you."

"When can we expect you?" he asked.

"I suppose I'll come tomorrow," I said, thinking hard.

"We'll have Carson ready for you. Just come to my office."

"I'd like to speak with him now if he's there," I said.

"May I suggest that you wait until tomorrow? He's rather upset and obviously worried about your reaction. I believe he's hiding out in the boys' room right now."

Now that sounded like Carson. I suddenly felt sorry for him. "Okay," I said. "Please tell him that Mom said everything is going to be all right. I'll be there by noon to pick him up."

I hung up the phone and took a swallow of wine. For the first time since my early twenties, I didn't know whether I should call Luke or not. I supposed I should start getting used to making these calls, informing Luke of our children's misdeeds and achievements by phone. I finally dialed his work number.

His secretary, sounding hushed and reverent, told me that he wasn't in and she didn't expect him back. I would have to get used to that too. Being the ex-wife. I dialed home next. I didn't expect that Luke would be there, and I assumed I would be leaving a message on the machine. I assumed wrong.

A woman answered the phone.

"Deanna?" I said in shock. There was a brief silence at the other end, and then she hung up. I pulled the receiver away from my ear and looked at it in disbelief. I quickly redialed. The phone rang until the machine picked up.

"Luke, this is your wife. Your son, Carson, has been expelled from camp. I'll be picking him up tomorrow. I suggest that you and Deanna find somewhere else to go. That is my house, I paid for it, and I expect you both out *immediately*."

I hung up, shaking, furious beyond measure. I suddenly thought of a thousand biting comments I could have made, a thousand threats and promises I could have left on the machine. I picked apart my five measly sentences and found them weak and pathetic.

I heard my mother laughing up on the widow's walk. I looked out the sliders and saw Tate and Gib happily digging a pit in the sand. My own house in Verona had been taken over; only this middle ground was mine, and it was filled with boxes and soon to be sold.

The pompano was probably delicious, but I could barely taste it. Everyone was having a good time, and I tried to pretend I was too. Vanessa went home soon after dinner, sensing that things were off. Once she was out of earshot Mother asked me about my call to the camp.

I downplayed Carson's expulsion and glossed over the fact that he'd actually started a fire. Carson didn't need Gib teasing him about it—the unfortunate *Carson* and *arson* rhyme was already going through my own head—and I didn't want Mother giving me advice about appropriate punishments either. Carson was going to feel punished enough on the way home when I broke the news to him that his parents were splitting up.

"I'll go get him," Gib offered. "It's only a few hours away."

"Absolutely not," I said.

"Why not? I drove Gram all the way up here and was fine," he argued.

"He drove very well," Mother agreed, and I gave her a warning look.

"For one thing, you never asked me if you could drive my car, and I would have said no if you had. For another, a parent has to pick him up, and since I can't get ahold of your father—"

"Would you stop calling him that?" Gib said, unmasked anger in his voice.

"No. He is your father, he will remain your father, and he's Carson's father too, no matter what my relationship with him is," I said, raising my voice. Tate and Estella edged away from the fire and I turned on them.

"Look, you both know exactly what's happening, so stop dancing away every time it's brought up." They stared at me in surprised silence, and I continued with Gib. "I know you're angry and upset, but I'm going to have to tell Carson about your father and me. He's much younger than you, and you need to be careful of what you say to him. There's no need to discuss what happened; he doesn't need to know any details. Understood?"

"I'm not stupid, Mom," he said, his face flushing crimson.

"Well, I know you're not stupid, Gib, but you're not always particularly kind to your little brother. He's going to be going through a hard time too, so maybe you could actually act glad to see him tomorrow?"

Gib rolled his eyes.

"I could go with you if you wanted some—" Estella began hesitantly, but I cut her off.

"Could you just try to keep Gib out of trouble? I don't want him to go in swimming too deep without me here."

I knew it was a cheap shot and Estella looked as if someone had hit her. I knew that Gib's bloody nose had been an accident, but the thought of them both in the water together without me there filled me with dread. I didn't want to explore it, I didn't want to work through it, I just wanted them to follow my wishes.

"He'll be fine," she finally said evenly. I gave her a curt nod and then marched past my disapproving mother and an embarrassed Tate and went straight up to the library. Luke never called me back, and I left a message for Angie about Deanna being in the house and asked her to call on my cell phone before noon so that I didn't have to talk with Carson in the car. I spent a fitful night tossing and turning on the mattress in the library.

I left before anyone rose in the morning and was on the interstate by seven.

Estella

I creep up the stairs to the library just after seven. I want to tell Connie about my decision before she leaves so that she can feel more comfortable on her way back, knowing that I won't be here. I've left everything too late. We all have.

I will leave the books. I will ask Mother to drive me into town. I will rent a car. I will drive back to Atlanta. I have it all planned.

It is Tuesday, so Paul will be turning new pieces. I will shoo the girls out for the night, give them money if I have to. I will prepare a surprise dinner, will wear the long black dress he likes though it is still too big on me, and will greet Paul at the door with a glass of wine. I've seen the look on his face in my mind and it makes me feel like myself again.

I am desperate to be me again.

I knock lightly. There's no answer. I crack the door just a bit, just a little more . . . she's not there. I can't believe that she left so early, but when I check beneath the house, the Escalade is gone.

I wanted to talk to her in person.

I will write her a note. It will be easier on both of us. Relieved, I wave good morning to Vanessa stretching in front of her dune, and plunge into the Gulf. Within a few moments, Gib is beside me. There is no horseplay this time. He turns when I do, changes his tempo when I do, and hauls himself out of the water when I do.

"Your mom doesn't want you swimming with me," I remind him as I ease myself down onto the sand to catch my breath.

"She's already gone," he says with a shrug, barely winded.

"Still," I say. "You should do what she wants right now. She's going through a hard time."

He blows water off his lips in lieu of an answer, and it is eloquent enough.

"Tell me about algebra," I say, searching for firmer ground.

"It's stupid," he says, and then follows with the age-old argument: "Besides, when am I ever going to use that stuff?"

I know by now that there is no answer that will satisfy him, except, "You have to pass it to graduate."

"Whatever."

I draw a simple equation in the sand. He looks down and runs his foot through it. I laugh and he grins at me. I draw another one. He studies it for a moment, and then hesitantly says, "X equals four, right?"

"That's right. See? That wasn't so hard."

"Those aren't the kind of problems on my tests," he says, kicking sand across the equation.

"I know," I say. "But if you can do that, I guarantee that I can show you how to solve the problems on your tests."

"What, is there a trick or something?"

"Well, maybe not a trick, but just a way of understanding. I think you might be making it a little harder than it is. If you break it down, algebra can be as easy as that equation was."

"No way. My teacher tried all kinds of ways to get me to figure it out."

"Maybe you could give me a chance? Come on. We don't even have to leave the beach."

He turns his head over his shoulder and squints up at the house. I have no idea what he's thinking, but I take a stab at it.

"Your mom won't be back until late this afternoon," I say, the prospect of playing with numbers with this child making me forget all about my plans to leave. He looks back at me and licks the salt water from his lips. "If you really don't think you understand more by lunch I'll never say another word," I say.

"Yeah, all right," he says, and I feel a surge of triumph. It feels like teaching again.

We begin.

CHAPTER EIGHTEEN

When I finally arrived at Camp Scherzando I had managed to compose myself into a concerned mother again. I wanted to be stern, wanted Carson to understand the severity of his actions and how disappointed I was in him. But as I got out of the car I heard him yell, "Mom," and my heart leapt.

He came pounding down the stairs of the office building, and I scooped him against me as though it had been years. His little body— thinner than I remembered, I could feel his backbone—was like a security blanket in my arms. I inhaled the scent of him. *My boy.*

I realized I had lifted him up and he was struggling to stay on his toes, and I released him. He turned his face up to mine and it pained me to see that he was trying hard not to cry. I rubbed my hand over the top of his head.

"Hey, it's going to be all right," I said, and he nodded, pushing the backs of his fists against his eyes.

"Mrs. Wilder, I'm Marshall Black, the camp director."

I hadn't even noticed the man waiting behind Carson until he stuck his hand out and introduced himself. He had Carson's bags and clarinet case ready and helped us load them before he said good-bye to Carson.

"I'm sorry to see you go, Carson."

Carson hung his head.

"No more fireworks, right?"

"Yes, sir. I mean, no, sir."

"Okay then, hop in, buckle up." He closed the car door for Carson and then came around to the driver's side. "Mrs. Wilder, I'm sorry about all this. I had hoped to speak with you during the parents' weekend. I feel you should know that Dan Hailey sent me an e-mail regarding Carson a few weeks ago."

"He did? That's interesting. He failed to mention it to me," I said, taking a deep breath. I knew I should have taken Carson to Big Dune. I railed at myself inside. And Dan Hailey was going to be sorry he hadn't listened to me.

"Yes, and then a week ago he e-mailed me again and told me about your meeting. I can assure you, he was very respectful of your wishes. And I have been also. I've kept Carson and his instructors focused on his playing, but it hasn't been easy. He can't help himself—I've had two instructors approach me with pieces he's written. He's very gifted, Mrs. Wilder."

"Where are they?" I asked.

"The pieces? I made sure they were returned to Carson. They should be with his other music. I would like to give you my e-mail address, and perhaps when you've had a chance to consider Carson's options—"

"Carson's options are none of your concern." I ignored the business card he held out. He nodded, but kept the card stretched toward me.

"I do understand," he said, his voice patient and formal. "I was in a similar situation myself as a child. Perhaps you might do a bit of research; there is plenty of information about me online. Part of the reason I run this camp is not to find children like Carson, but to make sure that when I do find them, they're protected. I'll be happy to send you copies of the e-mail exchange I had with Dan so that you're comfortable that no boundaries have been crossed. Please, take the card."

I tucked it in my pocket without looking at it. "I'll give it some thought," I said, though I had no intention of ever getting in touch with him. I climbed into the Escalade without another word and he held the door for me, tilting his head around me to smile at Carson.

"Take it easy, Carson. Be good on the ride home," he said.

" 'Bye," Carson said, waving as I pulled the door out of Marshall Black's hand and thumped it closed.

As we drove away Carson looked out the window, following a formation of drummers on one of the fields and waving to a group of horn players setting up on a small outdoor stage. They didn't see him and he finally let his hand drop.

"You liked this place, didn't you?" I asked.

"Yeah, it was really cool," he said, slumping in his seat. "Maybe I could come next summer? I'd be really good. I'm really sorry, Mom."

I looked over at him, so small in the Escalade, and wondered how he would feel next summer. He was in for a difficult year. I could keep him sheltered from the adults who wanted to use him, but I couldn't protect him from the fallout of his own parents divorcing. "I know, buddy," I said. "I think you've been punished enough. But you have to remember that you can't just go along with your friends if they're doing something dangerous. People could have been hurt, even killed. Do you understand how serious this was?"

He nodded, his eyes wide. "Did you tell Dad?"

"I did," I said carefully, taking a deep breath as we turned onto the interstate. "Sweetie, we need to talk about your dad. Things are going to be a little different when we get home."

"How?" he asked.

"Well, your daddy and I haven't been very happy with each other—" I began, and then stopped. I couldn't believe I was saying these things. I wanted to know when each step was going to stop being so painful. It wasn't something my lawyer could answer for me.

"Mommy?" Carson asked, his voice wavering.

"Oh, honey," I said, my voice shaking too. Gib's anger had been better than this.

"We're getting divorced?" he asked.

"It looks that way, Car," I said. I pulled into the slow lane so that I could concentrate more fully on Carson, could say all the lame things that parents said when they ripped their children's lives apart, about how it didn't mean that we didn't love him and his brother, about how it wasn't his fault, that sometimes mommies and daddies just couldn't live together anymore.

It made me feel sick, and it made Carson feel sick too. It made him feel so sick, that just as I was explaining how when we got home his father wouldn't be living at the house anymore, he suddenly, violently, vomited against the dash. I swerved and narrowly missed hitting a small sedan in front of us. Horns blared behind me as I jammed on the brakes, and a car whipped around me, passengers holding their middle fingers against the windows.

"Baby!" I cried, trying to watch the road, looking for an exit, while my son vomited again. The smell of it filled the car, and I rolled the windows down and then reached for napkins in the console. I handed them to Carson while he sobbed and dry-heaved as I took the exit ramp and pulled into a McDonald's parking lot.

I jumped out of the car and ran around to the passenger side, swallowing down my own reaction to the smell. Carson was already stumbling out, still crying and trying to apologize through his heaving. I picked him up like a toddler and took him to a grassy area next to the restaurant and held him until it stopped, whispering and crooning empty reassurances.

When he finally calmed down, I peeled his shirt off of him, turned it inside out, and tried to clean him up as best I could. I stuffed the shirt in a garbage can, then rummaged through his bags and found a T-shirt he could wear. I also pulled out one of Gib's old T-shirts that Carson used to sleep in, and ducked inside the Escalade to change my own foul-smelling shirt. Then we went into the restaurant, and I took him into the women's restroom with me, ignoring the disapproving stares.

I whispered to him as I cleaned him with wet, rough, brown paper towels, my arms and hands shaking. He had stopped sniffling and remained silent, merely closing his eyes when I rubbed his face, and hanging his head when I wiped his arms down. Once I installed him in a booth and got him a small soda, I went to the parking lot to deal with the Escalade.

The dash cleaned easily, and now that Carson was out of sight, I sobbed and cursed Luke as I scrubbed it, dropping the soiled paper towels onto the soaked floor mat. Once every surface was clean, I rolled up the floor mat and stuffed that into the garbage can too. I left all the windows down, hoping nobody would bother stealing Carson's bags and clarinet.

We sat in the booth for over an hour, splitting french fries when he felt up to it, then graduating to a burger. I talked, he mostly listened. I again explained all about us loving him, and watched carefully for another episode. I wondered if this was what was happening when the camp director told me he was hiding in the boys' room.

He assured me that he was okay, and we hit the road again. I tried to go slowly, tried to avoid bumps and sharp curves, and Carson finally fell asleep, his head wedged between the seat and the door. He woke about an hour before the bridge, and I told him stories about the island, about the pirate treasure, how Tate and Gib would take him fishing and show him the lighthouse.

He started to perk up a bit, and I continued, adding on swimming and watching dolphins and staying up late to watch the stars come out up on the widow's walk. I lied and told him that Gib and Mother had come up hoping that he would be able to join us, and that he could eat as many shrimp as he wanted.

By the time we arrived at the house, I had painted a rosy picture of a happy family waiting to cater to his every whim. The empty house made his smile waver, but when I opened the back door leading to the boardwalk, I saw the entire group on the beach and told him they were waiting for him. I walked behind him as he ran down the boardwalk. To their credit, as soon as everyone saw him they rushed to meet him.

He flung himself off the stairs and into Mother's arms, and from there to Estella, with whom he wasn't a bit shy. After Tate solemnly shook his hand, Gib hoisted him over his shoulder and marched him into the Gulf, shoes and all. Mother hugged me when I finally reached the beach, and I sat down on the steps to watch the boys play.

"How did he take it?" she asked.

"Not very well," I admitted. "He threw up in the car. We hung out in McDonald's until he calmed down."

Mother cast a worried glance Carson's way. I was glad to see that Gib was keeping him in the shallow water, and Tate and Estella were standing at the edge of the surf, watching them and shouting encouragement as they mock wrestled.

"I don't think he should be carrying on like that if he's sick," she said.

I sighed. "He's okay. I'm just happy to see Gib being nice to him for now. It'll end soon enough."

"I never understood why the two of them couldn't be better friends," she said. "Like you two."

I looked at Estella, clapping her hands and laughing at my sons in the water. "Mother, Estella and I weren't friends," I said.

"Of course you were," she said. "Don't be ridiculous."

"I don't know how you can say that!" I exclaimed. "You had to have realized how different we were. And you and Daddy sure didn't do much to help."

"What are you talking about, Constance? You girls were practically inseparable. You went through some periods like all siblings do—"

I laughed in disbelief. "Mother, I barely saw Estella after Daddy took her over. He made her into a freak—"

"Don't you dare speak of your father that way," she snapped at me. "I won't have it. He loved you both. He only wanted what was best for you girls, and he tried to steer you in the ways he thought you were naturally inclined. He did everything he could to see that Estella had people around her who could help develop her gifts."

"Oh, she got developed all right," I said, tempted to spill what I knew about Pretus. "And what did he steer me toward, Mother? Besides you."

"And I was so horrible?" she asked, her voice turning cold. "I made sure you had lessons, I made sure you had a good violin. You never once indicated that you were interested in anything else. The only one who stopped you from reaching your full potential was you, Connie. Feeling sorry for yourself again?"

"No, Mother, I just wish that once in a while you could . . . Oh, forget it." I stood and fled up the boardwalk.

She followed me, and I quickened my steps. But she quickened hers too, placing her feet just as emphatically as I placed mine. I broke into a jog; in a moment the absurdity of it hit me and I burst into laughter as she ran after me and caught me just before the door, throwing her arms around my neck as though to wrestle me to the ground.

She was laughing as I wriggled out of her grasp, catching my breath. It had been a long time since my mother had been so physical with me, and I suddenly remembered how she used to get down on the floor with me, especially after Estella was no longer my playmate. Her eyes now, as then, were full of playfulness, and I felt a rush of love for her.

"I'm sorry, Mom," I said. "You were great to be with. Thank you."

"Well, that's more like it," she said with a grin. "Now, shall we make this group some dinner, or will Tate and Gib go bring down a wild beach cow for us with their bare hands?"

"I think we can manage tonight," I said.

We worked in the kitchen together, making a pot of gumbo, listening to an old Aretha Franklin record, and good-naturedly getting in each other's way. The clatter from the boardwalk announced that the entire sun-weary group was coming in. The combination of laughing boys, bubbling gumbo, and Aretha was heady music, one I wished I could record and play when I was—as Mother so correctly, albeit cruelly, pointed out—feeling sorry for myself.

They stomped up the stairs, minus Estella, and I heard the rumble of a shower coming on downstairs. Tate, Gib, and Carson collapsed into chairs on the patio, talking like old friends. Tate was telling them about his pirate treasure theory, and Carson was rapt, wide-eyed and worshipful. I couldn't help but notice the contrast between his interaction with Tate and with his own father. I knew it wasn't fair, but I wasn't feeling very fair-minded at that moment.

Gib left them on the porch and began to flip through the box of albums. The few times we'd come to Big Dune for vacation neither of the boys had been interested in anything in the house. They were disappointed that they couldn't get to the widow's walk, and the library had been off-limits. They never touched the albums, preferring the CDs they'd brought from home. There were no fishing rods stored at the house—Luke wouldn't have known how to teach the boys to use them if there had been, and Gib in particular would never have been patient enough to learn from me.

In short, they'd been bored. And bored boys fight, and whine, and make life miserable for each other and everyone in their orbit. Luke had been as bored as the boys after the first couple of days of sunning on the beach. It was no wonder we'd stopped vacationing on Big Dune.

But the new shape of us, the crisis of their parents' marital problems, seemed to open the boys up, or maybe it was simply that they were older. It made me think, for the first time, that maybe I, we, could have a life without Luke. My hopefulness, hard on the heels of my self-pity, was a welcome relief, and I even felt my nebulous anger at Estella waning again.

"What's this?" Gib asked, holding up an old Embers album.

"Oh, put that on," Estella said, just reaching the top of the stairs as Gib asked. Her hair was still wet and lay in waves against her head. She looked toward the kitchen, sniffing appreciably, and caught my eye. I smiled at her, and she smiled back, her eyes widening in surprise. "Remember that one?" she asked me as she came in and lifted the lid to peer in at the gumbo.

I handed her a spoon. "Sure," I said with a grin. We'd listened to that record over and over again. It was the one Mother had taught us to dance to, and when we danced at night in the music room we'd whispered the lyrics under our breath until we were exhausted.

The first song came on, and Mother grabbed Gib by the hand, trying to get him to do the shag with her. Gib blushed and pulled his hand from hers, but she grabbed him again and slowly showed him the steps. Estella brought a spoonful of the gumbo up to her lips and gave a groan of pleasure as she sipped the spicy broth. Her hair stuck up a bit in back, and when I reached out to smooth it down she pulled away from my hand so quickly that she spilled the hot soup down her chin and gasped.

I pulled my hand back and gave her a napkin, my irritation flooding back as quickly as it had receded. I couldn't do anything right with her. Carson bounded in from the patio, Tate following, and they stood in line behind Estella, waiting for tastes, as Gib tried to escape Mother's undulating arms and snapping fingers.

"Carson," she commanded. "Get in here and show your brother how it's done."

Carson took a quick sip of gumbo and scampered into the living room, always ready to dance, always ready for music, and I felt my spirits lift again. Estella caught my eye and smiled and I couldn't help myself; I smiled back. Gib sat heavily on the sofa, while Tate, Estella, and I watched from the kitchen as Mother and Carson danced.

Estella started to sing under her breath, and then she grabbed my hand and we fell into the old dance as though we'd never stopped. I pulled her out of the kitchen, dancing backward, our opposing hands clasped, and we joined Carson and Mother in the living room.

Mother cried, "Switch," and we traded partners, me with Carson, Estella with Mother. Within moments, Tate cut in and danced with Mother, and Estella somehow coaxed Gib up, moving slowly, modifying the steps for him. When the song finally ended, Gib escaped to the kitchen, Mother and Carson collapsed on the couch, and Tate and I continued to the next song, doing silly dances from the seventies, making Carson laugh uncontrollably while we did the bump and the hustle to the beach music.

Estella cut in, and she and I danced again, spinning expertly until we were breathless, just as we had been as children. I finally called it over, throwing my hands in the air in surrender and lying prone on the floor, panting. Estella lay next to me, giggling and catching her breath, her hair dried into a nimbus around her head.

"When's dinner?" Gib called from the kitchen, dipping his spoon in for another taste.

I hauled myself up until I was sitting and leaned against the shelves, making the album skip. "As soon as everyone is showered," I said.

"Where's he sleeping?" Gib asked, nodding his head toward Carson, who looked at me as though he might start panicking again.

"You guys are going to have to bunk in together," I said.

"Mom," they both protested in unison. I shrugged.

"Unless one of you wants to sleep with your grandmother," I said, laughing at the looks of horror that crossed Gib, Carson, and Mother's faces.

"I can always come upstairs with you," Estella offered.

"Yeah," Gib said immediately, "then I can have my room—I mean, I can—"

"Nice try, Gib," I said. "You're not going to kick your aunt out of her room."

"No, I don't mind," she said. "If you don't."

I looked at her carefully, and finally said, "Okay. Well, Gib, you have to move her stuff up for her then."

"Done," he said, throwing his spoon in the sink and running down the stairs, closely followed by Carson. I could hear them arguing with each other but ignored it, thankful that neither of them was throwing up, sinking into a depression, or flying into a rage at the moment. They made several trips up the stairs, still bickering, their arms loaded with Estella's clothes and bags.

"Nice to have your own personal slaves," Estella said, watching them. "Do they do windows?"

"Only when threatened," I said.

Tate put another stack of records on, and an hour later everyone was showered and gathered on the patio for gumbo and rice.

"Can we go fishing tomorrow?" Gib asked Tate, and Carson lit up.

"Yeah, can we go fishing tomorrow?" he parroted.

"Not you," Gib said, shooting Tate a conspiratorial glance.

Tate frowned at him. "Of course you can come, Carson," he said. "You ever fished before?"

Carson shook his head while Gib looked shocked at the betrayal. "I got stuff to do anyway," he said sullenly.

"Like what?" Tate asked. "Don't you want to show your brother how to catch bait?"

Gib looked thoughtful, obviously considering the use he could make of his little brother, and finally nodded his head. "Yeah, okay," he said, and Carson bounced happily in his seat. "But you can't get in the way," he warned him.

"I've got a few houses to check out, so I'll come by late afternoon," Tate said, helping himself to another biscuit and breaking it into his gumbo. Carson carefully copied him.

"Good," I said. "I need you boys in the morning. We have to load the car and drop some things off to be shipped back home tomorrow, and then we have to get started on the downstairs." They both groaned, and Mother put her hand on my arm.

"Why don't you let the boys have tomorrow for the beach?" she asked. "Estella and I will help you."

"Mother, if you want this house cleared out by next weekend we can't keep acting like we're on vacation," I protested.

"Well, I'm supposed to be on vacation," Gib said.

"No, you, young man, are supposed to be in summer school, and you"—I turned to Carson—"are supposed to be at camp. If we're going to get everything done, then I need some help."

"I'm already signed up for summer school for when we get home," Gib continued. "And besides, Aunt Estella's teaching me, so I can pass it, no problem."

Estella looked up in surprise from her gumbo. She'd been staying out of the little skirmish, steadily eating her gumbo and biscuits in silence. "Oh, I was just showing him some things," she said. "I hope that's okay?"

"Of course," I said immediately. "Yes, it's very generous of you. Is he—are you getting it?" I asked Gib.

He shrugged. "The stuff she showed me I get," he said. "She explains it different."

Estella looked embarrassed.

"Well, thank you, Estella. All right then, Carson and Mother, you're my crew until we get this done."

There was an assortment of grins and groans, but I ignored them all, and when the phone rang I jumped to catch it. "Hello?"

"I'm sunk," Alexander said. "Nobody can do it."

"Oh, Alexander, I'm so sorry," I said. "What will you do?"

"I guess I'll have to cancel the performance, tell the manager, and rely on my audition."

"You'll get it, I know you will." I believed it, but I could tell that Alexander was sinking into one of his depressions. "Alex, it's going to be fine."

"It's not," he said. "It's not, and it's never going to be again."

"Come on," I said, losing a little patience. "It's just a performance. We've always been there, always done well; they're not going to cancel everything else and your audition is going to go well as long as you're prepared."

"Couldn't you—well, couldn't you maybe come home? Just for the night? Please, Connie, I can't . . ." He trailed off without specifying what he couldn't do.

"I have too much to do," I protested. "And now the kids are here—"

"June can watch them," he pleaded. "And besides, don't you want to check up on your house?"

"You're a big manipulator," I scolded him, but as I considered it I realized it wasn't impossible. I'd already made my case that we needed to get the house finished. I could stuff the Escalade and wouldn't have to ship as much and—yes, I could check on my house, could even have the locks changed.

"Let me think about it," I said.

"I have to call the board," he said, wheedling, whining.

"I'll call you in the morning," I said firmly. "Now, don't you even want to know about me?"

"I know. I'm scum. I'm incredibly insensitive. How are things?"

Aware of everybody on the patio, I lowered my voice and told him about having to pick up Carson and his reaction, how everyone wanted to play beach vacation instead of packing up the house, and how Angie had told me that Luke was resisting mediation. He made sympathetic noises, and by the time we got off the phone my self-pity had been mollified by his support.

"Mother?" I called out to the patio. "Could I talk to you for a minute?"

She encouraged me to go and promised that the boys would be fine, and my mind was made up. Feeling altruistic and motivated, I retrieved my violin from downstairs and brought it up, intending to practice in the library with the mute on so the sound wouldn't carry, but Carson was bringing his plate into the kitchen as I reached the second floor, and his eyes lit up at the sight of the case in my hand.

"Are you going to play?" he asked eagerly as Tate and Estella followed him in with their plates. They clamored for me to play too, and then Mother joined in, though Gib remained silent.

"Not tonight," I said. "I just need to practice. I'm going to run home Saturday, stay the night for the performance, and then I'll be back on Sunday." I half-expected the boys to insist on coming home too, but they merely nodded; Gib asked me to pick up his iPod. Carson was concentrating solely on my violin, tugging at the case as though he could get me to play if he could just show it to me, and I finally said, "We'd all love to hear you, Carson. Will you play for us?"

He ran downstairs for his clarinet. I made coffee while he got set up. Gib started to head to his room, but I gripped his arm and marched him to the couch, shoving a plate of cookies in his hand.

"Would you like to play something you learned at camp?" I prodded Carson, who was shifting through a stack of music. He ducked his head and pulled a few loose sheets of music out. We waited while he put the clarinet together, wetted and adjusted the reed three times, and briefly warmed up. Gib was getting restless, but I kept a death-grip on his arm.

Carson began slowly, sharp notes that quickly slurred into a softer, more advanced playing style. It was obvious that the short amount of time he'd spent at camp had done him good, and I waited patiently to recognize the piece he was playing. His face was red, and he was concentrating so heavily that his eyes appeared almost crossed from looking at his music down the length of the clarinet.

And then something magic happened: His eyes drifted shut, and suddenly the music lifted into a jazzy swing as he felt it. Everyone else felt it too. Gib went still beside me, and Mother and Estella were staring at Carson as if they'd never seen him before. I had to admit that I felt as though I were seeing him for the first time too.

My breath caught in my throat when I realized why I didn't recognize the piece. He was playing something he'd written himself. I glanced wildly around at everyone else, but nobody seemed to understand, until Estella looked directly at me and held my gaze. The piece was short, obviously unfinished, and he stopped abruptly, breaking the spell between me and Estella. He pulled the instrument from his mouth quickly, his eyes flying open to gauge our reaction.

Then Tate, thank God, stood and applauded, and everyone but me quickly followed suit. Estella nudged my knee with her leg and I stood rapidly, feeling light-headed. Carson let out the breath he'd been holding and grinned.

"See, that's what I was working on when I had to leave?" he said, making it a question. "The way it starts out, I didn't do that part real good, but I had already written the other part and it was easier when I closed my eyes, because I saw the music the way I wrote it, and then I had to stop. I mean it's not finished or anything." He trailed off, embarrassed by his outburst, but Mother rushed to hug him, and he beamed up at her.

"You wrote that? It was fabulous," she said. "Do you have more?"

"Yeah, but they're not really ready yet," he said.

"That's okay," she said. "Will you let us hear them when they are?" He nodded, and Mother turned to me with a look of wonder on her face. "Did you know this child was writing his own music?"

I nodded, my mouth suddenly too dry to speak. Estella pushed past me, making me sit back down on the sofa, and took Mother by the arm.

"Let's get this kitchen finished, Mother, and then we'll head up to the widow's walk."

I sat on the couch and watched while Carson packed his clarinet away. Tate left after promising to pick the boys up the next afternoon and giving me a quizzical glance, and Estella finally got me to move with a pointed look. We all trooped up to the widow's walk to look at the stars, a show of familial solidarity that relieved me.

I tucked Carson into bed in my old room, and his eyes closed the second his head touched the pillow. I smoothed his hair back from his forehead.

"When will I see Daddy again?" he asked without opening his eyes.

"Soon, sweetheart," I said, taken aback. "As soon as we finish up with the house. As soon as we get home, you'll see him. I know he misses you, and he can't wait to see you."

"Really?" he asked, opening his eyes a slit, checking for the truth on my face. I hoped it was there.

"Really. You know, you're going to be able to see your daddy just as much as you want to."

"Mark's dad never comes to see him."

"Well, Mark's dad is a jerk, and yours isn't," I said, hoping that it would turn out to be true. But it had not escaped me that Luke hadn't called to check on Carson. "We'll call him tomorrow, okay?"

"Okay," he said, closing his eyes again. He was asleep within a few moments, but I remained by his side, searching his face. Finally I rose, pulled the covers up over his arms, and softly closed the door. The light was on under Gib's door. I knocked.

"Yeah, come in," he said. He was lying on his bed with his arms crossed under his head, staring up at the spinning fan. I sat on the side of the bed.

"How are you doing?" I asked.

He shrugged a shoulder, still staring at the fan going around. "You're not—you don't *like* Tate or anything, do you?"

I laughed. "Whatever gave you that idea?"

He just looked at me, and then turned his attention back to the fan.

"Tate is an old friend. I do like him, and he's being a good friend to all of us right now. But that's all."

"How did Carson take it?"

"Not well," I answered. "He's going to need some extra attention from you. He's much younger than you are; he doesn't understand."

"Who says I do?" he asked.

I sighed. "I don't either. Go on to sleep, Gib. I'll see you in the morning." I stood, leaving him on the bed staring at the fan, and went upstairs to practice, hoping I could get Carson's music out of my head long enough to concentrate on somebody else's.

But Estella had different ideas for the night. As I climbed the stairs I heard her voice, low and strident.

"Why didn't you tell us?"

"You know now," Mother replied, as serene as Estella was agitated.

"What else is there?" Estella asked. I stopped in the stairwell, leaning against the rail and listening carefully. "What happened to your father?"

"Well, he died, Estella. Did you expect him to still be here?" Her voice lost a bit of its measure, and I stepped heavily on the next step, warning them that I was coming. As I entered the living room, neither of them looked at me, and I sank down on the sofa next to Estella. We gazed at Mother without speaking, and when I felt Estella's hand steal onto my leg I gathered it in my own, and we waited. Mother sighed and brushed the hair out of her eyes.

"You girls," she started, but then stopped. We said nothing. "Okay," she said softly. "Daddy wasn't a fisherman. Well, he was, but not a very good one. When he had money it was because he'd won a game. He played cards. He had . . . a thing. A thing he did, with the cards."

"He counted cards," Estella murmured. Mother smiled a sly smile and tilted her head with a nod.

"That's right," she said. "After the girls died, after we moved to Atlanta, it was all he did, and sometimes he didn't do it very well. He left me with the landlady when he was on the road. And when he got caught he'd go to jail, or sometimes the other players would take matters into their own hands. He came back once so beat up that the landlady got scared. She told him if he left me alone again she'd call the county. So he took me on the road with him. We traveled all over the South—the Carolinas, Alabama, Tennessee. We slept in the car if we didn't have money."

She nodded at us. "You know the rest. I met Sebastian at one of those games."

"Estella," I said to my mother, and my sister's grip tightened on my hand. "That's where it came from, isn't it? Your father?"

"Well, I've always imagined so," she said.

"Why didn't you tell me?" Estella whispered hoarsely.

"Because it doesn't matter," Mother said, leaning forward. "It was important to your father to think he had something to do with it. And why not? What does it matter?"

I couldn't answer. For me, it didn't matter. But Estella wasn't letting up on my hand.

"How did he die, Mother?" she asked. "Don't you dare skip anything now."

Mother stared at Estella and slowly nodded. "All right. He died in prison, Estella. He killed a man. In Macon. It was during a game, an illegal, big-stakes game, and the man came after him with a knife. He got it away from him during the fight and killed him. He was cut badly and almost died from blood loss himself. All the other players left; none of them called for help, too afraid they'd get arrested. A motel maid found them the next day."

"Oh, my God," I breathed.

"He was found guilty of manslaughter and was sentenced to fifteen years in prison. He was transferred to upstate New York and that's where he was when I found out. He died three years later from cirrhosis. Now that's it. I've said as much as I'm going to, and there's nothing left to tell."

She stood stiffly and went downstairs while Estella and I sat on the sofa in silence. When Estella finally turned to me, she said the last thing I expected her to say: "Would you play for me?"

"I—sure," I said. "Sure. I'll lock up, okay?"

She nodded and walked slowly up the stairs, stopping only to grasp my violin case tightly and bring it with her. I turned out the lights and stayed in the darkened living room for a moment, listening to the Gulf pound outside, wondering what kind of legacy my sister and my child had inherited.

Estella

I bring Connie's violin case upstairs and fuss around the library waiting for her to come up, unable to concentrate on anything other than the music that is to come. The case is heavier than I expected, and I unzip it furtively. I'm nervous just touching it. I know that good violins are insanely expensive, and the only place I am not a klutz is in the water. I touch the wood, run my fingernail down a string, and then hear footsteps on the stairs—eleven of them.

Three facts about eleven:

Eleven is the smallest two-digit additive prime.

There are eleven stars in Van Gogh's *Starry Night*.

Half of the first sixty-four partition numbers are divisible by eleven.

I quickly zip the case back up, lay it next to her bed, and then busy myself with my bedclothes as she enters the room. She looks exhausted.

"Are you okay?" she asks, and I nod. I am. I am . . . okay. I am explained, anyway. I am here, in the family I am supposed to be in. "Do you want to talk about it?" she asks.

"No," I say. "It makes sense. That's all I need. But Connie, we should talk about Carson." She lowers herself to the mattress on the floor and crosses her legs, then bites her lip and says nothing.

"You're making a mistake." I cannot help myself.

"But it's none of your business," she responds, and I nod, acknowledging the truth of that.

"This is the last thing I'll say—"

"Good."

"Okay. But you should know: Even if I'd known, even if she'd told Daddy, nothing could have kept me from the numbers."

"No. But you could have been protected from Pretus."

"But nothing could have kept me from the *numbers*, Connie."

We are silent.

"So, you have to go back?" I finally ask.

She nods. "I can't let Alexander down. At least Mother's here to watch the boys."

Of course. Because I wouldn't be able to. She might as well say it out loud.

She doesn't trust me with her children.

She pulls her violin case over and unzips it, pulls the violin out, and tightens the bow, rosins it, begins to tune. I love to watch her preparation. The look on her face is just as it was as a child. No matter how many times she'd done a task, she was always so careful, so studious.

My favorite memories of her are the ones in which she is pretending to play the little violin from Mittenwald. She was a tiny, perfect maestro, a wee prodigy even if not in the perfect sense of the word. Her talents were always so much more interesting than mine.

I loved that little violin. When I left for Atlanta, moved out of this house, my father magnanimously offered to let me have anything I wanted from the library. Considering the value of some of the books on these now-empty shelves it had been a generous offer.

But what I wanted was that baby violin.

I had my hands on it, I even picked it up, and then Daddy pulled out the first edition of Hemingway's *For Whom the Bell Tolls* he'd bought at Bauman's, in the collection—or so Daddy said—because of Donne's clod washed away by the sea, not because of Hemingway. His hands shook as he held it out to me.

What was I to do?

I put the violin down and accepted the book.

And now Connie begins to play, and she is wonderful. I close my eyes, remembering how I'd heard her though the walls, back when she didn't care if anyone was trying to sleep. I remember how it drove the patterns out of my head and filled it with music, just music, no numbers in it at all, just pure sound strung along, note to sweet note, ribbon unspooling, a Möbius strip, never ending.

CHAPTER NINETEEN

My heart was pounding as I pulled onto my street. The trip had been horrible. I couldn't get Carson's music out of my head; it was playing like a loop, driving me to distraction. Semis and massive RVs careened past me, buffeting the Escalade and making it difficult to steer. Stability and noise wasn't helped by the fact that I had the back hatch partially open the entire way so the huge damn Bokhara rug would fit.

I wasn't sure how I was going to get it inside the house. It had nearly killed Tate and Gib to get it downstairs, but Alexander said he would meet me so I didn't have to go in the house alone, and I thought I might be able to guilt him into helping. He was actually on time, standing in the street, watching me drive up. I grinned at him, but the look on his face made it fall away. I pulled next to him and rolled my window down.

"Hi, honey," he said. "Do you know about this?"

That's when I saw the sign pounded into my front yard.

FOR SALE

By Appointment Only

I forgot to breathe and drove past Alexander without a word. I pulled into the driveway, searching the windows for signs of activity. There were none, and the garage was empty. I pulled in, noting that Gib's golf clubs were still leaning against the wall, but Luke's three sets and their expensive stand were gone.

Alexander followed me into the garage and held my door open as I slid out. He leaned down to lightly kiss my cheek, and I absently patted him on his waist. I needed to see the house.

Luke hadn't turned the air-conditioning off when he'd left, and my arms broke out in goose bumps when I entered through the laundry room off the garage. I adjusted the thermostat a few degrees as I entered the kitchen, where everything appeared intact. My cookbooks were still neatly lined up, the blue Kitchen-Aid mixer stood where it had since Luke had given it to me.

I trailed my fingers along the island's marble top on my way into the living room. The big plasma TV was gone. As were the leather sofas, the coffee table, both end tables, and the surround sound system. He'd left all the plants—thirsting for water—and window treatments, as well as the art on the walls. No. There were some empty spots. The O'Keeffes. He'd taken those, of course.

Alexander whistled under his breath. "I take it you weren't expecting this," he said.

"Not exactly," I replied, walking through the living room to the sunporch. The patio set was gone, but the wrought-iron tables I'd used for the orchids had been left behind. The grill was gone. I reentered the house through the dining room doors. The table, chairs, and china cabinet were gone. The china itself was stacked in the middle of the room, positioned directly underneath the chandelier.

The rest of the house told a similar tale. The boys' rooms were untouched, as was one guest room, but every other room had been stripped of its major components.

The master bedroom furniture was gone, with the exception of the box spring, mattress, and comforter set. My clothes had been piled against the wall. Luke's side of the closet was empty. Everything of his in the bathroom was gone.

Alexander stood in the doorway of the bedroom and watched as I threw myself onto the mattress and stared, dry-eyed, up at the tray ceiling. Luke had left the fan. He probably hadn't known how to disconnect it. Alexander sat down next to me, making me roll slightly toward him like a rag doll.

Thank God I hadn't brought either of the boys. Alexander rubbed my shoulder, and I finally sat up and let my breath out like a leaky tire.

"Well, looks like this is it," I said.

"What about the for sale sign?" Alexander asked. In the shock of my denuded house, I'd almost forgotten about that.

"This is *my* house," I said, getting to my feet. I marched down the stairs, out the front door, and yanked the sign out of the lawn, leaving two gaping holes. I left the sign in the garage and pulled out one of the information packets for the agent's phone number, intending to call him immediately, but I changed my mind and called Angie instead.

We'd planned to have drinks after the performance, and when I couldn't reach her in person I just left a message confirming our appointment. I couldn't get the agent's lockbox off our front door, so I had to leave it, risking potential buyers showing up at any time.

I scrawled a note and taped it to the door: *This house is not for sale. I am the rightful owner, and you do not have permission to enter. Constance Sykes Wilder.*

Alexander helped me drag the rug out of the Escalade; we left it in the middle of the living room. I didn't bother bringing anything else in. I transferred my music, violin, and clothes to Alexander's car, and we went to his apartment to get ready. I took my rings off, as I always did, but this time I knew I would not be putting them back on. I rode to the library in silence, obsessively running the pad of my thumb across the dents in my ring finger until it was painful.

Hannah was already playing Waldteufel to warm up when we arrived, and as we joined her she kept glancing at me, concentrating on me just long enough to lag behind, making Alexander furious. He finally stopped playing and waited for her to notice.

"Hannah," he snapped. "Come on, could you concentrate, please?"

"Are you okay, Connie?" she asked, ignoring him.

"I'm fine," I assured her. "Really. I just want to help Alexander get through tonight. I'll catch you up afterward."

She didn't look convinced, but we got through the warmup, and when the director knocked on the door we were ready. The auditorium was filled to capacity, the lights low. As we walked onto the stage, silence fell before polite applause broke out. We nodded to the audience and got settled, breaking into Tartini perfectly.

I hit every note, my violin stayed in tune, Hannah kept up; by the time we'd moved on to Beethoven my only thoughts were of the music. My phrasing turned liquid, my fingers moving of their own accord, my bow arm lifting and falling, bringing first the frog to the bridge and then the tip, again and again and again, each note pushing bits of my life out of my mind, as if they were closing doors on the empty rooms of my house.

Hannah escaped to the bathroom at intermission to avoid Alexander's chatter, so he talked to me while he tuned, throwing my routine off. We were all touchy at intermission, full of music looking for an outlet, building up pressure, ready for the steam valve of the second set. Alexander used talk to relieve his nerves, and I was used to it. But tonight I couldn't stand it, and I envied Hannah hiding in the bath-room.

"More wine?" he asked.

"Huh-uh," I muttered, shaking my head, willing him to be quiet.

"Wiley's out there, I saw him," he said. Jason Wiley was the or-chestra personnel manager he was hoping to impress.

"Hmmm."

"David's here too. Did you see who he's with?"

"No."

"Bethy Simmons, that skanky pianist. You think they're actually dat—"

"Alexander, *please*." I turned away from him with a sigh.

"Oh, yeah, yeah, okay." He went back to tuning his cello. "But really—"

"You've got to let me be for a few minutes, Alex," I said, walking out the door with my violin tucked under my arm, my tuning fork and bow gripped in my hand, nearly running into Luke, who'd been about to knock on the door.

"What on earth are you doing here?" I asked. The sight of him, here, in this world, threw me off. I involuntarily took a step back. He looked like hell, his forehead shining with sweat and a three-day stub-ble turning his face into the dispirited, haggard face of his father. It looked as though he hadn't washed his hair, and his clothes—clothes I'd never seen before—were rumpled and gave off the odor of alcohol. I heard Alexander gasp and put his bow down.

"What the hell do you think you're doing? I just got a call from the agent saying he couldn't bring somebody in to look at the house." He swept his hand across his brow and into his hair, his signature gesture of stress.

"How dare you," I said through clenched teeth, pointing at him with my bow, not thinking. He grabbed it, hard, and I gasped as he wrenched it out of my hand. He held it captive, like a hostage, which indeed it was. I watched as he ran his greasy, sweaty palm up the length of its hairs. He knew exactly what he was doing. I held my hand out—it was ruined for the night but much too expensive to relinquish—but he ignored it. I felt Alexander behind me.

"Please give me back my bow," I said. "You've already got all the furniture."

"You're the one who left the house, Connie," he said with a shrug, clumsily flipping the bow in the air and catching it by the other end. "Your lawyer should have coached you better."

"Luke—" Alexander started, but Luke didn't let him finish.

"Back off, faggot," he said, jabbing the bow at him. I heard Alexander gasp and felt my knees weaken. Luke had never been a bigot, but he was unpredictable when he was drinking. He didn't drink often, and the memory of his broken-down father kept him sober but for a few episodes a year. And he hated himself on those occasions, knowing how his behavior—loving one moment, surly the next, and then suddenly asleep wherever he landed—would affect his children.

"Luke," I said, "I don't mind about the furniture. Everything will be added up in the end, and you picked most of it out anyway. You're obviously upset and you've been drink—"

"Oh, please," he sneered. "Don't start the Saint Constance act with me."

"Is that why you're with her?" I asked, unable to let it go, unable to resist jabbing him back. "She's willing to let you turn into your father? What a bargain she's getting. Expensive furniture and a drunk."

"I'm not a drunk," he said, emphasizing each word with another poke of my bow. "I just went out with a client for a few drinks, something *Deanna* understands."

"That's great, Luke. Now please, we can talk about this after the performance. Let's be adults about this. Let's be fair. May I have my bow back? Please?"

Alexander had backed off, but I heard him on the phone in the dressing room.

"Be fair? Fair? I don't think it was *fair* of you to freeze the accounts, you bitch. And you've got nothing to say about the house. You don't need all that room. I got a good agent. We'll split the profit."

"That's not the point," I said evenly. "You didn't even talk to me about it. And *my* trust fund paid for that house."

"I need . . ." Luke trailed off.

"What, Luke? What do you need?"

"That Escalade's in my name, and I let you take it," he said.

"Do you need money? Is that it? Maybe you should have thought of that before you stole from your own sons."

Alexander appeared at my back again. "The police are on their way," he said. "I suggest you give her back that bow and get out of here."

"You asshole," Luke said. His fist clenched around the bow, stretching the hairs, making it quiver under the strain. I quickly put my hand on his arm.

"Luke, please, give me back my bow and we'll talk about the Escalade tomorrow."

His stared at me, trying to focus. He was a stranger to me. An angry, volatile stranger. I wondered if I looked like a different person to him too. No longer his wife, just some woman who was trying to steal his rightfully earned money from him, preventing him from starting a new life with the woman he loved.

"If this is a trick I'm going to make your life miserable."

"You've already managed that," I said softly. It was the wrong thing to say. His jaw clenched, and then he held the bow up in front of my eyes and snapped it in half faster than I could flinch.

He dropped it on the floor, the two halves still held together by the hairs. I fell to my knees with a cry and gathered it up. He pointed a finger at Alexander but said nothing, and then turned on his heel and left, one hand trailing down the wall.

I slumped against the door frame, clutching my ruined bow, my hands trembling. Alexander pulled me into the room and shut the door before he took the bow from my hands and put his arms around me. I could feel his heart beating through his suit. I thought I might cry, but instead I just shook, and finally stepped away from him.

"Did you really call the police?" I asked. He shook his head.

"I called my house and left a message on my machine, so that if he killed me the police would know who did it."

I had to laugh. "He wouldn't have touched you—or me, for that matter," I said.

"Connie, he was drunk. There's no telling what someone is going to do when he's drunk and pissed off, and my neck's no thicker than that bow. Tell me you have your other one?"

I did, but it was of little comfort to me. It had been an expensive bow, my favorite, and from the way it had splintered I doubted it could be repaired. Alexander opened the door and looked around to make sure Luke was gone. Hannah appeared at the end of the hallway, checking her watch and rubbing her hands down her black skirt, working out her nerves and completely unaware of what had just happened.

"Are we ready?" she asked. I took a few deep breaths under Alexander's watchful gaze, and then nodded. I retrieved my other bow, quickly tightened and rosined it, and we tuned together.

"I guess so," I said.

The second half went better than I would have expected, but I played the Telemann and Danzi by rote, the music never taking me back where I needed to be to play my best. We received a fair length and decibel level of applause, and Wiley was waiting for Alexander in the corridor after our final bows. He shook hands with all of us, and complimented Alexander, saying he was looking forward to his audition before he left.

Alexander was ecstatic, Hannah was jealous, and I was exhausted. I still had a long night of divorce talk ahead of me, and I wished for it to simply be over.

Angie was waiting in the driveway of my nearly empty house when I arrived. I didn't bother introducing her to Alexander, but rather kissed him quickly on the cheek and told him I would call him from Big Dune. Angie loomed over me—she certainly topped six feet— and I suppressed a little smile. Tall women had always intimidated Luke. We shook hands and I invited her inside, ready to begin the official decimation of my marriage.

To my surprise I slept well, and in the morning I walked through the house slowly, breathing in the familiar scents of memories and growing boys and cleaning products, of long-ago dinners and recent arguments and marriage. What it didn't smell of was me. I loved this home, but I loved it with a family in it. Without one it felt huge and sad and somehow reproachful. Perhaps I would feel differently when I brought the boys back.

I packed a few suitcases, throwing in clothes for the boys as well as their CDs and video games, and by the time I was ready to pack the car I'd felt something shift in me, some reckoning and acceptance. I checked all the locks, set the air-conditioning, and hoisted a suitcase in my hand. My other hand stilled on the doorknob as I breathed in one last bit of air from the house and set off to start a new life.

I opened the door to the garage, nearly expecting a ray of light, or perhaps a soundtrack of uplifting music. Instead, what I was confronted with was an empty garage. I stared into the emptiness, willing the Escalade to appear. But it did not.

I set the suitcase down gently and opened the garage door. As it rumbled up I squeezed my eyes shut, hoping that when I opened them the Escalade would have somehow materialized in the driveway. But it did not.

I went back inside to call Angie.

An eight-hour drive in a rattling rental car provides plenty of time for thought, and my head was swimming when I arrived on Big Dune. Everyone was on the beach, and I took the opportunity to grab a snack, unpack, and take a shower. When I emerged, Carson was just coming in the door. He screamed, "Mommy!" and flung himself at me.

"Hey, baby," I cried, hugging him to me. He was followed in by Estella and Mother, and they both greeted me almost as enthusiastically as Carson had. While Carson showered, Estella and Mother followed me up to the library to hear about the weekend. Their wide-eyed shock was as comforting as their embraces.

"Where's Gib?" I asked once their questions had been answered.

"You can't peel him off Tate," Mother answered. "They're fishing down at the cut. Carson was down there with them, but I think he and Gib had words. He came back looking pretty down in the mouth."

"I'll have to talk to Gib," I said with a sigh.

"Every little sibling tiff doesn't need a *talk*, Connie," Mother said.

She was probably right. Without Luke around to keep things even in our family, Carson and Gib were going to have to work out a new relationship. And as much as I might want to help, they were old enough that much of it was going to have to get worked out without me.

It was an oddly satisfying realization. It stayed my hand from buttoning my shirt for a moment, and I stared at Mother. She gave me a puzzled smile, but I couldn't explain it.

"Estella," I said, "feel like walking down to the cut with me?"

"Yeah, sure," she answered.

We walked slowly, the destination only an excuse to get out of the house with my sister. The feeling I'd had in the library was expanding in my chest, and what I'd wanted to talk about for so many years could no longer be contained. It was suddenly greater than myself, and yet, it also seemed less important than ever. I understood, and now I needed to let her know.

"You know Mother thinks we got along growing up," I said as we walked through the surf. Estella glanced at me, and then looked out to the Gulf. She raised her hand to her temple and massaged it.

"Well, we didn't really fight the way most sisters do," she said. It was an answer I might have given before today, a safe, evasive answer, and I was having none of it. I stopped and put my hand on her arm to stop her too.

"No," I said slowly. I'd rehearsed a lot of speeches over the past thirty years, but none of them was right, none of them fit now, and I wasn't exactly sure what I was going to say. "It was worse. And it wasn't all their fault. It wasn't. At first, maybe, yes, definitely. We were young, but later we should have made it better ourselves."

"Connie," Estella said, "we didn't have a chance—"

"But we did," I protested. "We did. Especially that summer, remember? When Daddy took Mother to Europe. I thought we were really getting closer. But we lost it, and . . . and I don't know what happened. We just never tried to get it back. Why? Why didn't we try?"

She shook her head and started walking again, looking down at the sand, moving fast now. I stared after her for a moment and then ran to catch up, matching her pace. "What, Estella?"

"It was my fault," she said, her words strangling in her throat.

"But no, it wasn't," I said. "That's what I'm getting at. It was *our* fault, because that's what we'd done for so long, but—"

"Connie!" she shouted, stopping and turning toward me sharply enough to send a small spray of sand over my feet. "Why won't you just say it? I almost let you drown. That was my fault. And then I couldn't stand to look at you, I couldn't stand to see all that forgiveness in your face. Always looking at me like that, *Jesus,* since we were kids. You exhausted me. I loved you, but I couldn't live up to it."

"What?" I whispered. "What are you talking about? We were friends, we *were.*"

Estella covered her mouth with her hand as though afraid to say anything else. She stood there, her short hair gold in the sun, and she seemed vulnerable, ethereal, as though I could pass my hand right through her and she would disintegrate and disappear into the sand. I reached out, but she backed up a step.

"Connie, don't you remember what happened?"

"When?" I asked, shuffling through memories to find the one she felt so strongly. "You mean Daddy? Graciela?"

"No, Connie. That summer."

"That wasn't your fault, Estella. It was mine. I was the one who was drinking, you couldn't have stopped me. I was the one who got in over my head, quite literally. If it weren't for you, I would have drowned."

Estella slowly shook her head. "No, Connie," she said quietly. "No. If it weren't for *Tate,* you would have drowned."

"He got to me a second before you did," I said. "I don't blame you, Estella, I really don't, I never have. I know you did the best you could."

"No, I didn't do the best I could. You must remember, Connie," she pressed me, stepping toward me, her eyes intense. I took a step back, feeling the waves splash up my calves.

I remembered her eyes. I remembered seeing her green eyes. I remembered the relief of knowing she was going to save me, that my protector was there.

I remembered wondering what was taking so long.

"I *didn't* do the best I could. I was going to let you drown, Connie," she finally said, enunciating each word carefully. It was as though all the air on the beach had been sucked away, leaving only the echo of those words.

"No."

"I'm sorry, Connie—yes."

"But why?" I asked, beginning to cry, feeling as sick as I had that day, as sick as Carson had been in the car. "Why, Estella? Why did you hate me so much?"

"I didn't hate you," she said, not reaching toward me, not even trying. "I wanted to *be* you."

"I don't believe you," I said. "You wouldn't let me—let me die. Oh, no." I turned away from her, unable to look at her face, and saw Gib and Tate coming down the beach. I couldn't let them see me like that, see us like that. Estella turned and saw them too.

"Tate knows, Tate remembers," she said. "I sickened him. Why do you think he wouldn't sleep with me? I threw myself at him. He couldn't stand to see me."

"I—I can't—" I stuttered, unable to form a coherent thought, unable to stop the memory of her green eyes above the water, calmly watching me, clinically watching me as I swallowed water and went under. I stepped out of the surf, scuttled past her like a crab in a wide arc, and achieved the safety of the dry sand before Gib and Tate reached us.

"Hey, Mom," Gib said with a grin, genuinely happy to see me, his arms full of fishing equipment, his face open and sunburned, a tiny yellowish smudge of a bruise under his left eye. "Tate said we could camp overnight on Little Dune before we went home."

"Gib," I said, looking up at him miserably. His eyes widened and he took a step toward me. Estella stopped him.

"Gib, your mom and I are talking. Could you go back to the house?"

He shook her arm off and narrowed his eyes at her. "What did you say to her?"

"No, Gib, it's okay," I said. "Please, honey, go on back to the house."

He stared at me for a second longer, and I nodded down the beach toward the house. He turned to Tate, seeking his approval, and I was amazed again at how quickly he'd become so close to him.

"Let's leave them alone, Gib. Come on."

"Could you stay, Tate?" Estella asked, her voice tight.

"Why can he stay?" Gib protested.

"I don't know," Tate said. Then he added, "All right. Gib, you want to take the cooler?"

Gib snatched the cooler handle away from Tate and set off down the beach, muttering to himself and dragging the poles along with his other hand. The three of us watched him go in silence, only turning toward each other when the waves drowned out the sound of the sinkers clanking against the fishing poles.

"Connie thinks I saved her life," Estella said. "Tell her what really happened."

Tate sighed and pushed his hair off his forehead. It stuck up, spiky and near white. I couldn't see his eyes behind the dark lenses of his sunglasses, but his mouth turned down and he didn't respond for a minute. Estella and I watched him silently.

"What's the point of this?" he asked, his fists at his hips.

"She says she doesn't remember. She should know," Estella said.

He was silent again.

"Tell her the truth, Tate," Estella said quietly.

He shook his head and muttered, "Fine," before he turned to me, closing Estella out. "Yeah," he said. "It took me a minute to realize what was happening. I sort of froze for a second. I thought you were fooling around, and I knew Estella was there. She was so close, and she started to swim just as I realized that you were really in trouble. I jumped in, but it seemed like you were miles away. I never swam so hard in my life, Connie. I was getting closer, but Estella wasn't. She's telling the truth. She could have gotten to you before I did. She *should* have gotten to you before I did. Long before I did."

I swallowed hard, and swallowed again, dryly shoving unspeakable words down my throat. I couldn't speak. I knew it was true. I did remember.

I remembered her eyes.

Estella

She remembers. Her mouth is working, but she's not speaking, and except for the fact that she is upright and dry, it is like watching her drown all over again. Tate is watching her carefully, his back still to me, effectively shutting me out, as it's always been, as I know is completely appropriate this time.

"Connie," I say. Tate steps back, and I step forward, a small step. "Please, let me explain."

But she is too far gone. She turns and runs down the beach, stumbling in the loose sand and righting herself to correct her course, now running on the hard pack. It supports her, and now she is flying, but I am not pursuing, and neither is Tate. In fact, Tate is gripping my arm hard enough to hurt to make sure I don't chase her.

And I appreciate, now, that he cares for her. But he is no longer a part of this for me. Now that it is in the open, he is gone from my soul like smoke in the wind, attached to the confession that festered for too long. I shake loose, feel the bruise that will appear like a slave bracelet in a day or two, but I don't chase her.

"Why did you have to do that?" Tate asks. Now that it is in the open, things have changed for him too. There is no longer any good-natured, brotherly attitude toward me; instead, the hostility is laid bare, the anger he didn't let fly thirty years ago finally taking hold. "You haven't changed a bit, Estella. Why now, when she's at her lowest point? Why?"

"Because she had to know, and this was the time I had," I say. "And I owe you an apology too."

"Not accepted," he says and walks—no, *stalks*—away from me, the military evident in him.

I stay on the beach until I see Mother coming, and then I run too, toward her, and she catches me when I fall into her, and I realize that it is the first time I have ever let her catch me.

And I tell her what I did, and I beg for her forgiveness.

And then she walks me along the beach, holding my hand, and tells me more about her father, about the con man, the card counter. She asks for my forgiveness. And now, here we are, forgivable, forgiven, wrung out, and I know that I have more that I am keeping from her, but there is no sense in burdening her with it now.

We reach the cut, and I pull the smaller of Tate's canoes out of the brush for us to sit on. We gaze across the cut to Little Dune. I don't know what she's thinking. But my mind is empty. No numbers. No patterns. Not even any pain, though I know it will return. I would take the pain over the patterns, though they are both harbingers of the same thing.

But for now I am new.

CHAPTER TWENTY

Gib was waiting for me on the patio. I had stopped running and managed to walk up the steps without stumbling. He was too young to have learned how to camouflage the confusion obvious on his face, and I felt sorry for him. I knew how confusing family loyalty was, how it flexed and expanded, and then shrank and flattened to a hard line again.

"What'd she say to you?" he demanded.

I shook my head as I walked past him and into the house. I said, "Gib, don't worry about it, okay? This is something between Estella and me. You'll have things that will be between you and your brother one day."

He didn't seem to buy it, but he stopped dogging my steps as I made my way up to the library. I had priorities: I had a house to close up; I had a divorce to get through and two wildly different boys to finish raising;

and I had a life to figure out. That was enough. I cast my gaze about the library, desperately looking for something to take my mind off my sister; I didn't have room for Estella and her problems. I saw my violin case.

Haydn would keep me occupied. I prepped quickly, and then started the adagio cantabile, but the air wasn't moving in the room, and when the bow slipped I pulled the music from where I'd propped it on the piano and took the violin up on the widow's walk. I secured the music to the top of the open case with some binder clips, fitting them from left to right, adjusting the angle until I could see without stooping. There was a light breeze, but the back of the case was to it, so the pages fluttered only slightly.

I could see Mother and Estella walking on the beach—Mother providing comfort and aid to exactly the wrong person yet again—and then took a deep breath and began to play. I heard movement behind me, but I ignored it and concentrated on the music, hoping whoever it was, whoever needed something from me, would just go away and leave me alone.

I didn't bother making any notations, I just played the adagio all the way through, alternating between reading the music and glancing at the Gulf, drowning in the music rather than the water. I'd always played Haydn too correctly, forcing a rigidity where there was none, but I was playing loosely now, perhaps not perfectly, but letting notes flow like water from the end of my bow.

As I felt my sister's steps on the boardwalk reverberate all the way up through the house my playing changed, becoming angry and careless, as though punishing her with the music. Six pelicans, in a tight formation like feathered fighter jets, soared over me, dipping their wings on the eddies the Haydn made in the heavy air. They swooped below the edge of the house and came up again, and I leaned back to watch them, my chin just barely making contact, my bow nearly horizontal. I could almost smell them as they made their second pass, lifting the air and the music up, up, pulling the fury out of me, leaving me with just wonder.

I quickly found my place again, and now I reined myself in, making the transition easily, something I'd always fought with. I was an either/or player, but something cut the wires in me, and now I was playing naturally, beautifully, the way it was supposed to be played, the way it had been written to be played.

A small sound started behind me, filtering in under the violin, and at first I ignored it, but then it became louder. I turned my head slightly, nearly faltering when I saw Carson sitting on the widow's walk door with his eyes closed, his clarinet in his hands.

Once again the sound came, nothing Haydn had ever written or intended, but something my son heard and transformed. I turned back quickly, unwilling to lose my place and interrupt Carson. I was nearing the end of the music, and I looked for a way to loop it back. Scanning for the spot, I found it and made the loop seamlessly.

It was lucky I wasn't playing a wind instrument, because all my breath seemed to be caught somewhere below my heart, and somehow, now that I wasn't looking at him, wasn't seeing Estella superimposed on my youngest son's features, I was finally hearing him, hearing what everyone else heard, and my God, they were right. I wasn't going to be able to control this, or contain it.

The clarinet grew stronger, and soon I was hearing what he intended and I scaled back, softened my sound, and he compensated. This was music I'd never heard before. I let the transitions get loose, I let his vision guide me, and now I was part of it too, and if what I was feeling was even close to what Carson felt when he created it, then I would be a monster to keep him from it.

I looped back once more and finished it off softly, letting him help me down easily, and he sustained a final, perfect wavering note after I'd ended mine. I laid my violin and bow in my case carefully and turned, able to watch him at last, as he stopped and opened his eyes.

He pulled the clarinet away and grinned at me, wiping his lower lip. I whooped in laughter and swept him up and into my arms, his clarinet caught between us sideways, its bell sticking out of his ribs as though grown there.

"Carson," I cried, finally releasing him and grinning down at him. "That was amazing! How did you do it?"

He was still laughing, and his cheeks were flushed. He looked away from me, bashful at my reaction, but pleased with himself too. "I just tried it," he finally said simply. "You made it easy."

"*I* made it easy?"

He shrugged. "I don't know. I knew what you were going to do."

"Before I did it?"

"I guess."

"What are we going to do with you, Carson?" I asked. "You love it, don't you?"

He nodded enthusiastically, and then, to cover his embarrassment, he lifted his clarinet and played a little tune, bluesy and simple, marching away from me and around the railing. We stayed up on the widow's walk until the sun set, watching Gib walk up the beach and the boardwalk, watching Tate arrive from the beachside and then depart in his truck, disappearing into the brush of the interior. We said little, but I could nearly hear the music between us still, and the low hum of it felt like a conversation of its own.

Gib finally stuck his head up out of the door just as we were preparing to come down. "What are you guys doing? Dad's on the phone," he said to Carson without waiting for an answer, and my heart hurt to see Carson so excited. He nearly tripped in his rush to get down the steep stairs, but he caught himself on the banister. I followed more slowly after handing my violin case down to Gib.

"What were you guys doing up there?" he asked again, and I realized with a jolt of amusement that he sounded jealous, those tides of loyalty shifting in him again.

"Just playing," I said lightly. "You could have come up if you wanted."

He shrugged. "Yeah, I guess."

"What did your dad have to say?" I asked.

He shook his head and narrowed his eyes. "Nothing. Stupid stuff. Did you know he moved in with her?"

Of course I had known, where else would he have taken the furniture? But it still shocked me coming from my son's mouth. "Yes," I said. "You okay?"

He gave a disgusted little grunt. Answer enough. Carson came trudging up the stairs, his face troubled. "Dad wants to talk to you," he said.

"You okay?" I asked, searching his face.

Gib reached out and rubbed his shoulder and Carson brightened a bit. "I'm okay," he said, looking to Gib, seeking approval for his bravery.

Luke started off with a cough before he found his voice, ragged and tired. "I just got a call from my lawyer," he said without preamble.

I remained silent.

"I, ah, guess I shouldn't have taken the Escalade. I'd like to ask . . ." He couldn't finish the sentence.

"What, Luke?"

It took him a moment to respond, and when he did his voice was tightly controlled. "I would like to ask your *permission* to use the Escalade until mediation."

"Ah, so you've agreed to mediation, then? Why so amenable suddenly?"

Angie had warned me about this. It appeared as though Luke had very little to his name, though information was continuing to come in. To my surprise, I now held most of the cards. His lawyer must have come down hard on him after Angie called to tell him what he'd done.

"Jesus, Connie, you have no idea what I'm going through here."

"I don't care what you're going through, and I never wanted the Escalade to begin with. I did want my bow, though. You owe me, and Alexander, an apology for that."

He cleared his throat again. "I'll get you a new one," he said.

"With what, Luke? From what my lawyer tells me you don't have anything. Or do you? She'll find it, you know. She's very good at what she does."

"Keep pushing me, Connie—"

"And what? What do you think you can do to me now?"

"So can I use the Escalade?"

"Use the Escalade, Luke. You officially have my permission. The only thing I care about is how this is going to affect our children. You can call here to speak to the boys, but if you want to talk to me you'll have to go through my lawyer. Good-bye."

"Wait," he said. "Please, just wait. Listen, I wanted to talk to you about the boys before we got to mediation."

My heart stilled. If Luke wanted them, both of them, either of them, then mediation wasn't going to work, because I wasn't giving them up.

"What?"

"I have a feeling Gib will want to live with me," he said, his voice hesitant.

"Oh, I wouldn't be too sure about that," I answered. "And you'd better not even *think* about talking to them about this without me."

"I haven't," he said quickly. "But what do you mean? You don't think he'll want to?"

"You might not realize this yet, Luke, but I'm not the only one you've betrayed."

"Now look, I thought we—"

"Just because I'm making this easy doesn't mean that you haven't done a horrible thing, to me and to our sons. I'm trying to make it easy for them. You've got a long way to go to make this up to both of them."

"Well, it—it would be all right if he stayed with you, you know? I mean, I've got a lot to do, I have to start my life over too, and—"

"Good God," I said, realization dawning on me. "You don't even want Gib, do you? I know you have no interest in Car—"

"Stop right there, Connie," he interrupted. "That's not what I meant."

"Feel free to explain yourself then." I remained silent, listening to him fidget on the other end of the line.

"I'm just saying that it might be best if Gib—Gib and Carson, stayed with you at first."

"I wouldn't have it any other way, Luke," I said quietly. "But don't blame me if it takes years for your sons to trust you again. *Sons*, Luke. Remember you have two of them. My lawyer will be in touch."

I hung up and turned around to see Gib slipping away. I didn't call him back—there was nothing I could say to him to cover for what he had heard.

Dinner was subdued. Tate never returned, Estella pleaded a headache and skipped it altogether, and both Gib and Carson were near silent the entire time. Only Mother tried to lighten the mood by asking Gib and Carson to walk through the house and choose anything they wanted to keep. Both of them passed on her offer, and we all floated off to our own devices after dinner.

I walked the beach, unwilling to return to the top floor until I was certain Estella was asleep. When I saw the light wink out I walked back up the boardwalk just in time to snatch the ringing phone up.

"Hi, Connie," Paul said, his voice pleasant and soft, such a far cry from most of my recent conversations.

"Hello, Paul. How are you?"

"I'm doing all right. Missing Estella, though. Is she around?"

I hesitated. What did I care if I woke her up? But I said, "She went to bed early. Do you want me to see if she's awake?"

"Is she feeling okay?" he asked.

"She probably had a headache," I said, and I'm sure my irritation bled through in my voice, because he was silent for a moment.

"Is that happening a lot? Badly enough that she has to go to bed?" he asked.

"Sometimes she lies down, sometimes she doesn't," I said, not particularly bothered with what my sister did or didn't do. "Do you want me to get her?"

"No, don't wake her up, she needs her sleep. But can you please ask her to call me in the morning?" he asked.

I agreed, but when I woke the next morning she was already gone, swimming in the Gulf with Gib, reigniting my fury. I forgot to tell her that Paul called, but figured she knew when I saw her hanging the phone up that afternoon. She was agitated, flexing her fingers and blinking her eyes in that way I remembered so well.

She left for the beach when she saw me moving her things down to her old bedroom, transferring Gib to my old room, and moving Carson up to the library with me. She skipped meals and we stayed away from each other for the remainder of the week. The thunderstorms that returned didn't make it any easier, but while being forced to stay indoors didn't do much for our relationship, it helped with the house. We all worked. Mother gleefully threw things away, seeming to relish the task, and after Estella helped Gib with his algebra, they dove in too.

Carson stuck close to me. We practiced in the library in the mornings, when everyone else was down on the beach, then he helped me box and label in the afternoons. We made a couple of trips into town to ship things to Verona, but the boxes still piled up uncontrollably on the first floor. I didn't bother asking Estella if she wanted to ship the books—she could make her own arrangements—and so those boxes never moved.

Vanessa came to eat dinner with us most nights, along with Tate, who was scarce during the day. Two nights before we were scheduled to leave, he brought fresh shrimp, lugging his big cooler up the stairs through the thunderstorm that had rolled in. He toweled off in the kitchen, and Gib looked at him anxiously.

"We're still going to Little Dune, aren't we?" he asked.

"Oh, Gib, I don't think a campout is such a great idea now," I said.

"Mom," Gib protested. "You already said I could."

"Why can't I go?" Carson asked, for the twentieth time that week.

"Because you're not invited," Gib said.

"Hey, knock it off or I'll cancel it altogether," Tate said mildly. "Gib, if your mom says you can't go, you can't go. And Carson, you certainly would be invited, but your mom thinks that you might be a little young. You come up next year and I promise we'll go camping, okay?"

Carson was not appeased and stomped down the stairs to his bedroom. Gib glared at me, waiting for a decision. I looked out the sliders at the storm.

"Why don't you go downstairs and be nice to your brother," Tate said to Gib. "I'll talk to your mom."

Gib left reluctantly, casting dark glances over his shoulder, and I slumped down onto the cooler with a sigh. There were no chairs left in the house, and we'd been eating picnic style, cross-legged on the floor, wherever we felt most comfortable.

"Hey, Connie," Tate said. "It's almost over. You'll be back home soon."

I looked around at the empty house. "I don't know," I said. "I don't know if I want to go back yet."

He followed my gaze and laughed. "Well, it's a little late to decide that now."

I shrugged. I'd come to like the bare house, full of possibilities, emptied of tangible reminders of things I would now rather forget. "I guess so. What about this camping trip?"

"If you don't want him to go, he won't go," he said.

"What if it storms?" I asked.

"I've camped in a lot worse weather than this. I think Gib's hoping it will storm. Hell, it'll be good for him. Sort of a rite of passage, you know? He's learned a lot, and he really likes all this outdoors stuff. From what I gather, he's not that interested in much at home except football."

"That's true," I admitted. "It's been so nice of you to take an interest in him."

"No problem; he's a good kid. I'd be doing all that stuff by myself anyway, so he's company for me. If the rain gets bad we'll sleep in the lighthouse. He'd probably like that better anyway."

"You don't think it's dangerous?"

He laughed again. "God, Connie, when did you turn into such a wimp?"

"When I gave birth," I answered sharply, and then caught myself. "I'm sorry, Tate. I'm just so tired. I want to get all of this over with."

"I know," he said softly. "He'll be with me, Connie. He'll be safe. I promise. It's just rain."

"All right. We'll see you tomorrow then."

He winked at me and dropped a light kiss on top of my head before joining the boys downstairs. Mother came up and we shelled shrimp for dinner in companionable silence.

"Your sister's still not feeling well," she said. I grunted in reply and dropped another cleaned shrimp into the bowl. "She told me what happened," Mother continued.

"And I'm still not interested in talking about it, Mother," I said.

Mother sighed, a heavy, pitiful sigh. I turned to her, my hands dripping shrimp water on the floor. I wiped them on my shorts, not caring that I'd smell like shrimp for the night. "Why are you selling this house?" I asked. She looked startled, and I was a little startled myself at the vehemence in my voice.

"I've told you that," she answered. "It's quite simple. Nobody uses it and it costs too much to keep."

"I want it," I said, and it took the words coming out of my mouth for me to know it was true, the same way I'd known that Estella was too different to ever come back to me, the same way I'd known when I fell in love with Luke.

"You can't be serious," Mother said, her face incredulous.

"I am. Yes, I am. I want this house. This is where I want to be. I'll sell the house in Verona and buy it from you."

"Connie, this is ridiculous."

"This is the first thing I've known for sure in years, Mother."

"You can't afford it."

"Then don't try to make a killing off me."

"Well, that's—that's not fair. I would have to ask the fair market price, Connie."

"Then rent it to me, leave it to me and Estella, and when you die, I'll buy her out." The wheels were turning furiously now. Mother wasn't keeping up; she looked flustered.

"Connie, this is a big decision. At the very least, please think about this for a while. Sleep on it. And what about the boys? They won't want to be that far from Luke."

"For your information, Luke says he's starting a new life, and he's not interested in the boys being a part of it."

She looked stricken. "Surely he didn't say that," she said.

"Not exactly, but that was the impression he gave me. Mother, look at Gib. Have you ever seen him interested in doing anything other than playing video games and football? He's even changing his attitude toward Carson. I think I could be happy here, Mother. And I think the boys could too. Doesn't that matter to you?"

"Of course it does, Connie. I have to think about this. I am not at all convinced. And I think once you've had some time to think, you won't be either."

But she was wrong. As I lay in the dark that night, listening to my son sleep beside me, I knew that it was exactly what I wanted.

Estella

For the first time in my life I don't know what I want. I vacillate on the hour. Tough, then tearful, then angry, and moving on to desperate in less time than it takes me to recite the Millennium Prize problems. But it is worse than any math, it is family, and I am reminded once again that it is often simply easier to opt out of it altogether.

Gib watches me and Connie, darting his eyes back and forth between us like a spectator at a telepathic tennis match, as though we are volleying arguments back and forth without saying a word. And perhaps we are. I know I am sending her plenty of topspin-loaded thoughts, alternating between pleas for leniency and angry declarations of disinterest.

But I don't feel anything coming back.

When Gib splashed into the Gulf beside me this morning I almost walked out, but he simply began to swim, and after a moment I did too. I only have a few days left here. I only have a few more times to feel this exquisite weightlessness. I counted my strokes, divided and multiplied and factored on my flip, and then counted strokes again.

I've been swimming in numbers all day. I have stopped fighting it. There is no use in it; it is what I was meant to do, what I was born for, and no doctor can cut it all out of me after all. It is something of a relief to know where it came from. Daddy tried so hard to make us connect with his ancestors, but it was always a tenuous, counterfeit bond. I never really felt it.

But now I am connected to my mother's father, a cardsharp, a con man, a man who died because he encouraged the numbers to swim and play in his head. I wonder if he ever tried to make them stop, or whether he simply accepted it. Did he blame the numbers when he killed that man, when he heard his sentence read, when he died in some cell in upstate New York?

I blame them for everything.

"Estella?" I hear Connie call, and my heart jitters. "Paul's on the phone."

I walk upstairs listening to her make small talk with Paul, cringe when I hear her politely lie, "Sure, we're having a good time."

I pull the phone from her grasp, and her eyes widen. I say, "Hi, Paul, hang on a second," then hold the phone down at my side and stare at her until she turns away and goes upstairs, shaking her head.

CHAPTER TWENTY-ONE

"Paul, I'm fine," I heard Estella say. I hung back, listening, unable to help myself. She listened for a minute, and then continued, "A few days isn't going to make a difference."

Silence, and then, "You should be at your show."

Silence again. Then, "I miss you too. Yes, fine. I'll see you then."

She hung up, and I tried to look casual as I came back downstairs.

"Don't worry, Connie," she said. "I'll be out of your hair tomorrow. Paul's coming to pick me up."

It surprised me enough that I momentarily forgot my standoff. "What? Why?"

"Because he is," she said irritably. She shoved the telephone back against the wall and left the kitchen, heading downstairs and passing Mother in the stairwell.

"I'm leaving tomorrow. Paul's coming to pick me up," I heard her say.

"Whatever for?" Mother asked. "I thought Connie was taking you home on Saturday."

"Connie doesn't want to be anywhere near me, Mother, so I don't imagine that's a problem."

"But, Estella, what about the books?"

"Burn them," she said. Then I heard her race down the stairs; the beachside door slammed.

Mother arrived upstairs looking dazed, as if she couldn't understand how everything had gotten away from her so quickly. "What was that all about?" she asked me, as though it were my fault.

I shrugged. "She's a grown woman, Mother, you can't stop her."

Estella and Gib swam, with me keeping a careful eye on them from the patio, while Vanessa did her tai chi and Mother sat in the sand. The house was finally empty, and I had little to do but wait for Gib to go on his camping trip and give the house a final cleaning.

By that afternoon the house looked very nearly ready to place on the market. I walked through the living room and leaned my shoulder against the slider casement, gazing out at the thunderheads that had started to roll in over the Gulf.

Everything was gray: the water, the sky, even the white sand looked dingy and used. I wanted to drag my weary self upstairs, crawl onto my mattress, and sleep for days while rain lashed against the windows. I closed my eyes and listened to the muffled sounds of the surf, allowing it to lull me. Had Carson not run up the stairs, thumping a bulging backpack behind him, I might have drifted off standing up like a horse.

"I want to go camping!" he yelled at me, having worked himself up to confront me. He was red-faced and breathless, clutching his back-pack straps in one hand and already near tears.

I shook my head to clear the fuzziness. "Carson, lower your voice. I've already told you that you can't go. And besides, look, it's getting ready to storm. You're afraid of lightning and thunder."

It was the wrong thing to say.

"I am not! And if Gib gets to go then I do too—"

"No, that's not how it works. When you're older you can go, and I'm not arguing with you about this anymore. Now take your back-pack upstairs and stay there until you can calm down."

He stared up at me, his chin trembling. "I'm not staying with you anymore," he said, stomping off, dragging his backpack behind him. He pushed it off the top stair and it hit the landing with a thud. He took off up the next flight of stairs. Soon his clothes and pillows were flying down. It was a good old-fashioned tantrum, and I decided to ig-nore it.

As he sullenly moved all his things downstairs, I began packing food for the campout. Mother watched Carson in amusement.

"Don't you dare laugh," I murmured to her when Carson tripped over a stray tennis shoe.

"Why don't you just let him go?" she asked under her breath as he shot us a murderous glare and threw the shoe downstairs.

"I'd think you of all people would understand that children don't belong out in a storm."

She looked stricken, and I was horrified at myself. Everything was coming apart now. We were leaving Big Dune less of a family than we'd come to it. I reached my hand out and touched her arm, but she pulled away from me and followed Carson down the stairs.

By the time Tate arrived, nobody in the house was speaking to me.

"You in exile up here?" he asked as he reached the top of the stairs, raising his eyebrows at me.

I shoved a bag of sandwiches and chips across the counter at him. "So what else is new? Somebody has to be the responsible one."

He laughed, and I suddenly felt like crying. I turned away from him and dug in the refrigerator, pulling out a soda I didn't want and taking a long drink. Tate moved behind me and I fell against him as soon as his hand touched my back.

"Hey," he said. "Hey, come on, Connie, it's okay."

I shook my head and allowed him to hold me, fighting against tears. "No it's not," I mumbled against his shirt, breathing in the scent of the Gulf.

"Are we going or what?"

I jumped away from Tate as soon as I heard Gib's voice, but it was too late, and in fact, that guilty move only made things worse. He stared at both of us in fury. Tate wasn't as easily cowed by my son, and he took his time leaving the kitchen.

"You all ready?" he asked.

"I'm ready," Gib replied tightly, refusing to glance my way.

"Okay, here, thank your mom for making us sandwiches and take them downstairs. I'll be right there."

Gib grabbed the bag Tate held out, muttered something that sounded vaguely like a thank-you to me, and then whirled around and went downstairs.

"You know, it seems pretty natural that he'd be feeling protective of you right now," Tate said.

I snorted. "He's more worried that I'll take you away from him."

Tate cocked his head to one side, gave me a quizzical look. "I think you underestimate the kid, Connie."

I had no answer for him, and I turned away, clutching my soda.

"We'll get going then," he said lightly. "You want to walk down to the cut with us?"

I didn't, but Mother was at the stairs by then and she answered for both of us.

"That's a lovely idea," she said. "We'll all go. I'll get Estella."

After she forcibly wrangled everyone together, we trooped out of the house, a motley crew of teeming emotions. We spread ourselves out along the sand as though kept apart by magnetic fields. Mother threaded her way around each of us in turn, trying to herd us together before finally giving up and joining Tate, the only one unaffected by the collective sour mood of our family.

The storm had yet to break. Not a raindrop fell, but the air was heavy and the sand glowed in the strange, muted light that fought its way through the building thunderheads. I cast surreptitious glances up at the sky but marched on. If my son wanted to spend a wet, miserable night being munched on by no-see-ums on a scary, pirate ghost–filled island, well, let him.

I nearly relished the idea of him coming back in the morning trying to put a brave face on his bitterly fought-for camping trip. This was no posh Verona sleepover at a wealthy friend's house. He'd be dying to get back to his cushy life, I thought with satisfaction, and when I felt tears prick my eyes again I realized with dismay exactly how right Tate was.

I did underestimate Gib. Always, and with something that came close to hostility. A hostility that I should have been directing at Luke. The realization made me stop in my tracks. I froze and watched my family move away from me, silhouetted against the edge of the world. Only Estella looked back, then quickly turned forward again. I hurried to catch up, filling the widest empty space in my family.

"You have your cell phone?" I asked Gib, breaking the silence.

"Yeah," he said, glancing at me out of the corner of his eye, waiting for me to try to ruin something, change the deal.

"Well, call if you need anything," I said.

"All right."

"I still don't see why I—"

"Because your mother said so, Carson," Mother said firmly, and I shot her a grateful look.

When we arrived at the cut, Tate and Gib dragged the large canoe out from the brush, with Carson getting in the way as much as helping, and we loaded their gear just as the first few raindrops fell. I gave Tate a worried glance, but he and Gib just grinned at each other and hauled the canoe to the water's edge. I held it steady while they boarded, and then helped push them off.

The rain came a little harder as they started to paddle, and lightning forked in the clouds over the Gulf, lighting them up from inside like a Japanese lantern. It was followed by low thunder, and Carson sidled a little closer to me, his eyes watching the canoe intently as it slid away from the shore and entered the cut through a silver veil of rain. My oldest son raised his oar, clutched in both hands, over his head and screamed a savage male greeting to the storm.

Carson gaped after Gib; his face changed from admiration to hero worship when Tate raised his oar to the clouds to bellow his own challenge. The next time the thunder rolled, he didn't move closer to me, but instead moved toward the water's edge, waving his arms as the warriors made their way across the cut.

Dinner was somber. Carson was no longer angry but was dejected instead, pushing his food around and watching the clouds build in the Gulf again. The afternoon storm had been just an advance squall, and my worry came back with a vengeance, all thoughts of enjoying a repentant Gib gone from my mind. As dark fell the rain began again; this time there were no periods of docility—it came in aggressive sideways gusts, hitting the sliders despite their protective overhang.

Estella retired early, claiming her usual headache, and Mother followed her.

"You want to come up with me?" I asked Carson lightly, trying to give him an easy out.

"I told you I'm not scared anymore," he said, his face turning red.

"Okay, okay," I retreated. "I'm going to go upstairs and read. If you change your mind, though—"

"I won't."

I sighed. "All right, sweetie. Good night, then." I climbed the stairs slowly, waiting for him to follow me when thunder shook the house. He didn't. I slid into bed and opened a book, but I didn't get past the first sentence before I drifted off.

The phone startled me awake and I grabbed for it with my eyes still closed, convinced it was Gib. The voice was not that of a panicked young man; it was that of a panicked young woman.

"Connie, Luke told me to call you. You have to do something," she sobbed.

I held the phone away from my ear and blinked at it, certain I was dreaming. But the storm still raged outside, and when thunder cracked, making me jump, I knew I was fully awake. "Who is this?" I finally asked, though I already knew the answer.

"It's me, it's Deanna," she said, her voice shaking.

"What's wrong?" I asked, her panic beginning to infect me.

"They—he—Luke's been arrested," she said, her voice a mere squeak.

I was stunned into silence. Arrested? Could it have been something I'd done? Something I'd told Angie? The Escalade? Nothing made any sense, and the crying on the other end of the phone finally cut through my thoughts.

"Deanna, calm down and tell me what happened," I said firmly, speaking to her as though she were a child.

"He didn't come home," she started, and then at least had the grace to falter when she realized what she'd said.

"Yes," I said impatiently. "What then?"

"I was so worried, and then his lawyer called me and I had to go down to the jail, and the lawyer told me that they arrested him on some sort of fraud charges. He can't even get him out until tomorrow, and he said Luke wanted me to call and tell you because he would need for you to free some account. The lawyer said to call him tomorrow and he could tell you more. What am I going to do?"

Deanna dissolved, and I heard the phone fall and her scramble to pick it up. "Hello, hello?" she said.

"I'm here," I said quietly. "I don't know what to tell you, Deanna. Let his lawyer know I'll call tomorrow, if my lawyer thinks it's a good idea. There's not much more I can do."

"But—" Deanna started.

I gently hung up on her. After searching for what I was feeling, I realized that it was relief. I had no questions left about what I was doing. Angie would guide me through the official paperwork, but emotionally, I was formally divorced.

A crack of thunder made the windows rattle, and I swung my legs off the mattress and headed down the stairs to check on Carson, wondering what I was going to tell him and Gib about their father. I pictured him huddled beneath his covers, shaking, but too proud—or too scared—to brave the staircases up to the library in the dark.

Mother and Estella's lights were out, and only a night-light glowed beneath the door to Gib and Carson's room. I gently pushed the door open.

"Carson, honey," I whispered. "You okay?" The lump on his bed didn't move. I placed my hand on it, feeling nothing but blankets and sheets. I pushed harder.

The other bed was empty too, as were the closet and bathroom. I hurried to my mother's room and knocked frantically.

She opened her door, bleary eyed, squinting at the hall light. "What's wrong?"

"Is Carson in there with you?"

"No. He's not in bed?"

"No," I called behind me, already down the hall at Estella's door. I rapped just as she opened it.

"What's wrong?" she asked. "Are you okay?"

I didn't stop to wonder that I was her first concern, but instead looked past her, noting that her bed was empty before I even asked my question.

"Is Carson with you?"

"No. Did you check the bathroom?"

"Not there," I said and raced up the stairs. He wasn't in the bathroom off the living room, or curled up on the living room floor, and when I threw the sliders open to the storm, he wasn't on the patio. I ran back downstairs to find Estella and Mother in Carson's room, looking at each other with drawn faces, Carson's blankets clutched in Mother's hands.

"What?" I cried. Estella turned toward me.

"His backpack's gone," she said. "I saw it at the door when we came in this afternoon. It's not there, it's not in here, and the door's unlocked."

"Oh my God," I said. It only took a second for me to figure it out, but by then Estella was already pushing past me, racing to her room. I headed for the back door; before I was halfway down the boardwalk, Estella was hard on my heels. We ran through the storm, stumbling and falling in the sand, down to the cut, where we gasped for breath as we scanned the shore. Lightning flashed like a klieg light, illuminating the beach, and Estella pointed toward the brush.

The small canoe was gone.

Estella

Connie freezes when she sees the space where the little canoe isn't, and I see the horror that crosses her face when she realizes what Carson has done. Only the clap of thunder releases her, and she looks to me, the way she did as a child, because I always know what to do, I always know how to fix it.

It makes me move.

I head to the water's edge and kick my shoes off, my muscles screaming and pulling at me to *get in the water!*—but I make them wait. I wait and I watch as Connie clutches my arm and yells things I don't hear.

The lightning flashes again and now I am moving into the water, shaking Connie's hands off, scanning the storm-chopped waves.

Nothing.

Now thunder, and now lightning again, slamming almost directly behind us, and now I see it. It could be a trick of the rain, or my mind, or the stuttering white light of the lightning, but I don't wait to figure it out. I plunge into the Gulf and begin to stroke for the tiny thing I saw bobbing on the waves.

It is drifting more than halfway across the cut, and I can only hope to catch it before it is carried past the tip of Little Dune, before it is caught in the current that runs around the curve and out to the deeper Gulf. Before it moves beyond where I can go.

I can't see anything, but I aim as well as I can. For once I embrace the numbers that are racing inside my head—they allow my muscles to forget that they are exhausted within moments of fighting against the current—and plow on.

My mind is a machine in my damaged skull.

My body is a machine in the hostile waves.

I pause, just for a second, just for a breath, and when the lightning comes again I see it, and it is not a trick of the rain or my mind or the waves. It is the canoe, bobbing wildly. I can reach it; it won't get away from me. I am about to slam my battered body toward it again when I see something out of the corner of my eye.

Numbers split and crash back together like wild things in my head. And now I have to choose. Because while Carson is obviously in trouble in that canoe, there is worse trouble behind me.

Connie is in the water.

CHAPTER TWENTY-TWO

God forgive me, I hesitated. I watched Estella disappear into the water to save my son and I waited. It was only a moment, but it will haunt me for the rest of my life.

I waited.

But I followed her as soon as I caught sight of that canoe, and I was in trouble the second I hit the water. My arms weren't right, my legs weren't right, my breath wasn't right. I was still gasping from our panicked run down the beach, and when I threw myself at the water in imitation of Estella, I slammed onto, rather than into, a wave. My cotton pajama bottoms tangled around my legs, and I wasted precious moments wrestling them off with my feet while trying to keep my head above the water.

The rain stung my face, the salt water stung my eyes, and I swallowed enough of them both to make me choke. I caught occasional flashes of Estella's arms pinwheeling toward the canoe, toward my son, and I willed her on, even as I struggled after her.

The undertow was stronger than I'd ever felt it, the stuff of my nightmares. It seemed impossible that Estella was moving through it as quickly as she was. She was superhuman; she was strength and speed and fierce will. I made progress, but my muscles were tiring so quickly that I knew I would not make it.

But Estella would. My Sun, my ruler of planets and protector, would make it to my boy. She took my father, but she would give me back my son, and it was a trade I was more than willing to make.

I couldn't go forward, and I couldn't go back, but I could still manage small snatches of air, and I continued to catch sight of her moving inexorably toward my child. I made feeble attempts to get closer to them, knowing it was useless, but once in a while the waves were on my side and I was buoyed toward them through no effort of my own.

I went down, once, twice. I came up a third time, and saw Estella looking toward me.

No! I wanted to scream at her. *No!* But then she moved back under the waves and, relieved that she must have somehow heard me, I tried to float, tried to remember how to stay alive, how to breathe.

But my relief was wasted, because she didn't hear me, we had no telepathy, she was not going to save my son, she was coming for me. She was coming to save me and sacrifice my child. I struggled again, wheeled my arms, churned my legs, and then she had me, and she was yelling, but I couldn't understand what she was saying because I was choking.

And then she flipped me over like a turtle, like I weighed nothing, and I couldn't fight her, and she was tugging me along, hauling herself and me through the waves with one arm. Her legs fought under me and I realized that I was tangling my own legs in them. She had my head completely out of the water, and I tried to fill my lungs, tried to will my body to float up and out of her way, and it suddenly started working.

She tugged and jerked me, allowing me to catch my breath, allowing me enough of a rest to scream out, "Let me go!"

Waves crashed over both of us, but for once it didn't happen as I was breathing in, and my throat was nearly clear of salt water. I barely heard her scream back, "No!"

I found the strength to struggle, and just as I fought my way out of her grasp she allowed me to go, slipping her arm from around my chest, and then she was off like a shot again, with me flailing behind her.

Her ruthless rescue had given me enough of a break that I could fight my way through the waves again. As lightning flared I saw the canoe, and then Estella plowing her way toward it. She would reach it in moments, but it didn't matter, because in that instant of light I saw what I'd been too far away to see before.

The canoe was empty. There was no Carson huddled on the seat, no oar splashing futilely at the waves. It might have made me weak, it should have made me give up, but as soon as I saw that empty canoe a surge of pure adrenaline came over me and I exploded through the water in my own clumsy way, screaming a refusal to the waves and the undertow and the storm.

I felt an arm, felt Estella hauling me in, while her other arm clutched the rim of the canoe, rocking it wildly as she pulled me to it. I grabbed on with both hands, nearly capsizing it as we both struggled to breathe, and as the canoe rocked toward me, I saw him.

Carson stared up at me from the bottom of the canoe, hunched over on the floor of it on his knees, clutching his backpack to him, water sloshing almost halfway up the inside.

"Mommy!" he screamed, lurching toward me. I screamed back at him, something inarticulate and wild, but overlying it I could hear Estella screaming louder.

"No, Carson! You'll flip over!"

Carson froze, his eyes locked on mine. "Stay down, stay down!" I yelled, suddenly realizing that we weren't out of danger. We were holding on to a canoe that was nearly full of water and that was moving swiftly past the point of Little Dune and out to the Gulf. Estella crowded in close to me and yelled directions in my ear.

"Stay on this side, get to the front, and we'll pull it to the island."

I nodded, unable to speak. But she'd given me a chance, and now that I had something to help keep my head above water, I was going to be strong enough to save my son. She disappeared under the canoe and I walked my hands over each other and kicked hard against the current until I was at the front, where Estella was already waiting for me. She screamed "Swim!" at me, and together we swam, one arm clawing the water, the other hooked over the edge of the canoe, and finally we began to move toward the island.

All I could focus on was a palm tree curving up into the sky, its fronds dancing gracefully in the wind, as though it were a different wind than the one violently buffeting the Gulf. There was nothing graceful about the waves, but they seemed to recede as I concentrated on the fronds, and soon there was nothing else in the world but that palm tree. It filled the sky. It stayed where it was, and stayed where it was, and stayed where it was—and then it was suddenly closer. I was roping it in, pulling and pulling and pulling through the water.

When Gib appeared before me I stopped swimming, and the bow of the canoe knocked me hard enough on the back of the head that I went under. I knew that he wasn't a mirage only when he hauled me back up, sputtering and gasping, and threw my arms over the edge of the canoe. He grabbed ahold of the bow and began pulling hard.

We made the shore in minutes, the canoe fairly flying through the water. Gib hit the sandy bottom first, scrambling to his feet and hauling the water-heavy canoe while I tried to get my footing and get to Carson all at once. But Tate, hauling the other side of the canoe without me even realizing it, got there first, scooping Carson into his arms and up to the beach with me straggling behind.

Carson struggled to get down. When Tate released him, he ran to me, hitting me hard. I couldn't keep my footing and we both went down, slamming into the wet sand. I pushed his head back so I could see his face, scraping the hair out of his eyes. He squinted up at me, his tears indistinguishable from the rain.

"Are you okay? Are you hurt?" I asked, just as Estella reached us.

He nodded hard, flinging his hair back in his face, and then shoved his head into my shoulder and sobbed as Estella fell to the sand beside us. I leaned into her, and the three of us huddled there on the beach in the storm, trying to catch our breath. Gib and Tate dragged the canoe past us and anchored it in the brushline before coming back.

"Come on," Tate yelled over a low rumble of thunder, "we've got a fire going at the lighthouse. Gib, you bring up the back, make sure everyone stays together."

We stumbled after Tate, Estella first, Carson and I clinging together, and Gib behind us. Lightning forked brilliantly over the Gulf and thunder continued to make us jump, but once we were under the dense spread of palms the rain became less of a nuisance. By the time we arrived at the lighthouse we were all shivering. I was torn between going straight to the sputtering fire and getting Carson into the lighthouse and out of his wet clothes.

The fire won, and the heat felt delicious as we caught our breath and leaned into each other.

"How did you know?" I asked, as Tate draped a towel around Carson and me.

He pointed toward Gib. "June called his cell phone. I knew which way the current would take the canoe, but I didn't expect to see the two of you. My God, Connie, you could have drowned." At this last he looked over at Estella, who was curled over, her head resting on her knees, her shoulders shaking. He quickly put his own jacket around her and she clutched it, looking up at him gratefully.

"I almost did," I admitted. "Gib, are you all right?" I asked my silent older son. His face was grave, his eyes alternating between Carson and me. He bit his lip and nodded, and I could see his chin quivering slightly. I held an arm out to him and he ducked into it. I held my two boys, Carson now the calmer of the two, while Tate led Estella into the lighthouse.

By the time they returned, Estella dressed in Tate's jacket and boxer shorts and Tate wrapped in a damp towel, the three of us were dry-eyed and silent, having run out of a rushed jumble of *sorry*s and *forgiven*s and declarations of love. Luke and his problems had never been farther from my mind.

We took our turns in the blissfully dry lighthouse, making use of whatever clothing we could scrounge together from Tate and Gib's backpacks. I wound up in one of Gib's oversized T-shirts, Carson in a sweatshirt and shorts that were still eight years away from fitting him. Gib wrapped his sleeping bag around himself.

We were a ragtag exhausted bunch that met around the fire again, and Gib gave me his phone to assure Mother that we were all alive, though we couldn't get back to Big Dune that night. The two police officers who patrolled Big Dune were already at the house, and I spent entirely too long convincing them that a full-scale helicopter and rescue boat operation was unnecessary.

Mother was more difficult to calm down, but she finally accepted the fact that we were stuck. Tate and Gib shared the remains of their dinners, and we spent nearly an hour going over the night, from when I found Carson missing to the shock of Gib rising from the waves. But it wasn't until Tate led Gib, carrying a sleeping Carson, into the lighthouse that Estella and I talked about what she'd done out there and what I hadn't been able to do.

The rain had stopped, but lightning still illuminated the clouds and low thunder rumbled through the trees. We were on opposite sides of the fire, and it was difficult to see her face. I scooted toward her, but she merely stared at the fire.

"Estella," I said softly. "I don't know what to say."

"Don't say anything." She tilted her head to one side, and opened her mouth twice, as though about to speak, but the only things that escaped were small sighs.

"You saved my life," I said, talking over her when she tried to interrupt. "You did, and you saved Carson's. My son, Estella, you saved my son's life. And I don't care about anything else. I don't care about Daddy, or the books, or the house, or the violins. You can have it all, just—just—"

My voice was shaking too much for me to get the rest of the words out, and I finally closed my eyes and gave in to the sobs I'd managed to hold back in front of Gib and Carson. I pleaded with Estella in my mind, silently entreating her to reach out and touch me, to put an arm around me or just place her hand on mine. But the touch didn't come, which made me sob harder. I finally lifted my head, sniffing at the tail end of my humiliating breakdown, to find Estella staring at me.

"Do you still want to know about Pretus?" she asked.

"What?" I replied, unable to change gears so quickly. She looked away and then back, impatient with me.

"Pretus. You wanted to know—"

"Okay," I broke in, suddenly impatient with her too. Impatient with her distance, her inscrutability. "Fine, yes, tell me about Pretus, Estella."

"Connie, that summer, I didn't hate you. I wanted to *be* you. Not you the way you were every day—you *drowning*. You at that very moment. I wanted to die. I . . . Connie, I was pregnant."

I froze and it seemed that the rest of the island froze with me. The raccoons stopped shuffling in the brush, the fish stopped jumping in the Gulf, the palms stopped shifting in the wind. Even the fire seemed to stop crackling. Estella. Shy, strange, genius Estella. I saw her in my mind, remembered her as she'd been that summer. She'd become a woman, that had been clear, but exactly how much of a woman I hadn't realized.

"What happened, Estella? What about—the baby?"

She looked at me in surprise. "There was no baby, Connie. Pretus paid for it. Do you remember that I stayed with them for the rest of the summer? He took me to Atlanta. I had an abortion."

I couldn't have spoken then if I'd wanted to.

I thought about my miscarriages, the little lives I'd wanted so badly, and for just a moment, a brief, horrible moment, I turned against her. She was making it up, trying to excuse her behavior. Somehow she knew what flashed through my mind.

"Connie, I was young. It's not a choice I would make today," she said gently. "But it was the only choice then. I'd lost everything, don't you see? Seventeen, and I'd lost my mind. I lost whatever everyone saw in me, I lost my gift, my genius, my big future. Pretus knew it. And he made sure that Daddy knew it. Daddy gave the books to keep me in school and to keep Pretus quiet. Daddy bought my way through my last two years, Connie."

"Daddy didn't know, about the abortion?"

"No, of course not."

"You went through all that alone?"

"I didn't think I had a choice."

"So then, afterward, did it come back? The math?"

"Sometimes. It comes and goes."

"But how?"

She was silent for a moment. "I don't know. The doctors all say it's psychosomatic, that I have control over it. They say that in times of stress I either shut it off or turn it on depending on my needs."

"The doctors? You've been to a psychiatrist?"

She gave a short bark of laughter. "I've been to psychologists, psychiatrists, neurologists."

At this last I glanced at her. "That serious?" I asked. She nodded and looked away. "Then why, *why* would you want me to encourage Carson? You're abused and then spend years in therapy because of it and you think I should let Carson follow in your footsteps?"

"Connie, I would have spent years in therapy anyway. What happened to me isn't going to happen to Carson, because Carson isn't me, and because you're not Daddy, and because we're going to make sure it won't happen. I might have been protected from Pretus, but I still would have run to the numbers. And Carson will run for his own gift. This is what I was destined to be. This is *all* I was destined to be."

"Are you really happy?" I asked. She nodded, and I believed her.

"I needed to tell you this, because there's something else."

"Oh God," I said, dropping my head in my hands. "I don't think I can handle anything else, Estella."

"I don't think it's psychosomatic. I think I lost it because there was something wrong with my brain," she said, proceeding without my permission.

"What?"

"Sometimes I had headaches, bad headaches, and that's when the math would come back or go away." She shook her head, and I remembered her headaches over the past three weeks.

"So, is it here or gone right now?" I asked, thinking I was getting a handle on what she was explaining.

"It's back," she said, nearly whispering.

"Isn't that a good thing?" I asked, confused.

She shook her head. "No," she said. "I had surgery last year, Connie. I had a cluster of tumors removed from my brain."

If the island had seemed to freeze before, now everything exploded. I heard every wave, every rustle, every drone of every hungry mosquito. They all assaulted my ears at once, making me dizzy, drilling into my core until I felt it in my heart. I pressed my hand to the center of my chest and stared at my sister, unable to utter a word.

She reached out a hand, tentative, trembling in the glow of the fire, and I grabbed on to it as tightly as she'd clutched me in the water.

"I'm—" She stopped, took a deep breath, and then continued, her voice trembling as hard as her hand. "Everything's been clear so far, but it came back. The math, I mean. A month ago, and now the headaches are back, and I know—I know . . ."

She began to weep softly, and I continued to hold her hand for a moment, unable to move. I finally broke myself out of it and moved to her, gathering her in my arms. She bent her head down to my shoulder, and I cradled the back of it, feeling her flinch.

She sniffed, wiping her face savagely and pulling away from me. But she grabbed the hand that had been holding her head and guided it back up to her skull.

"Here," she said, pushing my fingers through her hair. I gasped, reflexively pulling my fingers back when they touched the ridge of scar across the back of her head, but she held fast to my hand and made me feel it. "You see?" she asked, finally letting go of my hand. "It's back, and I know the odds, Connie. I know the odds."

"No, Estella," I said, my words catching in my throat, unable to accept what she was telling me. "What do the doctors say? Do they say it's related?"

"The headaches? Sure, they tell me they're a legitimate symptom. The math they want to laugh at. They don't, but I know they don't believe it. Maybe they're right. It doesn't matter, really."

"Oh my God, Estella, why didn't you tell me? Why?"

"I'm telling you now, Connie." She sounded exhausted. And of course she was, we both were. She leaned against me again, and I held her to me, and we didn't speak, we just watched the fire burn itself down until the sun began to rise behind us. Somehow the universe had moved along just as if the previous night hadn't happened, as if it hadn't changed everything.

Estella

We move across the cut in silence. Connie is paddling hard up front, nearly frantically, while I paddle and steer in the rear. Carson crouches in the canoe's middle, gripping the sides tightly, though the water is so calm it's nearly flat. Tate and Gib paddle along effortlessly in their canoe beside us.

Everyone is somber, everyone is tired, and everyone—including me, I'm sure—looks exactly like they got less than twenty minutes of sleep on a desert island after nearly drowning. We can see Mother waiting for us on the beach of Big Dune, her feet in the water as though she just might wade out and meet us in the middle of the cut.

She grabs our bow as we glide up and hauls us up on the beach, her mouth going already. She grabs Carson to her, scolding him, then forgiving him, and the rest of us smile wearily at one another. She hugs us all in turn and presses for details on the trudge back home.

By unspoken agreement, Connie and I lag behind and allow Tate, Gib, and Carson to relate the events of the night before, and soon they are far ahead of us.

"So when is Paul supposed to get here?" Connie asks.

"Before noon," I reply. "It'll be good to get home." I say this last hesitantly. It was all I wanted before; now it means I must face up to the neurologist, the tests, the next step.

"Do you have to go? I mean, do you have to go today?"

"Paul wants me home," I say simply. I have fallen back to that, back to placing all of my decisions in Paul's hands. A year ago I had to, and now I will have to again. It is almost a relief.

"Couldn't he stay the night? I feel—there's so much more we need to talk about," Connie says, and she grabs my arm, stopping me in my tracks, sending up a little rill of sand where she's planted her stubborn leading foot.

I shake my head. "I don't know, Connie. Let's see how it goes, okay?"

She looks at me for another moment, squinting in the sun, making her wrinkles obvious, showing her age. I wonder how I look to her. I feel ancient. She nods and slowly lets go of me. We stare at each other a second more. A cloud slides across the sun, and for a moment, she is a teenager again.

"I'll try," I say, but I know better. It's time to go home.

CHAPTER TWENTY-THREE

Mother, unable to sleep the night before, apparently came to the decision that it was time to go home. Her bags were packed and by the front door when we walked into the house. I didn't say anything, ignoring them until I had organized the boys, sending them to separate showers and gathering breakfast supplies together.

Tate collapsed in the living room, and Estella began to haul her bags to the front door, stacking them beside Mother's. I was feeling deserted already. Mother watched me from the other side of the counter.

"You're too quiet," she said suspiciously, and rightly so, as usual.

"It was a long night," I said truthfully. "What's up with the bags?"

"I needed to do something to keep me busy last night. I was thinking—"

"Uh-oh," I murmured.

"Don't be smart. I was thinking that I might take the boys home a few days early—"

I whirled around, an egg-covered spatula in my hand. "What? Why? They're both fine, Mother. Everything is okay."

"I know, I know," she said. "I'm trying to do a nice thing, Constance, now be still and listen to me. I thought I might take the boys back to Verona a few days early, get them back to their friends, maybe do some shopping—they're both growing out of their clothes—and maybe give you a little break. You've been working nonstop on the house, and with Estella leaving, well, I though you just might like some time to yourself, to regroup, relax on the beach without worrying about those two."

"I don't know," I said. "Mother, Deanna called me last night."

"I know," she said. "She called back after Gib called. Drunk. She told me about Luke. Let me take the boys to Verona, Connie. You just talk to your lawyer and do what she tells you."

I almost gasped at the thought of Deanna and my mother having a conversation, but right then I didn't want to even know what was said. She was offering me a chance.

I thought over my options. I'd taken the rental car back the day after I'd arrived on the island, and I had no way to get home. "If you take my car I don't have any transportation."

"Take a cab into Parachukla and fly home. I'll pick you up at the airport. For goodness sake, Connie, I thought you'd jump at the chance. Stay as long as you want, bike to the store if you need something. You wanted me to be on your side—well, here I am."

I looked around the living room. I still had the stereo and the television, still had the mattress upstairs, still had electricity and water. She was right, the small island store was only a few blocks away and we'd left the bikes in the storage closet downstairs for the next owners.

"Okay," I agreed, noting the relief that crossed over her face. "But are you really sure, Mother—"

"Connie, if you continue to push me I'll just give up and take the cab and the plane myself. I am leaving this island today. Now let's go get the boys' things together. We can have a nice breakfast and be on the road by this afternoon."

"All right," I said. "Thanks, Mom." She nodded, the tension in her forehead relaxing slightly. I watched her back as she walked slowly downstairs, holding tightly to the handrail as though unsure of her footing. She seemed to have aged ten years overnight.

I spoke with Angie, who did not seem surprised that Luke had been arrested. She assured me she would speak to his attorney and that I would be wise to simply stay where I was until more information came in. Then I had to sit down with the boys and try to explain, in some sort of matter-of-fact manner, that their father was in trouble and they might not be able to see him for a little while. Gib seemed to have aged overnight too. He held Carson to him and told him it would be all right, while he looked over his head and gave me the same message with his eyes.

To my surprise, the boys wanted to go home, although I think that Mother might have bribed them after she'd spoken with me. Or perhaps they'd simply had enough of the island too. They left before Paul arrived, all of them anxious to get on the road.

Gib gave Tate a manly handshake good-bye, and Carson gravely followed his lead, breaking into squeals of laughter when Tate swung him up and across his shoulders to carry him down to the car. Mother handed Gib the keys, with a small, challenging smile at me, but I didn't say anything. Gib had already proven himself.

I hugged my boys hard, promising that I'd be home in less than a week, and then they were gone, crunching away down the drive and puffing up a cloud of shell dust and sand as Gib spun the car onto the road. I stayed outside while Tate and Estella climbed the stairs, and so I was the one who first saw the old Cutlass slowly working its way down the road. I walked out to the mailbox and raised my arms over my head, waving Paul in.

I'd hoped for a small break in the day, a chance for Estella and me to finally be alone. Paul exited the car wearily, with the shell-shocked look of somebody unused to driving the convoluted back roads of rural Florida.

"Hi, Paul," I greeted him, holding my arms out for a hug without thinking. We'd never embraced before, but the drive must have lowered his defenses because he immediately stepped into my arms, then just as quickly moved away and looked up at the house.

"Nice place," he said. "How's Estella?"

"She told me, Paul," I said quietly, placing my hand on his arm to keep him from gaining the stairs.

He eyed me warily. "Told you what?"

"About the tumors, the surgery. About the headaches."

He nodded. "Well, I guess I'm glad she finally told someone in her family. I did try to get her to tell you before."

"Thank you for that, and for everything else you've done. It couldn't have been easy."

"She'd have done the same for me," he said simply, and I knew he was right.

"Paul, I was wondering, hoping, that you might be able to stay for a bit—"

He began to interrupt, but I hurried on, suddenly seeing my opportunity in his concern for her. "For the night, at least. She just told me last night—last night! You don't even know about last night."

He looked confused. "Should I?" he asked. "Is she all right?"

"She's fine," I assured him. "But to be honest, I don't think she should travel until she's gotten a good night's sleep."

"Maybe I'd better talk to Estella," he said, pulling from my grasp and taking the stairs two at a time. I followed with a sinking heart. He was going to yank her off Big Dune so fast he'd pull the tide with him. He waited on the front porch for me impatiently, allowing me to open the door and precede him into the house.

"Estella," I called as I led him up the stairs. "Paul's here."

I heard the thump of feet as she came running. I flattened myself against the wall as she flew past me and into his arms, nearly taking them both down the stairs. He held her tightly, her face pressed into his collarbone, and they murmured to each other, words I couldn't—and didn't want to—hear. I hurried up the stairs.

Tate, ready to go home to his own shower and bed after once again finding himself in the midst of a Sykes family drama, sat on the steps to the third floor, yawning. I sat next to him, and he put his arm around my shoulders. I could have fallen asleep right there but for Estella one flight beneath me. The low thrum of voices had stopped, and then I heard steps, heading down, rather than up, the stairs. Tate groaned and fell back before hauling himself to his feet with a sigh when Estella's bedroom door closed.

"I want to do the polite thing here and stay to meet the guy—" he started.

"Go," I encouraged him. "Go home. Stop by tomorrow, I'll make you dinner."

He looked uncertain. "Are you sure? Is she still leaving today?"

"I guess so," I said, hoping I could convince her otherwise.

"Will you be all right here by yourself?"

I opened my mouth to answer and then shut it without a word. I would be by myself. I was *by myself*. Not just for the night. My life stood before me like an empty bookshelf, waiting for me to choose and place and rearrange. I thought of the boxes of books my father had chosen, waiting downstairs to be claimed by Estella. Perhaps we'd been too hasty to judge him for his seemingly flippant choices.

Violins and math, the sea and the South. He chose what was important to him and to his family. Perhaps he had seen how we'd fallen apart and it had been his own way of keeping us all together. Estella and I represented upon the shelves he gazed at every day, our mother and the island he loved protected by his carefully constructed jewel box at the top of the stairs, together with his ancestors rendered immortal in oil, languishing on the wall.

I had nothing. I'd surrounded myself with nothing. No wonder my house in Verona no longer meant anything to me, while this empty house ached in me like an arthritic joint. Would I be all right here by myself?

"I'll be fine," I said slowly. He gave me a half smile, and I shook my head. "Really. If I need anything I'll call you."

"Okay then," he responded.

I followed him downstairs, but left by the beachside door while he left by the front, and I was down at the edge of the Gulf before the sound of his engine died away. The storm had scoured the island clean during the night, and the only footprints on the smooth sand other than ours were from shorebirds and an occasional beach cat chasing a breakfast of ghost crab. The top layer of sand crunched beneath my feet, mixing with the softer sand beneath, sending a shiver up the backs of my legs when it tickled my tender arches.

It didn't take long for Estella to join me. I heard the hollow thud of footsteps on the boardwalk and turned around to watch her move slowly down to me. Her face was drawn, recently wiped clean of tears.

"Paul is taking my things to the car," she said quietly.

"Estella," I pleaded. But she was shaking her head.

"I can't, Connie. Paul's right. I need to get back to my support system, my family."

I flinched. "I'm your family. Can't we start over? Won't you let me just make you dinner?" My voice was rising, high and unnatural against the sound of the surf and the cry of the gulls.

Estella sighed. "Connie, I have to go. We may have left this for too long. I'm not blaming you for that—"

"I'll take the blame if you'll just give me a chance."

"You're not to blame. I have plenty of share in it. But I can't help what's happening right now. We'll work on it, okay? I'll call, I'll let you know what's happening. And I want to know about Gib, and I want to help with Carson . . . and you. It's—" She opened her arms wide in a shrug that encompassed everything—us, the beach, the Gulf—and then dropped them, her head drooping as she looked at her shoes. "It's the best I can do right now."

I felt the fire leave me, seeing her look so defeated, seeing her shoes in the sand next to my bare feet. Maybe it was too late, maybe our parents had screwed it up, maybe we'd kept screwing it up. It happened. It happened to families every day. Maybe the last great Sykes had been hanging on that wall of paintings. Maybe there'd never been any great Sykeses at all.

"Okay," I said. "What about the books? Should I ship them to you?"

She smiled. "Would you just take them, Connie? Please? I don't want them, I don't care about them, and they'd eventually be yours anyway."

"Don't say that," I said, but it was useless. "Will you call when you get home to let me know you got there safely?"

She nodded, and then folded me into her arms. It was a start. We stood there on the Big Dune beach, me grounded to it by skin, Estella separated from it by thick soles. And then she left. Paul didn't come say good-bye to me, but I didn't mind. He'd taken good care of my sister, and he would continue to, and I would always be thankful to him for that.

It was a restless afternoon. I couldn't relax, couldn't sink into any sort of comfortable feeling in my own skin. Late that afternoon I walked down to the cut and sat on the sand, gazing across the now-calm water to Little Dune. My eyes were drawn to the canoe tracks in the sand. *Fresh* tracks. I glanced back in the bushes to see that the big canoe was gone. Tate.

After a moment's hesitation I wrestled the small canoe from its spot and dragged it into the water. I was panting by the time I reached Little Dune, and I rested for a moment, allowing the little waves to rock the back of the canoe while its bow cut into the sand.

I finally got out and hauled the canoe up to rest beside the larger one, looking for Tate's footprints. There was a set heading north, toward the lighthouse, and drag marks of an indeterminate source beside them.

I finally came upon him cutting chicken wire to lay atop a turtle's nest just in front of a large bank of dunes. I watched him silently, his bare back muscles bunching and stretching as he cut the wire. He caught sight of my shadow and turned quickly, the wire cutters clutched in his hand as though he might have to defend himself.

He relaxed as soon as he saw it was me, but I didn't want him to relax. I was either going to break down or I was going to channel all of it—all my anger at Luke, my anxiety for my children's future, my fear for what might be happening to my sister—into a long-overdue surge of action.

"Con?" Tate asked, tilting his head to the side. "You all right?"

"No," I said. "But I will be."

He only protested once as I led him to the lighthouse.

"I'm not what you need," he said. "I told you, I'm not fit for it." He tugged me to a stop, and I whirled on him.

"Tate, I'm only asking you to be fit for one thing. We're adults now, aren't we?" He stared at me and nodded slowly. "Then let me worry about what I need. Take me to the lighthouse and be what I need for now—just for right now. Don't make me beg."

"No," he said, and I nearly walked away from him then in disgust, but he held tight to my hand and I understood. He pulled me to him, and when he kissed me, he kissed me hard, with his hands holding my head, and even if I'd wanted to escape then I don't think I could have.

We hurried to the lighthouse, and I found exactly what I wanted there. And I did not cry afterward, not for Daddy and Graciela, or Estella, or Luke, or my children . . . or myself.

Tate's arm was beneath my head, and he too was staring up into the cylinder of the lighthouse, a faraway look on his face. Was he feeling determined, as I was, to change something? Or, more likely, was he determined that things would stay the same? It wasn't in our deal for me to ask, so instead I posed a different question.

"Tate? Can I borrow your truck?"

He looked at me in surprise and tightened his arm, rolling me into him slightly. "Sure. What for?"

"I need to go to Atlanta."

Estella

Paul is waiting for me. I can just see him at the end of the boardwalk. He looks beautiful in the fading light, the moon rising behind him as a witness. I see him turn and I back away from the slider a
bit, but it is not me he is looking at. It is Connie, who is nearly
wrestling Mother down the boardwalk. Paul approaches them and
they have a brief powwow, which ends in Paul walking Mother down
to the chairs lined up on the beach.

He seats her next to Gib, who is even larger and more grown-up
than last summer. Mother and Gib lean their heads together conspiratorially, and I know she is complaining about being thrown out of the
house. Both my mother and my sister are making me insane today, but
Connie believes that it is only Mother. I let her believe it. I'm happy to
let her believe it.

It seems the sisterly thing to do.

Connie arrives back upstairs, breathless and determined. Capable. She catches me looking at her and suddenly grins. I start to raise my hand to adjust . . . something, anything, because what could she be laughing at, but she is not laughing at me. She is simply happy.

"Okay," she says briskly. "Everyone's here, let's get you together."

And everyone *is* here, including my students Chelsea and Lisa, who are eyeing Tate in a way that might make Connie jealous if only she would acknowledge how she feels. Carson is there with his clarinet, prepared to serenade me down the sandy aisle with a composition he's held closely guarded from everyone except the small group of musicians and instructors he's studying with at the college this summer. Musicians and instructors heavily vetted by Connie and me, who are grouped around him now with their own instruments, ready to make his astonishing music come alive as the moon begins its ascent.

And Vanessa is there with her son, who is visiting from Alaska and has been eyeing Connie in a way that might make Tate jealous if only *he* would acknowledge how he feels.

I'm working on them both.

And that, too, seems the sisterly thing to do.

Connie begins her own sisterly ministrations, adjusting the straps of my dress though they need no adjustments. She reaches up to smooth a curl of my hair.

"How do you feel?" she asks.

"I feel wonderful," I answer, and it is the truth. Yes, the cancer was there. But it was not nearly as bad as it could have been. The tests showed that it hadn't spread, but that a tiny bit had been missed. The doctors swore that it was stress, not a fast-growing tumor, that caused my headaches, and wouldn't even entertain the return of the math as a symptom. I'm getting there. Slowly.

So, yes, I was right. The cancer was there.

But so was Connie.

Despite her own problems, despite the divorce, Luke's arrest and subsequent conviction on fraud charges, and the sale of the house in Verona, Connie was there. And when I woke from a surgery to implant tiny radioactive seeds into the bit of tumor that was left, Connie was there, right beside Paul, telling me that everything was going to be all right.

I believe her.

I'd like to think I was there for her too. Paul has certainly been there, as though she were his own sister. This summer he helped Tate and Gib remove the shelves from the library—now Connie's bedroom—and install them in the space she found for her bookstore and gallery in Parachukla.

Paul's bowls and sculptures form a solid core on pedestals in the center of the gallery, while Vanessa's airy watercolors grace the walls that aren't already filled with bookcases. Once a month the pedestals are pushed aside to make room for a recital by Connie's string quartet. Occasionally they feature a solo by Carson, though she still keeps him heavily shielded.

All of us helped her arrange the books on the shelves, even Mother, who, despite her inherent distrust of the island, still visits more often than Connie can handle. Mother chalks it up to checking in on her property, and Connie has little choice but to grin and bear it. Just like she bore Mother insisting on rent for the past year, even while Connie was still living and winding up her affairs in Verona. Mother will always be a businesswoman, will always have a head for numbers.

Connie is still fussing with my hair. I gently push her hand away.

"I'm ready," I say.

"Well then," she says, holding her hand out to me. "Let's go."

I take her hand and grab a bouquet of magnolias off the counter as we walk past the kitchen to the stairs. I count the steps as we walk down, but I count out loud and Connie joins me.

"—nine, ten, eleven, twelve, thirteen—" and we are in the foyer, opening the door, crossing the porch, and moving down the boardwalk.

My math is back, but I've let it come, because the seeds have done their job and I am clear for now, and for now is good enough.

We stop at the head of the stairs and Carson begins his piece. It blends perfectly with the music of the beach and the Gulf, and it has never been more apparent that he is destined for the kind of Sykes greatness our father had wanted for me.

Connie will not screw it up. And I will be here as often as I can to make sure of it. Big Dune is in my blood. I tried to hide from it for too long, but now that I have given in, I will not allow it to happen again.

Three facts about right now:

I am healthy.

I am being given away by Connie, willingly this time, because we have a choice now.

I will always return here, to this island, under this moon, to dance with my sister.

READERS GUIDE
for
Catching Genius

Discussion Questions

1. *Catching Genius* opens when Estella and Connie are still girls, just before Estella's "genius" disrupts their lives. How does Estella's mistaken assumption that her "eyecue" could be catching, like an illness, affect her relationship with her sister? Can Estella's estrangement from Connie be seen as a way of protecting Connie? How is genius viewed as a gift in the story? How is genius viewed as a curse?

2. When Carson's composing talent is discovered by his music teacher, do you understand Connie's initial reaction? Given her family history and the tension with her genius sister, how else do you think she could have reacted? How does Connie view herself as a musician in relation to her son? What makes Connie come to terms with Carson's talent? How do you believe she will handle his future?

3. Mr. Hailey, Carson's music teacher, finds Carson's musical talent a given once he learns that Carson's aunt is a math genius. "Music is math, math is music," he tells Connie (p. 107). And at Estella's dinner party, the recurring debate over math enabling and supporting creativity comes up again. "Math is connected to creativity in all kinds of ways we don't completely understand," Estella tells Connie (p. 136). How do you see the two—music and math—connecting? How do they connect through the characters and plot of this story? Are Estella and Connie opposites, or more alike than they would realize?

4. Discuss why Connie and Estella's mother decided to keep her family's history a secret from her husband and children. She said she did it for her daughters. Do you believe this was necessary, in the face of the Sykes family legacy and fortune? Are there ever times when large secrets are necessary? And does it ever become imperative that secrets be told?

5. Connie had the Sykes eyes, "the eyes that said [she] belonged to [her father] and that divided [her] family down the middle" (p. 6). If Connie "belonged" to her father, why was her musical talent not encouraged in the way Estella's talent with numbers was? Do you believe that Connie would have been considered a genius under different circumstances? Did the so-called "Sykes eyes" mean anything to Connie's father, Sebastian? Did they mean anything to Connie? Why does Connie see Gib as Luke's son, and Carson as her son? Does this still hold true at the end of the novel?

6. At the start of the novel, Big Dune Island is a place both sisters don't want to return to. What are they expecting to find there? What has kept Tate on the island, and why is he more connected to it than Estella and Connie? Estella hasn't been to Big Dune in

twenty-six years. Why has she physically distanced herself from the island? Do you think physical distance can keep away the memory of what occurred in a specific place? For Connie, the return may have been easier, but it takes her a long time to realize she wants to stay on Big Dune. What was holding Connie to her life in Verona? What makes her realize that Big Dune is really her home, and a home for her children?

7. When Estella is about to face Connie after many years apart, she says: "I am clutching the banister, stuck between the upstairs and downstairs, between childhood and real life" (p. 129). What has kept Estella from her sister? And what has kept Connie from Estella? When Estella decides she wants to repair her relationship with Connie, she says: "Scars can be prevented when sewn up with care, but I've not been taught that particular skill. My stitches will be ragged, clumsily done. How many will it take?" (p. 193). If Estella had not saved Carson's life, do you think she would have been able to repair her relationship with Connie? Do you foresee irreparable differences between Gib and Carson? Do you think the divorce will change that? Do you think Big Dune will change that?

8. Why do you think Connie repressed the memory of how she was saved from drowning? How did learning the truth change her relationship with Tate? With Estella? How would things have been different had she never learned the truth? Do you think Estella should have told Connie when she did?

9. Discuss the motif of drowning in the novel. Connie almost drowns as a teenager; her mother survived a storm as child but lost her two sisters; and Estella saves Carson from drowning during the storm. How does this recurring theme work throughout the story? Did you expect Carson's near-drowning to happen?

Did you expect Estella to save him? When Connie decides to move ahead with pursuing the divorce, she says: "I felt like an island, with my family eddying and flowing around me, unaware that I had become immoveable" (p. 60). How do islands, both actual and imagined, show up in this story?

10. Why do you think Connie ignored Luke's infidelity for so many years? What made Deanna—the Escalade and the person—the last straw? Connie said: "I was the wife. . . . The only reason I put up with this over the years was because my position afforded me certain protections and guarantees" (p. 250). Do you think that Connie truly had "protections" and "guarantees" in her marriage to Luke? Do you think having such things is worth putting up with infidelity? How do you think Connie and Estella's parents' marriage influenced their daughters? Why does Estella wait so long to marry Paul, the love of her life?

11. Connie removes her wedding rings when she plays violin. About this, she says: "I'd never gotten the knack of playing with the rings on. It was too distracting for me, too invasive, and I rather liked the ritual of it, the trade of one life for another" (p. 45). What were Connie's two lives? In which life was she the happiest? Did other characters have multiple lives in a similar way? When Connie removes her wedding rings for the final time, before the performance with her trio, how has she changed? Do you think she would consider herself to be living only one life at the end of the story?

12. "We are family," Estella says about Connie after she learns that Connie is leaving Luke (p. 226). Why does Estella seem surprised when she says it? If she truly believes it, why, when she thinks she's facing another relapse, does she tell Connie that she's leaving Big

Dune and needs "to get back to [her] support system, [her] family" (p. 362)? Discuss what makes someone "family" to you. Is blood enough? Can a person who doesn't share your blood ever become your family? What do you believe author Kristy Kiernan is saying about family in this novel?

13. Do you agree with Connie's reaction when she discovers how her mother came to marry her father? Connie tells her mother: "It's like you were a horse to be traded or something! A poker chip to be won" (p. 79). Instead, Connie's mother argues, her father was trying to give her "the gift of a life" (p. 79). How does Connie's mother give her own children the "gift of a life"? How, in turn, does Connie do the same for her children? What sacrifices need to be made to ensure a child's future?

14. Estella got pregnant when she was seventeen, but she didn't tell Connie until many years later. Do you understand why she kept this a secret for so long? At the time, when she watched Connie about to drown in the Gulf, Estella thinks: "When she goes under the next time, I will go under too. . . . It is me who needs saving this time" (p. 13). Does Estella ever get saved? Does Paul save Estella? Does her math? Do her students? At the end of the novel, Estella says: "My math is back, but I've let it come, because the seeds have done their job, and I am clear for now, and for now is good enough" (p. 370). Why do you think she lost her math, and why do you think it returned?

15. Did you find the alternating first-person voices of Connie and Estella to be a successful way of telling this story? Why do you think the author chose to show both perspectives? How would the story have been different had we seen it only through Connie's eyes? Or only through Estella's?

16. Consider the epigraph at the start of the book: "If children grew up according to early indications, we should have nothing but geniuses." Does every child have the potential to be a genius? What can make genius possible, or impossible? How should a child prodigy be handled? How should any child's natural talents be handled?